Pandora's Orphans
A Fangborn Collection

More by Dana Cameron

Fangborn Novels

Seven Kinds of Hell

Pack of Strays

Hellbender

Emma Fielding Archaeology Mysteries
(now on Hallmark Movies & Mysteries)

Site Unseen

Grave Consequences

Past Malice

A Fugitive Truth

More Bitter Than Death

Ashes and Bones

Forthcoming from DCLE:

Exit Interview

(an "a/k/a Jayne" novel)

Anna Hoyt

Pandora's Orphans
A Fangborn Collection

Dana Cameron

"The Night Things Changed" First publication: *Wolfsbane and Mistletoe*, eds. Charlaine Harris and Toni L.P. Kelner (Ace, 2008).

"Pattern Recognition" First publication: *Murder and Mayhem in Muskego*, eds. Jon Jordan and Ruth Jordan (Down & Out Books, 2012).

"Love Knot" First publication: *The Wild Side*, ed. Mark L. Van Name (Baen Fantasy, 2011).

"Finals" First publication: *Alfred Hitchcock's Mystery Magazine* (Dell Publications, January 2013).

"Promises to Keep" DCLE Publishing LLC, 2021.

"Swing Shift" First Publication: *Crimes by Moonlight*, ed. Charlaine Harris, (Berkley Prime Crime, 2010).

"The God's Games" First publication: *Games Creatures Play*, eds. Charlaine Harris and Toni L.P. Kelner (Ace, 2014).

"The Serpent's Tale" First publication: 47North, 2013.

"Pax Egyptica" First publication: *Hath No Fury*, ed. Melanie R. Meadors (Outland Entertainment, 2018).

"The Curious Case of Miss Amelia Vernet" First publication: 47North, 2014.

"Burning the Rule Book" First publication: 47North, 2015.

For Charlaine and Toni.

For Josh and Jon.

And always, always, always, for James.

Contents

Foreword: The Moment Things Changed

Charlaine Harris and Toni L.P. Kelner

When Dana talks about the big shift in her fiction career—from writing archaeological mysteries to urban fantasy—she sometimes talks about an epiphany.

At a convention in 2006, we asked Dana to write an urban fantasy story for our anthology *Wolfsbane and Mistletoe*. (In fact, she was the first author we asked to contribute, mere minutes after we'd agreed to edit the anthology.)

Dana accepted on the spot. But when she began to plan the story, she hit a brick wall, she told us. There were no reference books to acquire! No authorities to consult! She would be able to make stuff up.

You might call that moment the one when things changed.

Dana told us this story later with gentle self-mockery, but we think she's being too modest. We were astounded with her story. When Dana decided to "make stuff up," she plunged into the deep end.

The Fangborn are unlike any other fictional werewolves and vampires either of us have ever seen, and trust us when we say we've seen a lot of werewolf and vampire fiction. Then Dana took that original concept, added historical depth, and extrapolated beautifully to create her world. It's an amazing achievement.

But perhaps more importantly, we think that the Fangborn stories and novels are when Dana started to come into her own as an artist. As new writers, we are repeatedly told, "Write what you know." And with the Emma Fielding mysteries, Dana did that to perfection, drawing on her own archaeological background to tell some really exciting stories. But after writing the Fangborn, a world she didn't know at all, Dana became even more adventuresome: she wrote her wonderful Anna Hoyt stories and the a/k/a "Jayne" stories, and she edited her own anthology.

She just keeps making stuff up, and it's glorious.

Dana gives the two of us more credit than we deserve for the Fangborn Universe. It's true that we as co-editors invited her to submit to two anthologies, and Charlaine invited her to submit to a third, meaning that we made some editorial suggestions along the way. But the startling originality of the world, the depth of the characterization, the rich historical background, and the beauty of the writing are Dana's alone.

We couldn't be prouder of our role in inspiring these stories, and are delighted that she's collected them for her many fans to have them together in one place, and for new fans to discover them.

Charlaine Harris and Toni L.P. Kelner
Proud Fang-y Godmothers

The Night Things Changed

This was the first Fangborn story I wrote and the second short story I had published. I began to panic when I realized I didn't have any reference books on werewolves on my bookshelves. I couldn't embarrass Charlaine and Toni, who are good friends and the editors who'd invited me to contribute! After fifteen sweaty minutes, I realized that, as a fiction writer, I could just make up my own rules—this after having written six novels! So I flipped the traditional tropes: vampires and werewolves are born into their powers ("fangs" + "born, not bitten" = Fangborn) and they work in secret to protect humanity from evil.

I pounded up the stairs to the roof and slammed open the door; the wintry air lashed my face. My sister the vampire was stretched out on her stomach, nearly naked, under the pale December sun.

She wasn't moving. I knew from her phone call the news was bad, but...

"Claudia?" I swallowed; my mouth was dry. "Claud?"

She stirred and opened her eyes blearily. Her face was drawn, she moved stiffly. Claudia relaxed when she saw it was me, fastened the bikini top behind her neck, then sat up.

I turned away, blushing. "Aw, jeez, Claud. Do you have to?"

"What? I'm covered. Gerry, take a pill. No one can see me up here. We picked the place for that very reason."

She was right; evergreen shrubs and dead, leafy vines—a forest of green in the summer—sheltered her place from every side, leaving the roof open to the sky. Despite the crust of snow on the ground, she wasn't even shivering.

It was such a small bikini, though. I kept quiet: she'd think I was being a prude.

"I don't even need to wear a bathing suit when I'm alone," she said, reading my face.

"Yeah, you do, as long as I'm your brother." I *am* a prude; sue me. No guy likes to think about his sister being ogled, especially not when she looked good enough to model that bikini. And I wished she'd cut her long dark hair. It was just too dangerous in a fight.

I changed the topic. "I got your message. I was worried."

She nodded; her shoulders sagging. "A bad one, this morning. It means work for us."

Things had been so quiet lately, it had to happen. "Tell me."

"It was in the emergency room." Claudia "happens" to go through the emergency room a lot, trolling for trouble. "This guy was in for sutures, a cut on his arm he said he got slipping on ice. He was giving Eileen a hard time, and I got a whiff of him. I asked her to send him to me for 'post-trauma assessment.'"

Claudia glanced at me; there were dark smudges under her eyes. She looked beat. "He barged into my office, got angry when I told him he had to wait his turn. Very aggressive, all id, defensive as Hell. Maybe there's a hurt little kid somewhere under all that armor, but he's being led by a really thuggish protector-self."

I hate when she talks like a shrink, but it's how she gets things straight in her own head. "Was he big?"

She nodded. "And he uses it. He doesn't mind threatening people, liked the idea he was scaring me. And then...when I stood up to him, he took a swing at me."

I nodded, bristling. She was obviously okay, but I hated hearing this kind of stuff. It was part of our job, and I knew Claudia could take care of herself, but it still chafed. Call me overprotective. "And?"

"He missed. That made him crazy. He tried again." She shrugged. "And then I bit him."

I nodded again; it didn't make me feel much better. If biting had cured the guy, she wouldn't have called me, just saved it for the next time we got together for dinner. "Anyone see you?"

"The door was shut. He knocked me down, then ran out of the office." She paused. "He's a really bad one—"

"We'll get him. We always get the bad guys," I said, confident.

She shook her head. "There was something weirdly, profoundly, wrong about him."

"You're just tired. We always—"

"No, Gerry!" Her sharp tone startled me. "This is different. His reaction...I can't get the taste out of my mouth. It's like...I could work on him for a year, and still not get anywhere."

Her eyes filled up, and I knew that she'd been thrown for a loop. Professionally and personally, Claudia is a proud person.

"Scootch over," I said. I didn't say any more, just sat down on the lounge and put my arm around her. I resisted the urge to take off my jacket and put it over her shoulders, because the sun was the best thing for a vampire in need of healing, even the weak sun of a Massachusetts midwinter. And besides, I needed my coat myself. I always seem to feel the cold.

Prudish. Overprotective. Chilly. In a lot of ways, we werewolves are just big pussies.

After getting Claudia's promise that she'd take it easy, I took the copy of the file she had and visited the address of "J. Smith."

J. Smith? Proof once again that evil is not creative.

I didn't need to get out of the pickup, but I did. As I figured, the place—a double-decker—was abandoned, my footprints the first breaking the new fall of snow surrounding it. As I nosed around, I picked up lots of strong residual scents, most of them unhappy: drugs and sex, pain and fear. There was something in the background, an ugly smell that made my skin crawl; I didn't know if our guy had been there, but the recognizable odor of evil called me to Change…

Not here, not now. Save it for tonight, when you might be able to do something about it…

I reluctantly followed my tracks back to my truck and decided to pick up the trail at the hospital. Construction and early holiday mall shoppers had turned Route 128 into a slushy parking lot, but the F150 handled well with her new snow tires. I tuned the radio to the Leftover Lunch on WFNX and crept toward Union Hospital in Lynn.

I like being a werewolf for the same reasons I liked being a cop. Sure, it's a lonely job and I see life's tragedies, but then I fix them. I help people, I make the world a better place, and I'm good at it. I *like* being one of the good guys. I get a sense of satisfaction I bet your average CPA never gets. Or maybe they do; what do I know? I'm just Gerry Steuben, regular guy, North Shore born and bred, with a CJ degree from Salem State, recently early-retired from the Salem PD. My tax forms say I'm a PI now, but I don't do domestics, insurance fraud, or repo. I'll go to the end of the earth to find lost kids, though, and never charge a cent. But I mostly stick to the Family business, which is eradicating evil from the world.

Sounds like I'm full of myself, doesn't it? Not if you know the truth about my type. Our type. The Fangborn, Pandora's Orphans, the ones the ancients called "Hope," supposedly trapped at the bottom of the box. But according to *our* legends, the First Fangborn got out, and it's a good thing they did, too, for when evil was released into the world, so was the means of destroying it. Vampires and werewolves, the first to clean the blood and ease the pain, the second to remove irredeemable evil when we find it. Our instincts are infallible, our senses attuned to evil. True evil—not the idiot who cuts you off in traffic or steals your newspaper—exists, and we're here to fight it. We're the ones evil can't touch, the superheroes you never see, if we do our jobs right. I believe that to the core of my soul, and it's the best feeling in the world.

Imagine the world today if we didn't put the brakes on evil. Funny, since the Fangborn have always been depicted as the most depraved killers in every mythology. My kind aren't the most fertile in the world—there are less than one thousand of us in the United States— and when you Normals turned from hunting to agriculture, you started popping out kids like it was going out of style. But we're the children of Hope, so we do what we can, and every bit helps.

As for those myths: It's not the turn of the moon but the call of evil that makes us Change, though I can manage it if I'm pissed off enough. I don't have hair on the palms of my hands, though for a while when I turned thirteen, I was afraid of that happening for other reasons. Claudia says I obsess about anyone touching my stuff, but can you name one guy who isn't territorial? When we order pizza, Claudia always asks for roasted garlic. She relies on the mirror by her front door to remind her to dress like other people when it's cold. She also *claims* she's allergic to silver, but that's because she thinks it looks tacky against her skin.

In reality, we're big on family and secrecy. Me and Claud live in Salem because eastern Massachusetts was where our Family was needed, back in the day. Grandpa had a sense of humor about it: "Ven ve move from de old country, I tink, 'Here, dey like tings dat go bump in de night, so ve vill giff dem bumps in de night!'" he'd cackle. I miss the old guy like crazy, but our presence has nothing to do with the witchcraft trials; it was just easier to hide a bunch of Germans with funny habits among the Polish and Russian immigrants in nineteenth-century Salem. Protective coloring is all-important. Around here, not only do you have tales of witchcraft, but there are rumors of a sea monster (a nineteenth-century gimmick concocted by ferry owners and innkeepers), pirate treasures, and haunted houses. What's the occasional sighting of a big dog by moonlight against all that?

The traffic finally nudged its way to my exit and I pulled into the hospital parking lot. Many Fangborn are nurses, doctors, shrinks, cops, even clergy. Any job that gets us close to the public, the people who need protection, is a good job for us.

I didn't even have to roll down the window. The stench hit me from outside the cab of the truck. It was all I could do to keep my hands from turning to claws on the wheel and my human brain focused on parking. I killed the engine as soon as I could, clutching the Saint Christopher medal that's been on my neck since my first Communion. I don't care whether he's a saint; I'm not that religious. My mother gave it to me, and it helps to have something to focus on when resisting the Change.

Claudia was right: this guy was a bad one. Smith had escaped her—which was saying something—and then left a trail that a Normal could follow, if he'd understood why he was suddenly feeling queasy and irritable. There wasn't a sound of bird or beast anywhere nearby, not even a seagull.

True evil has the smell of rotting meat, sewer filth, sickrooms. Add the feeling you get when you realize something life-alteringly bad is happening, something you can't do anything about, and you'll get close to what I felt. But my senses are a hundred times sharper than yours.

The good thing is that smell brings on the Change and that brings power.

I opened the door cautiously. The wind shifted and I found I could manage without going furry, so I visited the ER. The nurses told me the doc who'd treated "J. Smith" was gone.

I thanked them, then tried Claudia's office. The scent was stronger here, possibly because of his attack on Claudia, but there was something else I couldn't place: it set my teeth on edge. The assistant Claudia shared with the other shrinks told me I'd just missed my sister, that she'd been really shook up by a patient. I feigned surprise—Claudia could get into a lot of trouble for talking about the case with me, much less giving me the file—and said I'd check on her.

I tracked the scent back to the parking lot, where the guys at the valet stand said that a guy had caught a cab dropping someone off, a local company.

Just then Eileen came out, a tart little nurse who'd always had a cup of coffee and a kind word for me when I'd been on the force. Claudia'd said she was the nurse handling Smith's case. We exchanged hellos.

"You heard about Claudia?"

"Yeah." I exhaled, whistling.

"She's okay. Guy was a bruiser. Came in to get stitched up, said it was a slip, but I know a bottle slash when I see one. Street fight, probably."

I nodded.

"Claudia gave me the high sign, so I sent him along to her. A post-trauma chat, I told him. Oh!" Eileen said, remembering. "It gets better. Weems brought him in. Said he found him in the middle of the street, and hauled him in to get him patched up. Too bad you missed him, you guys could have caught up on old times."

She grinned a mean grin; everyone knew Weems and I hated each other.

"My bad luck," I said. I stuck my hands in my pockets. "Apart from this guy, you been busy?"

She shook her head. "Not the past two days. Not even a bumsicle." She glanced at the steely sky. "That'll change. Snow tonight."

I nodded; I could smell that, too. We both knew that between the cold, the holidays, and the law of averages, soon enough there'd be accidents, drunk drivers, domestic disputes, and the homeless who'd freeze to death. The usual.

"Well, the kids will like it." She zipped herself up. "They're out of school after today. Jumping out of their little skins already, the little monsters."

"Oh, come on," I said. "Kids should be excited about Christmas." I like Christmas. I like the effort people make. I like presents. I like the hope. Like I said, we Fangborn are all about Hope.

"Yeah, I guess." Eileen looked uneasy, though. "I've got this feeling, Gerry. Everyone's on edge. Maybe it's the low pressure or the full moon, but there's something up. Watch yourself out there."

The ER was always hopping during the full moon. My people aren't the only ones who feel its power.

"I will, thanks. And you take care. Keep up with the patch."

Eileen was startled. "How did you—?"

I grinned. "You've been out here for five minutes and didn't light up." I didn't tell her I could smell the difference in her clothing, see the slight weight gain, feel her nerves humming with the strain of not reaching for that crumpled box of relief...

We wished each other Merry Christmas and I left. The trail from the taxi was blasted by the mall traffic and the nearby landfill, so I headed to Ziggy's Donuts in Salem, where the cabbies hung out. It didn't hurt that Annie worked there, a girl I'd been kinda hung up on for a while.

I ordered a jelly-filled because Annie was on the counter. I had been trying to get up my nerve to ask her out on a date. It was one of my New Year's resolutions—from this year. But we chatted while she got my donut, and I didn't say anything dumb, so I counted it a success. Maybe even a sign. I found a seat before I did something impetuous and stupid. I'd have to soon: time was almost running out on my resolution, and I keep my promises.

It's hard, when you're a guy, to ask out a cute girl. I'm okay, I'm not hideous, though personally I think I look better as a wolf. I built my own house when our folks died, I have a decent income and a boat that's paid for, and my place is spotless because I don't like surprises.

But it's even harder, when you're Fangborn, to ask a Normal out. The two species can mate, though most of us Fangborn prefer to keep to our own kind. A mixed mating has a lower chance of producing a were or vamp than two Fangborn, but that's pretty low odds, too; how my parents lucked out and got *two*, one of each, I don't know. As far as I understand, it's all about recessive genes, but it doesn't make the initial discussion any easier. "Hey, sweetie? When I said my Family was strange, I didn't mean regular, dysfunctional-strange..."

My cabbie came in then, sweating profusely, probably thinking he was coming down with the flu; I could smell Smith on him, even though they'd probably only brushed fingers when Smith paid. I waited until the cabbie ordered his coffee—even Annie's smile didn't help him—and then I approached him. He wasn't supposed to tell me where he took his fare, but I slid a twenty across the table and got the address of a no-tell motel on the edge of town. Then I asked to check his cab, to see whether Smith had dropped anything, I said.

"Help yourself," he said, shivering around his coffee cup. "It's open."

I was feeling pleased with myself when Weems pulled up alongside me in the parking lot. As he locked up the cruiser, he didn't speak, but gave me a nod along with the hairy eyeball. I nodded back, and kept moving.

We had never liked each other, and now he harbors the deep suspicion most cops have for PIs. He's always made my hackles rise. I couldn't put my finger on the reason, so I did the best I could to avoid him.

Annie knew him, too. Well enough to know that she could look forward to a full six-percent tip.

I waited until Weems was tearing into his bear claw, then opened the door to the cab—

...the screech of brakes before a crash...a phone ringing at 3:30 in the morning...the gush of blood from a wound that is deeper than you thought...

I could barely keep myself standing. I slammed the door, and stumbled back to my truck, not even waiting to calm myself before I fled into the traffic and away from that cab.

"What's next?" Claudia said, when I returned to her condo two hours later. She looked a little better and was now dressed in shorts and a T-shirt that said "I ♥ Spike." She was barefoot, making us coffee. I still felt sick and I was freezing just looking at her. Her place is all white wood and glass and bare surfaces, which she calls "clean lines." The Christmas tree and lights looked out of place there, but I was glad of them.

I tried to get myself together. "After I left Ziggy's, I checked the motel. He paid cash, left no forwarding address. No luck at the other fleabags, either. I cast around for a while, but he wasn't doing any walking and I couldn't get anything from car tracks." I didn't tell her I'd driven halfway to New Hampshire before I'd gotten hold of myself, and used my work to keep from spinning into another panic. I wrapped my arms around myself, trying to feel less hollow, trying not to puke watching the cream swirl around the top of the coffee.

She saw me hesitate. "Gerry, what's wrong? You look like seven kinds of Hell."

I pushed the coffee away from me. "Every time I've caught a noseful of Smith, it's almost knocked me off my feet. You were right, he's bad."

"Yeah, bad. But why did I take so long to bounce back after I saw him? And you, you're always psyched up, all bloodlusty and rarin' to go, when you find a bad guy. What's different about Smith?"

"I dunno." I shrunk down into myself, not wanting to talk.

"That's not helpful." She went into psychiatrist mode. "Okay, you can't say what's wrong with *Smith*. What do *you* feel?"

"Claudia—"

"Humor me."

I shivered. She was right, but I really didn't want to discuss it. "Every time I think about Smith, I get sick, I feel confused. It's like the world's upside down, like I'm chasing my own tail—"

I shoved the chair back and bolted for the sink. I made it, just before the donut made a repeat appearance, and turned on the tap while I retched. Much as I wanted it to, the sound of running water didn't block out Claudia's exclamation.

"Oh, my God, Gerry. He's one of *us*."

"He can't be." I wiped off my mouth and turned to her.

"That's got to be it. It explains so much—our reactions, his, the way he went berserk in the office—"

"He's just a psycho," I said. But I knew she was right.

"No, Gerry." She took a deep breath. "He's evil. And he's one of *us!*"

"There's no such thing as an evil Fangborn, Claudia," I said. "Not in all our history."

"Maybe not in our history, but what about our future? I've got to check in with the Family, let them know what's going on. Maybe the oracles will have something for us. This is *amazing*—"

A sudden, childish urge hit me. "Claud, don't."

"Don't tell the Family?"

I nodded. I just didn't want any of this to be true.

"Gotta do it, Gerry. We can't let Smith get away, and if he's what we think he is, they all need to know. This is *big*."

I shrugged miserably.

She put her hand on my shoulder. "It's scary, yes, the idea of evil appearing in our form, with our powers. It's also a tremendous revelation. Gerry, it can tell us a lot about who we are, maybe more than the geneticists or the oracles can, and it can tell us about the nature of evil. It may even foretell the final battle against evil, Gerry. The one where we win. Who wouldn't want to be present for that?"

Her eyes were alight and her fangs peeked out with her excitement.

I hated her for being excited, but at least that helped shake off the overwhelming emptiness I felt. Time to man up, Gerry. We're still the good guys—

It's just that the bad guys had never looked like us before.

I nodded. "Okay, you contact the Family, and I'll hit the Internet. Smith's out there, and until we get a clue or a scent, we're just gonna have to wait."

We exchanged a look. Sensing the presence of evil is one thing. Being able to find it before it acts is quite another. And the idea of evil in the form of a Fangborn was just plain terrifying.

I went home, and no sooner opened the door than I was attacked by a mass of muscle and fur.

"Beemer, get off!" I peeled the big, brown-striped tom off my shoulder and dumped him on the couch. As a kitten, Beemer jumping from the staircase railing onto me was impressive and cute as Hell. Now that he was in the fifteen-pound class, it was less amusing. To me, anyway. Beemer still thought it was a riot. But even he couldn't cheer me up tonight.

As I heated a shepherd's pie I got over at Henry's Market, I listened to the police scanner, but didn't hear anything that would help. As Beemer washed himself on the leather couch next to me, I drank too much and flipped around the TV—a beaut, 40" plasma, with controls to put the *Enterprise* to shame—but there was nothing to keep my attention. Ditto the Internet and the new issue of *Maxim*. If you wanted proof that my kind are born, not made, just do the math: if we could turn Normals, not a single lingerie model would be left unbitten. Trust me.

Frustrated in every sense of the word, I didn't drift off until just before the alarm rang.

Groaning, I got up, dumped kibble into Beemer's bowl, and hit the bricks, not because I had a lead, but because I had a headache worse than any hangover. The memory of evil left unchecked is one of the downsides of the job, and I didn't even want to think about what Smith meant.

I walked by Ziggy's, but Annie wasn't working. The day outside matched my insides: granite gray, cold, depressing. Even the telephone poles were decorated to suit my mood: the neighborhood was papered with missing pet flyers. I knew how I'd feel if Beemer ever went missing: it'd be a crappy Christmas for the kids worrying about Kitty-Cakes or Bongo or Maxie...

Focus on the job, Gerry. Keep it together.

Down by the Willows, I caught a faint scent. The Salem Willows is an amusement park, very small and dated. It's mostly Whack-a-Mole and fried dough stands and rackety rides during the summer. In the winter, it's a wasteland, boarded up and abandoned.

It wasn't abandoned now: Salem PD, state police, and the ME vans were there. My vision and hearing sharpened, and my olfactory nerves went crazy. Smith had been here, not long ago.

Weems was also there. This time, he came right over to me.

"Steuben. Been seeing a lot of you lately." He only reaches my chin, and he's kinda pudgy, so short-man syndrome never helped things between us.

That's why werewolves and vamps have such crappy reputations. The local authorities always notice us sniffing around crime scenes and figure we're the bad guys.

I sipped my coffee. "Been seeing a lot of you, too, Weems. Funny, huh?"

"I ain't laughing." He crossed his arms. "What're you doing here?"

"I'm looking for the guy at the hospital who knocked my sister around."

His face softened, just a little. "Your sister, she's okay."

Suggesting I was not. "C'mon, Weems. I'm trying to catch an asshole here."

"And what're *we* doing?" For an instant, I thought he'd either hit me or have a heart attack. He balled up his fists and turned a shade of red that would have made Santa's tailors envious.

"You know what I mean." I tried to look desperate, no stretch, under the circumstances. "Man, come on. It's *Claudia*."

The stories would have you believe that vampires are incredibly alluring. It's true, they produce a pheromone that seems to make people around them comfortable, which helps vamps in their healing work. Add a good dose of empathy, and yes, vampires hold a definite attraction for Normals, who think of it as sexual.

Something about Claudia had long ago hit Weems hard, right

between the eyes. She'd hate me throwing her under the bus like that, but if it got me past his defensiveness…

I could see that Weems was torn, but he wasn't going to pass up anything that made him look good in front of Claudia. "We got one vic, and it's a wet one. Or it was, a couple of days ago: it's pretty dried up now." Weems looked greenish; he never could stand the sight of blood. "Chest sliced open…and the heart removed."

"Jesus." I swallowed. "Got an ID?"

"Homeless guy. My guess, he was either flopping in the shed over there, or he was lured in."

"You said *sliced* open?"

"You're a ghoul, Steuben." He sighed. "ME says a big knife, it looks like. They need more tests."

I nodded. If there was one thing we could agree on, it was the reluctance of the ME to spill details.

He hesitated. "The chest was opened up like…ah, jeez. It reminded me of one of those Advent calendars. The skin pulled back square, and the ribs broken to get the heart out."

Maybe he didn't like me seeing him queasy, maybe he just regretted telling me as much as he did, but Weems's face hardened. "Get lost, Steuben. I find you nosing around, you'll be sorry."

"Merry Christmas to you, too, Weems." I left.

"They found a body," I said, after I let myself into Claudia's condo.

Claudia was excited. "Yeah, I know, I just heard it on the news." It was her day off and while Claud was waiting to hear something solid back from the Family—who were going crazy over the news—she was trying to work out a profile for Smith. Maybe she was doing rote work for the same reason I was: to keep from thinking about our world being turned inside out. I still felt like I had the pins knocked out from under me and I hated that uncertainty.

"Down the Willows?" I said, surprised. That was quick.

"No, pulled from the harbor." She frowned. "The woman had been in there about a week. They said 'mutilated,' which usually means something worse."

"So was mine." I told her what I'd just learned from Weems. "They know who she was?"

"A local prostitute, was all they said."

"There's a chance it's not the same guy, not our guy—" I said.

"I'm not willing to bet on that."

"Me, neither."

"He's selecting people on the periphery of society," she said. "Going for those who live under the radar."

I considered where the trail had led me: the abandoned drug den, the dry spell in the emergency room, and—oh, Hell. Three missing cats in one neighborhood was just too much coincidence. I told Claudia. "I guess he's been doing this for a while."

She nodded. "And is escalating. He's refining his ritual, getting bolder, going for less vulnerable, more public targets. It's typical that he started with animals." The look on her face didn't bode well for Smith when we caught him. "Gerry, it's only going to get worse from here. I'm guessing that he's attributing some special significance to the date—the full moon, Christmas..."

Suddenly, I knew. "It *is* Christmas," I said. I told her Weems's description of the corpse, what he'd said about Advent calendars. "Doesn't that sound like what you're talking about? Little, uh, treats leading up to the big day?"

She nodded. "Right. Christmas. Good eyes on Weems."

I snorted. "He's my hero." But Christmas was just two days away. "My question is, why did Smith have to call a cab?"

"He didn't have a car," she answered promptly. "Weems brought him in, right?"

I made a face at her. "But if Smith is responsible for the murders, he must have a car."

"He can't afford to let it go out in public. Too many people could see...what?"

"Bloodstains? Cracked window?"

"Too recognizable," she said. "A truck with a business logo on it, contractors, deliveries—"

"Right, it's got to blend in, but not the sort of thing you'd drive for private stuff." I thought a minute, then an idea hit me. "Like a police car. Maybe it isn't Smith! Maybe it's Weems!"

"Gerry. Get real. Weems is your bête noir, and he's a dickhead, but he's not our guy."

"He was at the hospital." I ticked off my reasons on my fingers, *loving* that Smith might just be a garden-variety psycho, his trail confused by Weems. "He was at the donut shop. He's been dogging my tracks all day, and every time I saw him, I felt the call to Change."

"All places you'd expect to see a cop investigating the same case as we are. Have you ever wanted to Change because of Weems before now?" She put her hand on mine; it was warm as toast. "I know you don't like him, but you're getting distracted by this. You've always been so damned sure about everything—"

That was the problem: I couldn't be sure about anything anymore if Smith was Fangborn.

I pulled away. "I don't think so. I think you were picking up on his vibes, the same time you were dealing with some ordinary, run-of-the-mill loony, and that's why you thought it was Smith."

"You're wrong," she said. "Weems has nothing to do with this. I think you want it to be Weems so you don't have to consider that there might be an evil out there we haven't seen before. I get it, Ger: you want things to be cut-and-dried. But now we know...it can't be like that."

"Whatever." I turned away.

"Don't dismiss me, Gerry."

You know about that traditional conflict between werewolves and vampires? It's really just a sibling thing.

"Claudia, just because—"

"Sssh!" Claudia was pointing to the TV.

The news was on. A school bus, its driver, and six kids were missing from their daycare center.

"Okay," I said, "we've got the fake address at the Point, a murder at the Willows, a body in the harbor. Throw in the missing pets, and we have someone with a familiarity with the waterfront. That's a couple of big neighborhoods to cover."

"He needs space, and he needs a place where people won't hear...screams." Claudia was looking at the map spread out in front of us. "He's sticking with what's familiar to him, which is good for us, but he's also an organized psychopath, which is bad."

"The houses are too close together, here and here," I said, pointing out two neighborhoods. "That leaves the warehouses in the industrial park down at the Point and the coal plant down here." I pointed to a neighborhood that was near, by water, but on the other side of town, by land.

"A school bus is going to stick out in either place," Claudia said. "Is he going to take them out to sea?"

"If he is, we're pretty well screwed," I said. "Protective coloring—where can you take six crying kids and a school bus where no one will notice?"

We looked at each other, then simultaneously at one of the neighborhoods we had just rejected. A short distance from my own house, separated by large parking lots and a playing field, was the middle school, now empty for the holidays.

It's not that we need the moon to shift, though that helps. It's easier to run around as a wolf when there aren't many people around. It's easier to pick up a faint trail with the dust settled from the day. It's not that we need the moon, but somehow, it makes it easier for me, the same way the sun takes the poison out of vamps like Claudia. You'd have to talk to our scientists who are working out exactly how we Fangborn work, but if you think of it like a vulture's bare head helping to kill the bacteria they pick up, or photosynthesis, taking nutrients from the sunlight, that's probably close. All I know is that Claudia couldn't taste the blood and clean it, cauterize the wound, and numb the memory without sunlight to charge her up. And in the same way—don't ask me how, I'm not one of the geeks—I get recharged by the moon.

Plus, lots of bad guys also wait for night to work. Makes it easier on us all.

The moon was full and low on the horizon as we parked down the street from the school. We ran down the plan again: check the school and then call the cops if we find anything.

Simple, if we were right. If we weren't already too late.

"Got the gear?" I asked Claudia.

She nodded, held up the leash—her excuse for being out with a very large dog—and a charged cell phone. As for me, while I hate what people inflict on their pets—birthday parties, pedicures, Halloween costumes—I will always be grateful for the dog-clothing craze. And grateful to the guy who invented stretch fabrics: my Lycra doggie track suit makes it a heck of a lot easier if I have to Change back to human and don't want to be butt-naked.

Claudia doubled the knots on her bootlaces, tied her hair back, and we went into the schoolyard.

The bus was there, all right, on the side, cold and silent as an empty grave. Sure, school was out and it was night, but who notices a school bus outside a school? The schoolyard had been badly plowed, so there were no clear tracks, but it only took me a minute to find the basement door they'd used, the lock broken.

The reek hit me as soon as we got the door open. This time, I didn't resist the Change.

The rush of adrenaline and endorphins and other hormones blotted out whatever pain shrieking bones forced through evolutionary growth in an instant might bring. Nature wouldn't be so cruel as to put this burden on us without compensation. The bloodlust didn't hurt, either, and it was only Claud's warning hand on my back that reminded me not to howl with the delight of it.

Smith's spoor was worse than any I'd ever smelled, overwhelming the traces of new linoleum, old wax, and textbooks. It was nearly unbearable to my lupine nose, but one thought, a bloodthirsty, simple joy, cleared of all human doubt and fear, overwhelmed even that:

It was time to track and to tear.

I stepped out of my boots and glanced up at Claud, who was down on one knee; the reek was hitting her just as badly. It was always harder for her; vamps don't have the same chemical buffer that protects wolves. Her skin took on a violet cast visible even in the shadows, and her eyes were wide and bright. Her facial features broadened, her nose receded, and her fingers lengthened.

She stood up, shook herself, and nodded. As she packed my boots into her backpack, I saw the gleam of her viperish fangs extending, the glint of a streetlight on the fine pattern of snakescale, an armor of supple, thickened skin. Snakes have always been associated with healing and transformation—there's a reason they're on the staff of Asclepius—but they've got a rep for danger, too.

I whined and stared at her neck. Her hand went up, and she found the pearls she'd forgotten to take off.

"Thankths," she said, with a slight hiss. Still largely humanoid, fangs and a forked tongue make speech awkward, but not impossible. She stowed the necklace in her bag, and nodded.

I led the way, as stealthy as a shadow. I cast around, stopped, panted, and tried again, but with no luck. There was no one single track to pick up. Smith'd been here long enough for the basement to be so saturated with his stench that I could barely breathe.

I couldn't detect the children. I hoped we weren't too late.

Claudia nodded. She pointed at the first door, and we both listened. Nothing.

She tried it; locked solid.

The next was an unlocked closet. The stink was there, too, but less.

The bus driver was stashed in there. There was a pulse, faint and fading.

Claudia fanged down, called 911. We continued.

The next door opened silently; I could smell WD-40 recently applied to the hinges. No way to tell Claud, but she pointed to the duct tape across the lock, and I nodded. We went in.

The children were there. Even under Smith's foulness, I could tell they were alive. I felt a surge of delight.

They were drugged, only half-awake; a light on the playground offered just enough illumination for a Normal to see forms without detail. My nose told me of full diapers, fear, and baby shampoo.

Smith was nowhere around. We went quietly, just in case.

"Hang on," Claudia said. She Changed back about halfway, just enough to keep her powers on deck, but not so far that the first thing the kids saw was a pale purple lady with no nose and very big teeth.

She went over to them quickly. "Hey, you guys? Let's get you fixed up and we'll get you home, okay? My dog Chewie is going to do some tricks for you. He's really big, but he's really, really friendly. Chewie, come!"

That was my cue. I knew to play it dumb and sweet over in the faint light so the kids would focus on me. That way, they'd be less afraid and they wouldn't notice Claudia practicing her leech-craft. I spend my time fighting evil, not practicing party tricks, but whenever I fell over, the kids laughed, so it was okay. And as soon as Claudia got one kid untied, her razor nails dancing scalpels over the duct tape, I was there, his new best friend, and they were so busy patting me they forgot to be afraid. Under the guise of inspecting their wounded hands, she got to work, biting their wrists, narcotizing the pain, neutralizing their terror, sucking out Smith's drugs, dimming their memories. I could sense her body reacting to the blood and emotion she was taking in, her muscles rippling, nearly all trace of humanity lost from her features even as she healed the little ones.

She'd just finished the last one when *he* was on her. Even as I picked up on the fresh scent—snow mixed with spoiled milk and rotting fish heads—Smith rocketed from the shadows, moving faster than anything human.

If I knew he was there, it meant Claudia knew, too. She shoved the kid toward me as Smith landed on her. She rolled with him as far away from us as she could.

In spite of Claudia's ministrations, the kids whimpered. I grabbed the last one by the hood of her jacket and gently pulled her the rest of the way to the group. I stood between them and the brawl, nudging the kids to stand behind me, thankful Disney had removed their fear of large wild animals.

It took everything I had to keep from jumping in and ripping Smith apart, but I had to keep the children safe. And there's not much that can stop my sister when she's pissed and Changed; for all her tweedy skirts and bookishness, she's as much a warrior as I am.

Smith was putting up a pretty good fight and the sonofabitch knew how to use a knife: Claudia would need a week on the roof to recover from this. I was glad of the dark, that the children's eyes weren't as sharp as mine, that they couldn't see the amount of blood that Claudia was letting.

She was winning. Maybe Smith wasn't Fangborn, maybe just some kind of freak human genetic anomaly—

You could practically feel the energy she expended fill the room, almost blotting out the horror of Smith. Righteous violence in the cause of justice—

I let out a low growl; there was *too* much energy, the air was sizzling as if every Fangborn in New England was Changing next to me.

Claudia screamed.

Smith had Changed. An unholy transformation, something never before seen in the world as I knew it: evil taking on the shape of a werewolf.

If I'd had time for rational, human thought, I would have been slowed by what *shouldn't* have been happening, by what was impossible, but the pull to attack was so strong I almost burst out of my skin. I bunched up and launched myself at Smith.

Claudia threw herself out of the way as I bowled the other wolf out of the room. We skidded into the hallway, unable to get a purchase on the cold, polished cement floor. With a scrabble of claws, I was up, but he was just a second faster and knocked me down again, snapping at my eyes. I slashed at his gut and jerked my head out of the way, feeling his hot breath and drool on my ears. I whipped around and grabbed at his muzzle; I was bigger than he was and he almost pulled away before I closed my teeth. I caught him, barely, by the tender tip of his nose and the soft skin under his jaw. Teeth slid through flesh and I held on; he tried to push me away with his front paws, but was more effective with his rear claws, raking across my belly.

I smelled my own blood, but held on for dear life. He couldn't pull out of my grasp without tearing himself and I couldn't let him go.

The door opened and cold air washed over us. I heard a shout and recognized Weems.

He shouted again. I could smell Weems's fear. Weems drew his pistol. He was going to shoot.

Well, I couldn't let him shoot *me*. I let go and Smith hurled himself at the doorway and Weems.

Thoughts flashed through my head: If Smith landed on Weems, I could grab him before he did much damage. If he knocked Weems out of the way, or took a bullet or six, so much the better for me.

Damn. He bolted right past Weems. He couldn't afford to get caught as a werewolf any more than I could. The prospect of decades of lab experiments made a life sentence at Cedar Junction look like a week at Sandals.

Sweat-soaked polyester, terror, boiled coffee, and roast beef: Weems had had dinner at Big Freddy's. If I planted a dirty, doggy paw in his face as I chased after Smith, I'm sure it was an accident.

Smith was nowhere to be seen as I raced down the street away from the school, but it didn't matter: he was leaving a trail of blood that any Cub Scout could have followed, and his scent was so strong there might as well have been a spotlight on him.

I cut through snowy backyards and vaulted a chain-link fence: Christmas lights lit the snow and the smell of cooking meats and seafood wasn't even a momentary distraction. Another burst of speed brought me down to the historic district on the waterfront, the eighteenth-century houses decorated with candles and garlands.

The tear in my belly was bad; I could feel the shock of the cold air through fur even as my muscle reknit itself. There was a sharp pain whenever I moved my left hind leg. The icy snow, dirty with sand and road salt, packed itself in between the pads of my paws, slowing me down and throwing off my gait. Blood—mine and Smith's—was matted in my fur, and my jaw ached.

The trail of blood was getting heavier, though: Smith was also slowing down. In spite of my wounds, I sped up, eager to end this.

But part of me hoped Smith would never stop. If he stopped, I'd kill him, and my job would be finished. Then I'd have to think about what was happening. I wasn't sure if my frail human brain could deal with it.

I leapt onto a back porch, tensed, then sailed over the back of the deck onto the sidewalk of Derby Street. I skidded on the icy bricks of the crosswalk, and barely missed getting hit by an Escalade. I yelped, feeling the breeze as the SUV swerved past.

The waterfront opened up in front of me. The heavy clouds parted for an instant and the full moon shone down on the blood that led straight down Derby Wharf, which stretched out a quarter of a mile into the harbor.

Unless Smith wanted to swim in life-sucking cold water toward the winking lights of Marblehead, he had nowhere to go except back to me. I grinned, as only a wolf drunk on power can.

There was no one out, and I was glad; it was usually a place for evening strolls, the marks of lesser canines blazoned against the snowbanks. I padded down the wide gravel path, catching my breath, preparing myself for the last fight.

Smith was smarter than I gave him credit for. He timed his attack for the instant the lighthouse lamp whirled toward me, washing the shadows together and reducing my field of vision.

Keeping my eyes lowered and narrowed, my ears back, I made myself wait until the last moment. Then I sprang at him, just as hard as I could. I caught Smith with his head still up, and seized him by the throat, biting down with every bit of strength I had.

His momentum carried him over me, and as he fell, his own weight tore his flesh off in my mouth. Hot blood poured and he dropped dead at my feet.

He might have been a predator with a hero's weapons, but I was a hero with true purpose.

I spat out the fur and gore as the moonlight flooded the wharf and harbor. Steam rose from the wounds of the dead wolf, blood black on the snow. Power from the kill, from having slain one of my own kind, almost knocked me off my feet, and it was possible I was the first one ever in history to have experienced it.

Evil just doesn't exist in the Fangborn. At least, it hadn't before now.

I threw my head back and howled, my inhuman blood singing, the completeness and rightness of my triumph dizzying.

But somewhere in the back of my brain, the part that stays human, I knew it was the last time I'd feel that way.

On Christmas Eve, Claudia found me down in the basement of my house. It's finished with mats on the floors and walls so we can train in private.

"That's some sweat you're working up there," she yelled. She was wearing her T-shirt with the bull's-eye printed over her heart, the one that says, "Go ahead and try it, Buffy."

I was flaked out on the floor in three layers of sweats, my headphones on, music turned to eleven. I considered her statement, then showed her a finger.

She came over to the stereo, cranked it up to fourteen or twenty so I had to pull the headphones off, then she switched off the CD. She glanced at the player.

"*Disintegration*. Nice. And have you been down here since yesterday, moping out to The Cure? I'm going to take my old CDs away from you if you're going to behave like an adolescent."

"I am an adolescent." And I am, by my people's standards. Just a pup.

"I get that. Gerry, you *peed* on Weems's car!"

I shrugged. It seemed like the thing to do at the time.

After I'd returned, still wolfself, to the school, Claudia had sold most of the story to a suspicious Weems. She was out walking her dog when she saw the school bus. Not wanting to feel like a fool if it wasn't the missing children, she'd explored, then found the kids. The kids, still under her chemical thrall, had confirmed it: the scary man's dog had attacked the nice lady's doggie, who chased both the bad guys away. Weems later found Smith's body at the wharf, dead, without a mark on him save for his stitched-up arm.

She knelt beside me. "Gerry, Smith is a shock; I buy that. I was rattled, too. It's scary as Hell. The Family computer lists have been lighting up with the discussion, and none of the historians have anything like this. *Ever*."

"I'm not scared, Claud," I said. "And I get that this is major. It's just that..."

I took a breath; it was even harder to say out loud than it was to admit to myself. "I liked knowing that we Fangborn were the righteous ones, and that whatever we hunted was *always* wrong. No doubts, never. I always thought it was the payoff for the work we do." It also meant, no matter what my opinion, that Weems was at least nominally on our side.

She cocked her head. "You mean, in addition to the super strength, healing, and longevity?"

"Yeah."

"And the rush that comes after the Change?"

"Well...yeah."

She frowned. "You're young and you're being greedy and you're forgetting the First Lesson."

I scowled. "'The work is the reward.' You sound like Grandpa."

"There's a good reason for that. He was right." She hunkered down against the wall next to me. "Look, everyone reaches a crisis of faith at some point in his life. For me, it was trying to figure out if we had the right to live outside human law, learning the difference between *law* and *justice*. It's part of the life. It makes us understand what it is to be human, why that's precious and to be protected. Normals never get half of what we have, and go through life in doubt."

"We're not human, Claud. Never will be. And now we get the doubt, too."

She shook her head. "We're closer to them than anything else. Biologically and spiritually. We need that connection. And you know that killing Smith was right, even if he was one of us."

But no Fangborn had ever killed Fangborn before. No Fangborn had ever manifested pure evil before...I couldn't turn off the voice in my head.

Claudia talked for a long time about the community of the Fangborn, duty, honor, and all that crap. I listened. A lot of it made sense.

I nodded. "You're right. I need time, that's all. Thanks."

"No problem. I'm just glad I got here before you got into the Nine Inch Nails." Relief flooded her features, which told me exactly how rocky she thought I looked. "So. You packed?"

"No. It won't take me long." This year, our Christmas present to each other was tickets to Aruba. Expensive, but we both needed the sunshine right now.

She nodded, then eyed me sternly. "But you're gonna go to midnight Mass, right?"

"Probably. I gotta go for a walk, first. Clear my head." I hauled myself up, muscles stiff not from the fight, but from lying around. Any harm I take while wolfself heals rapidly, as long as I remain wolfy, but any hurt I get while in human form reappears when I revert back to human form.

"Good. I'll see you there. And Gerry?"

"Yeah, Claud?"

She wrinkled her nose. "Take a shower, would you?"

I flipped her the bird again, and got my jacket. She smiled as she left, and I knew I had her convinced. That's the good thing about having a shrink for a sister: you learn what they look for and you can give it to them.

Yes, her words made sense. They just did nothing to take away my pain.

I pulled on my duck boots, hat, scarf, and gloves. I probably didn't need so much—it was over thirty degrees—but ever since the fight, I just couldn't get warm.

I walked a long time and found myself at the foot of Derby Wharf. I went out far enough to let the holiday lights of the street fall behind me, until I was alone in the frigid dark. Bloodstains blurred the snow, which had been trampled by the locals looking for the serial killer's savage dog. A fierce hellhound roaming Salem, one more myth in the making.

I watched the lighthouse beam skim the surface of the dark water. Listened to the soft slap of waves against the stone wharf. Anyone with a lick of insight could feel the remnants of the power that had been expended here.

In our Family's annals, there was nothing like this, but now I had to wonder: Who else had we missed? Or if this was a really new development, what did it mean? The only thing I knew was that my certainty about my place in the world—my armor and my sword—was shattered.

I felt the silence all around me, city noises muffled by the snow, and tried to find the bottom of the sea of pain I felt. The uncertainty was crushing, the loss of faith like the loss of a limb. I felt broken and made a fool of, mocked by the universe for my belief.

I took a deep breath, the kind you take at the crossroads when the dark man shows up and offers you the world in exchange for your grubby soul. As I watched the obsidian water, I took another breath and realized that if I couldn't manage the leap of faith that Claudia described, then I had to make a leap of another kind.

Down the street from Derby Wharf is a little bar called In a Pig's Eye. It's a local joint; there's no television and they pull the best pints in town.

Annie works there nights.

It was about half full, the folks who were getting one more drink in before Mass and the ones whose family were the other strangers on bar stools.

"Jeez, Gerry, you been sick or something? You look kinda peaky." She set down a coaster in front of me. "Winter Warmer?"

"Thanks. Just...out of it, I guess." I suddenly remembered my rank-smelling sweats and two days' growth of beard, and kept my jacket zipped. Hell.

"I bet. I read about Claudia in the paper. You must have *freaked*."

One of the things I've learned to live with is the fact that I'll never get credit for being on the scene, for doing the job. "I worry about her, but she's good at taking care of herself." Then I couldn't resist, sweats or no. "And besides. Chewie wouldn't let anything happen to her."

She put the dark beer down in front of me, a perfect half inch of froth at the top. "No. He's a sweetie."

I felt myself flush, remembering the perfume of Annie's ankles, her hand on the back of my neck as she talked to Claudia one summer night. We'd been coming home from work and I'd still been intoxicated by the kill when we ran into Annie. It's one of my fondest memories. "You like dogs?"

She shrugged. "Depends. Like people, really. You gotta take them one at a time, you know?"

Ask her out, I told myself, *ask her out right now, coffee, a drink, anything, or so help me, I'll—* "How do you feel about Aruba?" I felt myself go red again: that was not what I meant to say. It was too much, too soon, too pimp, oh shit—

Annie stopped wiping down the bar.

Suddenly, the bottomless water seemed a better choice. "I'd prefer to start with a drink, maybe dinner," she said slowly. "That is, if you're really, actually, *finally* getting the guts to ask me out?"

"Uh...yeah." I swallowed. "That okay?"

"Yeah. But it took you long enough." She glanced at me. "You tough guys, you're all just pussycats. You aren't always a big pussycat, are you, Gerry?"

Mostly I'm a big wolf, I thought giddily. "Never again," I vowed. "How's tomorrow night?"

"Can't." She looked at me funny. "It's Christmas tomorrow, remember? I'm going snowshoeing at Bradley Palmer State Park in the morning."

I wrinkled my brow. An odd tradition, but nice, I s'pose...

She blew out her cheeks. "You know I'm Wiccan, right? I like Christmas, but I observe the Solstice."

She looked a little defensive, but I could barely contain myself. I forced myself to take a deep breath. "Trust me when I say that mixed relationships are not a problem for me."

She relaxed, then gave me a look that warmed me instantly, straight through. "If you invite me over for breakfast, I'll ditch the snowshoeing. But I have to leave by noon, because I promised Kelly I'd take her shift at the shelter so she can be with her family."

"Breakfast is at nine o'clock!" I could barely get the words out fast enough.

"Claudia won't mind?"

"Nah. I'll call her when I get home." Claudia had been pushing me to ask Annie out from the first time I'd mentioned her. "She's good people, not an evil bone in her body," Claudia'd said. And Claudia knows bones, good and evil.

"I'll be there." Annie smiled, so sexy I felt my knees go to jelly. "I made a batch of my famous chocolate-chip muffins; I'll bring them."

Into nature, civic-minded, and a cook? I realized I was grinning like an idiot, so I drank the rest of my beer, to keep from proposing to her right then and there, my head ringing with every Christmas carol ever written.

Pattern Recognition

This story represents one of the moments when I realized that the Fangborn world was expanding, and that "oracles" were becoming a more powerful part of it, being capable of telekinesis, and maybe even necromancy. Like "Love Knot," the idea that the Fangborn are magic—or not—comes into play when powerful beings are revealed as the Family is threatened. I began thinking that there might be a more conservative faction of Fangborn, and played around with the notion of "strays," Fangborn who didn't know what they were and raised outside the culture—like Zoe Miller, the protagonist of the Fangborn novels.

Joel's eyes went straight to her breasts, then lower, where they loitered. The next moment was a blur of arousal, interest, and, when his brain caught up with his spinal cord, curiosity, followed by concern and building fear.

Naked, was the first word that came to him. Then *girl, dirty, crazy.*

She *was* naked, save for a scarf draped over her head. She stood on a rickety wooden chair in the middle of the room, skinny arms outstretched wide before her, shaking with the effort of holding them up. Her brown hair was long and tangled and she looked like something out of ancient history class.

Joel felt a rumbling beneath his feet; maybe it was the train passing nearby.

Her eyes finally opened, wide and unfocused, as if he'd wakened her from a dream. She glanced around, looked right through Joel as if he wasn't even there, then mumbled something.

"Didn't catch that," he said, wondering if reaching for his cell phone would set her off. *She didn't look like much,* he thought, *but you couldn't be too careful. Not with a serial killer on the loose.*

"Thought it would work," she said, swallowing. "This time."

He pretended to look around, shook his head. "Nope. I guess not."

He didn't want to know who she was, didn't want her to be his problem. He held out a hand, hoping she'd get down and leave.

It halfway worked. She climbed off the chair, but then sat down.

He stepped toward her and his foot slipped. When he looked down, he saw olive oil covering the floor. All over her arms, dripping down her legs, the empty container in the corner, as if it had been flung away.

Joel tamped down burgeoning panic as he tried not to think of the ridiculously expensive olive oil. It had been one of the last things he and Lenore had argued about before she left.

The anxiety that plagued him so constantly—had he locked the door? Had he been offensive to the waitress? Had he really cut someone off in traffic?—was somewhat at bay since he'd just come from therapy. Maybe this was one of those opportunities his shrink had mentioned, about climbing out of his own head to help someone else.

"You got a name?" he said, flinching. He hadn't meant the question to come out so brusquely.

"I don't think so." She stood, and to Joel's relief, went over to a pile of clothing on the floor, just out of range of the pool of oil that was being sucked into the hungry, rough wood planks. "This isn't your place." She seemed fine now, blotting herself with the scarf, as if she remembered nothing of standing naked in a stranger's presence. As if she'd suddenly realized how cold and drafty the room was.

"No." The apartment was his cousin's, loaned to him on condition he admit the bead shop staff downstairs every day, and lock up at night. "It's not yours either," he said. Not aggressive, really, he thought. Maybe a little nudge, a hint of assertiveness. Nothing anyone could take offense at, surely?

She didn't seem so dangerous now, in an old pair of cargo pants, a hoodie, and Docs. The sodden scarf was wrapped around her neck, forgotten.

"No. I..." She faltered for the first time, looked around her. "I don't know where I am."

"How about we get someone to come pick you up?" Joel was emboldened by the idea of his authority. It had been a while. "Is there someone we can call?"

She opened her mouth to speak, then shut it. After half a minute, she said, "I don't think so. I think I'm trying to hide."

No shit. I would, too, if I was crazy as you, he thought. He immediately regretted the uncharitable thought. "Um...okay. We won't let anyone hurt you. I'll call a friend of mine." The more he thought about calling Dr. Steuben, the more it seemed like a good idea. "She'll be able to help you sort things out."

And if not, she can check you into the cracker factory.

"Okay." She went over to the window, looked out into the winter dusk, and shivered. "This is Salem?"

Joel fumbled with his phone. *And I'd been so close to taking the doctor off speed-dial,* he thought. "Uh, yeah. Massachusetts. March, 14, 20—"

"Yeah, thanks, I got it." She interrupted him with a frown that said "asshole."

"Hey, I'm not the one standing naked on chairs," he said then immediately regretted it. What if he set her off? What if she got violent? He of all people should be more sympathetic. "Sorry. I'm sorry. I just didn't know...what else you didn't know."

She shrugged. "Me, neither."

Luckily, Dr. Steuben answered just then. Joel told his story, and after confirming neither one of them was injured—as far as he could tell the woman was perfectly fine, just lost in thought—Dr. Steuben asked, "Did you ask if she knew your cousin? If she'd been given a key of her own?"

"Ummm..."

"It's like we discussed, Joel. Stick with the basics, what's most likely. That will help."

He imagined he could hear her impatience and felt chastened. "Okay, hang on a sec." He covered the phone. "You don't know Diana, do you?"

"Who?"

"My cousin, the woman who owns this apartment? And the bead store downstairs?"

"No." That seemed to worry her.

Joel returned to the phone, feeling vindicated. "Never heard of Diana."

"Tell me again what the woman was doing."

He turned away, as if to conceal his words from the woman herself, and described the scene. "It was, I don't know," he finished. "Like something from the History Channel? Ancient looking?"

He felt stupid as soon as he said it, and when his therapist didn't say anything, he was sure her concern about him had cranked up a couple of notches. He could hear a keyboard clattering in the background, and wondered if she was taking notes. On him. "Can I bring her to see you?"

"Do you think she'll come with you?"

"Sure. She seems—" He turned around to check on the girl—woman, he corrected himself automatically.

She was gone. The door leading to the back alley stairs was hanging open.

He went over, and looked down into the alley. No sign of her.

"Hey, it looks like she took off." His relief to be rid of this problem was tinged with regret. He couldn't have said why.

Both relief and regret were short-lived.

"Find her, if you can," Dr. Steuben said, surprising him. "I'll be there in ten minutes."

My sister Claudia insisted on driving, which was fine. She drives at least as fast as I do, if not as cautiously. She's a vampire—with all the speed, agility, and coordination that implies—and if she gets pulled over, she can always charm the cop.

I can't charm cops. They shouldn't be allergic to me, but they are. There's a serious mistrust for ex-cops who go to the dark side. Not 'dark side' because I'm a werewolf—most of the guys I know would think that was pretty cool, once they got done pissing themselves. Even cooler if they learned I'm Fangborn, born to a Family of supernatural beings dedicated to the protection of humanity and the eradication of evil. No, I went to the dark side when I retired from the force and became a PI. That's when the love got lost.

So I let Claudia drive and tried not to flinch as she changed lanes, slipping into a nearly nonexistent space between cars.

"My patient, Joel Weeks," she said, "is working on issues with grief, depression, and separation anxiety. No real breakthrough, no catharsis, yet—there's a lot of denial there—but it's nothing I can't fix with talk therapy and a little vampire boost. It's the woman he found in his apartment I'm interested in."

"Why? You said he'd never met her before."

"Her posture, the oil, the nudity—it's a hunch, Gerry, that's all." Claudia's hunches are pretty good—honed by her training as a shrink and vampire intuition—and while I didn't say anything, I agreed with her. There was something about this whole situation that got my spidey sense tingling, too.

"When we get there," she said, "I'll ask him what he saw, and distract him while you track the girl. We need to find her."

We arrived at the shop and I didn't need to hear Claudia's gasp to tell me plans had changed.

Outside the construction site for the local museum's new wing, a hapless-looking guy—just a citizen, weedy, remarkably unimpressive— was frozen in his tracks, gawking at another man trying to drag a young woman away. The late winter snow had started again, muffling the sounds outside. The jerk dragging the girl outweighed her by at least seventy pounds and looked like he enjoyed his job. When she actually managed to wriggle out of one of his hands, he cocked his head. Then he stepped in, yanked her by the other hand, and gave her a slap so hard it knocked her head into the concrete foundation.

"Gerry!" Claudia warned.

I stopped growling, unfastened my seat belt, then Changed halfway as Claudia stomped the accelerator. The rush came over me as it always does, adrenaline gearing me up for battle. A glance in the rear view showed we were alone. It also revealed my inhuman face: muzzle filled with teeth; furry, upright ears; a wolf's predator eyes. Red Sox cap.

"I'll get Joel," she said, as I unlocked my door. "You get the bad guy."

"Fastball special, coming up." I've had a lot of practice, talking around fangs.

My sister accelerated, then pulled the handbrake, sliding in alongside the sidewalk and blocking the struggling couple from Joel's view with the BMW. I threw myself from the still-moving car, tucked, and rolled. Because my reflexes are about a hundred times better than a human's, I landed right at the jerk's feet before he realized it.

I stood up, driving my fist into his chin with all my 200 pounds behind it. When his head bashed into the same wall he'd just bounced the girl against, I thought it had a certain kind of poetry.

Something freaky happened: an overwhelming urge to Change completely to wolfself hit me. It was all concentrated at the base of my skull, though, like I'd never felt before, Pop Rocks and Alka-Seltzer buzzing my brain. I was losing control like I hadn't since I was a kid, damn near drunk on the glory of fangs, fur, and the pursuit of evil.

Then, a loud, metallic crack, high overhead. I grabbed the girl and threw us both to one side.

A tangle of rebar crashed down from the construction site to the sidewalk. If I hadn't moved, the girl would have been dead for sure, and I'd have looked like roadkill for a week, at the very least. The jerk was extremely dead, a mess of metal rods and hamburger.

"Hey, you guys?" Claudia spoke calmly, as if she only wanted to get out of the wet snow. "Let's get out of here. Joel, could you get us some coffee at your place?"

I felt the tug of her vampiric suggestion, and wondered why my sister was pushing so hard. Maybe she was afraid the girl was going to run again, but she still seemed pretty dazed, maybe concussed. Maybe she was worried Joel would freak out at what he'd just seen, but he only nodded.

We followed him a few doors down to one of those old brick warehouses converted to apartments and shops. As we entered, something told me to look back down the block.

If I'd been a Normal, I might have told myself it was a trick of the light. I knew better. The rebar on the sidewalk had been twisted into the shapes of perfectly formed snowflakes, as delicate as the ones falling around us.

Joel found himself making coffee in the apartment over his cousin's shop. He felt calmer now, probably because Dr. Steuben and her slab of a brother seemed to be taking charge. Fine with him; he'd never been a leader. He was still fuzzy about what had happened on the street.

Dr. Steuben was talking softly with the woman, when he emerged from the tiny kitchen. They looked up.

"Hey." He set down the coffee, glanced nervously at Dr. Steuben. He always felt so...useless...around her. "Um...any luck?"

"Nope." Dr. Steuben smiled, and his anxiety vanished. "She seems to have suffered some kind of massive trauma. The first thing she remembers is asking you where she was."

The woman shrugged. "Apparently, I put on quite a show when I've suffered a trauma." She was trying for casual, but fell a mile short, her laugh nervous. She was shaking now.

Joel wasn't sure what to say. Fortunately, Gerry looked up from the smart phone he'd been studying. "There's been an unusual number of missing persons cases lately. I've been keeping an eye on them, and so far, every one has either stayed missing, or..."

"Or?" the woman said.

Gerry hesitated. "Was found deceased."

Joel stirred his coffee, frowning. "You mean the ones who were macheted to death? It's been all over the papers. Some kind of gang war, I thought."

Gerry shook his head. "Maybe. I doubt it."

Joel felt the hair on the back of his neck stand up and swallowed hard.

"Any luck on a name for our friend here?" Dr. Steuben said.

Gerry tapped the keys on his phone. "I think so: Alexa Thompson, White, age twenty-seven, brown and brown. Sounds about right. Reported missing three days ago when she didn't show up to her IT job at the college."

The girl—Alexa—swept her arm out and knocked her coffee cup to the floor. She took a deep breath, then began to cry.

Joel booked it for the kitchen to find a towel; he had no problem leaving this kind of emotion to a trained professional. When he returned, Alexa was calmer, but Dr. Steuben was downright agitated.

"—Gerry, it doesn't work like that," she was saying to her brother. "She's had a blackout—without any symptoms of post-traumatic confusional state—but with no sign of injury. Exhibiting both anterograde and retrograde amnesia, at the same time she now recognizes her name? It's not medically...usual."

"If she's telling the truth," Gerry said.

"Of course I'm telling the truth!" Alexa said, snuffling. "Who would make this up?"

"She's telling the truth." Dr. Steuben gave her brother a glance. "But this is just *not* what happens with a concussion or even the stress of having been mugged."

"I don't think I was mugged," Alexa said. "I don't have a bag, but I don't have my coat either." Her face brightened. "Something must have happened inside."

"Something you can't recall."

Dr. Steuben ran down a list of questions, with no luck: Alexa didn't drink to excess, never touched drugs, no history of mental or physical illness.

Agreeing to meet back at the apartment in an hour, the Steubens left to check Alexa's apartment for clues. Joel reluctantly agreed to keep Alexa until the Steubens returned; the incident with the guy on the sidewalk had left everyone shaken. Locking the door behind them, Joel couldn't stop thinking about what it must be like to be cut with a machete.

"I notice you didn't encourage them to call the cops," I said. "I also notice they're not even questioning our involvement."

Claudia pulled on her latex gloves as we returned to the site of the attack. She'd Changed halfway, the better to examine the corpse. We both hoped the street would stay empty; a bipedal, female herpet-American with fangs and purplish scales was no tourist attraction, even in Salem. "I didn't want the cops near them," Claudia said. "And yes, I gave them a little blast of suggestibility pheromone. This is *our* brand of weird, Gerry."

"Because it's magic?" I stared at the iron snowflakes, ranging in size from three to five feet tall. The detail in them was astonishing, more than man-made. Definitely not natural, definitely not an accident.

"No way. If Normal humans knew about the Fangborn, they'd think we're magic. We're not. Science just hasn't caught up with us yet. And Alexa didn't use magic, either."

I looked at the rebar, twisted into impossibly delicate, graceful shapes. "Science had better catch up quick. This is fucking weird. Almost, you know." I made booga-booga hands. *"Magical."*

Claudia hissed faintly, as she searched the body. "Gerry, it's only our ultra-conservative cousins who live in caves and cast bones who believe in magic. There ain't no such thing."

I crossed my arms. "And yet, a werewolf and a vampire stare at an instant modern art installation in the middle of the sidewalk. What's the deal?" I nodded to the wallet and other pocket detritus Claudia had collected from the corpse. It had been a difficult job; the body had been impaled about a hundred different ways from Sunday. When the cops finally arrived, they'd have a bad time with this.

"The name Ronnie Platt mean anything to you?"

I took a deep breath. "He works for Diego Cesar, a guy the Normals don't want to even think about."

Claudia showed me his cell phone: Hells. Ronnie had called in to his boss. But I was willing to bet he didn't actually know Joel, or where he was staying, if he was after Alexa. There was no connection between the two I could see.

"Any reason Cesar or Platt would be slicing up people randomly?" she asked, as I pocketed the phone.

"Usually profit involved." I stared at the rebar. "I've heard Cesar has a strange kink about mystical stuff, though. An unattractive habit of getting live goats and chickens from East Cambridge to...open up. To...examine. I can't make a case for him killing the missing persons, though."

"Haruspicy—divination by the examination of sacrifices? That's an archaic kink." Claudia thought about it. "Assuming Alexa has never done this"—she nodded to the transformed rebar—"before, what's the time-line for the four other murders?"

"Nothing before last week."

"Something must have happened then, to trigger...whatever this is." She bit her lip. "Were any of the others in pairs?"

I started to shake my head, then stopped. "Not really together. But two were found in one neighborhood, and the other two in another."

"Pairs—maybe they were trying to find each other?" She stared, thinking.

"What?"

"You didn't notice? When I was alone with Joel, he was the same as all our therapy sessions: passive, depressed affect. And when I was alone with Alexa—nothing. But when he was near Alexa, and she was in danger...something happened. It felt like the call to Change, focused right in my brain stem. But like it was going to take over, not like I was driving." She stared. "The two of them *fit* together somehow. Linked."

I considered. "You don't think they're like Fangborn oracles? Like the Triplets?"

"Oracles tell riddles about the future and sometimes they're lucky. And none of them have the telekinetic power to move anything bigger than a coffee stirrer." She nodded to the rebar. "You ever see an oracle do anything like that?"

"No."

"Right. Something else is going on here." She put the wallet back and pulled off the gloves. "Got a spare phone?"

I nodded, and pulled out a prepaid phone and tossed it to her. She called 911 to report the body. She'd ditch the phone later. "You go ahead to Alexa's apartment, it's not too far. Make sure no one's waiting for her. I'm going to do some research."

I nodded innocently, and raised my eyebrows. "Maybe check in with the cousins who live in caves?"

She gave me a look that said *bite me*. "If you have time, you might see if there are any similar patterns occurring outside Salem."

"But...we shouldn't go to the Family with this?" She paused before answering. "Let's make sure we have something real before we involve the rest of the Family."

I left thinking—or trying to not think—about how the body of Ronnie Platt was pinned down like a bug on a board.

An hour later, having done all the possible tidying up, Joel summoned his courage. "So. Any idea what you were trying to do? Up there on the chair?" *With no clothes on?*

"Nope," Alexa said. "This is freaking me out as much as you. Maybe not; I don't actually remember what I was doing." She glanced around the bare room. The only decoration was an ornate ceramic vessel on the mantel. "So how do you know Claudia?"

He felt himself go red and she cut in. "I'm sorry—that's personal."

"No, it's okay; I've been having trouble getting past my wife...leaving. That's why my cousin let me stay here while she was on vacation. A change of scenery—"

There was a rattle, the sudden sound of many heavy feet, then a pounding at the back door and the alley stairs.

Alexa froze. "What's that?"

"Someone's trying to break in! Quick, downstairs."

Joel pulled out his phone, but with all the jostling down the front stairs, he got the wrong screen. He hit another button and, when she answered, he said, "Dr. Steuben, get back here *quick!*"

They stumbled through the shop door, pulled it shut, and locked it.

A massive hand landed heavily on Joel's shoulder. He staggered under it, and briefly saw a shaved head and piratical eyebrows. The hand righted him, and slid under his chin, holding him in a headlock. He felt powerful muscles in the arm tightening under his chin and didn't dare swallow.

"The entrails of my birds led me to the other magical pairs," a deep voice behind Joel rumbled. Alexa froze in her tracks, staring at the giant of a man. "When they couldn't show me what powers they had, their human entrails led me to you. I could smell their power; I can almost *taste* yours."

"What the hell?" Joel gasped, struggling to twist, but he would have needed a crowbar and three men to move the arm from his neck.

"Whatever you want—the cash register?" Alexa stammered, backing away. "Just take it."

Cesar shoved Joel toward her, holding him like a kitten by the scruff of his neck. "You have power. Show me. When I understand yours, maybe I can access my own."

"Are you kidding me? I don't—" She halted, having backed into one of the shelves of beads. She reached back, groping for a way to escape, but her hands brushed only against partitioned shelves of beads. A few fell to the floor, bouncing and rolling.

"Either prove what you are, or he'll die."

Joel felt the hand tighten and thought he heard bones start to grind in his neck. "Alexa!"

Her eyes went wide. "You're crazy—!"

"You crucified my man on the pavement," Cesar said, "a study in elegance and brutality. Show me how." He pulled an eight-inch knife and held it before Joel's eyes. "I need to know where this power is coming from."

A tiny red crystal bead rolled across the floor, bumping Joel's shoe.

Alexa was crying now. "I didn't do anything! I can't—"

Another bead, smaller than the first, flew across the room. It smacked into a window, making a tiny *ping* before it vanished.

Impatiently, Cesar jabbed the knife deep into Joel's side. Joel screamed. Blood spurted, poured down his leg, and soaked into the rough, antique wood, swallowing up and obscuring the red bead.

Joel dropped to his knees and clutched his side, trying to hold the flood back. His hands were scarlet and slippery in an instant.

Alexa flung a hand out in front of her, as if to protect herself from the sight. "Stop it!"

The sound of fighting and screams—howls, really—came from upstairs.

"Best to show me, my dear." Cesar hauled Joel up by the shirt, and jabbed the knife again. "Your friend will die soon, otherwise."

Another squirt of blood. Joel whimpered.

Alexa's hands swung up, palms out. Her eyes rolled back.

A black-faceted bead flew across the room, bouncing off Cesar's nose.

He swatted in front of his face. "Please. How can I make this plain to you? You'll *both* die if you don't—"

Alexa moaned. A skittering across the floor, and tens of thousands of beads converged, rolling up Cesar's legs, swarming over his body, their colors rippling and...glowing.

Cesar was able to brush whole handfuls of the tiny assailants off, but they were quickly replaced. The more beads swarmed, the more energy energy they summoned, and the more they multiplied.

The doorway heaved and splintered; Joel saw a wolfman in a flannel shirt and jeans and a purplish snake-lady with fangs break through. Joel was certain he was hallucinating from loss of blood, because they both looked like they'd been in a fight. The snake lady looked like Dr. Steuben.

More than that, the beads were changing their original colors and shapes, forming a giant scarlet snake encircling Cesar. Beads rolled into his ears, piercing his eardrums, boring their way into his brain. As he tried to scream, a flood of animated glass rushed down his throat, their facets causing a thousand tiny scratches as they filled and distended his stomach. His eyes bulged under the pressure of vitreous fingers; he sank to his knees. The shimmering red snake continued to constrict around him, even as his lungs were so full they could no longer compress.

Filled with power and unable to control what she'd inadvertently summoned, Alexa directed it to the next threat: the vampire and the werewolf in the doorway. Waves of glass, crystal, wooden, and plastic beads turned on them, lapping up the walls like flame.

The vampire hissed, "Joel, she'll listen to you!"

Joel hauled himself up, trying to ignore the patterns his blood now made, a living arabesque dancing across the floor.

He was going to die; that was clear. But he had to end this. "Alexa! Knock it off!" It sounded weak as soon as he said it, but the sound of his own voice helped him focus. "Alexa, you're gonna kill us all!" he screamed hoarsely.

The beads and blood continued their dervish dance, and the apartment walls shuddered horrifically, as nails trembled within them. The porcelain urn on the fireplace mantel shattered. The ashes flew into a whirlwind, hovered for a moment, then skipped across the floor.

A piece of bone emerged from the maelstrom. More fragments followed, mixing with the ash. A shape emerged from the swirling cloud, a woman's form, more and more cohesive with every second.

Lenore! Joel thought.

He struggled to get up and failed. He dragged himself toward the gray-veiled form of his dead wife. As Joel disturbed the patterns of blood still writhing across the floor, the droplets flew up, adding body to the shape of the woman.

Halfway to his goal, Joel collapsed. He'd lost too much blood. He raised a hand, gasping for breath.

"I'm sorry, Lenore! I can't." He sobbed. "I'm sorry—Lenore, I love you!"

The shadow reached out for him. With everything he had left, Joel reached for his wife's hand. A faint smile, benediction in the dusty whirlwind.

Joel collapsed.

Alexa looked up. She blinked, once, twice, and the wildness left her eyes. The wind stopped. Ash and bone fell to the ground and a million beads scattered across the floor. Silence filled the room.

"What," Gerry said, gasping, "the skedley *fuck* was that?"

"Telekinesis, pattern sympathy, I don't know—heads up, Gerry!" Claudia shouted.

He turned in time to catch Alexa as she swayed and fell.

"Shit!" He set her down carefully, checked for a pulse. "She's alive."

Claudia crossed to Joel. "So's he, but not for long. Call 911!"

"Hey, Dr. Steuben? How was that for a cathartic event?" Joel smiled as his heart slowed, then stopped.

Joel woke up in a hospital room, he didn't know how much later. He had a scrubby beard that itched. The room itself was nice and it was private. He couldn't hear anything. Nothing beeping, no intercoms, nothing.

The silence worried him. Cesar's hideout? A hospital? One way or another, he didn't like the quiet.

He was giving serious thought to just leaving, in spite of the backless gown, the tubes running out of both arms, and the unbelievable pain in his chest and gut, when Dr. Steuben opened the door. Joel's muscles relaxed, and his panic subsided. She looked like the woman he knew:

no fangs, no purple hair, no scales. Killer bod under a white lab coat. Her brother Gerry appeared behind her, blocking the sunlight streaming through the doorway.

Dr. Steuben looked at his chart and monitors, and smiled. "You're healing up. No permanent damage, no infection. Good."

"Where's...how's Alexa?" he asked.

Gerry shut the door, and pulled two plastic chairs to the bed. "She's why we're here."

"Oh, God, she's dead, isn't she?" Joel sagged. He'd had enough of death. "What the hell happened, back there?"

"No, Alexa's fine," Dr. Steuben said. "She's confused, of course. Asking for you."

"Oh. But something must be wrong, if you're both...staring at me like that."

A flicker of surprise before she concealed it; he'd never challenged her before. "Not wrong," Dr. Steuben said. "An opportunity, if you want it."

She paused; her brother said, "Give him just a little push."

"No, Gerry. No suggestion. This has to be done right." She took a deep breath, looked deep into Joel's eyes. He might have been turned on or terrified at other times, but now...he was just focused.

"Alexa is a telekinetic, at the very least. She appears to control objects when she's in danger. And then there was that thing with your wife's image...and, well, we're still working on identifying exactly what the range of her talents is."

Talents? This was nothing like playing the piano or twirling a baton, he thought, not knowing what to say.

"Thing is, me, my brother...we're Fangborn. Our people work in secret to fight evil, so we know about power, trust me. But Joel...we've never seen anything like Alexa. She claims not to know anything about the snake imagery she created, but we sure do."

Claudia handed him a notebook, filled with images of women holding snakes. He'd seen one of them on a show about excavations in Greece, a bare-breasted woman, wearing a headdress, holding two serpents. Another was a stone from Sweden, much more stylized, but similar. There were pages of them, from all over the world, throughout time.

"Um, good." He looked at the IV bag, feeling woozy; these were some quality painkillers they were giving him.

"But since we've separated you two, there's been no trace of Alexa's power. Nothing. We've talked to her about it, and we've all agreed. It has to do with you."

"I can move stuff with my thoughts?"

"No, she needs you, for some reason, to access her power. You're her focus. Alexa wants to help us, so we need you to consider our proposal, too." She shook her head. "There may be others like Cesar out there, looking for their own telekinetics. Think about them opening up the prisons of the world with their minds, and worse than that. And if it was true necromancy we saw Alexa perform...the idea of someone like *him* raising the dead, raiding Hell for an army? We need *you* on our side."

Gerry got up, began to pace. "Look, man, it's like this. Either you want to join us werewolves and vampires and oracles, and try to protect Normals using Alexa's freaky powers—shit we've never even *heard* of—

or you go back to your old life, and remember none of this. Claudia will wipe your memory."

He turned to Claudia. "You can do that?"

"Yes. No pain, no trauma. No memories."

He was about to ask whether they'd just kill him, and go about their business, but somehow he knew Dr. Steuben wasn't like that. And her brother; apparently he'd taken on Cesar's men when they broke into the apartment. They seemed to be telling the truth, as weird as it was. "You think I can handle it?"

"I do. And I can tell you believe us."

"I know." He scratched at the bandage on his arm. "This is a lot to take in. Do I have to answer right away?"

"Yes."

Gerry held out his hands, fists closed. *"You take the blue pill—the story ends, you wake up in your bed... You take the red pill, you stay in Wonderland and I show you how deep the rabbit-hole goes."*

Dr. Steuben showed the first signs of temper. "Gerry, don't. This isn't the time for—"

Joel understood. "No, it's okay, I get it." He looked at Gerry. "It's that big? Like Morpheus says in *The Matrix*?"

Gerry nodded. "It's how we spend our lives. I figure, something pretty Hellish is coming, for Alexa—and you—to show up *now*. Something activated you and her and we need to find out what that is. There may be more like you, and probably, others like Cesar coming. How did he know to go looking for you, when we didn't? This is all new, and we need to get up to speed on it, like, yesterday."

"You—and Alexa—really need me? This isn't the drugs?" He shook his head. "I can help."

"Yes."

Joel had been depressed, he knew, and less than useless. But he'd seen Lenore and he'd desperately needed that. He needed to repay Lenore for that last blessing.

"If you say no, well." Dr. Steuben nodded resolutely. "We'll see if there isn't someone else out there with whom Alexa can work."

He looked at them, remembering Dr. Steuben as a vampire, her brother the werewolf.

Anything would be better than feeling this sad. This...alone. Maybe I can do something. Lenore would like that.

He pulled himself upright, as best he could.

"Sign me up," he said. "Give me the red pill."

Love Knot

When writing this story, I was toying with ideas about what constitutes "magic." The Fangborn would seem magic to us, but most think of themselves as "as yet unexplained by science." I also wanted Claudia to have a story where her habitual self-possession was at odds with her great power—and the more she gives in, the more those around her respond, and the better it gets to her. She's a nice girl, and I shouldn't have been so mean to her.

Justine sat at the table and stared at the small parcel wrapped in plain brown paper. The only light came from a single bulb in the cheap motel lamp, but it was enough. She hated the sight of the package.

She pushed it farther from her, wincing as she did so. She was pretty sure something had been torn in her arm. The long-sleeved shirt meant to hide scratches on her shoulder and arms only stuck and made them itch worse.

She shifted her weight, gingerly, regretting it as she did so. Her back...her legs...simply *everything* ached. But she had to decide what to do with the hateful thing on the table. Now on her eightieth hour without sleep, the eightieth hour since the parcel had come into her possession, she could barely keep her eyes open. But she didn't dare fall asleep, not without deciding what to do.

She couldn't just throw the thing away. She'd already tried destroying it, with dire results. She was fearful of bringing it to the Family: despite the oaths she'd sworn and the loyalties she owed them, she couldn't trust them with it. Especially not them. If power corrupted even the best of people, then this thing…

No. She couldn't go to the Family, but if they found she'd had the box and hadn't brought it to them…

She shuddered, and *that* hurt all over.

Well, that was just one more item in a long list she couldn't let happen.

She had to do something. Whatever it was, it would be a chance.

She had an idea, rejected it, then reconsidered.

She was going to call Claudia.

Shit.

As Justine punched the number with a shaking hand, she tried not to think of what she would be doing to Claudia.

But if you couldn't bring this kind of trouble to your friends, well, you were just out of luck.

Four hours later, Claudia Steuben checked the security monitor in her kitchen before she answered the door. Her friend Justine looked every bit as bad as she'd sounded on the phone: Her auburn hair was a tangled mess, her eyes were bloodshot, and athletic figure drooped with fatigue. Her skirt and jacket were rumpled. She had no luggage besides a briefcase and a small, sturdy plastic cooler.

She shoved her way past Claudia and went straight into the kitchen. She pulled out the carefully stacked and color-coded plastic containers from the refrigerator and threw them on the floor. She shoved the cooler into their place, then slammed the door shut. She walked, unseeing, past Claudia, collapsed on the couch, and began to cry.

Claudia watched for a moment, frowned briefly at the disrupted order of her kitchen, then nuked hot water for tea. She cleaned up the kitchen floor and threw out whatever wouldn't last in the freezer or on the counter so she would not have to re-open the refrigerator. When the tea water was ready, she set it to steep. She poured the tea into two mugs, laced them both with honey and lemon, then poured a stiff shot of whiskey into each one.

By the time she returned to the living room, Justine had calmed down. Her face was streaked with tears, and she stared straight ahead, only seeming to recognize Claudia when she was handed the mug.

"It's hot. Also spiked."

"Thanks."

They drank. Claudia curled up in the leather chair and waited for Justine to start talking.

After a long shuddering breath, Justine looked up. "I'm sorry."

"For what?"

"Look, that...thing...in the refrigerator...?"

"What is it?"

"It's dangerous. Worse than that. There are men after it. I don't know who they are, but they mean no good."

Claudia could be patient. "Why not bring it to the Family? Why not destroy it?"

"I can't. Neither of them. I've tried destroying it, and...I can't."

"You can't."

Justine shook her head. "You'll...you'll see what I mean. I don't dare hide it. And frankly, I think you'll understand why I can't bring it to the Family."

Claudia watched Justine carefully. Clinically. "And?"

The question was obvious. Why didn't Justine take care of the situation? It should have been well within her capabilities. Their Family—the Fangborn—was made up of vampires, werewolves, and others, all dedicated to tracking and destroying evil. The humans they protected never knew about them, though myths of monsters and murders swirled up around them. Justine's strength, speed, and intuition should have been more than enough to deal with whatever the problem was.

Justine's hands shook as they held the empty cup. "Claudia, I promise you. It was all I could do to evade them, and make it up here."

"So why bring it to me?"

"I trust you." Justine's eyes flicked away. "You'll find a way to deal with it."

Claudia nodded. Her friend was lying. "Deal with what?"

"You'll see." Justine set her cup down. Her color was better now, but she still looked desperately tired. "Take the cooler out of the refrigerator. Open it up. I want to reassure myself that the damn thing isn't witching me. I want to make sure it's real, that I'm not going crazy."

Which I'm not ruling out, Claudia thought. Justine looked like seven kinds of Hell.

Willing to humor her a little longer, Claudia retrieved the cooler from the fridge. It had a few sparkly stickers on the outside. Unicorns and stars. Claudia looked up.

"The kids got them out of the cereal," Justine explained.

Claudia nodded, feeling slightly ridiculous. "They're safe?"

"With their dad. I told them I had an out-of-town appraisal. Didn't want to worry them." Parenting was tough on Fangborn, even after their children understood their special role in the world.

Claudia nodded again. She put the cooler on the kitchen table. She swung the handle back and removed the lid carefully, noticing as she did so that Justine was unconsciously turning her head away, pressing herself back into the cushions of the couch.

What the Hell is in here?

She set the lid aside, and peeked in.

A small box wrapped in brown paper, taped up and addressed, as if it was ready to be mailed. The address was faded and illegible, and the tape had been replaced several times, leaving dark ghosts of the adhesive on the furred brown paper.

Claudia relaxed. It looked like nothing at all.

She fanged up, briefly, just enough to allow her nails to grow and strengthen, her skin to turn pale violet. She slashed the tape on the package, removed the paper, opened the cardboard box beneath. That done, she returned to her human form.

Inside was another box, this one much older than the cardboard she'd just discarded. This was 19th century, carefully dove-tailed, travel-stained, perhaps the size of a stack of three hardcover books. She didn't recognize the exotic wood.

Claudia lifted the top of that box and suddenly was relieved. Everything was going to be perfectly fine. She was completely on top of the situation. There was nothing to worry about. In fact, she felt like she'd had three quick shots of tequila.

Inside was an object wrapped in layers of antique cloth, nestled in layers of utterly modern acid-free paper.

Justine was standing across the kitchen table now, breathing shallowly, her eyes wide. Claudia glanced up. Justine looked much better now. Everything would be okay. Claudia reached out, brushed the hair from her friend's cheek.

Justine's hair smelled of orange-blossom and honey. Claudia leaned over to breathe it in. Her lips brushed her friend's hair, her teeth grazed her ear. She could see Justine's neck muscles tighten, and the curve of her breast just below the collar of her silk shirt.

Startled, Claudia pulled back. Then she caught a look at Justine's shoes.

Oooh, Jimmy Choo! Pretty, pretty...

Justine kicked away her chair and grabbed Claudia's arm, Changing into a sleek wolf-woman in a Chanel suit. The expenditure of power involved in Justine's Change shook Claudia to her vampire core, and in response, she Changed, too. Her eyes widened, her nose receded, the outline of scales appeared on her violet skin, and her fangs grew long and bright.

It was both better and worse. Claudia's Fangborn senses were heightened, but her head cleared, and she knew she was being heavily influenced. It wasn't the whiskey in the tea. Her tongue flicked out from between her fangs. She tasted the air and it was exquisite. Beguiling.

She also now understood that whatever was in the box was affecting her, affecting her so deeply that she was producing a level and complex of pheromones that would slow down an army. Ordinarily, it would be just enough to calm whoever she was trying to cure—that's what gave fictional vampires the charisma and allure they seemed to have in the movies and comic books. Now...

Justine had taken off her jacket and had undone the top button of her blouse when Claudia managed to damp down the chemicals she was producing. Justine growled, confused but relieved, and that allowed Claudia to concentrate even more. Vampires can produce a range of effects on other living creatures, and to a certain extent, control their own body chemistries and those of the people around them.

With an effort, Claudia got hold of herself, slammed the lid back on the box, and shoved it back into the cooler, panting. Justine collapsed onto a kitchen chair.

After a moment, she caught her breath, and blushing, buttoned her shirt. "See what I mean? It's not just me, is it?"

Claudia shook her head. And if Justine had been exposed to it for even longer than the drive from New York to Salem...

"When did you find it? Where did it come from?"

"The museum." Justine worked as a curator at one of the premier art museums in New York City. "It was my turn to be on the desk, you know, to answer questions the public might have. Identify the artifacts they bring in. Break the bad news that it's just Grandma's knockoff souvenir and not a real Romanov egg." She took a deep breath.

"A guy came in, and he looked like shit. I immediately thought 'junkie looking to sell an antique,' but he was okay: I didn't pick up any smell of drugs on him, or any trace of evil. I told him I'd look at it, but he said he had an appointment. He barely stayed long enough to give me his name and contact information. Practically knocked a guard over, trying to get out. Then I thought: 'toxic divorce.'

"I opened the box."

Claudia reached out toward the cooler again, but Justine held up a hand. "Please. Don't. I can't...I can't take any more."

Shaking off an unexpected regret, Claudia sat back down, controlled the impulse. "What happened?"

"At first I assumed that I was just, you know. Feeling the lack. Two kids *will* put a speed-bump in your sex life. But it wasn't going away, and I found myself leaving work early. Since when do I play hooky? It got worse. I started eyeballing guys on the subway. I was actually contemplating following one home when my stop came up. Thank God. I managed to get up to the apartment and lock myself in. Until Ben came home. I'm still worried about what he thinks."

Claudia tilted her head. "You didn't tell Ben?"

"What, that I got a weird artifact at work, and suddenly, I was horny as a teenager?"

Claudia hated the word "horny."

Justine continued. "My husband just took it as a pleasant surprise. We didn't quite break the bed before the kids got home from day camp. The next day...the next day, I thought it was just a quirk of hormones. But when I got back to the museum, a couple of things happened. For one thing, even though I'd packed the thing up in secure storage, there was an awful lot of...friskiness...going on."

"It's been a wet summer, and it just turned sunny," Claudia mused. "Could it be a delayed spring fever? And didn't you tell me there were several couples working together?"

"Yeah, but this...was definitely beyond PDA. It wasn't so much casual Friday as swollen, engorged Friday. Even with that thing over there locked up, folks were getting positively rampant in the back offices."

"Then I tried to call the guy back, give him my report. Unusual, but not valuable, certainly not something the museum would consider purchasing. His name, the number, the address—all fakes."

Claudia digested this. People might abandon wrecked cars or dump garbage by the side of the road, but why go to a museum to lose something you didn't want?

"Then, I got the weirdest call. Someone asking to speak to the guy who left the box, using that fake name. I told them they had the wrong number, but then the caller got angry, said I'd be sorry I'd not been more helpful."

Justine took a deep breath. "I brought the thing—and the paperwork I'd filed on it—home with me. Maybe the guy who left it there thought it would be safe, but I didn't dare leave it at the museum."

Claudia nodded. If anyone could handle this, the Fangborn could. Better to keep civilians out of it, as much as they could.

"I left early again, and let me tell you, by the time I got done with him, Ben was no longer complaining about missing 'Dirty Jobs.' I'm sure he's still walking funny. I was about to tell him about it—after I'd hidden the thing so no one could find it—when I saw the newspaper. A man had been found, under a subway car. The body was unrecognizable, identification was through dental work."

"How do you know it was your guy?" Claudia said. "If you didn't know his real name?"

"He had my card in his pocket. Cousin Dmitri—down at one of the fire stations?—had been on the call. He palmed it and called me. Told me the guy, whoever it was, had been *tortured*. He noticed marks that weren't made by the train, and said the stink of whoever did it was pretty awful. I called in sick, grabbed the box, and told Ben I got a call from the Family, and would be back in a couple of days."

Claudia nodded.

Justine took a last sip of cold tea. "Someone bad is after this. I can't risk just leaving it somewhere. I've tried breaking it, but...I can't. Somehow, I can't. And now I realize the extent of its power, I don't dare hand it over to the Family."

Claudia got it right away. "So you came to me? Please tell me, it's not because I'm a vampire."

"It's not. It's just..."

"Honestly, Justine, if we can't keep our own Family from believing the myths—"

"It's not that you're a...it's not the *vamp* thing—"

"The vamp thing," Claudia thought. *Wasn't that just like a werewolf? Fuzzy simpletons. No subtlety, not one of them.*

"It's not that." Justine shrugged miserably. "I didn't know what else to do. You have your head on the squarest of anyone I ever met. And...you're...you've...you've got good self-control," she finished apologetically.

Claudia knew what she meant, knew her own appearance (professional, but tailored to the point of severity) and reputation (serious and studious) were often misinterpreted. She found this even more galling than the human beliefs about vampires and their reputed hyper-sexuality. "Go to Hell."

"No, seriously, I'm not being bitchy, it's just...if anyone's got the brains to deal with this, and the willpower to...not succumb...you do."

Brains and willpower don't automatically make one virginal, Claudia thought. But people sure assumed it did.

"Besides, everyone knows you're...seeing...whatshisname?"

"Fergus O'Malley." Seeing was about all they'd been doing. Claudia, having met Fergus during a difficult time, had wanted to take this relationship slowly. "He's out of town, at the moment. Did you find anything that did work? Anything that kept you from...giving in?"

Justine's face lightened and she answered eagerly. "Anything distracting is good. Something rote, if you can keep your mind on it. I did our quarterly taxes. That worked. Until I stopped."

Claudia nodded.

Justine tried to keep the hopefulness off her face. "Well?"

"I'll help you with this," Claudia said finally. "But for now, you need some sleep. I've made up the spare room—"

"No!"

"It's no trouble—"

"Another time, I'd take it in a heartbeat. But now..." Justine shook herself. "I just need to be away from people. I don't trust myself near *that* any more, and I need sleep. Can...can I leave it here tonight?"

"Yes, of course, you may. Where will you—?"

"Blue Harbor Inn. It's actually wonderful, but the owner...well, he just gives you the impression you're messing up his beautifully run, historically significant house. Cold fish, your basic taciturn Yankee. He's *exactly* what I need right now."

Claudia made a face. *Another stereotype.* "Hey, I'm a Yankee and I have manners *and* I can be downright loquacious when I need to be. I know Mr. Dow—he's just rude. He must be a thousandy-seven."

Justine was ready to cry. "Claudia, fine, I'm sorry. I just...really need some sleep now."

Claudia nodded. "I'll see you first thing in the morning."

Ordinarily they would have hugged goodbye, but tonight they didn't, by unspoken agreement.

Well, Claudia thought as she closed and locked the door. *I've got the reputation. I might as well put it to work. It'll be easier, now that I'm alone.*

In the kitchen, she opened the cooler, stripped back the layers, then ran her fingertips around the edges of the top of the old wooden box. It resisted before it came off in her hands. She peeled back the acid free paper, then steadied herself. Just as she'd discovered with Justine, there was real power emanating from the thing. The fabric, rotting and faded silk, centuries old, fell away to reveal another, smaller wooden box.

Claudia sensed the age of the nested box, would have sworn she felt it quiver in her hands. As if it were alive. Humming, almost vibrating, though she couldn't hear a thing. Whatever was putting out the power, was in here.

It couldn't be alive, could it?

She felt herself grow warm. She was only delaying the inevitable. But the suspense about what the object might be was almost as pleasurable as knowing. The brink of discovery is intensely exciting, and there is always, always a moment of hesitation before revelation.

Claudia ran the back of her hand across her forehead, and then the back of her neck. Sweat slid along her spine as she ran down the list of things it might be. The box was oblong, so she immediately considered the possible contents: a Shiva lingam or Greek or Roman good-luck phalluses, or pre-Columbian pottery decorated with figures engaged in sexual activity. Then she wondered if it mightn't be older than that, and thought of the variety of Stone Age fertility goddesses.

The lid of this box was heavily inlaid, though the ivory had shrunk and cracked and discolored. It was smooth under her fingertips, and she had to sit down, because her knees would no longer support her. Her breath came in shallow gasps.

Finally, curiosity overcame prudence. She caught her breath and tore the box open.

And stared.

It was a vase.

There were no obscene figures, no runic inscriptions. Nothing in the least suggestive, from any point of view. It was porcelain, a white body with a blue floral decoration.

It was a perfectly ordinary bud vase, maybe nine inches tall, and two across at the base. Hexagonal, sides gently curved upward, it couldn't even be properly called phallic.

It was, in a word, "mumsy." A dust-collector, out of date and pretty and curious and innocuous.

There must be something on the base, perhaps inside the thing.

Claudia picked it up—

POW.

Her head snapped back. She flooded with wave after wave of warmth that started from between her legs and radiated out. A rushing in her ears and the kitchen vanished, replaced with a delicious oblivion. She tasted salt and sweet and felt herself sag. She moaned.

With the last scrap of will she possessed, she hurled the vase across the room.

It careened off the wall, banged onto the stove, and bounced onto the floor.

There was no tinkle of broken pottery. There was no need to get the dustpan and brush. There was nothing to clean up.

Claudia, gasping, staggered to her feet. Porcelain, in her experience, did not survive flinging. It did not, as far as she understood, bounce.

She picked it up, and ran across the room. She slammed it into the marble countertop.

Nothing. Not so much as a crack.

Before the thing could completely cloud her judgment again, she seized a heavy aluminum frying pan and bashed the vase with every ounce of supernatural strength she possessed.

The frying pan was badly dented. Williams Sonoma would have wept to see its perfection marred. It would never again toast hazelnuts or sauté shallots or sear pork.

The vase was completely intact.

We are so *screwed.*

Claudia picked up the vase, and holding it as if it were radioactive, ran across the room and slammed it into its nest of boxes and wrappings. She stuffed the whole thing back into the cooler, then shoved that into the refrigerator.

As she leaned against the refrigerator door, out of breath, she reconsidered and took the thing to the deep freeze in the basement. Best not to take any chances.

It was not the first thing to be hidden in the padlocked freezer. It probably would not be the last.

There is no such thing as magic, she told herself, on the way back up the stairs. *We don't believe in it, not most of us, anyway. Our past, which is longer than that of humankind, would have produced physical evidence.*

The scientist in her reasoned: there are plenty of earthly, human objects we don't understand. We still don't know, entirely, how the pyramids were constructed. We don't understand why some ancient metals defy spectrum analysis. The Fangborn—we can't explain ourselves yet, or our place in this world, but it doesn't make us magic. There are a thousand unexplained things in the world; science just hadn't caught up with them...or survived the ravages of time.

Suggestion, she thought, though the idea was absurd. If she had to guess, after talking with Justine, she would have assumed a kind of psychological thrall. Perhaps she was missing subliminal clues, something outside their Fangborn abilities of detection?

But how could the vase look so normal, appear to be made of human materials that were well familiar to her, and yet resist destruction? Claudia could very nearly bend steel in her bare hands, and this thing...

Harmonics was another idea. Perhaps sound communicated directly with the parts of the brain involved in sexual desire and response.

Whatever it is, she thought, *it is terrible. Something that strips the will, clouds the mind, drives reason away.*

A terrible thing. In the wrong hands...disastrous.

Justine was right not to go to the Family with it. They'd both seen the effect it had on super-sensitive Fangborn. The Family was at a politically sensitive juncture, right now: this thing would be the end of us all, Fangborn and human.

She remembered what she felt like, tearing through the wrappings to get to the vase. What it felt like to handle it.

She'd never smoked, but now she would have killed for a cigarette.

Claudia took the report to bed after a long, cold shower, and crawled in, shivering but clear-headed, to read.

She flipped past the description of the object on the forms in the front, noting that it had been assessed as "Dutch workmanship imitating Asian decoration for the export market." Which wasn't much of a clue as to its pedigree or manufacture; that would describe a thousand objects from any maker, any place...

She dozed off with the lights on.

The dreams were horrifying and wonderful.

As if to punish her for resisting or trying to destroy it, the vase exercised an awful vengeance. Though Claudia didn't believe in booty calls, if he'd been anywhere within a hundred miles, she would have called Fergus. Hells, if she'd known there were any willing males nearby, it would have been all over for them.

Fangborn have to be very careful mating with humans and Claudia was not sure her self-control was all it should be. Would ever be again.

She woke up in a sweat, trying to forget her dreams. After an hour, it was no good. She gave in. She opened the drawer and found Señor Peter Rabbit. She clicked it on. No dice: no batteries.

Claudia Steuben was a responsible environmentalist, but she'd forgotten to plug in the battery re-charger. And after looting the remote control, the doorbell (God help anyone who came to the door tonight), and the flashlights, she failed to find the right sized batteries. Finally she thought of the hurricane kit in the basement.

If this isn't an emergency, she thought, ripping out a fresh, non-rechargeable battery pack, *I don't know what is*.

Claudia woke from an uneasy sleep, about two hours later than she ordinarily would have. It had been a rough night.

Thank God it was summer; she had an early meeting at the office, since it was August, she had no patients. With any luck, this ordeal would be over by the next time she had regular office hours. She didn't want to think what might happen to her own therapist's reserve and discretion after prolonged exposure to the vase.

She would drive to the meeting, get out ASAP, then find Justine. The two of them would get rid of the vase. Curiosity about its origins was banished by fear of this being unleashed on the world.

At first, she felt much better being outside, away from the terrible drive of the object in the freezer. The short commute from Salem to Lynnfield along Route 128 would be packed with annoyances that were anything but provocative.

The first one met her at the foot of her driveway. Landscapers were among Claudia's pet peeves—why did they have to start mowing, chopping, and mulching first thing in the morning? The racket, their unkempt appearances, the way their trucks took up an unreasonable amount of space on the narrow and twisting and busy roads of Salem, were constant sources of irritation.

She pulled over to tell them exactly which noise ordinances they were violating. She'd been meaning to for some time, in any case. *That one, over there. He was obviously the foreman or the team boss or whatever. Had to be. Look at the size of the brute, the sleeves were ripped off a dark green work shirt to accommodate his biceps. Not an ounce of fat on him, and he was sweating already, rivers running down the inside of his collar, getting lost in the dark chest hair...*

She froze.

What the Hell am I doing?

Claudia caught herself, turned, and all but ran back to the BMW, which was still idling. She tore out of the driveway, leaving the confused ground crew staring after her.

The guy in the green shirt yelled, "Hey lady! Did you want a card, or something?"

No cards, Claudia thought, shaking. *Definitely no "something." You wouldn't survive it, my friend. Not in the state I'm in.*

Being in the car helped—clearly, the residual effects of contact with the vase were enhanced by human proximity. She recalled Justine's warning and began conjugating Latin verbs. *Ero, eram, erat...*

Which worked until she got to the construction crew slowing the highway traffic on Route 128. They inspired desperate fantasies of faceless men, singly or in pairs. Then there was the distinguished man being driven in the town car—she could imagine the fine wool of his excellent suit tearing beneath her nails as she rode him into Boston, the coarse feel of his grey hair under his tongue as she licked the side of his head. The young driver of the empty school bus, straddling her on the back seat, the smells of ancient vinyl and petroleum and sticky spilled soda around them...

Claudia abandoned conjugating verbs and tried to recall the succession of Hittite kings: *Labarna, Hattusili, Mursili, Hantili, Zidanta, Huzziya, Telepinu...*

As long as she kept her eyes straight ahead and her brain distracted, she managed. Things took a turn for the worse when she had to pause next to the cop directing traffic around the roadwork—the uniform, the sunglasses, the gun, the *handcuffs...* All she had to do was roll down her window, given him a blast of her vampiric glamour, and the poor man would have leapt into the backseat where she would lash him down with the safety belt and then...

The cop, far from being under a sexual compulsion, rapped on the window and screamed at her to get a move on, startling her out of the reverie. The spell broken, she hit the gas and sped into the now-moving traffic.

Justine was right. There was no way the Family could manage something like this, no matter how good their intentions. Imagine the vampires, besotted by the vase, unable to control themselves, and then unable to control those Normal humans around them. Things would spiral out of control, into a beautiful, sexual chaos...

Okay, but we're not going to think about that now, are we? Claudia thought. *Because that would be the start of it.*

Thinking about starting the end of the world worked. Claudia forced herself to turn the radio to a shock-jock show she absolutely hated, and between that and jaw-grinding determination, she made it safely to the hospital.

She didn't dare stop at Starbucks. There was no way she was adding caffeine and energetic young baristas to this mix.

The hospital helped. Her empathetic sense registered the pain and grief and fear there, which diverted her from...everything else. She kept her head down over her clipboard, grateful at last for her reputation as a grind.

"Hi, Claudia," the receptionist, Marlene, called. "Staff meeting in ten."

Not looking up, Claudia mumbled something, and locked herself in her office.

The meeting was excruciating. Fifty minutes of iron-willed self-control and superhuman—Hell, super-Fangborn—concentration was needed. Claudia stared at her notebook, scribbling the alphabet in Greek (ancient *and* modern, uppercase *and* lower). When questions were addressed to her, she kept the answers as brief as possible.

Finally the meeting was over. She was almost in her office when Dr. Schmidt came over. "You okay, Claud?"

"Just a little...something I ate." She noticed he washed with Tom's of Maine almond soap, his clothes smelled of Arm and Hammer. Intoxicating.

He waved a cupcake. "Then you shouldn't probably eat sugar and chocolate on top of it. I was going to tell you, Marlene has some leftover from her birthday party."

She began to salivate as he described the party. She heard not a word of it. She couldn't take her eyes off the cupcake as he ate it. So chocolatey there wasn't room for another bit of cocoa to be wedged into it. Frosting, white—she could smell the butter, vanilla, and was that just a hint of mint?

She watched, transfixed, as he reduced the overhanging frosting with little, nibbling bites. His tongue flicked out and he smoothed the edge of the frosting like he was licking an ice cream cone. He caught a large crumb that came away; it vanished into his mouth. Then he peeled the paper cup away from the cake, one pleat at a time, with a barely audible "pock" as the paper straightened.

He ate it with splendid and complete attention, his teeth, strong, straight, clean. Another day, his deliberateness and precision might have been an unnoticeable tic of personality: today, to Claudia, it had an admirable and consuming appeal.

She felt weak and sagged against the door. She couldn't stop thinking about his mouth and his...attention to detail.

"Anyway," he concluded. "You look like you could use some sun. Say, can you and your boyfriend get away to the beach this weekend?"

The thought of Fergus, their as-yet-unconsummated relationship, and a beach, made her look up. She'd gotten to know Fergus in Aruba. Dr. Schmidt's cupcake was replaced by the memory of Fergus in a bathing suit, climbing out of the ocean, water running down his chest and belly, following trails into the waistband of his trunks.

With a wrench, Claudia turned her mind to the elements of the periodic table. *Hydrogen, helium, lithium, beryllium, boron...*

"I really think I need to get home," she managed to gasp, after a long moment.

"Get straight to bed, then," he agreed, then wagged a finger at her. "You take good care of yourself, Doctor."

Thinking of the battery charger on the counter at home, Claudia turned and fled.

I'm going to kill Justine, Claudia fumed, on her way to the inn with the box. *She knew perfectly well what that thing would do to a vampire.*

She made the least of bad choices, the rational part of her brain tiredly reminded her.

She can bite me. But before that thought could jump the rails, she arrived at the Inn.

Claudia relaxed. Mr. Dow was at the front. Something about him calmed her.

"Morning."

"Morning. I've come to see Justine Nash—"

"Can't."

"I'm sorry?"

"She never came home last night."

"Do you have any idea where she might be?"

Mr. Dow pursed his lips as he sorted the mail. "I never pry into my guests' comings and goings."

He's not even curious, Claudia thought. "Is there some way I could check her room? She was supposed to lend me a book." She stepped closer and used just a little vampiric *push*, just enough subliminal influence to overcome his reticence.

He put his mail down, his eyes a little glassy. "Sure. No harm in that." He handed her the key, listing a little as he did so.

She opened the door. The room had been trashed. Someone had been looking for the object.

Her phone rang; it was Justine. She answered, and heard heavy, masculine breathing on the other end. "Who is this?"

"We have your friend. We want what she took from us."

Claudia stalled, trying to think. "Who is this? What are you talking about?"

"Your number shows up three times on this phone last night. We know she told you. Bring the box to Boston, tonight at eleven if you want to see her again." The voice gave an address and then hung up.

Claudia cursed briefly and thought furiously. She cast about the room for a trace of Justine's abductors. There were three of them, at least.

"I left after I didn't find my friend," she dictated to Mr. Dow, giving him a story to replace his reality. "I never went into her room." Tired and scared, she pushed just a little.

"I would never let you do that," he agreed, his dewlaps shaking with his head.

"The men who came here? Did you see them? Describe them to me."

"I didn't see any men."

"Okay. You were alone all morning."

"It's how I prefer it." He nodded with satisfaction. "Alone all morning."

It was then Claudia noticed that the terrible strain that had been hag-riding her was gone. She looked at Mr. Dow with curiosity. Nothing there, no thoughts about sweeping him behind the desk and having her way with him. The idea was more than unappealing. Still susceptible to her chemical manipulation, the vase itself seemed to have no effect on him. Or her, near him.

He was still under her thrall, and stood smiling absently, waiting to be dismissed.

No time for speculation. She needed to get to Boston.

She sent him on his way, and had a quick look in the parking lot. It was gravel, and there were no tire tracks. She got into her car, and headed south.

Claudia thought about the disruptive power of the vase. Fangborn seemed to be unusually affected by it, but Normals—if Justine's account of the ruckus it had caused at the museum was any indication— were affected by it, even at a distance. Even when they didn't know where it was, or that it was even there. Everyone but Dow.

So imagine it in the hand of someone with a political agenda, of any kind. If it was ever analyzed, its secret found and harnessed, it would make a weapon of unspeakable power.

Your enemies would never even think of pushing the button; they'd never have the time. They'd never pick up a weapon. They'd never see you coming.

For a split second, Claudia thought: *What's so bad about that? Wasn't all the music and art and literature inspired by and devoted to crazy-making love? What if this is the key to world peace? What if this is the way to let the Fangborn reveal themselves to the Normals? What if we all learn to love our enemies?*

Right, she shook off the thought. *Get a grip. Love them right through the mattress or until you all die of terminal bedsores? Not very likely.*

This thing had to be absolutely destroyed.

She spent the day observing the warehouse on the pier, but saw no way to set up a trap for Justine's captors without being seen by the legitimate traffic on the wharf. She returned after dark, closer to the appointed hour, and hid her car, but as early as she was, they were earlier. There was only one truck in the parking lot, now. The truck was unmarked and unremarkable, but after she broke in, she found it was registered to the largest pharmaceutical company in the Northeast. Of course they'd want the object: if they could crack its secret, they'd rule the world.

She saw they'd left the door to the business office of the warehouse open for her, the way to them clearly lit, but she continued around the building anyway. She fanged up, the job keeping her focused and she slung the backpack with the vase over her shoulder. She searched until she found a weather-beaten section of wall. Her fingers, now elongated into sharp claws, found the cracks in the brick and mortar and she climbed silently. A window showed there were at least six of them.

She listened, her keen ears picking up snippets of conversation. Apparently, the man who'd brought the vase to Justine had stolen it from the gang, who'd stolen it from a private collector in Switzerland. The original owner, quite mysterious about the object's origins, had made the mistake of showing it to the head of the pharmaceutical company's office in Berne, who instantly ordered its theft.

The men below knew what they were after, and its value, even if they didn't know who was after them.

There was no sign of Justine.

Claudia took a piton from the pouch on her belt and drove it between two bricks. The mortar crumbled, but it sank in and wouldn't move. She shrugged the backpack off, and, with a silent click, slid a carabiner attached to its handle over the loop of the piton.

The thing was safe enough, for now. Let them figure out how it got halfway up a sheer wall.

She climbed down, Changed back to her skinself, and went in the way they expected her to.

In addition to the six men she saw, there was another, clearly the leader. A tall blond, he was armed. She presumed the others were, too.

First things first. "Where's Justine?"

The leader was in the center of the room. As she approached, two of the others moved over closer to her, never getting between her and his gun. She decided to call the one on the left Bruiser and the one to his right, Stretch.

The others she named Red, Knuckles, Scab, and One-Eye. Unimaginative, but mnemonic.

The leader stepped forward. "Where's the box?"

"Not until I get my friend back."

"She's only safe if I call in. If I don't call my man in ten minutes, with the box, she's dead."

"You're lying." And he was; Claudia could tell. His heart rate was up, and she detected the faint odor of anxiety. She realized he, Bruiser, and Stretch were battered and bleeding. From claw marks. Justine had Changed, fought her way out, escaped.

Claudia wondered whether Justine was okay. She could have used her friend's help.

"I don't need her." He lifted the pistol and aimed it at Claudia.

"Shoot me, and you never get the location of the...object."

"I can shoot you a little." He aimed at her knee. "Just a little. It doesn't have to be much—"

He was so sure of himself. He was a talker.

She thought, *good*.

By the time his finger tightened on the trigger, Claudia had Changed halfway. The surprise of seeing her skin and hair turn violet, her fingers elongate into claws, and her face shift into something serpentine filled two rows of sharp teeth, slowed the rest of them. She struck out at Bruiser, who was closest to her, landing a good uppercut on his chin. She pivoted and kicked Stretch, and when he bent over, she sank her fangs into him.

She'd only meant to give him a jab of poison, a quick injection of venom that would keep him down and out of the fight. It should have gone:

Dart at the leader, two quick punches. Disable him, lose the gun. Guns leave trails that can be followed by the Normal police. Punches and kicks and quick-healing vampire bites don't.

Spit poison at Red when he closed in, then twist, slamming him, blinded, into Knuckles, who would come from behind. Then two steps to kick Scab in the breadbasket, blocking One-Eye's punch before kneeing him in the head.

Interrogate the leader, using her chemical arsenal to get him to spill his guts.

That's how it should have gone. Claudia was good at this. And if she happened to exercise a little more self-control in her personal life to prevent the unjust employment of her powers, if she seemed to her Family and friends to be uptight, rigid, prudish, a little conservative, well, this was the part of the job where she loosened up.

But fatigue and worry caused her to misjudge. What happened, alas, was this:

As she bit into Stretch, her lips brushed his neck. The electric shock of his skin, the tiny hairs on the back of his neck standing straight up, the blood rushing over her tongue, made her gasp. She bit harder still, her tongue flicking, and the man collapsed, moaning. He tried to turn around to embrace her, but the friction of his body against hers had such an effect on Claudia that she released a flood of air-borne chemicals, which knocked him to the ground, limp, spent.

That had the effect of rebounding on her, intensified by the power of the vase. Even a hundred feet away, it called to her, possessed her, drove her. She'd been exposed to it for so long, it no longer needed close proximity to work.

Oh, shit.

She tried to stop, but it was too late. She managed to block Red's punch, shoving him away. She kicked straight out in front, aiming for Knuckles's sternum, but her speed was off and while most of the kick connected, Knuckles stumbled forward, still holding onto her leg. She managed to stay standing, but he was now at her feet, one arm locked around her leg, his other hand sliding over her thigh, as he kissed her knee, utterly besotted.

The closer the others crowded, the worse it got. Their anger and aggression were channeled into sexual excitement. The more they got turned on, the more Claudia's empathy picked up on it. And then threw it back at them, amplified by the residual effect of the vase.

Red approached again, his pistol in his outstretched hand. He wept openly, adoringly, his other hand down the front of his pants.

Outraged at this breach of her control, Claudia slammed the pistol into his face. He went down with blood on his teeth, a smile on his lips, a stain on his jeans.

Scab said, "Oh, man. That bitch can fight."

One-Eye nodded, and reached over to caress Scab's face. They locked in a tight embrace, each struggling to take the clothes off the other while not breaking their kiss.

By this time, Claudia was blinded by her own desire/emotions/conflicts/lust. The more she tried to resist, the more tangled up things got. She knew she was supposed to stop the men, but now that they weren't actually attacking her, and were, in fact, pretty much willing to do whatever she wanted, she couldn't find it in herself to send them into unconsciousness.

Worse, all those desires, all those bodies, all that energy, all packed in together, was starting to get very good to her.

She found herself giving in, and tried to resist. The heady combination of control and resistance only colored the experience and heightened the experience for her.

What do you do when your strength is the very thing that is undoing you? Laying you bare, shredding your will—

For Christ's sake, Claudia! Focus!

Trying desperately not to watch One-Eye and Scab, Claudia felt herself pulled under by the waves of desire threatening to overwhelm her. She saw the leader was confused, but somehow, like Mr. Dow, unaffected. He screamed at his men, but getting no response, turned, heading for the door.

He'd get away, and Claudia couldn't let him escape with his knowledge of the object. With the tangle of men at her feet, she could barely move. She didn't really want to move...

What do you do when you can't go with strength? Go with weakness.

She focused on the power of the vase, and increased her attack, tenfold. She absorbed the emotions of the men, and used that against them, too. Claudia gave in to her baser instincts, and let fly with every bit of glamour, chemical and pheromone, hint or suggestion in her vampire's arsenal. She might have invented a few new ones.

In the midst of it all, Claudia felt an extraordinary power coursing through her. She was a thousand places at once, an avenging angel in the depths of Hell, corrupting demons to the cause of good.

She pointed at the leader. In a powerful, echoing voice, not her own, she said:

"That man could use a hug!"

Immediately, Red, Bruiser, and Knuckles tackled their leader, knocking him to the ground. Scab and One-Eye were crying, and

Stretch had a blank look of joy. They cuddled their leader so effectively that he couldn't move. They snuggled him into submission.

The leader struggled under the onslaught of affection. "What the fuck—? What's wrong with you? She's a witch! Don't listen to her—"

Some little part of Claudia knew that she had to make this stop somehow. The more she got, the more powerful she became, and the harder it was to wrest back her self control. Either she would consume the whole world, as she drew others into her web, or eventually, she would die of sexual exhaustion and starvation.

She felt a buzzing against her hip. It broke her concentration on maintaining her spell, just the merest bit.

That's good, she thought. *My phone. It's a good distraction. I need a distraction. I need that. I need it...I need it to move down, and a little to the right...*

The phone stopped vibrating and her disappointment was so great, it snapped her concentration. She fanged down, and suddenly, the flow of wonderful vibes was cut off. It didn't matter. Some of the men were unconscious, a few were weeping, and the rest just collapsed in a limp, damp, sated hamster pile on the floor.

Claudia staggered over to the wall, and shuddered. Her concentration was better now, and she found the leader, who was still squirming beneath his men. Somehow, like the innkeeper, he was unaffected by the presence of the object. He would be, however, affected by the chemicals she produced.

Better not to take any chances, she decided. *Don't want to get that whole thing started again.*

Before she could talk herself into getting close enough to glamour or bite him, she kicked him in the head. That shut him up and sent the three other men on him into orgasmic fits.

She went outside, and sagging against the wall, took out her phone. There was a message.

It was from Fergus. His lovely, growling brogue almost set Claudia off again.

"My flight was late, but I'm at Logan, now. Call me, if it's not too late for me to see you." She pressed speed dial, and got him. "I'm at the waterfront. I need you." She gave the address and hung up.

She was still confident there was enough residual power in her voice to have Fergus come running.

By the time Fergus arrived, out of breath, Claudia had disarmed the men, and handcuffed them, using zip-ties from her belt pouch. In a daisy-chain along the wall, most of them were too stunned to say a word. All of them were still trying to figure out what had happened.

Claudia was on the phone. After a few more words, she hung up. Before Fergus could ask, Claudia began in a rush: "That was Justine. She's okay. They managed to get her into the back of their van by creating a roadblock, but after she came to, she Changed. They were on their way here when she came to, and busted out the back of the van. She made it off the highway to the Middlesex Fells, where she can heal undetected. We'll meet her back in Salem."

"Good," he said, puzzled. "But what do you need me for? You've got it under control, far as I can see."

Claudia took a deep breath. "I have to interrogate them, find out who else knows about this thing they were after. Then I have to wipe their memories. If you see me…getting too deep, too involved, you need to stop me. Any way you can. If I can't wipe all of them, we'll have to kill them, and I'd rather we were able to hand them over to the police."

"Claudia, what—?"

"And then, once we can call the cops—I'll have them tell them that they were beat up by a rival antiquities gang—we'll split up. Meet me at the Charles Hotel in Harvard Square exactly one hour later."

"Um…okay?"

She sighed. "I'll explain it all later. I swear, Fergus."

He looked at her, and nodded. "Man, you sure do know how to tease a guy."

"You have no idea."

Two hours later, Fergus O'Malley nodded to the doorman as he entered the Charles Hotel. He carried a battered overnight bag over one shoulder and a heavy shopping bag from Cardullo's. Not wanting to risk being even a little late, he'd bribed the cabby with an insane amount to get him to Harvard Square, then, being a gentleman, or at least knowing what was good for him, stopped at Cardullo's to buy a bottle of champagne. Then, thinking of his own proclivities, threw in a loaf of bread, smoked salmon, and crème fraiche. But since it was a celebration of sorts, he threw caution to the wind and asked for a tin of Sevruga, not bothering to inquire about the market price. But perhaps Claudia was more of a sweets girl—? He tried to remember whether she ordered dessert when they saw each other, and realizing time was wasting, grabbed a box of chocolates from Fauchon and some outrageously expensive apples.

The clerk observed the tell-tale groceries, the little bag from the pharmacy sticking out of his pocket, the burning desperation in Fergus's eyes and the impatient tapping of his foot, and decided that wishing the gentleman "good hunting" would be too cheeky.

"Have a good evening, sir." And he meant it. There was something about the guy...he usually went for blonds but had to resist the strongest urge to lean over the counter and run his fingers through the customer's dark hair. And a man with an Irish accent was almost too good to resist.

Fergus resisted looking at his watch again, while he waited for the elevator. He had no idea why he was so nervous: either Claudia would have sex with him tonight, or she wouldn't. He had been willing to follow her lead so far, and didn't think she was the kind to punish him for being a few minutes late, but he was not taking any chances.

The elevator door opened. A wretched thought hit him, and suddenly, Fergus's world came crashing down. Claudia wasn't inviting him to consummate their relationship, he realized. She'd asked him over to help wrap up the loose ends of the gig, deal with the aftermath, cover their tracks. He was acting like an adolescent eejit, and she—she of all people—would be able to tell.

Oh, God.

Then he braced himself. It would be hideously awkward, but maybe he should bring up the subject...they were both adults, they could...

He entered the elevator, and practiced what he'd say. *I don't want to rush you, and I'll wait as long as you want. You're worth waiting for. But I think we're both ready to try this—*

He practiced all the way down the hall; it sounded more and more pathetic, and he resigned himself. The door to the hotel room opened.

Claudia stood there in a white robe, her hair wet from the shower, the light of madness in her eyes, her fangs glinting.

He stammered, but started his speech. "I don't want to rush you—"

She grabbed the front of his shirt, pulled him toward her.

"You want to have sex?" Her voice was uncharacteristically husky.

He nodded quickly. "Uh, yes, please."

"Good. I want sex. Let's have sex."

She pulled him all the way into the room, her lips fastening on his. His overnight case and the bag of groceries hit the floor. The apples rolled across the floor as, in between kisses, Claudia promised to repay him for the shirt she'd just ripped off him. The door slammed shut.

Three days later, they joined Justine back at her B&B. Justine entered the room to find Claudia and Fergus sitting on the bed, their fingers entwined. The box containing the vase, recently liberated from the safe at the Charles, was at their feet.

"Well." Justine gave Claudia a pointed look.

"Here's the plan," Claudia said, ignoring her. "Tell me if you have a better, because this is pretty weak. We've tried everything from a junkyard car crusher, to acids, to explosives, and nothing's worked on the vase. All I can think to do now is take my brother Gerry's boat out as far as we can, load this thing down with weights, and lose it off the coast. With any luck, it won't be rediscovered until we have some way to combat it."

"But we need it! We need to take it to the Family," Fergus said.

The argument went round and round: if they couldn't destroy it, they couldn't trust anyone with it. Even involving Gerry was a risky move.

"It just can't be that hard to destroy," Fergus said, picking up the box.

He had it opened before either of the women knew what he was doing.

Claudia and Justine lunged toward him at the same time. "No!"

A voice came from behind the door. "Doesn't that look nice?"

Claudia, Justine, and Fergus turned. The innkeeper, Mr. Dow, was behind them. They exchanged uneasy glances; this was going to get messy. At least most of the guests were gone for the day—

"Just the thing for a little nosegay, right there in that corner."

Claudia was as astonished to hear him say so much, so positively, as she was to learn he knew the word "nosegay." She could only nod.

"I really like that," the innkeeper continued. "I'd be happy to buy it from you. Is it Chinese? Or an English copy?"

The vase seemed to have no effect on him, save one. For the first time since Claudia'd met him, a shy grin cracked his face.

She sputtered. She recalled the leader of the gang, who'd also shown no effect from the object. Maybe some people were just more resistant to it than others.

Justine said, "I don't know. I picked it up at a little shop in Boston."

"Well, it sure is pretty. They don't happen to have another, do they?"

"It was the last one," Claudia said. *I hope.*

"Oh, well." The innkeeper did not withdraw into his habitual taciturnity. He just whistled tunelessly, plucked a curtain back into place. "I guess I have to stop decorating some time. It's only that I'm about to retire, and my son will take over. He's a lot like me, and I thought if they had another, he'd like it. In any case, I'll be happy to bring you more towels, if you need them, Mrs. Nash."

"Oh, that would be lovely, Mr. Dow. You know, " she glanced at Claudia, who nodded. "You know, now that I'm looking at it, I don't think it will go with my living room. The color's not quite right. I've had such a good time here that I'd like to give it to you."

Claudia stepped closer to him and pushed the flimsy story with a little blast of chemical conviction. Would that be enough to get him to take it? She even reached out to the vase for a little help, but there seemed to be a hollow place in the world, now. In Mr. Dow's presence, it was just a vase.

"Why, that's lovely of you!" he said. "Thank you!"

Fergus met Claudia's eyes. "I'd only ask that if you decide to sell it or give it away, you'd give us first refusal." Claudia nodded and kept encouraging the impulse.

"I'd never think of letting go," Dow said, and he meant it. "It's just too lovely."

None of them felt anything but relief.

A few months later, Claudia received an email from Justine, who reported that the vase was safe and sound. A temporary solution, hiding it in plain sight, they'd all agreed, but if it was neutralized by Dow and his family, it was the best they could do for the moment. Justine checked up on it periodically—just business, she'd told Claudia—but each time she'd brought her husband Ben and now they were expecting their third baby.

"Thought you'd get a kick out of this," Justine had written. There was a link to a "Hidden Treasures in Massachusetts" website.   Blue Harbor Inn was voted "most romantic."

Finals

I overheard a couple of young people talking about how they used to dare each other to go up to the grounds of what had been Danvers State Hospital (also known as the State Lunatic Hospital at Danvers)— reputedly one of the most haunted sites in the United States—at Halloween. I liked the idea of Claudia and Gerry being reluctant to visit such a place, not because they were afraid of ghosts, but because they were trying to fix something that was already spiraling dangerously out of their control. It was the first time that I thought about what training would look like for the Fangborn young.

"Gerry, dammit, if you don't clean your room *today*, I will scream!"

"You're already screaming, Mom," I said. It wasn't wise, given my mother actually swore, a rare, bad sign.

But then, I wasn't very wise: It was 1992, I'd just made the successful transition to a new high school for my final two years, and I was feeling full of myself. I already towered six inches above my mother, which I knew she hated; so I leaned over and wrapped my arms around her head and shoulders, engulfing her. I rocked back and forth, pulling her off balance. "There, there. Shhh. You'll be okay."

Mom patted me on the shoulder, then broke free; she's pretty strong. "I'm late for work, I need to stop at the store because you and your sister have emptied the refrigerator *again*, and I have second shift tonight, too. I do not have time to ask you seven times to do something you are old enough to do without being told. Clean your room, Gerhardt."

Quiet was worse than screaming or swearing, and she'd used the full form of my name, which I hated. She and Dad had been tense for days. They both worked two jobs, which sometimes made life tough.

So I sulked. "I have things to do, too. What if I like my room like that? What do you care? It's my room."

Too far. Mom was silent as she packed up her lunch. I crossed my arms, determined to out-silent her. No good.

"I'd rather go with you, on second shift," I said, finally cracking. "You said I—"

"I've said you can go on second shift when I'm certain you're managing school and chores. Not before." She didn't look up as she said this, spent too long smoothing out a crease in the white coat she wore to work in the local pharmacy. "So I strongly urge you to clean your room. As in, yesterday."

Something—maybe the Hayes case—was really bugging her, which made me want to go all the more. I didn't say anything, but let my head roll back. I sighed hugely, suggesting I'd eventually comply with her wishes, but in doing so, I'd be joining the ranks of ageless martyrs.

She reached up on tiptoe, kissed me, and left for work.

My sister came in, looking like something you'd clean out of a drain, all stringy black Goth layers and shit, with mascara that made her look like a raccoon.

"Yo, 'sup, bitch," I said, gathering my books into my backpack.

She set her empty o. j. glass on the counter, then turned and spit at me.

Full-on venom. I could feel my skin tingle, then go numb in the places where the venom hit. I started to feel sleepy. "Claudia! Mom's still upstairs!"

"Ha!" She crossed her arms, even as her fangs retracted. "That was weak. Even *you're* not stupid enough to say something like that if she was in the house. And I know Dad's already at the courthouse."

I staggered over to a chair, trying not to give her the satisfaction of falling over. "No unsupervised powers in the house! And you're cranked up way too high—even I can feel it!"

"Well, don't call me *bitch*!"

"All right, I'm sorry!" I pretended to mouth the b-word again, just to watch her bristle.

But she crossed her arms, a smirk on her face. "And here I was going to take you with, this afternoon."

"Where? Claud, you *have* to take me!"

I knew she was talking about the Fangborn Family business, which involved tracking down evil and protecting humanity. I wanted in.

A vampire, like Dad, Claudia had passed Qualifiers last year, but only by the skin of her teeth. She had the equivalent of a Fangborn learner's permit, which meant she could go out on patrol with Mom or Dad on their "second-shift" jobs and she could even track bad guys on her own, as long as she then reported to an adult. But she was still on probation, and couldn't use her glamouring powers or venom unsupervised for "an unspecified period," until her Finals, which didn't sit well with Claudia at all. Which is why, despite her high grades and ability, she had only barely passed. Her attitude needed adjusting in the worst way.

"What the *Hell* does that mean?" she'd stormed. "I passed all the tests, I can do the work! Why do I have to *wait* to go out on my own?"

"Rules are rules," Mom had said. "Watch your language."

Many stormy sessions had followed, complete with slamming doors, loud sessions with The Cure, and sobbing. But disappointed as she was, Claudia went out every second shift she was allowed.

Back in the here-and-now, she said, "I don't *have* to take you. You'd only slow me down."

That was baloney. Werewolves are just as fast as vampires, and I could *more* than hold my own in a fight. Well, in scrimmages, anyway—I'd never seen real action.

I made a face like I didn't care.

Claudia shrugged. "Whatever. I'm going right after school, so if you want to go?" She wrinkled her nose. "Lose the Public Enemy t-shirt, Gerry."

I ran upstairs to change my clothes, not only because this t-shirt was my prize possession and I didn't want to ruin it, but also because it was too noticeable—with all the news about shootings and lyrics recently, rap put too many people on edge.

My taste and opinion didn't matter. Fangborn rules were to be invisible whenever possible. Even Claudia would tone down the dreary, lost-soul look.

On my way back down, I frowned, slowing my steps. It occurred to me that if Claudia was willing to take me, she thought she needed backup. And if she wasn't going with our folks, what she was doing was probably not only illegal by our laws, it was downright dangerous.

That afternoon, after school, we followed Route 114 out of Salem and into Peabody. Claudia's car was a far-cry from the BMW she'd asked for on leaving St. Cuthbert's Academy—what we called Fangborn

Academy in front of Normal humans—and moved onto Salem High two years ago. The car was used and navy blue, but was reliable enough to get her back and forth for her last year of Normal high school. Claudia had added little touches, like the skull seat-covers and a black-lace graphic film bordering the windshields, and I knew she'd spent hours banging away under the hood. But the car still looked like what it was: Mom's hand-me-down dressed up like the Batmobile. I thought the Sadmobile was pretty pathetic, but I kept my yap shut, because I didn't want to take the bus until I got my license.

She drove lead-footed, relying on her tweaked reactions to save us from crashing into everything on the road. Shortly after we pulled onto Route One, just as I was about to ask her to use her hands for steering and not dramatic gestures, I saw where we were going.

The complex of Danvers State Hospital loomed just over the rise. Gothic brick towers with boarded-up windows towered over the hill, and you couldn't get more of a cliché for a haunted insane asylum if you tried. It had recently closed down, along with nearly a century and a half of horror stories.

No one goes up that hill without a good reason, and usually an audience. When those of us from Salem felt as if we had something to prove during Halloween, that was our pilgrimage. If you live in a town that has a reputation for ghosts and witches, you have to amp it up. The old hospital—reputedly one of the scariest buildings in the world and within spitting distance of the site of the 1692 witchcraft hysteria—was our proving ground.

I'd been up there once or twice. What did I have to be afraid of? Better than most folks, I knew there was no such thing as ghosts. It was helpful to lead an expedition as the new kid in school—as almost every

Fangborn kid is, at some point, transitioning from Fangborn Academy to the Normal world. And getting a good rep gave me an in with girls, which I made the most of.

Claudia never went up there. She hated the place and didn't care about dares or getting with the in-crowd, so I couldn't imagine what drew her now.

She parked off the main road, and we walked to one of the outermost buildings, which had a door busted off the hinges. We stepped in, our footsteps echoing against the cement. Abandoned and vandalized, the windows were broken and the walls covered in amateurish graffiti and colored with minerals leaching out of the water seeping in. There were cracked tiles everywhere, and behind that, exposed rebar reminded me of the bars on the windows.

I shivered. Sure, I'm a werewolf, and I know there's no such things as ghosts. But the place was *spooky*.

I was trying so hard to act cool, I wasn't paying attention. I just about jumped out of my skin when I heard scuffing footsteps come from the other direction.

Claudia glared at me; I should have smelled the girl coming long before I heard her. In all the Lessons, Rules, and Laws of the Fangborn I'd spent time studying, somewhere on those lists is a variation of "pay attention to all your souped-up senses you have and maybe you won't end up dead." Staying alert to my surroundings was something I "needed improvement" on.

As she appeared, I realized I knew the girl—her name was Amanda—by sight only, from school. She was in twelfth grade, with Claudia, but I doubted they were in any classes together, unless it was gym or art. I sniffed once, twice, wincing. Amanda was high on something, and anxious to get more.

"Hey, Claudia." Amanda scratched her arm, and looked around, unable to focus on one thing.

"Hey, Amanda." Claudia gave her a single up-tilting nod, looked around. "I thought we were meeting today."

"Yeah, something came up." She frowned. "How did you know I'd be here? It's not exactly the library."

"You said you come up here, sometimes." Claudia was improvising, I could tell. "I was worrying about you."

"Yeah, well, you don't have to. I'm meeting someone." Amanda frowned and looked around again. "Ryan's not here, though."

If "Ryan" was the loser I knew, she was better off without him.

"How about a ride back?" I could tell Claudia was giving Amanda a little vampiric push, just enough to make Amanda think Claudia's suggestions were good ideas. Not cool; she'd be in deep shit if she got caught using more powers than a Normal had.

Amanda shrugged. "Okay." She only seemed to notice me then. "Who's that?"

"My brother. He's okay."

Amanda smirked. "Yeah, but who died and made him Vanilla Ice?"

Maybe I'd gone a little overboard with the hair product, but that was cold, an insult to my Adidas. "Screw *you*."

"Gerry!" Again, Claudia pushed, too hard. I could almost feel her willing Amanda to chill out and come with us.

"Whatever. Can you give me a lift to the mall?"

"Sure. Let's go."

I paused as they went outside, and sniffed the air, hard. The smell might have come from the heyday of the hospital: fear, pain, sickness, and chemicals that had no business anywhere near human bodies. But there was something else: a smell like a dumpster so nasty, no seagull would dare scavenge there. I got a cramp in my stomach that would have floored a Normal, and I couldn't help but growl a little. There had been something bad, here, and it wasn't ghosts. It wasn't just bad; it was *evil*. The brand of evil we Fangborn specialized in stopping.

We dropped Amanda at the mall, then drove home. "So, what was that all about?" I asked.

"I'm worried about Amanda. She was there to meet Ryan Sheppard." Claudia had both hands clenched on the wheel, a sure sign she was deep in thought.

Sheppard was a low-level low-life at school: a dope dealer. "You wanted to 'suggest' he not deal anymore."

"No."

"Don't bullshit me, Claud."

She shook her head and frowned, looking over her shoulder as she backed into the driveway. "I wanted to get a look at him since I suggested he stop dealing...a few days ago."

I swore to myself.

"Gerry." She set the brake, killed the ignition. "I know what I'm doing. It wasn't even a bite, just a suggestion. A little whiff of pheromones, that's all."

I bunched my fists, tried to keep my panic out of my words. "You know what could happen. You go before a group of Elders and they decide whether to subject you to Examination. Maybe even Shedding."

"Only if I fail." But she didn't look as brave as her words.

"The Examination is bad enough, but the removal of your powers is the worst thing that can happen. They'll *do* it, you know."

"Only if I fail *and* they catch me." She looked away. "You gonna help me?"

"Why, if everything's okay? Why, if you're not gonna fail? Why do you need help looking for him?"

"Because he hasn't been seen since I spoke to him. Hasn't been home, not to school, not to his job. No one's seen him since he left the cafeteria, at lunch on Friday."

We sat there in the car, listening to the tick-tick of the engine cooling down.

"So? You gonna help me?"

"Do I have a choice? Of course, I—"

"You *do* have a choice." I was kind of surprised at how angry she was, since she was the one getting us into all of this. "Don't *ever* think you don't. You can ignore everything I've told you. You can go to Mom and Dad. You can help me. There's at least three choices right there."

"Yeah," I said finally. "Yeah, I got your back. Because what else is a werewolf for, but to track some ill mothah and beat him *down*?"

"Thanks." She nodded, smacked me on the shoulder. "And never, ever attempt to speak street near me again."

I asked around at school on Monday, but had to be careful. I couldn't make out like I wanted to question Ryan and I wasn't known to be one of the toking crowd. Dad said that the best way to flush someone out was to make him think there was something in it for him, and Dad was right.

I made up a story about needing to warn Ryan about someone pissed off at him, and that seemed to work the best. People opened up, willing to believe there was someone meaner than me looking for Ryan, which got me wondering if someone actually might be after him.

On the other hand, my strategy didn't work well enough. No one had seen Ryan since Friday.

So I did what I could, using Normal methods, or at least those available to a Normal high school kid. We spent a lot of our last year at Fangborn Academy doing "Ethics," which was full of rules and I eventually started to get why we Fangborn had to fly under the radar. But sometimes I have to ask: Why be a werewolf if you can't go to town?

I knew, in daylight, at school, I couldn't really afford to get caught doing anything too weird. Didn't mean I couldn't sniff around.

I can pull some of my wolfy senses on-deck while I'm still skinself. Not everyone at the Academy could do that right away—use *some* of their powers without fully or partially Changing.

I started where Ryan was last seen, in the cafeteria. Trust me, it wasn't easy, picking out one sweaty teenager out of 1400, not with the smells coming from the kitchen. Don't get me wrong, I'll eat anything that doesn't crawl off the plate too fast, but tell me: Where exactly on the chicken does the "patty" come from?

"Gerry Steuben!"

I jumped a mile. It was Mrs. Santangelo, who ran the cafeteria. "Hi, Mrs. S."

"What are you doing?"

Think fast... "Claudia lost her watch. I have a study, so I told her I'd look for it."

"Nothing in the lost and found," she said. "I haven't seen Claudia since last Friday. She was talking to that Sheppard kid. She's not dating him, is she?"

"No."

She nodded. "Good. She can do much better. Anyway, the late bell rang, she and Ryan both left out that door. I'm not supposed to let them, but Friday afternoons, I look away."

"How about Monday afternoons? Maybe I could just look outside around real quick?"

"Can't do it, Gerry. Get back to your study, and next time, make sure you have a hall pass."

I went back to study hall, and tried to focus on calculus, but all the equations swam around.

Claudia had said she'd last seen Ryan Friday noon. Mrs. S said she'd let them go out the cafeteria door at the late bell, Friday afternoon.

Claudia had lied to me.

The rest of the day, I walked through classes like a zombie. During lacrosse practice, however, I kinda caught a break. The wind shifted, and I got the faintest whiff of something that made me want to hurl. It was so bad, so wrong, I stopped dead in my tracks, trying to pick up what it was and where it was coming from.

"Steuben! Whaddya doing? We're in the middle of a play!"

Coach was seriously pissed, but I was so caught up in trying to figure out the scent, I'd zoned. "Huh?"

"Nevermind, 'huh!' You can't concentrate, you give me laps! Move it, mister!"

I hate laps, almost worse than suicide sprints, but I started running. At least I could shut out everything else and concentrate on that scent. Faint as it was, it was identical to the one I'd picked up the other afternoon at the old asylum. Had whatever was after Ryan Sheppard followed him here?

The stink was bad enough to make me want to blow chunks, but I didn't dare puke, not after only half a lap. Should I fake being sick, to get out of practice and track the scent? No, if I threw up, Coach would call my parents. I tamped down the urge to Change, and kept on running.

Finally, practice was over, and I got changed as fast as I could. I booked it outside, and around back to the school. It was the same scent that I noticed during practice all right, and it took every bit of focus to keep from losing my lunch. I pared away the overtones of teen angst and exhaust fumes, and focused on the signature, which gave me something to recognize next time I encountered it. In skinself, I could only get two things from the scent: I recognized it from when we'd seen Amanda at Danvers State, and there was a strong note that was not actually a part of the signature, but associated with it, and that one quite familiar. Meth.

Claudia had said Amanda was going to meet Ryan to score, but broken as he was, "Ryan the Herbmeister" didn't drive me to want to Change, not like whoever this was. This scent had come from someone else. I risked a quick look around, and reached into my pocket with one hand. With the other, I held onto my St. Christopher medal and concentrated.

I half-Changed. Even retaining my bipedal, upright form, I felt the surge of adrenaline, the flood of endorphins, the rocket-fueled rush of righteousness as my bones changed their shapes and my muscles shifted to accommodate my wolfy head, pelt, and claws. I was grateful my baggy jeans and fleece concealed most of my shaggy coat.

It wasn't dark enough, really, to risk any Change, but even with just half my powers on deck, my sense of smell and the ability to analyze scents went off the charts. So I kept my head—now complete with a muzzle full of sharp teeth and topped with pointy ears—down low as I crouched down in the weeds. I sorted through the smells of wildlife in the grass, and more recent passersby, trying to isolate the pertinent smells. The molecules disperse and break down, and with practice you can pick out the ones that are of a certain age. I got high marks in tracking at Fangborn Academy.

"Steuben, is that you?"

Have I mentioned I got *shitty* marks for Ninja-like concentration and awareness of my surroundings at FA? I had to work on that, because my Qualifiers were in the spring.

Coughing, I turned away, and praying like mad, Changed back to skinself, hoping the trees, weeds, and failing light had shielded me from view. I was sweating, my pulse racing, as I pulled my hand out of my pocket and dropped a small box to the ground.

Cursing, I went to grab it, but Coach Weems was faster. He snatched up the red and white box of Marlboros I'd dropped.

"I was looking for my sister's watch," I said. "Uh, that's not mine."

"Son, why on earth would you want to start with that poison?" He stuck the cigarettes into his pocket. "My boy Scotty is a few years older than you. I caught him smoking, once, and you know what I did?"

"Uh..."

"I made him smoke his way through the whole pack, until I knew he'd never want another one of those coffin nails ever again."

"Sorry, Coach." I tried to look guilty, which was easy enough, but I was much happier he think I was out here smoking than turning into a wolf-man. I held my breath, hoping I wouldn't get busted too bad.

"Show up for practice a half hour early tomorrow. I didn't see you light up, so I won't give you detention or bench you, but I ever catch you again, that's it. You got it?"

"Yes, Coach."

"Okay, then." He turned to go, then paused. "You need a ride home?"

"No, Claudia's supposed to pick me up. Thanks anyway," I said.

"Well, wait for her out at the drive. G'wan, now."

I booked out of there, glad to have avoided detection, but I didn't need super-senses to hear the click of the lighter and the smell of confiscated tobacco burning behind me as I left.

Claudia was waiting for me out front, in the Sadmobile. The school's doors burst open, though, and suddenly I was overcome...

...by cheerleaders.

They brushed past me in a flock, in their Salem "Witches" black and white uniforms, with those insane little skirts. The girls pretended not to notice me, but too casually for even a Normal to buy that. Legs, legs, legs as far as the eye could see, and the *sweaters*...

They smelled incredible. So incredible...

The world swam.

The world *hurt*.

I found myself sitting down, my butt hurting as much as my head did. A cement post was right in front of me. I'd never even seen it.

Their laughter surrounded me, and I felt my ego shrink to nothing. Then, mercy of mercies, two ran over to help me up, concern mingled with amusement on their faces.

"Awww! Gerry, you gotta watch where you're going," Nicole said, patting my shoulder. She and Jen K helped me up. Their hands on my arm sent thrills through every part of me.

"Just finished practice," I said, feeling distinctly wobbly again, but not from a blow to the head. The girls were so close…I could feel my fangs starting to nudge out…

Claudia honked impatiently, and my focus snapped back into place. She didn't care if I had a concussion or was bleeding to death or anything. But I was glad to get my senses back under control. Horny and wolfy is a bad combination.

"Probably just bonked. From practice," I finished lamely. I was barely under control now. "Thanks."

"I have a granola bar," Jen K said, a little breathless. "If you want it."

I stared into her eyes. She didn't look away. The world went swooshy again…

Hoooooonk! Honk honk honk honk—

I shook my head, as much to clear it, as anything else. "No, thanks, Jen. I gotta go. I think my sister is developing a brain tumor, or something. See you later!"

They both giggled. I didn't feel a bit bad about throwing Claudia under the bus, if it would help me escape with some dignity intact.

I waved and they waved. I got into the car with a big fat smile on my face.

"Smooth move, Ex-Lax," Claudia said, as she tore out, with a screech of tires. "Way to avoid drawing attention to yourself. Way to keep control over your senses. Way to focus—*not.*"

"Claudia—"

"Shut up, Gerry!"

"Why are you so mad at me?" I asked. "I've got more right to be mad at you."

"Like Hell."

She was driving like a maniac again, taking all the back roads from the school to our neck of Salem. Lots of narrow streets and hills, twisting and turning like a roller coaster. I knew she probably wouldn't get us killed, but there had been a few too many close calls recently.

"Slow down!" I yelled. "I know you lied to me about the last time you saw Ryan Sheppard! You said lunch, and Mrs. S said she saw you later—"

She slammed on the brakes. "Get out."

"Come *on*—"

"Get out of the car now or I will make you get out, Gerry!"

Claudia didn't make idle threats, and I didn't need another dose of venom to mess with my already fragile self-control, so I got out. Whatever she was doing, she was still trying to cover her tracks by lying to me. I slammed the door wicked hard behind me, but barely had the chance to get out of the way before she peeled out, leaving me stranded.

"You are such an asshole!" I yelled after my sister. The Sadmobile vanished around the next curve, so I got started on the long walk home.

Once at home, I spent a little quality time with the refrigerator and microwave.

I went up to my room, wondering whether Jen K would go out with me, if I asked her, and whether I wanted to ask her. I crammed my sandwich in my mouth so I could open the door.

Mom was sitting on the bed. Saying nothing.

Like I said, with Mom, quiet was bad. Quiet was bad, with all my middle names implied.

After a million years, she said, "The regimentation of Fangborn Academy is to build habits in you that will help you in our work. But even at home, we're still Fangborn and that means we always have to be prepared. *Always.* So when I ask you to clean your room, it's not because I'm trying to boss you, or I'm indulging some whim of mine. It's because I think orderliness might save your life someday."

I took the sandwich out of my mouth. "Mom, I—"

In an instant, she was in front of me. "Pow!" She clapped her hands together. "I'm a bad guy who's seen you investigating a crime scene. I've followed you home. What's your move?"

Since I knew better than to actually drop the sandwich and milk on the floor, which would be the right thing to do, I aimed a half-hearted kick at her, to make the point.

She grabbed my foot and held on; she's strong—she's a werewolf. I was left hopping, hands full, helpless.

"You need distance, and your primary weapon should be near the door," she said. Where is it?"

"Mom, I get—"

"Where is it?"

I knew she had me. My "fake" katana was only fake in that it was meant to look like a cheap imitation of a long samurai sword. It was way on the other side of the room, where I'd been screwing around, practicing it. Okay, maybe striking poses in the mirror. Even if my foot was free, the way was blocked by the weight bench and weights I hadn't re-racked. "Mom, I *get* it. I'll clean my room."

"Good." She let me go; my milk sloshed over my hand. "Then you can sort the laundry and wash the cars. You'll have a lot of time after you're done with your homework, because you're grounded this week."

I knew better than to argue, but I did anyway. "Mom! I was thinking I could go on second shift with—"

"Not for a week. You can spend the time thinking about why I'm so hung up on you doing as I ask."

She reached up to kiss me, but I wasn't having any of it and wouldn't stoop down. So she poked me, hard, in the gut. When I doubled over, she kissed my cheek and left.

That's Mom: All about the tough love.

Later, Mom, Dad, and I ate dinner in silence; Claudia had called, saying she was at the library. You could almost feel the tension. I knew it meant something big was going wrong with my parents' case. They were trying to nail an asshole named Jimmy Hayes, who seemed to think Salem's criminal community could be better organized under his exclusive direction. He was making no bones about advertising the fact with the bodies of those who tried to resist him. I'd snuck a look at the file; the pictures of Hayes' victims were pretty gross.

Claudia picked the wrong day to mess around. If she didn't watch out, she was not only going to be in serious trouble with the 'rents, she also risked delaying her Finals—or worse. I prayed she didn't screw up; screwing up would mean someone discovering the unauthorized use of her glamouring powers.

Shedding isn't talked about much among the Fangborn, but it happens, and they make sure we understand why. Examination before a group of Elders, the first step in any serious investigation, is awful: A vampire drains the examinee of blood and fills him with the urge to tell the truth, so far as he knew it. The terrible thing about the Examination is that the combination of the blood loss and the chemicals isn't deadly. You only wish it was. The pain is awful, lasting months under the best of circumstances. That's why we need to do it with the consent of a quorum. It's why we do it so reluctantly.

Shedding is worse: The vampire keeps draining until the powers of the Fangborn are *permanently* removed. It was the punishment meted out for the worst of crimes: the deliberate misuse of powers or deliberately endangering another Fangborn. Also, unauthorized use of powers by a minor.

A friend of mine's cousin had seen a guy with his powers stripped. He was just a Normal, basically, my friend said. He went through the day with this sort of sad, glazed look on his face, and eventually we heard he lost the will to live out his hypernaturally long life.

Shedding meant we took one more Fangborn off the front line of the fight against evil.

It was pretty goddamn awful. I didn't like that Claudia was skating so close to this.

There was enough food on the table for six, but even with just the three of us, I ended up not having to put away any leftovers. Mom went upstairs to change for second shift.

"How much homework do you have?" Clearly, Dad, as beat as he was from a long day of handling defense cases, was getting ready to go on second shift, too.

I sensed a chance. "I've finished almost all of it, and I have a study first thing tomorrow. And I started on my room, so I thought that maybe I could go with—"

"What did your mother say?"

I didn't quite hang my head. "I'm grounded. A week."

He nodded. "So why are you trying to talk me into something we all know won't happen?"

"Uhhhh...I'm an optimist?"

"Nice try, buddy. We're taking the Audi tonight, so once you finish the rest of your homework, you can work on washing the minivan." Dad shifted back in his seat. "And son?"

"Yeah?"

He shook his head sadly. "Never try to scam a vampire."

The minivan was a pain to clean, had more glass than the Hancock tower, and after years of ferrying kids, corpses, loot, and unwilling informants, had a *lot* of ingrained dirt. And smell. It was the least cool vehicle on the planet, after the Sadmobile.

And I was to be its bitch for the next two hours.

With a sigh, I picked up the bucket and sponge.

I'd washed the beast and was just starting an eternal purgatory with the Windex and newspaper when the phone rang. Desperate for any reprieve, I ran for the kitchen. "Hello?"

"Gerry? Gerry, I need help—"

It was Claudia. She sounded awful, wrung-out, like she'd been crying or fighting. "Mom and Dad are on second shift, Claud. What's wrong?"

"No, I need you, I need help now! I can't wait, I can't let them—oh, Gerry, you have to come!"

"Claudia, I'm on lock-down. For a week." If I left the house, there'd be Hell to pay.

"If you don't come...Gerry, I need you. *Please.*"

Her voice was strained, and although Claud dressed like a ghoul and pulled stunts I never would dream of, she didn't wig out for no reason. Something bad was going down.

"Okay. Where are you?"

"I'm at a gas station, on 95. But meet me at the hospital—"

"*Which* hospital? Salem or Union—?"

"No, Danvers State."

Oh, jeez. Where Claudia had been trying to find Ryan, where I'd first encountered that horrible smell. If she was this freaked out—"What do you need?"

"I...I don't know. Just *come.*"

"Okay, as soon as I can." I hung up and looked around, adrenaline pumping at what I was about to do.

This is why Claudia and I needed to get some of those new cellular phones, I thought as I gathered up an emergency kit, *so we won't lose time trying to find a pay phone.* Mom and Dad, the uncles and the aunts had them already, and they were even smaller than the one Michael Douglas had in *Wall Street.* Mom could totally hide hers in a not-too-big pocketbook, and Dad was working on some kind of a holster so his wouldn't show under his jacket.

I made a mental note to add that to my argument, next time I tried. I got the kit, filled with weapons and other emergency gear, grabbed my jacket, and turned around. How was I going to get out there? I didn't have a driver's license, only a permit. My racing bike was hanging from the ceiling; it would take me forever to ride all the way out there, and Claudia said she couldn't wait. The dreaded minivan was right in front of me, dripping wet, mocking me with its lumpy lines and dull respectability. My folks would kill me if I took it out. I could turn wolfy, and run, but that would take only a little less time than the bike, and I'd have to change into my sweats and Claudia had said right away...

I was reaching for the keys to the minivan, when something else caught my eye.

Dad's vintage BMW motorcycle. The Toaster. A 1970 "Slash-5," with a 750 cc engine, 50 horses at 6400 RPM, and a top speed of 110 MPH.

Dad had taught me the basics of riding it as a reward for when I'd finished my time at Fangborn Academy. The memory of how it felt to tear along the quarry road, all alone, almost turned me into a wolf. It was a beast—handled like a dream and went like a bat out of Hell.

If the folks come home, I reasoned, they might not notice the Toaster was missing. They'd see right away if the big blue whale was missing.

The motorcycle would be fast and discreet, two laudable Fangborn qualities.

I'd get to Claudia faster.

Maybe Jen K would see me on it...

I decided on the BMW. If I was going to break curfew, and get busted for driving a vehicle without a license, it might as well be for something really good.

I pulled the tarp off the Toaster, my mouth dry. I wheeled it out to the drive, and started it. I pulled the helmet on—just because I healed fast didn't mean I could come back from spilling my brains all over the road—and revved it. The rumble of the engine filled my universe, and I was in love.

I tore down the winding roads of Salem, showing a minimum of restraint until I hit Route 114. I unleashed the bike, and, as I rocketed onto Route One, I gave in and howled.

I rode up the twisty, hilly road, glad for the light and noise the bike made. For as much as Dad tuned the bike so it was very quiet, there was something about that place that begged for happy noise. Something to chase away the shadows, the gloom—

To keep from talking myself into a panic, I killed the engine and dismounted. I wheeled the bike over behind a tree, and began to track Claudia. I didn't want to start shouting; she might be trying to track someone herself, and I didn't want to give us both away.

For a minute, I was frozen: how was I supposed to do this again? I'd only left Fangborn Academy a few months ago...

Rote memory kicked in.

Breathe. You can't do anything if you can't breathe.

Wiggle your toes. If you can't wiggle your toes, the rest of you is too tense to move the way you'll need to.

Smell. What is nearby? Danger? Even if you can't smell it, are you afraid?

Move. If you don't see or smell anything, start to cast around the area.

I'd started moving even before I finished the list, reassured by the habit of it. I made sure there was no one around me, and Changed half-way, to my wolf-man form.

The confidence and power that came with the Change helped me a lot. Plus I look pretty awesome as a wolf-man, especially in my black t-shirt and jeans; I hated not being able to show off—once in a while, anyway. As I began to cast around, my newly-sensitive wolfy nose alive to every smell of leaf mold and rotting mortar, I remembered "Scenarios" was my favorite class at Fangborn Academy, and it calmed me a little. "Scenarios" was when our instructors set us loose on simulated crime scenes and we had to try and figure them out. It was like playing "army" for hours at a time, and I was good at it. After ten years of training, we'd been thrown into so many different "Scenarios," it was easy to imagine we young Fangborn had been prepared for everything.

Nothing could have prepared me for this, though, the real thing. My nose started twitching, and the smell of blood was thick on the air, long before I came to the clearing. My hackles rose, as I passed the last tree and saw—

Blood everywhere. The remains of Ryan were scattered, no— *festooned*—hanging from the trees and bushes. I identified him by the grunge-inspired flannel shirt and cowrie shell necklace he always wore. Then there was the smell of him, somewhere under the blood: a disgusting and musky cologne; a whiff of the hand soap they used in the auto shop; urine and feces. Faintly, far below the threshold of Normal olfactory capacity, I detected a whiff of dope, and something I knew only from FA was meth. The smell of whoever—whatever—had done this to him was the same I'd picked up at school.

Whoever—bigger and meaner than me—had been looking for him, had found him.

The world spun around me, a horror.

Deep breath, Gerry. Through the mouth.

I focused on my breathing, trying to shove the fear to the back of my mind. I'd seen things like this in "Scenarios" before, but this...this was real. If I screwed up, no one was going to come out from behind a bush and lecture me about what I did wrong. Now, people might die, if I messed up.

I might die.

Someone, *something*, had executed Ryan. Your average perp kills and runs, or tries to hide the body. I was pretty sure this display was meant as a warning. I remembered my parents' case file and remembered: Jimmy Hayes made examples of those who had resisted him.

When the Normal cops got here, they were gonna freak. I was considering it, myself.

Where was Claudia?

I could identify Claudia's tracks, but faintly. She should have been here already, long before me, even using evasion techniques.

A scream broke through my confusion.

It was Amanda.

I began to run, crashing through the weeds and low branches.

A hiss, followed by a noise like a quiet whipcrack. Claudia, outraged, spitting, too hard, at someone.

I smelled two kinds of vampire venom, the fading first was to heal, the second was to attack. My brain kicked in and I realized what had happened was this: Claudia had found Amanda, who'd seen the remains of Ryan. She'd worked to calm Amanda, then someone intruded, making Amanda scream. Claudia was fighting for her life.

I ran faster.

And stopped when I reached the next clearing.

A truck's lights cast weird shadows against the brick wall. Amanda was sinking to the ground; Claudia had been working on her, no doubt trying to remove some of the panic and fear brought on by finding Ryan's remains.

Now, exhausted from trying to heal Amanda, Claudia had half-Changed and was now a violet-skinned, fanged and clawed bipedal snake-creature. She was fighting, barely holding her own against a guy twice her size.

The smell from behind the school, from the site of Ryan's death, hit me like a ton of bricks. The guy beating on Claudia had killed Ryan. It was Jimmy Hayes.

He was the evil I'd been training to fight, all my life. He was the thing I'd been born to destroy.

Instinct drove me; I launched myself. I lost control, and the full Change overtook me midair; there was a bite of autumn cold in the instant between when my new, shifting muscles tore through my shirt and jacket and the next, when the coarse fur replaced naked skin. I'd never confronted true evil on my own, and the Change made me drunk with power.

I landed, three feet from the asshole who was about to drop my sister with a punch, and growled.

The noise startled Hayes, who instead of following Claudia down to the ground, pulled back.

Good for Claudia, not good for me.

He yanked out a .44 Magnum and shot me.

The bullet slammed into my shoulder, a ten-pound sledge hammer gone supersonic. I rocked back, gasping at pain I'd never imagined possible.

Another shot; I staggered, hit the ground. My head flung back and cracked on a stone. I shifted to my wolf-man form.

Through watering eyes and blurred vision, I saw the guy raise the gun again.

Werewolves are tough, but not immortal. We can be killed, if we lose too much blood before we can heal. I was pretty sure the next bullet would be the last thing I felt, ever. Didn't even need to be silver.

Claudia reacted faster almost than I could see. She tackled Jimmy

Hayes, slashing at the hand with the gun.

He dropped it, screaming to someone I couldn't see. "What are you waiting for? Get out here!"

Five more men emerged from the building. "We couldn't find—holy shit!"

I had to giggle at the looks on their faces—maybe it was shock. The sight of a teen-aged vampire dressed like Robert Smith fighting with their boss—and a bleeding wolf-man—would have stopped anyone dead.

In that moment, the pain began to fade to a manageable level as my body healed itself. When I realized I wasn't going to die immediately, I got angry. I picked myself up, and lunged at Hayes. Biting down on his other wrist got his attention. As he screamed, Claudia made the most of the moment. With the last of her energy, she sank her fangs into his neck and tore the carotid. She collapsed onto the corpse of Jimmy Hayes, blood everywhere.

I hauled her to her feet. "C'mon, Claud! Can't give up now—!"

She nodded blearily, staggering a little. Vampires are tough as nails and mean as Hell, but they do need to know how to pace themselves, especially when they're young. Claudia hadn't managed her powers tonight.

The five guys were going to figure out any second that we were vulnerable. We might have had a chance during the day; there'd have been no stopping Claudia because vampires suck up energy from the sun. Now, with the days getting shorter, and school taking up so much of her time, and me still bleeding pretty heavy from two gunshot wounds...

We were toast.

The five men started to fan out, surrounding us. "What the hell is this?" one said. "Halloween?"

I saw weapons: three guns, a knife, and a baseball bat doctored up with some nasty looking nails.

"One," Claudia whispered. There was a tiny "shiiing," and I knew she now had a fistful of hira-shuriken, ready to throw.

"Two." I almost imperceptibly nodded at the pistol by Hayes' body. If Claudia wanted to fight rather than run, I sure wasn't going to leave her behind.

Claudia never said "three."

She opened her mouth—

I saw her body tense, *I* tensed—

A wolf mowed into one of the men, knocking him into the next one.

I dove for the gun.

Claudia let the shuriken fly. One man screamed and shot blindly. The bullet's ricochet rang against the brick wall to our side. Two of the projectiles had found their marks, one embedded in his forehead and one in his shoulder; he collapsed. A tinny "ting," and the third bounced away harmlessly.

A walking snake-creature—in a UMass sweatshirt and jeans—as fast as, well, a darting snake, sank his fangs into the neck of the man in the middle.

Growls and screams as the wolf wrestled with the two men on the ground. They soon went quiet.

I grabbed the gun and, as I stood, put the momentum and the whole of my weight behind an uppercut that lifted up the guy in front of me. He fell back, and I stepped forward, my finger on the trigger, ready to—

"Gerry."

It was the snake-man in the beat-up sweatshirt. It was Dad.

I nodded, only half hearing him. The rush of the Change, the fight, of not dying, filled my world, and for a moment, I was Michael Keaton in *Batman*, or maybe Jean-Claude van Damme. "I'm on it, Dad."

"Gerry. Put the gun down. It's over. We won."

I felt the hand on my shoulder, and then a kind of a mental nudge, chilling me out. I relaxed, swallowed, and secured the pistol, realizing everything *was* under control now. A movement to one side, and I saw the wolf pause to kick disdainful dust over the prone men before loping off into the trees. Mom was going to find her clothes and Change back.

I followed him over to where Claudia was lying, breathing shallowly. There was no sign of Amanda anywhere.

Panic filled me. Claudia had acted on her own before her Finals. She risked Examination and maybe even Shedding, unless I could come up with a story.

"Dad, I can explain all this. Amanda called Claudia, all in a panic, and we had to—"

He knelt down. "Just a minute, son." He felt Claudia's pulse, and then closed his eyes. It might have looked pretty funny to an outsider, but I was used to Dad in his fang-form. Snake-headed people, wearing sweatshirts and healing the wounded, weren't anything new to me.

He nodded, finally, and I felt relief: Claudia would be okay. Dad had emitted a chemical to ease her into sleep. Her wounds were already healing on their own, no need for him to bite her to heal.

"She's just exhausted, poor thing," he said, standing and brushing off his jeans. "She needs to learn her own limits." He turned to me. "Now you were saying?"

"Well, Amanda—who's not here now—called Claudia and we—"

Just a look from those cold black eyes was enough to stop me in the lie. "What did I say earlier this evening?"

"Never try to scam a vampire." I sagged; Claudia was doomed. "Dad, you can't let them Examine Claudia. It's not *fair*."

"No one's going to Examine anyone."

"How do you—?"

"Hang on a second, son. One of them is coming around."

Business comes before explanations. He moved to the first two of the men who were returning to consciousness. "Hold the one on the left, would you, Ger?"

I took the one who was still mostly out of it, and sank a sleeper hold on him. Dad grabbed the other, and stared into his eyes.

"You and your friends were ambushed by a rival drug dealer and his men. He had a pit bull, which is how you got bitten. You saw no one else, and you should probably tell the cops what happened. Also, it might be a good idea for you to get out of the game."

The guy nodded, moaning. Dad repeated the same thing to the guy I had, then again, in fluent Spanish, to the next one.

Before he moved to inspect the corpses, he paused, and Changed back to skinself. His hair was rumpled and he looked tired. But I guess this was the end of the double shifts: these were the men they'd been after.

I couldn't stand waiting any longer. "Why won't Claudia have to face Examination? Are *you* going to lie?" Maybe Dad could scam another vampire, *maybe*; but it just didn't seem like something he'd do.

"This is Claudia's Final."

"Say *what*?"

"Your final test, the one that tells other Fangborn you're an adult, is when you're willing to risk all, including your life, more—your Self as a Fangborn—to save a human."

That pulled me up short. "Are you kidding me? There's no Shedding?"

"Yes, there is. It's rare, but it's our last punishment. I hope you never meet anyone who's suffered it."

"But...you tricked us into thinking that—? We have to *disobey* you, risk *everything*, to graduate?" I shook my head, looking for the words to express the enormity of my disbelief. "Dad, I can't believe you'd let us go along believing that! That is the *shittiest* thing I've ever heard in my life."

He only nodded, ignoring my language. "I agree. When you think about it, it's no different for humans." He was all "Attorney Steuben" now, his face as serious as a heart attack.

It struck me. "You and Mom...you *knew* this was going to happen! You knew Claudia was about to go off and do something dumb! That's why you've been so wound up lately!"

He nodded; a burden had been lifted from his shoulders. "Becoming an adult is a huge responsibility, and it's terrifying. There are consequences to acting as a mature person. We Fangborn need more of a test, given the powers we have. But it's really the same thing. You graduate—you grow up—when you take the risk and accept the results of your actions willingly.

"Claudia put her life on the line, and she knew what would happen if she did so. She passed." He looked down at the corpse of Jimmy Hayes, wiped my prints from the Magnum, and put it in Hayes' hand. He looked at me. "And so did you."

"Me? I was just trying to make sure Claudia didn't get killed."

"And you risked Examination in doing so. You thought about the risk, right?"

I nodded. "Yeah, well. There was no choice."

"There's always a choice, Gerry. Always." He fanged up briefly, and worked on the last guy, giving him the story he'd told the other survivors. Our trail was covered now, and if we hadn't been in time to save Ryan, maybe we'd keep a dozen others like him safe from Jimmy Hayes, put them on the straight and narrow.

"I'm going to take Claudia's car, to see if I can locate that Amanda girl. Your mother will take Claudia in ours. You want to come with me?"

Oh, *Hells.* "Um...I took the motorcycle up here."

My father blinked once, slowly, processing that information. "My motorcycle."

"Uh, yeah." My heart thudded—once, twice—then seemed to freeze solid in my chest.

"Then you better drive it back," Dad said finally. "When I get home, will I find it washed, and in the near-mint condition in which I left it? As if it had never been moved at all?"

My heart started up again. "Absolutely!"

"Change your shirt, then, and clean up some of that blood—you did bring an emergency kit with you, correct?"

I nodded, not believing I was going to get away with this.

"It takes about thirty minutes of careful driving to get home. I'll give you forty-five, if you promise to stop by Treadwell's to pick up some ice cream. Claudia likes mocha chocolate chip, right?"

I nodded again, a little numb. Jen K worked at Treadwell's. Half my class would be hanging out there tonight, seeing me as I rode up on—

The awesomeness of it all was almost too much to bear.

"Forty-five minutes to get home, Gerry," Dad repeated, bringing me back from Fantasyland. "And the bike will be *pristine*." Then he vanished into the night.

A couple of days later, I zipped up my fleece against the early November wind and went out to the driveway. Claudia was messing under the hood of the Sadmobile, and despite the cold, she was wearing only a black tank-top and leggings with her Docs, the better to soak up the autumn sun. She'd completely healed and looked good: her face was clean of the black makeup, but smudged with oil; her eyes were clear.

"'Sup, bitch?" I said, pulling up one side of her headphones and snapping it back. "You look like a plucked chicken."

"Ow!" Claudia exposed one fang, and showed me one finger, but that was the extent of her protest. She switched off her DiscMan; the CD slowed its revolutions and stopped.

"Bite me." She threw the socket wrench down, and wiped her hands on a rag.

"So. You heard?"

"Yeah." She paused. "And you're welcome. I'm open to gifts of appreciation. Cash is always appropriate."

I snorted, but I knew what she meant: she'd passed her Finals and was a full-fledged Fangborn, now—all the paperwork had gone through and the ceremonies scheduled. And because I'd done essentially the same, I'd also passed. I still had to get through my Qualifiers in the spring, and technically I was still just a pup, but the news had come down today. It was pretty much a done deal.

Claudia began to sort her tools, cleaning them and replacing each in the appropriate drawer of the red tool box. I lowered the hood of the car, and frowned: the Sadmobile hadn't needed tuning up. I still had a scar from helping her work on it three weeks ago.

I realized Claudia needed something to keep her from thinking about Amanda.

Amanda vanished that night; Dad followed her tracks to the highway, where he assumed she hitched a lift. Nothing had shown up on the computers, and I knew Claudia was still searching.

Despite my conviction my sister would one day find the missing girl, Claudia blamed herself for losing Amanda.

I was about to say something, when it struck me: Claudia wasn't holed up in her room, listening to Joy Division. She was outside listening to Joy Division, but she was working on the car, which I knew she did when she was trying to solve a problem.

She'd be okay, I realized. She was working it out. You can't assume your full adult powers without being willing to make the sacrifice and take responsibility for it all. That has to come voluntarily.

You have to graduate yourself.

Promises to Keep

The Fangborn compulsion to track and tear evil is strong, usually unavoidable; it occured to me that there must be a point at which exhaustion sets in. I supposed that whether the Fangborn would break off the search to rest or to push on would depend on the character. I wanted to follow Claudia to that point for this story.

"Pomp and Circumstance is my least favorite tune ever," my friend and colleague Renata Hoffman said as she walked me into the Psychology Department lounge. "It's one of the hazards of teaching. And if you have as many nieces and nephews as I do...it becomes unbearable. Torture and sweaty sunburn. At least here—" she gestured around her. "At least here, we have air conditioning and no damn Elgar."

"And champagne!" another professor added. "Who needs more?"

Replies came from offices where faculty were working while they waited for the main ceremony in the stadium to be over, and for the departmental graduation ceremonies to begin. Family and friends would return here to cheer for the group of matriculating undergraduates, a few Masters students, and one doctoral hooding. That was the reason I was here; I'd been an advisor on Astrid Elliott's dissertation and she'd invited me to join her for the big day.

Astrid had been so excited when she asked me. "The main program at the field is about two hours long, and yeah, I'm going. I know it's not terribly important, but I want the full day—all the celebration. A half hour after that ends, everyone will collect at the department. The university caterers will have hors d'oeuvres and drinks for the guests—but you know all this!"

I laughed. "I promise I'll be there."

And so here I was. I glanced at the clock, remembering Astrid's schedule. "I need to stretch my legs, Renata," I said suddenly. I was exhausted and needed some time in the sun.

"Okay, don't lose track of time," Renata said. "I want to sneak over to the City Lab Innovation Center for their party tonight. It's their first graduating class, and I have a mentee who's marching."

I nodded and sighed with relief as I went down the stairs. As nice as it would have been to celebrate with friends, I needed time to recuperate. I was still hurting from yesterday's overexertion and fights. I was glad that my academic robes hid the bruises that were still healing.

I felt a wave of relief as soon as the fresh air hit me; it was gloriously hot. Yes, I am a vampire, but if you know anything at all about my kind, the Fangborn, you'd know that we vampires recharge from the sun. You'd know that with our werewolf and oracle brothers and sisters, we protect humanity from evil, and you'd know that while we're not immortal—oh, we can be killed—we age slower than humankind. But since most humans aren't ready to know about our existence, we work in secret. We're the first on the scene of the crime because we're tracking the bad guys, not because we are the bad guys.

And for some reason, the past week had been chock-full of evil-doers, in addition to my psychiatric practice. Not only did it seem that there was more than the usual amount of crime, but one especially vicious specimen had eluded my brother Gerry and me two nights running. This guy was always a step ahead of us, which was unusual. Your average criminal has the intellect of a bruised eggplant, and the evil genius is very nearly a myth.

I don't get to wear my regalia often, as I'm not actively teaching, but I end up being on a lot of dissertation committees, mostly for psychology and sociology students. Of course, I agreed to advise Astrid, because I knew what it took to pass such a long course of training. Anyone, but especially a woman starting her professional career, needed all the support and celebration she could get.

And as she'd completed her work, I wanted to be here for Astrid, now, in spite of my ridiculous schedule lately. It was a vow I'd made myself, a long time ago. My own advisor had been boorish and misogynistic—later, I learned that the clinical term was "dickhead"— and he hadn't even bothered to appear at my hooding. I swore, after I finished jumping through his hoops, that I'd never be like that with any student of mine. So I actually didn't mind Elgar and pomp and circumstance and the whole nine yards: It marked someone's success.

Outside, I needed an Audubon Guide to correctly identify all the different specimens of academics, resplendent in their colorful regalia. A few had medals or fur trim and were probably from the older European universities.

Another sigh as the sun hit me, and I searched for a place on the stairs to sit a moment. I took a deep breath—

A grim feeling suddenly overwhelmed me, a despair that felt like my soul was being drained away through a hole in my heart. My brother, Gerry, always described the call to track and tear evil in terms of terrible smells—rotting fish and medical waste—but for me, that smell was always preceded by a sense of profound hopelessness.

Hopelessness makes me angry, and anger makes me act. The scent was so strong, an oracle could have followed it. A human should have been able to sense it, at least feel an inexplicable sense of unease, but there were so many other emotions on this day—gratitude, relief, excitement, and terror of what comes next—that no one would notice. I realized that it was also the perfect cover for any kind of evil: the huge crowds, the uniformity of the gowns, the distraction of it all.

I reached the main street and stopped, confused: there were two scents, coming from opposite directions. At first, I thought it was one trail, leading from east to west, but detected two different...flavors of evil, neither of which was close by and both of which were fresh and strong and overlapping each other.

Two killers, perhaps, intent on two targets? It could be anyone, anyone in the entire university, tens of thousands of people...

I shook my head; I was so tired, I wasn't thinking clearly. Two minutes of reasoning might make all the difference. Who couldn't we find here every other day of the year? Parents? Maybe. Students, faculty, administrators, maintenance were here every day. But today was special.

Who were the invited guests?

The usual suspects: A conservative judge, who'd been widely picketed by students but was immensely popular with the faculty and donors. An entrepreneur known as Wall Street's "Tech Tiger" because of his seeming prescience and aggression in making acquisitions. A sculptor who was a star with the art crowd, but largely unknown to the general populace, despite being a "Genius Award" recipient. A mathematician who'd made a breakthrough that even other mathematicians couldn't understand—but who also had a popular show on math and science in history. The "First Lady of Folk Pop," an accomplished musician who'd been outspoken on human rights, feminism, and the positivity of witchcraft, much to the dismay of traditionally religious folk.

To the east was the performing arts school. To the west, the business school. Two solid possibilities to follow that lined up with the scents.

Pick a direction, Claudia. The Lady or the Tiger?

The Lady. The Tiger would have his own security and there'd be extra on deck because of the wealthy alum who'd be there. The singer would have security too, but...

I was running east before I realized I'd made up my mind. Other things being equal: save the artist. CEOs are replaced every day.

A whole range of things flooded my mind: I had to move quickly through a vast crowd, but couldn't be caught in my snake-woman form which was my quickest. I had to manage to find the source of the evil and neutralize them without being seen. Or if I was seen, I needed to avoid causing a riot in a crowded auditorium. Basically, I had a lot to avoid and not a lot working for me. My venom was badly depleted, I was fatigued, and I knew from sad experience that a vampire pushed past her limits could injure herself if she didn't take the time to recover.

I couldn't think about that now.

The quad was between me and the auditorium, full of graduates and their delighted parents. There was security at the doors checking special passes. There was no way I could get there in a hurry...

The administration building was immediately adjacent. I noticed a few folks with their windows open over there, hoping to catch a glimpse of the singer.

I ran into the administration building and out onto the roof. It was hot and sunny and all I wanted to do was strip down and take a nap and recuperate. But...first things first. I stuck my robes into my bag and took a quick look around, to make sure no one was watching. I took a few steps back, tucked my bag securely under my arm, and Changed.

Changing was almost the best part of being Fangborn. I felt righteous, I felt canny, and though I knew I was badly tired, I felt strong. I'd take the feeling, even if I was running on fumes.

I took a deep breath, ran, and jumped across the alleyway to the roof of the auditorium. It wasn't a long jump, not for me, and I found the door that led from the roof to the interior.

I took a moment to pull my robe out of my bag. It was great camouflage today, being dark colored and ubiquitous. After a couple of false tries, I found the door that led to the sounds and lights control booth and the catwalks and such. Down below me, I heard the SFA speeches commence.

"Hey, you! What are you doing there?" A surprised whisper came from behind me.

I raised my hand to smooth my hair and saw with horror that I had neglected to Change back to my human form. Clearly, I was in bad shape, if I'd forgotten so basic a rule. I Changed back, turned, and saw one of the custodial staff. He was pushing an empty trash bin and cleaning set-up. We were a long way from any of the classrooms.

I allowed myself a small smile. "Same thing as you, I think? I'm a huge fan, and I had a couple of hours before my next event. I was hoping I could sneak a peek."

He blushed hard. "Yeah, me, too. I'll be working late but I came in early to watch."

"I won't tell if you won't."

"Deal."

My nose twitched, and I knew where my target was. I had to play this carefully. "Wait, do you see that over there?" I could see her well enough; she was dressed in dark colors and had a handgun. A look of hatred corrupted her face. She scowled as she listened to the dean's speech, waiting for the Lady to take her place at the podium.

The custodian squinted, then his face widened with shock. "Oh, shit!"

I pushed a little convincing pheromone his way—not a lot, my levels were low. "You go call the police. I'm going to see if I can distract her."

He nodded and hurried away, not asking what I was going to do to distract her, not asking me if that was a good idea. But the truth was, I had a much better chance of stopping her—and quietly—than the cops did.

I was directly across from her. I ran around toward her, and managed to do it quietly, ditching my robe and bag near the exit. I noticed a sleeping bag in a corner; she'd sneaked in here before the event had begun.

I must not have been as quiet as I usually am: She turned and pointed the gun at me. "Get out of here. This doesn't involve you." Maybe in her sixties, White, she had a tight gray perm all but concealed by a red baseball cap. She was wearing a kitten sweatshirt that was desperately at odds with the hate in her eyes and the gun in her hand.

"It does now."

"I'm trying to save her soul. Your soul."

My hand went up to the little gold cross at my throat. "Best start with yourself."

"I'm trying to save you all from your sins." She glanced down at the stage. The Lady was about to begin her speech, a radiant smile lighting her face, Bantu knots peeking out from under her tam. "America needs to return to its white, Christian, god-fearing roots—"

Why was the woman still talking? Why didn't she shove me away, shoot me, or—?

She was stalling—why?

I Changed. Before she recognized that I was now a snake-woman, I darted in. Sinking my fangs deep into her neck, I injected just enough venom so that her death would look like she'd had a heart attack; careful as I was, I felt something strain at the back of my throat. She sank down; I caught her as she fell.

"He said someone would be here, looking for us, he knew it." She coughed. "But he said he'd have my back? This wasn't—"

The Lady broke into an a cappella version of her hit "Sacred Circle," and the would-be assassin died hearing the music of the woman she intended to kill.

I caught myself staring, too long. I'd had no time to rest and replenish my venom. I was beat, but the stink of evil remained in the air, and I needed to follow it.

I couldn't catch a break this week. It's not that I resented my Fangborn calling, but there were times when it was nearly overwhelming.

I grabbed my stuff and climbed back to the roof. Luck was with me, and the custodian hadn't come back. I jumped, but stumbled and fell upon landing.

Two deep breaths, my cheek resting against the sun-hot pebbled roof. I pushed myself up. Changed. Pulled my robe on. Descended to the quad and pointed myself to the business school.

I'm no werewolf, but I can track almost as well. Maybe it was exhaustion, but I couldn't seem to find a clear scent. The track repeatedly doubled back on itself, almost as if the asshole was chasing their own tail. I'd never been so confused; it was familiar and unidentifiable, as if a base scent had been mixed with other contrasting notes.

I was in the middle of trying to untangle it all when I saw someone skulking behind a clump of bushes, a young woman with green hair. They clearly weren't my target, but something was going down. In front of me, a fleet of black SUVs pulled up, the Tech Tiger's entourage. The campus in front of the building was emptying—everyone else who was there for the commencement was already filing inside. Of course he wouldn't arrive a minute before he had to. I saw, to my horror, that a young man in cap and gown, probably his son, was with him.

Several things happened at once. As the figure behind the bushes stood, I began to run, my robes fluttering. The motion, quick as it was, drew the attention of the bodyguards and the Tiger himself. Confused, seeing two people advancing on them from different angles, they drew their pistols.

"FREEZE!"

It took very nearly the last of my energy to project the authority and suggestion in my voice at the group, but all of them froze. I felt a kind of snapping in my head, as if I'd pulled a muscle in my brain. A migraine was starting to take root behind my eyes.

I glanced at the young woman, who was wearing a t-shirt that read "Allergic to Billionaires." In her hands, she held...

A pie. And a cellphone. Bloody Hell, she was going to get shot for throwing a pie at him.

"You stay put," I said. I didn't even need to add anything to it; she was young and terrified and excited. That was good, and I was glad for the break. But there was still work to be done.

I turned to the bodyguards, who were less expensive copies of their boss: White, middle-aged, aggressive. "You four: Listen to me," I said. "You are all too ready to escalate things with gunplay, and that's a very bad habit to get into. There's a kid there! There are families, young people just starting out, and you're pulling your Glocks? Shame on you! Take the extra second to notice that a young idiot with a pie and a slogan t-shirt is not the same kind of threat as some self-appointed jackass with a rifle playing the hero in badly fitting body armor."

They looked abashed and nodded silently.

With that, I slipped through them to the Tiger himself, in a suit that probably cost as much as one of the SUVs and ridiculously intricate facial hair. I grabbed him by the side of the head, as if I were going to kiss him, but whispered, injecting a little emphasis into my command.

"Just because you are not irredeemably evil, doesn't mean you're not a real asshole," I said. "Do better. Pay your workers a living wage. Stop pillaging the planet. You're a clever man, or so you're always announcing. Do something with that brain of yours. And your son looks miserable. Find out what he really wants to do, and let him do that."

The Tiger looked stunned; I'm sure no one ever spoke to him like that in his life, or at least, not more than once. But he nodded quickly. "Yes, of course, it only makes sense."

"Good."

I turned back to the would-be activist. "You know, enough people are angry with billionaires; you don't need to draw attention to them with cream pies. Or was this to draw attention to yourself? Well, take all that energy and work with other people. Write some emails, get people registered to vote. Go to law school and figure out how to tangle up his counsel so much, they'll quake at the sight of your letterhead or email address. I know you have better ideas than this."

"What if I don't?" she said. "I'm not very bright, and I lack charisma, but I'm willing to work hard."

Definitely suggestible, to tell this much truth. "Then find someone who can use a ready pair of hands and a good heart."

She nodded.

"Okay, go home. And you—" I turned to the Tiger. "Go in there and be inspirational."

I sagged briefly as the entourage left, then straightened up, trying to locate the trail I'd been following. At this point, the scent seemed to fade, which made no sense. I stared out at the river, watching a faint mist rise as the day clouded over and cooled.

I turned to head back to the department. I still had fifteen minutes before the ceremony, and if I couldn't follow the trail, I could be there.

Chance or instinct made me look up at the top of Harkness Hill. I saw the glint of glass. My hackles went up.

What had the would-be killer in the auditorium said? "He said someone would be here."

Curse me for an idiot…The guy we'd been unable to catch had figured out, somehow, that someone was looking for him, so he deliberately muddied it. He'd positioned the woman at the auditorium on one end of campus, and had moved to the other end, to watch both buildings with binoculars. He hadn't seen me going into the auditorium because I hadn't gone in through the doors—and I didn't leave that way, either. But when he saw me follow his trail just in time to stop the mischief planned by the protester and then talked four armed men and a powerful man into dispersing, he knew he'd found his tail.

The binoculars lowered briefly, and I imagined that we were connected, him recognizing me as his tail, me recognizing my quarry.

I felt myself tense, waiting for a bullet that never came.

He'd vanished.

It started to rain, damn it all. Of course it did. I almost started crying right then. I knew I wasn't his target, but I didn't know who was. It was too much to ask: I was run down, dangerously weak, with virtually nothing left in my vampire arsenal. I couldn't think straight, but there was no one to step in and help me in time. I'd only come for the graduation party...

No, do better, Claudia. Same as this morning. Think, for thirty seconds...

He went down the back of the hill, to the river and the boathouse. Either he's going to take off—and I won't be able to track him—or he's going to his real target, thinking I won't be able to get there in time to stop him.

What's upriver? The city.

Downriver? The social sciences building, where I'm supposed to be in fifteen minutes. But why would he go there—?

Oh. The social sciences building was just down the way from the new City Lab Initiative Center that Renata wanted to see. A place dedicated to using the resources of the university to improve life in Harkness. A place full of eager young people, ready to get to work promoting social equality, diversity, inclusivity, and every other "-ity" that my two villians would definitely hate. He was going to harm the young people who were dedicating themselves to making the world a better place.

That was it. The last time Gerry and I had lost him, he'd been near the university president's house and the class night for the CLIC students. At the time, I hadn't made the connection.

I couldn't let it happen. But even running at top speed, I'd be there far too late. And I couldn't, not in my human form. But If I could stop him before he got there...

I looked around me. The Tech Tiger's drivers were sitting there, idling. Time to put one of them to work.

I got in, pulled the door shut. I said, "Drive me as fast as you can to Harkness Beach. As safely as you can—no one is to get hurt."

Harkness Beach was the most likely place he could land the boat, just shy of the Center.

He gave me a look that suggested my earlier command was wearing off. Summoning up all my reserves, I repeated my command, with the last bit of my pheromone. My head throbbed and my vision blurred, but he nodded once and started the engine. A wave of relief washed over me; I didn't feel very strong, but at least I was moving forward.

I glanced down at the dash. "Those flashing lights and the siren are illegal, aren't they?"

"Yes, ma'am. But the boss likes to put on a show, sometimes."

"Use the lights; they'll keep people out of our way, but we don't want the siren to clue him in. When we get to the beach, you're going to slow down, let me jump out, then you do a u-turn and return to your boss, quietly and carefully. And forget this ever happened."

I stuffed my robe into my bag and pulled my hair into a messy knot so that it would stay out of my eyes. Ordinarily, I'd do the driving—I love driving fast—and my brother Gerry bails out, something he calls the "Fastball Special." But this time, I was on deck. I pulled my expandable baton from my bag and took a couple of deep breaths.

"Here you are, miss. Have a lovely day."

"Thanks."

I pulled the door open, threw myself out. Hit the ground hard and rolled. Just as I asked the driver, he reversed and turned, pulled the door shut, then very sedately, headed back to the business school. I dropped my bag and looked around.

The stink got very strong then. There beach was no more than a scrap of rocks and cobbles below a bit of lawn where students would sunbathe. I would have missed him altogether if I'd been relying on sight alone. The rain was heavier now, and as tired as I was, as much as I hurt, I knew this was working for me, too: We were out of the way, and anyone on campus would be intent on going from one place to the next, speeding along, heads down.

He was pulling the boat up on the shore, tying the line to one of the bushes. White, medium height, brown hair, but muscles that looked like they'd come from training rather than the gym. His gear was minimal— the better to blend in—but when he checked it, he definitely seemed to be comfortable with it.

I Changed. My headache didn't fade much, but I was stronger in my snake-woman form. I snarled and extended my baton.

He saw me and charged, roaring like an angry bull. The easiest thing to do with a bull is to step out of the way at the last moment. I am very fast, but while I dodged him, he stopped on a dime. He managed to grab a fistful of my skirt and pull me off balance. I spat at him; the ache in my throat told me that was the last of my venom. It wasn't much, but it made him claw at his eye.

I was going to have to rely on my fighting skills and hope that I managed to take him down before I collapsed.

I swung again with the baton. He still managed to dodge my baton, but I evaded his counter punch and brought the baton back to strike again. He was well trained; it made sense, if he was smart enough to listen to his instincts when he thought he was being followed.

Not your average bruised eggplant, then, damn it all.

"Get away from me, you freak! You witch!" He pulled out a knife and whipped it up toward me. If I hadn't moved quickly, I would have been gutted like a fish. He kept advancing and it took everything I had just to keep up my defenses. He was used to fighting and even in my vampire form, I was starting to gas out.

I lucked out. I landed a blow on his wrist, making him scream and drop his knife. He grabbed my baton and wrenched it, throwing me off balance; I slipped, and he slipped—the bank was quite muddy by now. He tossed the baton away and pulled out a pistol.

I was so close to the end of my strength that I considered trying to jump into his launch and getting out of there. But he was between me and the boat.

He shot me. I went down, not even feeling the wet cobbles beneath me.

I had nothing left. My healing ability had been eroded by my exertions. Everything hurt. My vision narrowed.

I was going to die. God help me, I'm dying.

I heard him curse, as he tried to collect himself. He pulled a case out of the boat, the shape of a rifle, and then began to load it.

My phone buzzed somewhere. It was almost certainly Renata, wondering where I was.

"...gonna be a pain in the balls to handle this with one good hand, but I will. I made a promise, to put this country back on track. No more fucking mongrels and PC bullshit; time to clear out the leeches and freeloaders. And now you freaks. I took an oath and I'm damned well going to keep it."

I tried to get up, and couldn't. I was scared to realize I felt...numb. But his words seeped through my mental fog.

An oath? I'd taken oaths, too, to heal people as a doctor, and to protect them from evil, as a Fangborn. I promised Astrid I'd be there for her hooding. If I fail, the students and bystanders at the City Lab will die. They're starting their lives in the service of others, and this asshole is trying to ruin that. I'm not going to let this bigoted shitheel get away with that. I'm not dead yet, and if that's what's going to happen today, then it will be fucking him up as much as possible.

Hopelessness makes me angry, and anger makes me act.

I groped and found a good-sized cobble under my right hand. Suddenly, my vision cleared, and I felt a world of pain.

I couldn't suppress a groan as he readied himself to walk the rest of the way.

He paused, curious. I raised my left hand, and he focused on that.

"What the ever-loving fuck are you?"

I slammed the cobble into his foot. His scream was music to my ears. I dropped the rock and grabbed the front of his thigh as he buckled; I rolled to my knee, anchoring my weight on the claws in his thigh. I sank the claws of my left hand into his back, and literally dragged myself up to a standing—or at least, leaning—position. Blood spurted from his arteries, washing away with the rain. As he toppled, I grabbed his head and twisted, snapping his neck.

"Motherfucker!" It left my mouth as more of a gasp than the scream I'd imagined.

I staggered over and texted Gerry, who'd be on his way home by now. *Cleanup on Harkness Beach; I can't stay.*

My phone told me I was now two minutes late for the ceremony. No problem; ten minutes with a portable UV light in the restroom, and I'd look bad, but fell-down-in-the-rain bad. Not shot-in-the-shoulder bad.

Good thing my robe was reasonably dry; it hid a multitude of sins.

I called Renata. "I'm on my way—a patient with a crisis, but I got him some help and he's safe now. And of course, it started raining and I slipped. I'm going to clean up but I'll be there in time for Dr. Elliott's hooding. I swear."

"No, I'm fine, really. A little beat up, but I made her a promise."

Swing Shift

I first had the inspiration for this story when I heard a piece on NPR about the murals by George Biddle in the Department of Justice. "Society Freed by Justice" features a large, wolf-like dog next to a family saying grace over a meal. It made me think of the Fangborn as they might have appeared through history—and how sometimes, artists sneaked images of the Fangborn into their work. It was also the origin of the TRG, the Theodore Roundtree Group, a secret government agency that appears in the Fangborn novels.

Jake Steuben knew it would be easy to find Harry amid the crowd at North Station. All he had to do was find the highest density of pretty girls; his friend would be within fifteen feet.

Sure enough, there he was, ten feet away from a group of secretaries by the newsstand, watching as they chattered about the stars on the cover of *Life*. Jake picked up his valise and edged his way through the crowd. He leaned over and whispered into Harry's ear.

"If you get into trouble and you can't get out, it'll be because of a girl."

"There are worse reasons." Harry startled, his morose stare gone, and stood up to shake Jake's hand. "Train was on time. Any trouble?"

"What trouble would there be? It was crowded but quiet; I stood in the vestibule most of the way."

Harry looked askance. "No doubt the conductor made you stand out there—that's the ugliest hat I've seen in quite some time, my friend."

Jake took off his hat to look at it fondly. It was a little shiny, stretched, and the brim needed reblocking. "It's just getting broken in."

They walked out of the train station, past drunken sailors staggering to Scollay Square, then a few blocks to the Boston Common.

Harry said, "How's the wife?"

"Sophia is fine, thanks. How's the war effort in Washingt—?"

"And the baby's doing well?"

Jake couldn't help smiling. "Cutting his first tooth, so he's a handful. Say, Harry, what is it you—?"

"Good, glad to hear it. And everyone in Salem?"

Jake looked around. There was no one to overhear their conversation, so why did Harry keep interrupting? Politeness was all well and good, but he had come to Boston on the double. "Real good," he said slowly. "Thanks for asking."

They settled on a bench on the Common. The leaves on the trees were starting to turn, and would soon fall, but for now, the sun was warm and high.

Harry looked around carefully, then sighed. He shoved his hat back, mopped his forehead with his handkerchief. He sat forward, clapped his hands together, but didn't say anything.

Jake had had enough of waiting. "So, what's the problem you couldn't wire me about?"

Harry shifted uneasily. "I got a case I can't crack. It's a doozy. You've got a knack for getting into the tough ones, seeing angles I don't."

"Tell me." They'd worked occasionally as deputies for the Essex County sheriff until Harry started with the Bureau, and Jake inherited his family's farm near Salem.

Harry hesitated. "It's not easy. You know I deal with...government secrets."

"Are you sure you should tell me, then?" Jake enjoyed the sun on his face. His feet ached inside his shoes. The grass of the Common looked inviting.

"It's okay," Harry said, a little impatiently. "I cleared it upstairs. And got you clearance, too." He took a deep breath. "It's one of the research facilities, over in Cambridge. There's a bad leak. I can't pin it down."

"And what do you think I can do that the FBI can't?"

"I...I think I'm too close to it. You're outside." Harry looked up. "Like I said, you see angles no one else would. Remember the Beverly Slasher, how you knew he was the guy who found the first body? I wouldn't ask, but we got two strikes, two outs, bottom of the ninth. I don't find a DiMaggio soon, it's gonna be my fat in the fire."

"Sure, Harry. You know, I'll do whatever I can."

"Thanks, Jake." Harry smiled for the first time since Jake had gotten off the train, but it didn't reach his eyes. "The security is tight enough, I've been watching for weeks. I just don't know how the information is getting out."

"What do you think's going on? They've somehow learned to walk through walls? Use *magic* to whisk the secrets away?"

"Stop razzin' me, Jake." Harry shook his head, dead serious. "You know the Nazis are involved with some pretty unsavory investigations into the paranormal and mystical. The trips to Tibet, the archaeology, their obsession with skulls...don't even joke about it. My boss, Mr. Roundtree, has stories that would curl your hair." Harry shuddered.

"Nope, I'm hoping like heck it's good old human sneakiness and greed. I want you to get in there, see what I'm not seeing."

Harry pulled an envelope out of his jacket and handed it to Jake. "Your credentials, the location of a boardinghouse, description of your job. And a new name; we're not going to suddenly introduce a new guy with a German name. No offense."

Jake nodded. "Where will I be, and what will I be doing?"

"Janitor at a computational research lab. We want someone who will blend in, who no one will take too seriously. It's all in the file." He stood up, began to pace. "I should get going."

Jake was surprised. He wondered when his friend last slept through the night, ate a square meal, or bathed: his aftershave was faintly, nauseatingly sweet. "Hey, wait a minute! What do you think will happen, someone will go 'Psst, hey bud, want some government secrets?' You're gonna have to give me a few more—"

"Look, it's all in the file!" Harry said. "Wise up! I called you in because I need help. I can't sit around babysitting you; I got a job to do, an *important* job. There's a war on."

He mopped his face again. "Sorry, Jake. The pressure's killing me. I'll stop by your room in a couple of days. We can talk then. Okay?"

Harry stood and held out his hand. Jake stared at his friend, nodded slowly, and shook. He was genuinely worried now. His friend wasn't telling him the entire truth.

"Yeah, sure. Don't take any wooden nickels, Harry."

Later that night, Jake sat on the quilt-covered bed in his rented room, reading the file. Harry was right. He'd covered all the bases— waste disposal, deliveries, repairs—and checked some less obvious ways.

Harry was a good agent for the same reason he'd been a good deputy: he had a mind like a criminal, and though he went to extremes, he was thorough. Harry had already followed several of the potential suspects: the secretary who'd been complaining about the rationing complained about everything else. The technician who seemed to have an unlimited supply of gasoline for a car with an A sticker was found to be siphoning fuel from his brother's trucking business. No one was obtaining the information any way he could see.

It was time to call in reinforcements, Jake decided. He went down to the drugstore and called his cousin Vic, arranging to meet him at the boardinghouse in two hours.

When Vic arrived, the cousins set out for a walk along the Charles River. Jake explained everything, not sparing the details. "I want you to follow up on what Harry started. You and Rosalie tail the employees, sniff around, see what you turn up. It can't be magic that's getting those secrets out."

"Hey, there could be vampires," Vic said. He waggled his fingers, widened his eyes. "Turning into mist and going under the doors."

Jake shot his cousin a dirty look. "Stop clowning." Then he began to worry that Vic might not be too far off the mark.

Vic nodded. "Okay, you want Rosie's sister—you remember Olivia?—to cuddle up to anyone? She's got a real knack for making men want to please her."

Jake thought about it. Olivia might get Harry to reveal what he hadn't told Jake. As badly as he wanted to know, he shook his head. "No, thanks. Best not to raise our profile, now of all times, if we can avoid it."

After confirming their plans, Vic left for downtown, and Jake went about assuming his new identity.

Every day for two weeks, Jake—wearing Coke-bottle-bottom glasses and coveralls—swept, emptied the trash, and did odd jobs at the research facility. Even though he had access to almost everyone and everything, he still couldn't figure out how the information was leaving the lab. Rosalie and Vic had no better luck.

After two weeks working the day shift, Jake switched to the swing shift. The second night, he was mopping up in the office area when he heard a hiss from the doorway to Section Sixteen.

"Psst! Hey, buddy!"

Half convinced Harry was playing a joke on him, he looked up from the bucket to see a stacked redhead in a white lab coat beckoning to him. He recognized her as one of the computers, the women who operated the large, impossibly complicated analytical machines that were behind the locked door.

He made a point of looking over his shoulder, turned back, and raised his eyebrows—surely *she* couldn't mean *him*? She nodded vigorously, waved at him to hurry. He could barely believe his luck at this break. Supposedly, all the computers, mostly women, had the highest clearance, but maybe—

"Hey, I'm not trying to borrow money," she whispered. "I just need someone with good, strong hands."

Jake knew what she meant, but stayed in character. He backed away a step or two, holding his hands up. "Sister, I may be on the dumb end of the mop, but you move too fast for me."

The redhead blushed six different shades of mortified. "I...I didn't...I never...oh, golly, I just need you to help me fix something, and quick!"

"I'm not supposed to go in there," Jake said. No sense appearing too eager. "I don't have clearance."

"I've hidden all the sensitive material," she said, bouncing a little with impatience. "Unless you think a bearing that's come out of a rotor is top secret. And you're cleared to be *here*, right? I need to finish this set of calculations tonight, mister! Please?"

Jake shrugged. "You're the boss."

When he entered the long, wide room, the racket almost floored him. One side of the room were rows of shelves of electronics, bulbs and dials like 10,000 radios. The other side, a spaghetti mess of wires, all the way down the wall. The heat from the analytical machines was oppressive; a few curls stuck limply to the redhead's cheek.

"It's over here," she said and handed him a screwdriver. "If you could get that bearing back on track, I'd owe you."

Jake saw the problem right away. He grimaced; his hand was too big to fit comfortably, but she was right. All it took was brute strength to get the bearing reset. When it snapped into place, the woman's face lit up.

"Oh, thanks a million! I'd just gotten the—well, I can't really say. But if you hadn't been there, a lot of hard preparation would have gone down the drain, and some of our boys would have been in a real jam." Satisfied the machine was in order, she ushered Jake back to the administrative area.

The door safely shut behind her, she exhaled. "Phew! Thank goodness you were there. Those machines are so twitchy! Anyway, thanks."

"My pleasure." An idea blossomed. "Say, how do you manage when

I'm not here?"

"Oh, I'm usually on the day shift. There's a supervisor to help out then. And funny, they don't think they need one after five o'clock. Sometimes the fireman on duty—you saw how hot it gets? Sometimes he helps me." She stuck out her hand. "I'm Ginny."

Jake shook her hand, being careful not to crush her delicate fingers. "Stuart." He grinned. "Call me Stu."

"Well, Stu, I'd be happy to buy you a cup of coffee. I've got a ten-minute break coming up."

Good thing he'd hidden his wedding band under the lining of his bag at the boardinghouse. "Why, thanks, Ginny. That sounds fine."

They drank the coffee, didn't even miss the sugar. Ginny unwrapped a piece of newspaper, offered Jake a molasses cookie.

Sighing deeply, Jake said, "I sure am glad we met! What a treat."

Suddenly shy, Ginny said, "I'm covering for my friend Ida. Her boyfriend got the night off. They went to see Duke Ellington at the Roseland. And tomorrow, they'll see Sabby Lewis at Le Club Martinique."

Jake perked up; he was a fan of jazz and the local bands. "The boyfriend's either missing a leg, an eye, or is about a hundred and forty-seven."

Ginny laughed. "It's not that bad. He tried to sign up—three different recruitment stations—but they all caught on to his bad leg and marked him 4-F. But we can use every pair of hands we get. This place is always humming, always something new. Eddie—that's the boyfriend—he's the head of grounds services, here." She smiled, compressing her lips hard together. "So many boys gone…if a gal gets the chance to go on a date, you help her out."

There was such a wistfulness in her voice. Jake asked, "And your young man?"

"It shows, huh?" She nodded. "Italy. Or last I heard, two months ago."

"That's tough. War won't last forever, though." Jake thought a minute. "Ida and Eddie must get to take lunches, breaks, together, though. He helps her out with the, er, machinery in there?"

"Oh." Ginny looked around, nervously. "That's how they met, actually. And that's why they keep it quiet. We're supposed to be really strict about access."

"Mum's the word," Jake said. He mimed turning a key in front of his lips, then throwing it away.

"But you and he couldn't even be in this building if you didn't check out, right?" she said, now obviously wondering whether she'd made a mistake. "And I'm usually pretty good at telling the good eggs from the bad."

Jake believed her; he was good at reading people, too. He laughed. "I got more papers than a show dog, and to do what? Push a broom, wash windows. Even with these cheaters, I can barely see three feet in front of me. Nah, just be careful with everyone else." He stood up. "Thanks for the coffee, Ginny."

"Thanks for the company," she replied. Then she winked. "And the help."

Jake finished his shift, then went back to the boardinghouse. He had warmed-over dinner—meatloaf and green beans—for breakfast, went up to his room, took off his shoes, and stared at the peeling paint on the tin ceiling. After about an hour, he thought he had it pretty well figured out.

It was all just a little too easy, like it had all been laid out for him. And that made him nervous. He decided he needed to go to Le Club Martinique that evening.

Jake crossed the bridge over the Charles River to Boston, and walked down Massachusetts Avenue. The neighborhood was still bustling six hours after the close of regular business. The clubs and bars on this end of town drew Whites and Negroes, all dressed in their finest. Music seemed to create places where Jim Crow occasionally blinked. Jake appreciated that; he knew something about not fitting in.

Down toward Columbus Avenue, past the Savoy and the Hi-Hat, was the place Jake was looking for. Le Club Martinique might not have had the size or the garish splendor of the Roseland Ballroom, but it was hopping. Every time the door opened, a blast of swinging trumpet music threatened to knock passing pedestrians off their feet. Jake put it on his list to visit, after this job—maybe he'd even be able to talk the tin-eared Harry into coming with him. It was the kind of place where famous musicians would come after their sets to jam until morning.

A uniformed doorman tipped his braided hat as Jake entered. A big band was playing on the stage; they were good, not cluttering up the music with an unnecessary vocalist. The dancing couples got more and more daring with flips and twirls, putting aside care for a few hours, banishing worry with the joy and audacity of the music. They'd pay for it in the morning, but for now, it was worth every sore foot and hangover-to-be.

Inside the club, Jake saw a number of extravagantly long and baggy zoot suits. He wondered whether the uniformed soldiers there would call out the wearers as unpatriotic and wasteful as the beer flowed and the evening grew more raucous—

Jake's attention was drawn suddenly to a couple sitting alone. They matched Ginny's description of Ida and her boyfriend, Eddie.

The band tore into a version of "Cotton Tail" that would have done Ellington proud. Drinks were set aside, and the dance floor was mobbed.

The couple sat still, though Ida looked like she wanted to dance, too. Eddie, a weasely-looking fellow, said something to her. She pouted; he refilled her coupe with champagne—Jake could see the French label—and patted her hand. Ida smiled, and Eddie limped over to another table.

Jake thought about Eddie the groundskeeper pouring French champagne.

Unless the dolly sitting at the table was Eddie's sister, Jake thought, Ida was right to pout. The other girl was all done up in blue satin and had on more rouge than was smart. Jake couldn't really tell—the smell of beer and chicken mingled with cigarettes and liquor sweat—but he would have bet she was wearing too much perfume, too. Eddie was leaning in a little too close; she let him. When their hands disappeared under the table simultaneously and stayed there for too long, Jake began to understand.

The drum solo ended, the horns jumped in, and a burst of energy surged through the club. Eddie stuck something into his pocket. The girl put an envelope into a satin clutch with rhinestones bigger than a Packard's headlights. Everyone's eyes were on the dancers or the band; Jake was the only one who'd seen the transaction.

The couple, Eddie and Ida, left then; she was protesting, but he was having none of it. Jake thought about following them, but realized there were bigger fish to fry. He had to keep his eyes on the glamour puss in blue satin. He waited about twenty minutes.

When Harry came into the club, Jake cussed and ducked behind a pillar.

If things had been so plain to him—how Eddie was working and why—why hadn't they been plain to Harry? And what was he doing here now? He *hated* jazz.

Afraid he'd botch Harry's plans, Jake stayed hidden, watched his friend go through a similar routine with Glamour Puss, hands under the table, swapping envelopes. Only this time, the girl wasn't so pleased. She and Harry exchanged heated words, to judge by their expressions. They were lucky the band had started in on a rowdy version of "Bugle Blues," drowning them out. Finally, Harry left, the girl looking more irked than ever.

Jake knew he could come back any night and find the girl sitting in her evening gown at that same table; he'd only have this one chance to find out what was up with Harry. He decided to follow Harry, intending to straighten this out, once and for all.

Two toughs grabbed Harry as soon as he reached the front door. As they dragged him outside, the song ended, and the dancers mobbed the bar. Jake struggled to get through the packed ballroom.

When he reached the street, Jake paused. It had rained briefly while he was indoors, but that wasn't what stopped him. What was a guy supposed to do? Let his best friend get roughed up—maybe even killed—or blow his cover? Jake knew a thing or two about discretion, and knew it was just as important to Harry the G-man.

If it took blowing his cover to save a friend, Jake would do it. The risk came with the job.

But he was going to pick his moment, if he could. No sense in undue haste.

Jake spat out his gum and followed the two goons who had Harry—they were professionals, no doubt about it, keeping things quiet while they were among the crowds on the street. Had Harry done something so stupid he'd gotten on the wrong side of a mobster? Jake recalled the glamour puss in the club. Harry should have known better, doing the work he did. Dames like that didn't sit alone for no reason.

If you get into trouble and can't get out, it'll be because of a girl.

Jake picked up speed; the trio was heading into a shady-looking neighborhood, even darker than normal because of the enforced blackouts. Things would happen quickly.

They were in an alleyway, now, and it wasn't to talk. At first, Harry played it smart and got in a few good punches; Jake hoped he could keep himself out of it. But two against one was too much, and Harry faltered, went down. The darkness made it the perfect place for trouble; there'd be no rescue from anyone on the street.

Jake couldn't wait any longer. He had to get in there.

Jake took a deep breath and concentrated, Changing only halfway. Tissue rippled, and bone stretched; the slack of his suit was filled with new muscles and thick, rough fur. The wolf-self, contained too long by the city, by the cheap shoes, by Jake's cover, was let loose. The joy of the Change ran through his body, from lengthening teeth and pointing ears to sharpened nails. Jake couldn't resist chuckling, a guttural, inhuman noise. The stink of evil was strong on the two goons.

He felt traces of power crawling through his system as he sized up the men. One, a guy the size of a moose, had a shiv that looked a mile long, sharp as sharp could be. The shorter one—Jake thought of him as

"Cagney"—had just laid a cosh upside Harry's head. Harry looked like he was down for the count.

Good, Jake thought. *That will make this easier.*

Jake growled. The goons ignored him. Guys like that don't scare easy, and they were busy.

He hurled himself on them. They couldn't ignore that.

Jake landed on the back of Moose; best to lose the knife first, especially if the thug was any good with it. Moose kept his head, even as found himself slammed into the brick wall, slimy with rain and God knows what else. He twisted fast, ignoring the blood pouring from the side of his forehead. He held onto the knife, tore it along Jake's arm. Jake pressed his face close, so the other man could see the teeth that didn't belong in a human mouth, feel the heat of a lupine mouth as it tore his ear.

Moose yowled and clutched his head, as Jake took the steel blade and snapped it like a cheap toy. It fell to the ground with a tinny clink. Moose turned and ran, screaming bloody murder and bleeding like a stuck pig.

No time to waste; even in this crummy a neighborhood their racket would bring unwanted attention. His hat went flying as Jake bounded to the end of the alley and tackled Moose. Jake tore out his vocal cords with another slash. There was only a wet gargling noise, now.

Jake turned to Cagney, who was going through Harry's pockets. The guy must have feared whoever he was working for more than he feared what was happening to Moose, because he had worked all through the fight—

Cagney suddenly looked up. His eyes were wide and unfocused, and his face slack. At first Jake thought he might be drunk, or a little soft in the head, but then the sweetish smell worked its way past the filth of the alley. Jake knew Cagney was high on opium.

Jake recognized another smell now. This was a stronger version of Harry's sickly aftershave.

Jake knocked the cosh out of Cagney's hand with one paw while raking claws down his cheek with the other. Cagney screamed, his hands flying up to his face as much to block as to hide from the Anubis-like monster before him. Jake's face had lost nearly all trace of humanity: elongated snout, fangs and a row of jagged teeth, ears sharply extended above his head. The fur wasn't the worst, or the whiskers, Jake had been told. It was his eyes. Somehow it was wrong that such human eyes should be set into the face of a slavering animal.

But Moose's screams had brought interest; Jake heard automobile engines and police sirens moving closer. He couldn't just leave Harry in the alley; one way or another, he was responsible for getting him out of the trouble he was now in.

Jake leaned over, grabbed his hat, and picked Harry up effortlessly. He slung him over his shoulder and turned to leave when a car pulled across his path, blocking his exit. He loped to the other end of the alley, but a Cadillac screeched to a stop there. The headlights from both cars lit the narrow lane; Jake was trapped in the middle near a couple of rank-smelling ash cans. The five men who spilled out of the cars brandished revolvers, aiming them at Jake and the unconscious Harry. Crazy shadows made many-armed monsters on the walls.

The three toughs at one end stumbled over the bodies Jake had left behind. There were exclamations, and one of the men retched at the sight and smell.

"That's the guy, Mr. MacLaren." At the other end of the alley,

Eddie limped behind a large man in a flashy, double-breasted suit. He gestured to where Jake was trying to melt back into the shadows. "I'd recognize that cheap suit anywhere. I watched him eyeballing Sadie at the club while she was dealing. Then I followed him here, when I saw *him* trailing Sid and Joey as they hauled off that deadbeat Harry Gray."

Then Eddie got a look at what was left of Sid and Joey at the far end of the alley. He moved farther behind MacLaren.

"Wait a minute," MacLaren said. "Gray is the junkie? He's a Fed—he was at the big bust two years ago! The new boss is going to be very interested in what Gray knows about us!"

Jake was in a bind. He could run for his life, but leaving Harry behind with these goons would be tantamount to killing him. Jake could Change back to his human form, maintain his cover, and although he'd be able to fight, the chances of Harry and him surviving the armed gang were slight.

Jake adjusted Harry over his shoulder and pulled his hat lower. He'd try to make a break, hoping that in the mayhem, no one would notice a werewolf too much.

Fat chance.

He tensed himself, ready to spring, when he heard the clatter of ladies' shoes on the pavement at the top of the alley.

He froze. It was Rosalie and her sister Olivia.

It wasn't until the ladies called out that the gunmen noticed the two women had passed the cars and were right smack in the middle of things.

"Jake? You there, Cousin Jake?" Their voices couldn't have been more out of place in that dirty alley.

MacLaren didn't lower his pistol. "Ladies, this is a private party. Best you turn right around and get yourselves home."

"I think not," Rosalie said. "Not without Jake and his friend." She and Olivia were dressed for an evening out. They stood primly, in their best coats and hats, between the two groups of gangsters. Their arms were linked, their gloved hands folded over their handbags. They might have been strolling to church.

The other gunmen didn't bother stifling their laughter. Even MacLaren grinned at the ridiculousness of the situation. He snapped his fingers. "Walt, Jonesy, Studs."

The men moved forward quickly. Walt stepped behind Rosalie and shoved her hard to the ground. She didn't raise her head, and she was shaking.

At the same time, Jonesy grabbed Olivia by the arm.

"Take your hands off me!" Olivia demanded.

Jonesy laughed again but did as he was told.

"Jonesy! What are you doing!" MacLaren said.

When Jonesy realized what had happened, he looked at his hand and shook his head. "I don't know! It was like. . .I didn't have any choice!"

"Well, get them out of here," MacLaren said. "Or shoot 'em. We ain't got time for this."

Jonesy grabbed Olivia again and yanked her into him. "C'mon, you! You'd better scram—argh!"

Olivia had turned in to Jonesy and latched onto his neck with her mouth. As he screamed, perhaps Jake was the only one of the men capable of seeing her skin change, becoming violet snake scales. Her eyes enlarged, her nose diminished, and her teeth became. . .vampiric.

Studs and Walt tried to pull Olivia off Jonesy; she lashed out at them with razor-like claws. With a growl, Rosalie hurled herself from the ground and landed on top of the men attacking her cousin. Rosalie's face was like Jake's, now: furred, fanged, furious. Her little hat fell to the mud as she and Olivia shredded the gangsters. Bones crunched, blood ran.

As surreptitiously as he could, Jake deposited Harry behind the ash cans.

MacLaren was smarter than his men. He stared for only a moment, then aimed his pistol at Jake.

Jake rose up and threw an ash can at MacLaren, bowling him over. Jake turned to Eddie, who had the sense to run. Jake hesitated: Eddie now knew Harry was a government officer with an opium problem. Jake couldn't let him get away. But MacLaren was already scrambling up, his pistol cocked and ready—

A flash of fur. Something bounded over the Cadillac, knocking Eddie over. A large wolf, wearing a red union suit, grabbed the dope dealer by the back of the head and shook.

Jake dove for MacLaren, who managed to fire a shot. Jake clutched his shoulder but landed on top of MacLaren. The mobster screamed, the fear widening his eyes as Jake lowered his wolfy head toward him and snarled...

"Jake, no!" Olivia placed her hand on his back. "Don't kill him!"

Jake growled, thinking what MacLaren was: he would have killed Harry, he was a poison to his community, he was betraying his country by stealing secrets. "Since when are you squeamish?" Jake said, his voice made harsh by his elongated jaw.

"We need him for the FBI to quethtion. So Harry can wrap up his cathe." She, too, spoke awkwardly around a mouthful of sharpened teeth and two long fangs.

MacLaren, unable to see past Jake's head, still had it in him to be offended by mercy from a lady. "What makes you think I'll talk, sister?"

Olivia leaned down so MacLaren could see her. Her black eyes narrowed, and her head swayed slightly, fixing MacLaren with her gaze. He almost screamed, but stiffened, stared as if in a trance.

"You'll thing like a canary, when I get done with you," she said. No one hearing her would have doubted her, even with her hissing lisp.

A thrill of power rushed through the air. Vic had Changed back to human form, shivering in the night air wearing only his union suit. "Hey, Jake, we got to finish up quick. I left the car a few blocks back after I dropped off the girls, and tried to make sure the coast was clear for us to join you. But we won't stay alone forever."

"Right," Jake said. He got up and Changed back to his skin-self, handed the shivering Vic his jacket. "You and Rosalie move the bodies so it looks like they were fighting each other. The big guy down the end was a knife man; use that to cover up the worst of the claw and bite wounds." He turned to Olivia. "And how about you lay one of your Lamont Cranston–Shadow whammies on MacLaren? Suggest he remember this was a fight among his own men, and we were never here. And that he's dying to confess to the FBI, starting with who the 'new boss' is. I'm willing to bet he's a Nazi, or linked to them, if he's dealing in top secret calculations."

"Right, Jake." She pulled MacLaren up by the lapels and slammed him against the wall. "I know what evil lurks in the hearts of men."

She sank her fangs into his neck; MacLaren went limp, his eyes wide.

"Jake?" There was a weak voice from the sidelines; Harry struggled to pull himself upright. "Jake, what the heck—?"

"Harry, it's all right!" Jake tried to reassure him, but Vic was standing in his long underwear and a borrowed suit coat, and Rosalie was Changing back from her wolf-self, mourning a run in her last whole pair of stockings. Olivia, still a purple vampiress in a muddied coat, was whispering to MacLaren, who nodded eagerly.

Harry rubbed his head woozily. "Jake, there was a wolf-man. And he was wearing your ugly hat..."

"Harry," Jake said. "We're Fangborn. And we're here to help. Give us a hand, Olivia?"

She turned from MacLaren, delicately licking the blood from her fangs.

"We need to clean up my friend. And please give him a good story about how he followed Eddie from the club just in time to see the fight among MacLaren's men. How he flagged down the local cops and brought them here."

Olivia cocked her head. "It'll be tricky. It's harder to alter the blood chemistry of an opium addict. And he's concussed." It sounded like "concuthhhed."

"Do your best. We'll alert the Family down in Virginia to keep an eye on him. They'll give him more forget-me juice, if he shows signs of remembering us too well."

After they rearranged the bodies to suit their story, they loaded the still-dazed Harry in the back of MacLaren's Cadillac, his head cradled in Olivia's lap.

Jake handed Rosalie into the front seat and, after she smoothed her skirt around her knees, got in beside her and shut the door. He leaned around to the backseat. "Hey, Harry? How'd you like a kiss from my cousin Olivia?"

Harry's head ached from the beating, and the need for a fix was almost crippling. He looked up woozily at the lady who was stroking his hair in the dark. He couldn't see her well, but he knew, somehow, she was pretty.

He did like a pretty girl.

"Okay," Harry said. Was it his imagination, or was the pain that consumed him lessening?

Olivia leaned down to him, her lips slightly parted. Harry imagined a glint of white teeth. She brushed right past his lips and went for his neck.

By the time her fangs had pierced his skin and his blood was flowing into her mouth, Harry was so overwhelmed by a sense of wellbeing and comfort, the pain and the call of the opium needle was as remote as Shangri-La. There was room for only one thought:

That's some A-1 kissing...

In the front seat, Vic peered into the night, navigating their way back to his car. "So the girl, the computer—Ida? She was letting her boyfriend, Eddie there, into the lab?"

"She thought Eddie was just helping her out," Jake said. "But he was helping himself to the calculations *and* the information about who they were for. We were looking for some criminal mastermind, not Eddie trying to keep his junk supplier happy. MacLaren's men, well, let's say they didn't just deal drugs. I'll be surprised if they weren't being encouraged to expand their businesses by the Nazis. The Bureau will track down the rest, shut them down, as soon as they find MacLaren's 'new boss.'"

Jake continued. "Harry couldn't afford to reveal himself as a Fed to

MacLaren's men. He couldn't admit to his boss that he was taking opium. So he brought me in to get the evidence, while he kept himself out of the picture."

A voice came from the backseat, as if from a great distance. "Wow," Harry said.

"How you doing, Harry?" Jake asked. Vic and Rosalie exchanged tense glances.

"Well, I don't mind telling you, Jakey, I'm feeling pretty fine. But, tonight I saw a wolf-man wearing your darned hat. I saw a giant dog kill that cut-rate hood Eddie. And Olivia, well, apparently, she's a vampire—but nothing like what you see in the movies, let me tell you! At first, I thought I was high—who knows what that lovely, wicked Sadie has been giving me?—but I hadn't fixed. And it all seems so clear now. Like that time, up in Salem, when you—"

Time for Jake to step in. "Yes, Harry, my Family is full of werewolves and vampires, but not like in the movies. We're the good guys."

"Gee." Harry sighed. "That's swell."

"Olivia?" Vic said quietly. "You got the mix a little off. A little rich on the truth-telling serums and light on the memory blockers."

"Hey, it's a complicated case," she said, weaving a little. She was drained and giddy from the night's work. "But I'll take another crack at it." She smiled blearily and regarded Harry. "C'mere, lover boy."

A week later, Harry was back in Washington, whistling his way down Pennsylvania Avenue, his second-best suit cleaned and spruced up, a brand-new fedora cocked jauntily on the back of his head. There was a spring in his step that would have been out of place during wartime, save that everyone who saw him was suddenly filled with encouragement. Everything about his attitude shouted: *We can do it!*

Something had changed him in Boston. Maybe it was solving the case, maybe it was seeing his old friend, maybe it was getting hit on the head in that filthy alley, but Harry hadn't had the urge to use since then. It was days before he even noticed. Before Boston, he would have described himself as possessed by opium.

No more of that, now. Never again.

He'd already convinced his boss, Mr. Roundtree, to keep him on the job. In a month or two, Harry'd be back on track to run his own projects. Heck, he'd win the war from this side of the Atlantic!

He was still whistling as he entered the Department of Justice. He'd be hunting and pecking his way through another night at the old Smith Corona, and his fingers would be sore and stiff from jabbing the heavy keys. But his work—with Jake's help—had been a significant break, uncovering a major conduit for drugs and industrial-military espionage in the Northeast.

Something stopped him in his tracks. It took one minute to realize he wasn't ill, another to wonder what the problem was. But there was no problem. It was the image of the family sitting at the cloth-covered table, joined in company, sharing food, giving praise. On the left-hand side was a large, scruffy, shepherd-like dog, his head happily uptilted to the woman serving coffee.

He had passed the murals every day, had never really taken the time to examine them. Too tied up with work and then the pursuit of the needle, he'd barely bothered to look up. He did now. Amazing.

It was the dog that caught his attention. He wasn't much for dogs, didn't like the way they slobbered and jumped all over you—

In the alley. In Boston. Something had attacked MacLaren's men. Harry had been rattled, his head half-caved in, but he hadn't been high, and he knew what he saw. A wolf, standing on two legs, wearing a suit and one damned ugly hat—

The hat had been Jake Steuben's. He'd have recognized it anywhere.

As Harry stared at the mural, he remembered it all.

Jake had pulled a Lon Chaney in the alley, turned into a wolf-man. And Jake's friend Olivia had bitten him in the neck, just like Dracula. Only Harry was in better shape than he had been in years, and clean, to boot.

The first thing he thought was: *Oh, no. I don't want to have to get high again...*

And when he realized the idea left him with distaste, rather than that burning desire, he took a deep breath and considered. He'd done shady things to feed his addiction, seen horrors on the job. And now he realized Jake and his Family were something out of a Saturday matinée.

But he'd trusted Jake with his life on more than one occasion. And Jake had always come through. Olivia had taken the most terrible burden from him, given him his life back.

Jake and his Family *were* the good guys. They were patriotic, and discreet, too. Had to be.

Harry decided that there was nothing monstrous about them. He was eternally grateful to them.

It took him a while to find out the name of the mural—*Society Freed Through Justice*, by George Biddle. It struck him as particularly appropriate. He wondered why the artist had included the dog. Wondered how many more—Fangborn?—there might be out there.

Harry thought long and hard. If Jake and his Family could defeat MacLaren, and save a lost cause like Harry, imagine what they could do with a little help from the Federal Bureau of Investigation. . .

He made an appointment to discuss the matter with Mr. Roundtree. He had a feeling that after hearing what they could do, these Fangborn would suit his boss down to the ground.

The God's Games

I got a lot of my ideas about the Fangborn cultures from travel, and after a trip to Greece and Turkey, I was inspired by the idea of the Olympic games as religious festivals, with as many opportunities for commerce as prayer and sacrifice. The Greek tales of "metamorphosis" seemed to suggest that the Fangborn were part of them. It was also an opportunity to explore two other interests of mine: mixed-martial arts and the depiction of ancient life on Greek pottery.

When your oracle sends you on a quest, you don't drag your feet. I'd made the dangerous sea voyage from Halicarnassus on a crowded cargo ship, then risked bandits overland, to get to Olympia in a little over a week. Even traveling as fast as a mortal can go, arriving on the third day of the Games, I will admit I was reluctant walking the last miles from the boat landing. We who are born to the Fang work in secret, in the shadows. The idea of being among the thousands attending the sacred Games and holy rites at Olympia made me very uneasy.

Secrecy and peril is a fact of life for my kind. We may be gifted with extraordinary powers of longevity, strength, fast healing, and even metamorphosis, but we need those powers to fight evil and do the gods' will. So wherever an oracle sends you, there'll be adventure, danger, and glory. Which is why I'd done my duty and made love to Thyia, a girl of my village, so that if I should die, another born to the Fang would follow me. Although our women are like Amazons and fight alongside us, we must also take care to preserve our race.

Secrecy and peril; adventure, danger, and glory. Our life is never simple.

The Korax I was directed to was posing as a lowly fortune-teller at the Games. I found him easily enough in a nasty tent of dirty leather and gave him the letter from my oracle at home. After reading it, he scratched himself and threw another stick on the fire. "Okay, that jibes with what I've been seeing, my boy. Your Korax foretold a defiling of the Games on the fourth day. I saw—" He nodded at his tripod and a pile of herbs so rank they made my eyes water. "I saw a merchant named Keos plotting to kill his own brother to enrich himself."

I made a warding sign against the horrible notion; he did the same.

"Clearly, the gods have put us both on the same path: You're to prevent the murder and therefore the potential defiling of Zeus's holy Games with fratricide. Better if you can also expose the would-be murderer."

I cracked my knuckles and shifted uncomfortably on my stool, missing my hammer and my chisel. Stone working was an art, but it was straightforward. Not like human intrigue, not like the gods.

Not like oracles.

"Here," he said, handing me a small knife and a bit of wood. I hadn't seen them before they appeared in his hands. "Stop fidgeting like that."

I took them gratefully. You don't just pull out a knife in front of an oracle. And if he hadn't given me permission, it would have been disrespectful of me to carve while he spoke, as if he deserved only a fraction of my attention. "Thank you, cousin."

He grunted and poked at the fire. Without thinking, I began to carve and soon revealed the eagle trapped inside the wood. A symbol of

Zeus. See? I am a straightforward man.

I said, "But if my oracle saw danger at the Games, less than a month ago, why didn't the vision go to—?"

Fatigue and hunger made me foolish enough to even frame such a question.

The Korax was in a forgiving mood, however, or was less strict than the oracle back home. "To someone nearer?" He shrugged. "I don't know, Lycos. Just give thanks someone foretold trouble, and that you're here to stop it."

Lycos isn't my name, of course, any more than *Korax* was the oracle's. It simply means that when I transform, I take the shape of a wolf. My kin who change into snakes, and are healers, are called *Ophis*. *Korax* is "raven." Ravens and crows see far ahead and lead wolves to prey.

My people, those born to the Fang, and those born to the Sight, serve the gods on Earth. As we fulfill our roles in protecting humans and eradicating evil, some of our people say we take on the aspects of the gods themselves. Some of us, like the Korax, have the Sight, or luck, to direct those of us who fight, who track and tear at sinners. That service comes with a sacrifice, and while we must act in secret and keep apart from ordinary mortals, it is a blessed life.

"Thanks for this." He nodded to the bundle beside him, which contained the letter as well as a gift of cakes, a tradition among our people. "Go, get yourself some dinner, make your offerings, then come back."

I looked up; I was tired and hungry. Also eager to see Olympia, fabled for its temples, statues, and—

He shook his head, as if reading my mind. "We've a long day

tomorrow—the fourth day of the Games. I've seen that's when the murder can be prevented. And to do it, you need to participate in—and win—the pankration. I've already had a word with the judges; you're entered."

My jaw dropped. "Me? Fight in front of all those people? I won't be able to turn into a wolf, or even a wolf-man! How can I possibly—?"

The oracle only gazed at me across the fire. This time I had stepped across the line of respect.

We who are born to the Fang never question an oracle. Never. I bowed, intimidated by the fury in his eyes. "My apologies, seer, I am fatigued. I will do as you say. And I *do* excel over all my kin in the pankration."

Which was ironic. *Pankration* means "all powers." I could fight my opponent by any bare-handed means: boxing, wrestling, kicking. No weapons, and any fighting strategy was permitted, save biting or eye-gouging. Or turning into a wolf-man.

How could I serve the gods properly without using my one unique power?

He nodded and, with a gesture, dismissed me. He turned to his tripod and flung a handful of those awful herbs onto the pan. "Hey, Lycos!"

I turned. His back had gone rigid, and he seemed to be staring at the hide walls of his messy little tent. A true vision was upon him.

"Stay away from women."

Crazy old man. Of course I wouldn't go catting about; I was on a mission from the gods. But I'd already offended him once, so I bowed to his back and thanked him.

"I'm serious. Boys, too. But I've just seen—while you're here, you need to lay off the pussy."

I bowed again and backed out.

I straightened myself, dusted twigs and herbs and spiderwebs from my shirt. There was nothing on earth holier—or crazier—than one of our oracles.

Dismissed for the moment, I was left to explore the Olympic village. When I say *village*, I don't want to mislead you—it's far more than a few houses with a well, an altar, and a market twice a week. This place was almost incomprehensible to me, and I've seen many cities. I could be accused of telling travelers' tales, but it's well known what the village is like during the Games.

The noise, the sights, from all over the world. There are fine pavilions for the merchants and better sorts, who are here to have their fortunes told, make sacrifices, make deals, and show off, too. Then there's where the rest of us live, if you can call it that: crowded, dirty (in spite of the baths), smelly (in spite of or because of the latrines), and loud, with drunken brawling and celebrating well into the night. Try to get some sleep there, in your blanket under the stars. You'd think the athletes would be focused on preparation, but most of them, as much as they crave victory, also want to drink hard and try to persuade the whores to sleep with them for free.

Despite the sanctity of the Games, there's no false modesty here: Everyone is strutting, everyone is trying to sell you something. The athletes are pretty bad, with the posing, the oiled muscles, the slagging off their opponents, all in the search for a benefactor to pay their expenses, even if it's just a meal and a night's drinking. The poets are worse, on their little platforms, with their piles of trophies and awards at their feet, bellowing out their latest works for all to hear. You'd think old men would have weaker voices, but they're looking for patrons, too, and that must give them the strength to belt out an epic or two. Or perhaps Apollo is granting them sound lungs and carrying voices, as they claim. But the philosophers are even more aggressive and will get into fistfights over their rhetoric. They might as well sign up for the boxing matches.

The prostitutes do a bang-up business, as there are no modest married women in the village, and no women at all allowed to view the Games. Oh, sure, a few sneak in dressed as men, but if you're a father of a virgin, you keep her away, or risk coming home with a debauched daughter or a hungover discus thrower for a son-in-law.

Everyone showing off, but me. I had to pretend to be *less* than I was. By choice, I would never compete against an ordinary mortal in the Games—that didn't seem fair. And yet it seemed impious *not* to use all my powers.

But when an oracle speaks, you do what he says. Denying them is tantamount to refusing the gods.

Committing murder would pollute the Games, which was like spitting on Zeus Thunderer himself. I had to prevent it from happening. It would bring the god's wrath—famine, wars, earthquakes—on all of us, not just the sinner. Not only would I have to win the pankration, without using my ability to change, but I had to stop the murder and expose Keos.

First things first. I bought a cage of pigeons—at a seriously inflated price—and made an offering at the Temple of Zeus in gratitude for my safe passage. Then I privately sacrificed to Herakles, to whom I felt most close. There were tales that Herakles was also born to the Fang, and he was certainly the first pankratiast.

Duty satisfied, I could honor my stomach. I was ravenously hungry and detected burning charcoal and grilling meats. My nose, acute even by my people's standards, led me to a most promising food seller. Lamb, fat dripping and sizzling, seasoned with wild thyme. The aroma almost drove me beyond my control, but I calmed myself and, hearing the other prices from other vendors, estimated what I'd have to pay.

"Greetings! I'll take—" I was about to say *everything*, but that would have been excessive, even for an athlete in training. "Er, three of those, please."

"Ah, you know good cooking!" The vendor grabbed a couple of grape leaves and pulled the skewers from the grill.

I sniffed approvingly. "You're from near Miletus?"

"I am!" He glanced up and down at me. "You know your food. Based on your dress, your accent, you're from around there, too?"

"Near Halicarnassus."

"Then I'll take off a quarter from the price. Always good to see someone from near home."

Miletus was about two days' travel from Halicarnassus, but we were both so far from home, it practically made us brothers. His price was fair enough—just twice regular cost, with his discount, but standard for festival rates. The aroma of the meat was heavenly. "Thank you!"

"Excellent. If you want wine, nicely watered for a good boy like you, go over there." He jerked his head to a vendor nearby. "He's a Cretan, but his wine is good, and he won't rob you too badly."

I nodded my thanks, barely able to remember to open my purse and pay the man before I wolfed down the meat. And then—

Was it Heaven itself that made me look up? My attention was drawn, like an arrow to its mark, to a curtained litter being carried down one of the makeshift roads. Past the rough-and-tumble of the temporary thoroughfare toward the gaudy colors of the pavilions, I could sense *her*, almost as if she were standing in front of me.

The thick blue silk curtain parted for just a moment, and despite her veils, the distance, the crowd, our eyes met.

Her eyes were lined with kohl; I knew she and her garments were scented with roses. Skin soft as a peach, pale as ivory...

A shiver went down my spine.

The curtain settled, the entourage passed by.

"Who—?" I said, scarce able to catch my breath.

"That's Phryne, the courtesan," the vendor said reverently. "One of the most famous *hetairai* in the world. She won't be at the Games, but she attends her master, Tenes, and is the centerpiece of his life. Tomorrow night, for example, her master's brother, Keos the merchant, will throw a party for the day's victor in pankration." The vendor turned the skewers of meat and sighed. "But this is as close as either one of us will ever get to her."

That was it, then: I had to win in order to attend the party to get close to Keos, and stop him from killing Tenes.

So much the better, if Phryne were there...

As if my wishes were coming true, I felt a soft hand sliding along my arm. "Hmmm, I like muscles. *You* wouldn't leave me wanting, would you?"

I looked down. A little prostitute had appeared out of nowhere. They'll do that.

"Leave me." I jerked away, too roughly. "Sorry, I can't—"

She spat. Short, dark, pretty, and common. Slightly buck teeth. "Yeah, right. Like you'd ever get next to *that*." She jerked her head toward the litter. "Not even with that nice fat purse."

I realized I'd left my purse gaping, the coins on view for all to see. "I... I have been told to avoid women, during the Games. That's all." I stashed my purse safely in my shirt. I cursed. More than most, I knew better caution than that.

"Hey, prostitutes don't count, right? Come find me, if you ever find yourself at loose ends. I'm cheap and clean, the best bargain at the Games. Ask for Cythereia."

The vendor snorted, as he made sure *his* money was safely tucked away. "Yeah, right. *You're* named for Aphrodite. Get out of here; let my customers eat in peace."

An argument ensued, and I departed. I stopped at the Cretan's and bought wine, then ate and drank absently, a rarity for me. I tried to remember a snatch of a poem I'd heard years ago, at home.

"*...Helen with the light robes and shining among women...*"

I'm better with stone than words, but that was how I felt looking at Phryne.

I tried to put her out of my mind. I dusted the crumbs off myself and a thought struck me. Perhaps I could find a way to prevent the murder without competing.

Eagerly, I began to cast about—nothing obvious; I didn't want to be seen to look as though I were tracking something by scent. Also, in a crowd like this, latrines overfilling, bodies unwashed, trash heaps made less appealing with vomit and bloody bandages, no one—especially someone with my sensitive nose—wanted to breathe too deeply. I found nothing that would help me.

I did break up a fight before it could get ugly—one look at me and my muscles, and the would-be contestants thought better of their brawl.

"Save it for the Games, boys."

A little farther on, I saw a cut-purse at work. I could've snapped his wrist easily, to teach him a lesson, but I wouldn't draw attention to myself. I settled for picking *his* pocket and then redepositing the stolen purse in the rightful owner's shirt. Smooth as oil and quick as a cat.

All of this made me feel better but did nothing to help me with my goal. I headed to the pavilions of the wealthy. The stink wasn't so bad here; in fact, it was downright appetizing, what with the delicacies being prepared for the evening's celebrations, the perfumes everyone wore, and the general cleanliness of the place. The food reminded me I'd had only a very scant dinner, and could use more.

I nosed around as much as I could without raising the guards' suspicions—some of the affluent had private armies for their security, in addition to cooks, maids, grooms, and such. One guard took too much interest in me, so I backed off. I could have taken him easily, but that wasn't my job.

So intent was I in looking harmless, I stepped on something.

"Ow!" An irate female voice accompanied a hard shove to my back. "Mind yourself, oaf! These sandals cost more than you earn in a year!"

"Iris! Softly, softly, please. We're here to create pleasure, not cacophony."

"Sorry, my lady." Her contrition lasted only a moment. "But this great, ugly brute—"

A glance from her mistress silenced her.

The sight of her mistress struck me dumb.

It was Phryne, my Helen. Walking with her ladies, on her way to— It didn't matter where. It would be Elysium, while she was there.

My mouth went dry and I shook as I never did, even confronting the cruelest of villains. I'd forgotten my purpose, smitten by her beauty.

And she, a perfect Grace, *smiled*. She was used to such admiration, and yet did not mock my amazement, as she might.

I dropped my eyes and bowed. And was rewarded: A silken scarf, the color of lavender, had drifted to the ground unnoticed.

I picked it up; it floated like mist on the night air. Daring greatly, I handed it to Phryne directly, rather than to her cross maid.

Another smile sent me dizzy. A soft thrill ran through me as her elegant nails brushed my dirty, callused fingertips.

Phryne opened her mouth, perhaps to thank me, perhaps an invitation to—

Her eyes hardened slightly at something behind me, but her pleasant smile remained fixed on her face. A sickness creeping through my gut had nothing to do with the finer feelings Phryne inspired.

I glanced behind me, just in time to see a meaty fist crashing down toward me.

Though I'm taller than most, I'm very quick, even without shifting my shape. I stopped his hand before it struck, and stood with his fist trapped in mine. He was strong, though not through honest labor like mine. Nearly as tall as me, with narrow eyes and a hooked nose that gave him an unkindly look. He was one of those sleek boys who imagine they're owed something.

His carefully arranged curls and expensive clothes made me acutely aware of my broad features, my sunburned skin and unruly hair, and my rough, country garb.

I still had manners. "I beg your pardon, my lady," I said, never taking my eyes from his. "I meant no disrespect."

"Eleon! You are very quick to a lady's aid, even when there is no need." The words were gentle and commanding. "But I thank you for your assistance."

Eleon relaxed, but the outrage in his eyes never dimmed. He liked hurting people, I realized.

He nodded to Phryne. I released his hand.

She glanced at me. "And thank you, too. You rescued my favorite scarf."

Delight mingled with the continuing sick feeling. I could only nod.

"Tell me your name, that I might hear of your success in the Games."

"Nikodemos. Of Halicarnassus, my lady."

"Well, Nikodemos, you have the thanks of Phryne, and her best wishes." She gestured, and her ladies continued on their way to the pavilion. Iris with the bruised toes shot me a dirty look as she passed.

"You keep your eyes off her, dog!" Eleon said, once they were out of earshot.

"You keep your hands off her, goat!" I answered.

That time, he did not hesitate. He fell on me, with fists like hammers.

I laughed to myself; fighting was a welcome release for my sick confusion. Pummeling bullies was my specialty.

But as I fought him, I got weaker, sicker. I, who had never been bested before, who had the strength of a demigod, fell to my knees. That was when his friends joined in.

The pain was bad, but the queasiness was worse. What was happening to me? I could throw five ordinary mortals in a fight, and enjoy the exercise. I was struggling with three now.

Finally, I stopped resisting. They dragged me away and chucked me into a sty. I landed in mud and filth, eye to beady eye with a piglet.

"If he cannot find his own way out, at least the pigs will have a good meal of him," said Eleon. His friends laughed, as they walked away.

As soon as he was gone, I started feeling better. I had never been defeated before; the humiliation stung. I'd make him pay—

My training caught up with me. I wasn't here to fight over-privileged thugs; I was here to serve the will of the gods.

I rested until I felt nearly better. One growl from me, and the piglets and their sow kept to the far side of the pen. The growing dark helped: My bruises faded, my cuts healed up, and the ache in my side, where Eleon had kicked me, finally eased. The illness faded, and at last, I could think straight.

There was no time to ponder my strange and sudden indisposition. A stench like that of our storm-tossed ship, filled with sick men and rotting meat, stopped me cold. It was far worse than the clean animal stink around me.

My people can smell evil and are compelled to seek and destroy it.

I growled again. The pigs were perfectly silent in their fear.

A glance around me—no one was there.

A prayer to Herakles, my special benefactor, and I allowed myself to change halfway between man and wolf. I could walk upright but was covered in fur and had a wolf's head, teeth, and claws. I would have nearly my full power but be less noticeable than in a wolf's shape.

That metamorphosis—what can I tell you? It is truly a gift we share with the gods, but no gift from them is a completely unmixed cup. We must undertake our duties in secret. The stories you hear, of Narcissus, Arachne, and Actaeon, Changed permanently as punishment? We born to the Fang lose our ability to transform if we ever reveal our other selves.

We track evil and are obliged to continue until we defeat it, unable to turn away. Our hybrid and animal forms are a sort of constant prayer to the gods: perfect service. But if we observe our laws and are faithful, the power that accompanies our transformations cannot compare to earthly joy.

I felt stronger, almost immediately, and faster. My wolfish nose picked up a trace of roses. Phryne. I shook my head, keeping to the shadow and following the awful trail, until finally, luck was with me.

That foulness followed the same path as the perfume. My half-wolf's heart did not know the same lust as a man's but I was filled with a sense of well-being by the fragrance of roses, even as the evil reek drove me forward.

Past the better camps, to the finest; it became harder and harder to move undetected. But I was patient and was eventually aided by the drunkenness that increased as the night's parties wore on. Even a stealthy wolf-man could pass unnoticed, or unremembered.

A thousand odors assailed me, but most were of human folly. I had no time for loose women or badly behaved men, no time for those who served nothing but their own appetites. The disgusting stench compelled me to true work.

The pavilions were located on the driest ground, above the river. Some were simply large shelters; somewhere a series of connected tents, creating grand, houselike structures. My trail ended close by the largest. There were many guards here. I recognized two of the guests as Eleon's toughs.

A nervousness overtook me, similar to my earlier sickness, but I remained resolute. Fortune smiled; the wind was picking up, so three of the tent walls were down to protect the celebrants. I could spy on them unseen from behind the heavy curtains.

I saw such a display of wealth that I could scarcely believe it. Seeing this, Midas might have felt a pauper and Croesus might have hung his head in envy. The sights and smells were wonderful, and strange, and vulgar, like an overpainted whore: enticing, exotic, and repulsive all at once. Perhaps my lack of education made me think so: I had no idea what the rich might think fashionable or well done. Fortunately, in wolf form, I could note such things but not be intoxicated by them. My senses were close to overwhelmed by the excesses here, but I retained enough of a man's mind to concentrate.

The closer I got, the stronger the evil was, and my odd weakness grew. No time for illness: I'd found my prey. Three people were at the center of the activity, in the places of honor; a prosperous merchant, Keos, the would-be fratricide, was the source of the evil I sought.

And there was Eleon—damnation! He clearly was Keos's pet athlete, his muscles glistening in the torchlight, his hair bound in a circlet for the feast.

Beside the merchant Keos was a man who looked so similar, it was clear they were brothers.

When I saw Phryne seat herself near the third man, I also knew I'd found my potential victim. She attended her master, Tenes, brother of Keos.

I'd found my prey, his intended victim, and my goddess, all in the same place.

The opulence of the surroundings reminded me I could never hope to win a woman like Phryne...

As if that were all that stood between us. Not a sacred oath to the gods, not a warning from the oracle, not my commission...

I caught myself growling. Luckily, the music of the players drowned out that noise. *You're here to prevent a murder, not moon over girls. Steady on, Nico.*

Fortunately, the urge to duty was stronger than the stirrings of a mortal heart. My attention was drawn by Keos, who excused himself. Eleon followed.

I hurried after, hidden by the darkness outside the pavilion. Soon the two men were joined by another, an Egyptian, by his dress. He handed a cup to Eleon.

Eleon made a sour face.

"Come on now, it's not so bad!" the Egyptian said. "Making a face like an infant—and you some tough pankratiast! Drink it down; it will keep your humors in balance, you lunatic. If you don't take care, and take your medicine, you'll run mad again. *And* lose Keos's patronage."

Eleon was a pankratiast, too?

Eleon looked like he might slap the cup aside. Instead, he snatched it up, took three great gulps, and then flung the cup from him.

It landed with a crack of breaking pottery. One of the larger fragments bounced over to me.

I whimpered. A wave of nausea, and all thought of pursuit left me. I was so dispirited, I wished my life would end. My joints went like wet twine. The very strong felt any physical setback acutely, because they were used to strength. I knew it to be true. My people suffer little illness or lameness, usually dying violently.

The cup contained whatever was making me so ill. By drinking it, Eleon had gained a kind of power over me. Or rather, my great strength and quick healing were no good against him.

And yet I needed to get closer. Maybe if I avoided that damned cup…

I circled around, padding lightly. As I did, my head cleared and the strength came back to me. But I could get no nearer to Keos, not with all these people around and Eleon so close to him.

By the time I'd skirted the edge of the pavilion and dodged a party bent on some private debauchery, I realized the Keos and the Egyptian cupbearer were moving away from the torchlight.

Keos dismissed Eleon. I turned away, hoping that if Eleon saw anything in the darkness, it would be a man's form rather than my wolf's head. He stomped right past me, unseeing, muttering in a childish rage.

The Egyptian handed Keos a packet; my keen nose wrinkled. Carefully trained to identify the odor and taste of drugs and toxins, I could scent a foreign poison from my hiding spot. And they might have thought themselves out of any mortal's hearing but could not trick my sharp, pricked-up ears. Progress at last.

"Sire, if you use that tomorrow night, at the full of the moon, its powers will be at their fullest."

"And his death will seem natural?"

The Egyptian nodded. "Perhaps too much celebrating, a heart attack. No trace at all, nothing that will lead to you."

Keos clapped the Egyptian on the shoulder, and the two parted.

I now knew when and how the murder would be perpetrated. I sneaked down to the river, exchanged my wolf-man form for a man's, and ran to the Korax's tent.

"Weak in the knees, huh? Sick to your stomach?" Korax said. "What did I tell you about staying away from women?"

"It was after she'd gone, and they were beating me. Then later he drank something that made it worse!"

"No idea what it was?"

I shook my head.

"And you couldn't bring it back, eh?"

"It made me weak just to breathe it!"

The old man went to the door and whistled. A kid came running up, and the old man whispered into his ear. "Don't get caught."

About an hour and another bowl of food later, there was a bird whistle from outside the hut. The old man trotted out, and trotted back in almost as quickly, wiping his hands quickly.

He sat down, looking a century older. "It's worse than I thought. That stuff in the cup was black hellebore, which is toxic to our kind." He ran his finger along his nose in a gesture that indicated he meant our secret race. "It's one of the few things that will weaken or kill us, so keep that piece of knowledge to yourself. It's used to cure madness—and by your description of his temper, Eleon needs a lot of it. Problem is, it's not good for mortals, either. So they're probably making him worse with each dose."

He spat. "Damned Egyptian quacks and poisoners! Give me an honest physician from Kos, any day." He sighed. "The only thing you can do is keep as far away from Eleon as possible."

"But he's going to fight in the pankration tomorrow! Not only will I be fighting... as a man... but that damned black hellebore of his will make me even weaker!"

Korax nodded. "Yep. But you have to win to stop Keos and get the proof of his intentions."

A tiny grinding click of pebbles under sandals...

Old Korax didn't hear it over the drunken revelry outside, but I rushed out to look for eavesdroppers. I saw a page in Keos's livery shoving through the crowd.

The prostitute, Cythereia, stood right in my path, negotiating with a customer. No way to get around her; there was a juggler on one side and the food vendor packing up for the night on the other.

I jumped onto the vendor's stool and vaulted over the john's shoulders, like one of the bull-dancers of Crete. I landed with barely a stumble, but not in time. I watched as the eavesdropper broke through a hole in the crowd.

Cythereia brought me back to the here-and-now; I'd driven away her trade. "You'll jump *him* in the middle of a crowd, but you won't give me the time of day? Thanks a lot, mister!"

That brought laughs from the crowd now gathering around us. With any luck, her antics would help people forget me—I was supposed to be a pankratiast, not a gymnast. I heard some murmured discussion of the pankration bouts tomorrow, and some bets were exchanged. I'd lost my quarry, shown too much of my ability, and suffered a bad blow to my pride, all in one day.

"Listen, you! What did I say about avoiding women?"

I turned to see old Korax. "He got away. He must have spied that kid you sent nosing about and followed him back."

"Don't worry about it, Lycos. Anything he heard us discuss of our Family business would only confuse him. So your cover's not blown. Get a good look at him?"

I nodded. "But I'm sure he heard us. He probably ran straight to Eleon to tell him I'm susceptible to hellebore." I'd never felt so downcast. Korax led me back to his tent.

"What if I can avoid the fight—and Eleon?" I said. "I can try to break in tonight and find proof of his master's treachery. I almost made it earlier. You know my powers."

"And you know mine. My vision says there's no sneaking in. The only way in for you is to beat his favorite at the pankration and be invited to the celebration after. That's what I saw. My gift gets clearer as we go down this path."

I'd had enough of defeat today and was anxious to avoid a fight against that hellebore-swilling Eleon. "This the same gift that tells me to stay away from women?"

He was a frail old man, but his hand hit my cheek before I could blink, and with such force it knocked me over. I heard a crack of thunder outside. I'd gone too far.

"That's for impiety and impudence. You don't have to like me, but you don't question my power. An oracle sent you here, and you crossed half the known world to obey him."

I didn't dare correct him: He knew from my letter that our oracle was a woman.

"Never challenge me again."

I prostrated myself. There was no denying that the sound of thunder had accompanied Korax's displeasure. He was no crank: Zeus was acting through him. "No, Korax. My apologies. Forgive me."

"Get up. Get out."

I nodded, picked up my blanket and bundle, and turned for the door.

"Get some rest," he said gruffly. "Down by the treasuries isn't too loud. If the gods are willing, you have a long, painful day ahead of you tomorrow."

Pankration is the most popular sport of the Games—and why not?

Two well-muscled young men, naked and fighting in the mud, to the best of their ability? The idea is as beautiful as the reality is brutal. A live match is nothing as pretty as the scenes you see painted on pottery. I've heard it compared to being a kind of a dance, but that's bullshit. Pankration is a style of fighting so savage, it appealed to the god Alexander's army and to the bloody Spartans. That was why it appealed to me, too.

The next morning, after prayers, the *skamma* was prepared: Water was added to the sandy ground where we would fight, making it muddy, unstable, and challenging. A priest passed around the urn filled with the lots. I drew, and didn't look, but prayed some more. There's always room for one more prayer, and what better place than at the Games?

Finally, the lineup was announced. I drew an alpha; I swore. Eleon drew an alternate lot. That meant he could get through all the rounds never having to fight, if he was lucky. He'd be fresh for the last opponent.

My lot meant that I'd have to go through four different bouts, and win them all, before I even stood a chance of facing him. The odds were stacked even higher against me now.

I almost protested, knowing what I knew about Eleon, his patron Keos, and their plans. There was too much room for cheating, and I had so long to go today. We who are born to the Fang are blessed with stamina and strength, but fighting four fresh opponents, under the battering heat of a summer sun in Olympia—while the crowds watched in comfort from the cool, shady hillside, mind you—was a task worthy of the demigod Herakles himself.

I saw the Korax shake his head ever so slightly. I hadn't thought he could read my mind, but then, he's an oracle and I'm no actor. I kept still.

I sized up my first opponent as we nodded to each other and the prayers were made. He was no great matter. I don't know how that bare-faced youth thought he would survive today, but it seemed a shame to subject him to a fast defeat. Perhaps he was looking for a new, well-off lover and wanted to impress some older man in the audience. I'd been in that position before myself, so why deny him a chance? I let him make the most of a blow to the chin that caught me by surprise—the inexperienced fighter is the most unpredictable, and therefore dangerous—so he had a moment to shine. Then I submitted him by sweeping him off his feet and into the mud, seizing his ankle in a lock from which he could not escape. I didn't want it thought I was toying with him.

The next was another matter altogether: short and squat and all muscle. At first I imagined he would be easy to dispatch. I had a longer reach and legs and was certain I would be the better wrestler. But he surprised me with a speed and nimbleness that literally took my breath away. Before I could blink, he'd flung himself at me and, having thrown me to the ground, was inching his way up my body, never releasing me. He was strong as Hephaestus himself, and just as ugly, with two cauliflower ears and a nose that had been flattened by years of combat. If I didn't act quickly, he would find a choke hold on me from behind.

He countered every move of mine, all the while strengthening and solidifying his own position. I tried to sneak a hand under his arm, to break his hold, but his grip was iron, in spite of the oil, sweat, and mud that covered us. Keeping my head tucked was the only reason I'd kept him from sinking that final, match-ending hold. Worse, I had to fight off the urge to transform into my powerful wolf-man form.

The trick now was to keep moving, keep him busy hanging on until I could find an escape. I drove an elbow into his gut and was rewarded with a grunt. He shifted, losing some of his advantage, so I did it a couple more times. I felt him loosen, just a moment, and twisted hard. I made it to my knees. He managed to stay on my back, though his attack was less organized than before. I braced myself and stood up.

Then I slammed us both backward.

The geometers might have had some fancy formula for describing the speed at which he'd hit the ground and the impact he made. I didn't know the equation, but anyone who moves heavy weights—say, a load of stone—understands the power of falling masses.

My breath whooshed out as my head slammed into the earth. But as bad as it was, I landed on top of *him*. I felt his hands fall away from me and his legs go limp. His breath made a whooshing noise that sounded like life leaving a body.

I staggered to my feet, the world spinning, my stomach sick. It was becoming easier and easier to maintain the pretense of human vulnerability.

A movement from the ground. I looked down. My opponent had raised his hand weakly and let it drop on my foot. I waited. His eyes were closed, his nose was bleeding—my neck and shoulder were covered in his blood—and there was a swelling in his ankle. He'd twisted it under himself when we fell to the mud. No more Games for him, at best; a life-long limp, at worst. I could see welts rising on his gut where my elbow had found its mark, and tried not to think of the bruises welling on my body.

His hand hit my foot a second, then a third time. When he held up his finger, I knew he'd surrendered.

The priest acknowledged my victory. Cheering from the audience, and money changing hands—I'd made some men money today and perhaps made others poor. I'd have to watch my back; people weren't above trying to save their gold by hobbling the fighters.

I shambled off the *skamma*. Korax was there and placed a cloth soaked in cool river water on the back of my neck. It was as welcome as it was a shock. "How many left?"

"One more, in about..." He glanced at the other part of the field. "About, say, ten minutes. One of them is very strong, one of them is smart and lucky. Don't know which I hope you get."

I nodded. "And Eleon?"

"Hasn't left his bench yet. Fresh as a lily. He might be considering a snack."

At the word *snack*, my stomach growled, despite my hurts. I was as hungry as any of my kind can be. We need a lot of food to sustain us through our exertions, even when in human form.

Korax and I watched the match that would decide my third opponent. It didn't take long; I saw a brief struggle in the mud, then a scream. One man hopped up; the other signaled submission and had to be helped off. The loser's ear had been torn off.

The victor swaggered to meet me in our match. His body was hard-muscled and showed wear from years training at the gymnasium. But I knew he was trouble because his face was unscarred; he ended his bouts quickly and decisively, before he had the chance to get marked up.

After the ritual prayer and at the signal, I ran toward him, and he toward me. I moved as if I would kick at him with my left leg, but when he moved to defend himself, I suddenly stepped forward and swung my right knee into his back. He fell forward, and I was on him, grabbing his wrists and planting my foot in the small of his back. I pulled on his arms.

He wouldn't submit, never said a word, but there was nothing he could do against me. Finally, the priest ended the bout, declaring me the winner.

I had no time to enjoy my victory. Another splash of cold water from Korax, a cupful to my lips. "Remember: The hellebore will keep weakening you until he sweats it out. But you have to hang in there, no matter what. Go get him!"

It was time to meet Eleon.

Anyone watching from the hillside could have smelled the hellebore on him, but there was no rule against that. Everyone took potions meant to make them stronger.

I felt dispirited just walking to the *skamma*. I still hurt from the last bouts, and the hellebore was slowing my usually quick healing.

The priest had barely signaled the start when Eleon was on me. No greeting, just a hard tackle to my gut.

Tired and low I may have been, but rudeness was too much. I struggled to resist the urge to transform, but my anger lent fresh strength to my limbs.

I went back several paces but then found my footing. I drove my feet into the ground like posts, and leaned into him, so that while his hands were around my waist, my entire weight rested on his neck and shoulders. I grabbed his waist. Born to the Fang or not, hellebore or not, a stone-carver has muscles and bulk. I stopped Eleon.

The problem was, the closer we were, the weaker I became. I lost my grip, his foot slipped, and we broke apart, stumbling away from each other.

The logic of fighting told me I must get in close. The logic of not poisoning myself said otherwise.

I couldn't let him decide for me. I rushed in, and when he hunkered down for another tackle, I took one last step, pivoted on my foot, and kicked him in the side. He grunted—it was a solid blow—but had the presence of mind to grab my leg.

My head swam with the hellebore; I didn't have much time. I kept my balance well enough to stay upright and beat on his head. The blows weren't accurate, or terribly hard, but they weren't love-taps, either.

With a bellow, he shoved me aside. He slammed his fist into my balls.

A shock of pain through them, and then a hopeful lull, and then a new agony, rushing in a wave through my entire body. I couldn't breathe. I fell to my knees. My eyes blurred with tears; the world swam. My body refused to obey my commands to get up, get up or face worse.

A collective, sympathetic groan from the audience. More than one man there instinctively covered his groin and flinched.

I crawled like a beast, trying to catch a breath, trying not to vomit. Distantly, dimly, I could see Eleon reeling around, blood pouring from the cuts on his head, making his face a gory mask. He wiped at it repeatedly, nearly blinded.

His weakness pleased and inspired me.

Pulling myself to my feet, every movement of my legs a chorus of agony through my belly and bruised balls, I lurched over.

A final rub on his face left a horrible smear. "Come on, donkey! Going to kick me again? Too afraid to wrestle?"

I noticed that the sickness I felt was now mostly because of his last punch, less from the hellebore, which was leaving his system as he sweated. His exertions were helping me.

He ran his hand over his face again and slicked his blood-wet hair back. "What are you waiting for?"

There was something on his right hand that hadn't been there before. He'd concealed a spiked ring in his hair. I knew in an instant, he'd kill me with it.

The crowd was getting anxious, and the priests, too, ready to call the bout on Eleon's behalf if I didn't start fighting again. That they hadn't found the weapon concealed on him during the pregame examination suggested the match was fixed. Perhaps they'd even slipped it into his hair when they were supposedly searching him.

I needed to win. The gods demanded I fight and win, or die trying.

In spite of it all—sacred duty, civic duty, and yes, human pride—I hesitated. I didn't want to die. I recognized the hellebore on the barb of the ring; Eleon knew my weakness. I knew it would stop my heart if it pierced my skin.

I thought about the oracle at home, and the Korax's orders, and yet I hesitated.

Father Zeus, aid me now. I can't rely on the animal powers you gave me, just my human ability—

A movement in the stands caught my eye; a flutter of familiar blue silk on a litter.

Phryne was among the spectators.

It was like a flag signaling the call to battle. I put my head down and charged.

My opponent, incensed by my refusal to quit, also charged.

The crowd roared approval.

I kept one eye out for that right hand and the deadly spiked ring.

His first punch landed on my temple. I fought badly, clinging to his right wrist. I flailed at his head, his body, but he was crazier than ever, made wilder by my defiance.

I twisted again, to keep him from kneeing me. I couldn't win, fighting purely on the defensive. I was going to lose...

It began to rain, a downpour. A crack of lightning and a low rumble across the heavens.

The rain swiftly washed away the rest of the hellebore from him. My head cleared somewhat, though every inch of me was bruised and broken...

I made a decision. A bad choice, but my only one. I maneuvered, still fighting poorly, giving Eleon every opportunity to do what he wanted to do.

Finally, he got an ankle behind mine and hooked it out from underneath me.

We went down into the mud, him on top of me. I held his right hand with both of mine, the spike only inches from my chin. I wrapped both legs around his waist and pulled him even closer to me.

I swung my left leg over his neck, his right hand pinned against my chest. I raised my hips and, still holding his arm, used the weight of my leg to roll him off me. Now he was on his back, my left leg over his neck, my right leg over his chest, his arm trapped in my hands.

He should have known what was coming, but he kept struggling. He'd have to be a far more sophisticated fighter to escape me now. As it was, he was tired and sore.

Insanity and rage will only take you so far.

I arched my back, pushing my legs down against his body, until I felt his elbow bending the wrong way.

He screamed, but didn't submit.

I arched more, his arm bending backward over the fulcrum of my body. He was risking a break and a dislocation now.

A low animal moan and he went limp. I couldn't tell if it was asphyxiation or pain, but he was unconscious.

I shoved his arm well away from me and rolled over onto my belly, breathing heavily. The mud squelched, and I remembered the pigs in the sty. I growled low and wolfishly in his ear. The crowd couldn't hear; their cheering drowned out even the thunder.

The priest glanced at Keos and shrugged. He stepped forward and placed the olive wreath, cut from Zeus's own grove, on my head and tied red ribbons around my arms and legs.

My heart soared. My hurts dulled and healed, and I felt like a god.

Or perhaps, with the hellebore washed away, I was merely regaining my ability to recover.

I glanced up to the litter, but it was nowhere to be seen. A thing that large, with attendants and bearers, doesn't just vanish...

It came to me in a moment: Of course she'd never been there. Women aren't allowed to watch the Games. Like the rain sent to wash away the hellebore, my prayer had been answered. Some god had sent a vision of Phryne to spur me on.

The crowd rushed the field. I found the Korax among them.

I should not have expected *him* to be smiling. He was shaking a finger at me.

My job was only half done.

I'd never seen anything like the celebration feast that evening at Keos's pavilion, much less been the cause of it. The Korax even bought me a new gown for the occasion. Not my taste, but fancy enough, and certainly cleaner than anything of mine.

My people tend to be conservative in their ways, downplaying our deeds, chalking them up to a day's work. Which they are, but I have to say, it was novel and pleasing to have someone celebrate my accomplishments—and as a *man*, not one born to the Fang. For something not only laudable by my people, but celebrated across the civilized world.

A heady wine, and unwatered.

After the third or fourth song, I put aside intoxicating pride and returned to business. Keos had not yet appeared at his own party, so claiming the need to relieve myself, I went to the privies. Seeing no one around, I made the transformation into a wolf-man.

The metamorphosis brought with it that godlike sense of purpose and righteousness that dwarfed the childlike adulation of mortals.

Hugging the shadows of the pavilion, I heard footsteps behind me.

"Forgive me, sir. I was sent to help you find your way—"

It must have been the wine, or my head had been turned by the fuss, or I was still weak from the day's events to have let the page get so close. I turned, snarled, and leaped on him.

The poor fellow fainted dead away with one look at me. Which was just as well.

In my new form, it was easy to pick up the trail of Keos. I followed it to a curtained-off area at the far end of the pavilion, near the line of tents used as storerooms. Two armed men watched there.

Wait—why would extra guards be needed at a storeroom, in this secure place?

I came on them quietly. One was unconscious before he spoke. The other was so amazed by the idea of a wolf-headed man that he spent too long agape in fear. Made it easy for me to incapacitate him.

No more guards, no alarms, and I opened the door to the room, certain I was about to complete my task—

Phryne looked up and saw me. She was stooped over an opened strongbox, an open lock and a small flask on the floor beside her. Keos was also on the floor, unmoving.

Her shock was momentary, confusion followed by awe. She prostrated herself before me. "Tell me the right thing to do, whatever god you are, and I will do it."

I was so startled, I slid from my transformation and was a man once again. Curiosity overwhelmed fear of discovery. "What are you doing?"

She did not look up, her voice muffled by her robes. "Only what I was bid, by my lord and master, Tenes. Sent to recover a document that would prove his brother Keos was a traitor, asking for Egyptian poisons to kill him. I beguiled Keos into bragging and I begged to see the poison."

"Is he dead?"

"No, just unconscious. He's not the only one who can use potions and poisons."

I thought quickly, made my voice as deep and... godlike... as I could. "We work to the same purpose, then. How will you convey the letter to Tenes?"

"No need, lord. I bring it to the edge of this encampment and deliver it to a priest. To sully the holiness of the Games... it will be enough to have Keos banished."

She was telling the truth, I could tell. I would watch her from a distance, make certain the exchange was effected. My goal would be achieved.

Without thinking, I stooped down and took her hand, raising her up.

As she raised her head, she gasped. "It's you!"

"Uhh—" As I've said, I'm no actor.

She drew back, as far as she could. "You had the head of a wolf! Are you a Neuri, from beyond Scythia, who change to wolves? Or a descendant from cursed Lycaon, who offended Zeus by feeding him a child's flesh?"

I instinctively made the sign to ward off evil. "No! You and I share the same ambition, to serve the gods and preserve the sanctity of the Games."

"Huh," she said, dryly. "I meant only to serve my master."

It suddenly occurred to me that with Keos gone, Tenes would inherit his estate and become one of the wealthiest men in the world. And Phryne would be richly rewarded.

"Tricking Keos was your idea?"

She looked down demurely. She had the craftiness of a man.

"So much cunning behind that lovely face," I said, shocked.

"And what of you?" she snapped. "Lying, sneaking about, abusing the hospitality of Keos, your host? Who knows what kind of sins you committed, to be so cursed with a vicious double nature?"

"I serve the gods!"

"And so might not I? Who knows how I was directed here, if not by the gods? I was succeeding before you arrived!"

A shout: The boy who'd fainted early had come around, no doubt. No more time to waste.

"This way." She stuffed the letter and pouch into the front of her gown and hurried out the door. She led me down through the labyrinth of pavilions. We ran into guards running toward the strong room; she neatly ducked out of my way. I threw one aside and used the other's own shield to bash him.

"Down to the river!" she said. "No one will think to look there. Hurry."

She took my hand; I followed. She knew the maze of elite lodgings well and was clever at avoiding detection. A few moments later, she stopped and waved me away into hiding. She ran to a man; when he removed his hood, I recognized him as a priest. He took the parcel and bowed to her with more respect than I expected. She said a few words, then returned to me.

"Thanks for your assistance. He will escort me safely to my master. And Keos will be taken away for questioning."

"If it hadn't been for me, you wouldn't have needed help with those guards." I realized her plan *had* been perfect, until I'd come along.

"If you hadn't come, there wouldn't have been any ruckus, and I might have been discovered missing from the party," she said impatiently. "Don't try to second-guess the Fates."

She reached up, kissed me on the cheek, and then hurried away with the priest.

I turned into a wolf. I ran, the rushing wind in my ears. It helped blot out my tumult of emotions as I made a speedy escape.

I was past the pavilions when I heard a hiss. "Hey, boy! Over here."

Korax was dressed to travel. He had my bundle with him.

"We gotta get out of here. I arranged for a horse at the edge of the village."

I shifted back to a man's form. "But everyone will know I broke in—"

"No. I chucked a gown identical to yours in the pigsty, then told a guard I'd seen Eleon dragging you back there." The old man cackled. "He'll have a hell of a time explaining—" He stopped abruptly. "Hades. She kissed you, didn't she?"

"How did you—?"

"That woebegone look. The whiff of roses. Also, I had a vision, which is why I am so prepared to run. Didn't I tell you to stay away from—?"

"But I'd completed my task! The proof of Keos' treachery is in the hands of a priest—"

Korax took my hand, his eyes rolling back in his head. "Okay, I know that one. He's no true seer, but he serves his temple honestly." He blinked, then returned to normal. "I said, no women!"

"Keos was stopped, the Games preserved!" I protested.

"Yes, yes," he said, dismissing my words. "But if you hadn't let her kiss you, you could have sneaked back to the celebration and enjoyed an entire night devoted to praising *you*. Now you're running from the greatest victory a man can know, in the middle of the night, with a crazy old man. And in every nymph you sculpt, every scrap of wood you whittle, you'll find *her* face. You'll pine for Phryne as long as you live. I'd hoped to spare you that, at least."

He was right. I'd forever hear the songs about the mighty athlete who was murdered the night of his greatest victory and have to pretend it wasn't me. I'd claim no prize money. I'd remember beautiful, clever Phryne with longing, forever.

Difficult enough, O gods, to make me a man who was also a wolf— why complicate things with oracles' riddles and a *hetaira* with the mind of Odysseus? Why give me all the powers I had, then force me to fight without them? Why also send Phryne to do the work I was sent to do? Why inspire me with a vision of her, when I could never have her?

It was as though the gods set rules for us, and then made sport of us.

It wasn't for me to question any of this, I realized, as we fled through the raucous crowds. Zeus could play us however he chose. It was his Game.

The Serpent's Tale

Friends were discussing the weighty, occasionally terrible, decisions that parents must sometimes make, and it prompted me to consider how this would be complicated by the fact of being Fangborn—especially when they are forbidden to reveal their kind. I asked myself what Fangborn pregnancy looked like, and how would the Family behave in a time when demons were believed to be real? The possibility of "evil" Fangborn appears in "The Night Things Changed," and I wondered whether the Order might be responsible for them.

Sir Hugo of Godestone's manor wasn't large, and his house, although fashionably moated and possessed of several buildings, wasn't terribly grand. Still, it was by far the largest in the village, a bit removed from the center and the church nearby, and with woods and fields behind. It was also very carefully planned, if not actually fortified, in case of troubles from the outside world; these seemed to come too often. The fields and houses of the peasants lined up in front of the house, two nearly neat rows. A ditch and a road bounded the fields behind one line of houses, and the river marked the line behind the other, forming a rough triangle. The village of Godestone was located to advantage, with many roads and a navigable river nearby that kept it in contact with the larger city of Ipswich.

When the villagers petitioned for Hugo to hear their worries, he was bound to hear them. As it was early autumn, and still very warm, he invited four of the villagers to join him in the garden on one side of the house.

Hesitating only a moment, they situated themselves respectfully. They knew full well that some men of Hugo's rank would not be so approachable, nor so accommodating, and thus treated him as a man worthy of respect, not only of his station, but of his great learning and fearful responsibility. A few of the younger men held him in awe.

Alice watched her husband. She had learned from him that it was always best to have more than one person's opinion to consider. Having offered the villagers beer, he bade them to take stools near his chair, and then sat to listen. Alice retired to the kitchen, ostensibly to mend a shirt. She could see and hear quite clearly, even if her maids, sitting next to her, could not.

Observing him from a distance reminded her of the first time she'd seen him, at the Twelfth Night celebrations her people held. Sloshed wine threatened to spill onto an inattentive lady's lap. Rather than wait for a page, Hugo wiped it up himself, saving her costly dress. Alice had recognized it as an act of quick thoughtfulness and practicality first, and gallantry second. Although Alice was determined to marry him then and there, Hugo had taken a little more convincing.

Her husband was no egalitarian and knew very well the necessity of distance between the differing sorts of men. But sitting in the shade made men comfortable, and when they were comfortable they were likely to grow past their shyness and, when past reticence, confide what they might not otherwise.

"It's like this, sir," the blacksmith said. He was large, and quiet for his size. He twisted his soft hat in his hands, which were blackened and rough, scarred by long days by the forge. Alice liked the smith's fine work, like the new handle he made for their chamber door. "A few weeks ago, things started going missing—"

"Now, we do not know for certain that all these deeds are done by one person, Sir Hugo," the priest broke in.

Alice suppressed a grin; redheaded with a small space between his front teeth, Gilbert was impetuous and impatient, certainly for a priest. He was short and hale, and seemed more at home in the fields and the forest than in the pulpit. None in the village would argue he was anything but a fine cleric, even if (or because) his sermons were a little shorter when the fishing and hunting was best. His interest in his vows seemed to have more to do with action—serving the poor and righting wrongs—than study or contemplation.

"I'm sorry, Father, but let me hear what everyone has to say," Hugo said. Tall and graying blond with a warrior's body, he looked and sounded the part of a leader of men. "It may be I can see a pattern to these facts not immediately visible to those in the village who have been living among them."

"Forgive me, sir." The priest bowed his head, but walked out into the sun to surreptitiously stretch. He winked at Alice.

As Father Gilbert was a kinsman and dear to her, she took not the least offense. Alice believed Gilbert's earthiness and her own directness were complements to Hugo's patience and diplomacy.

The smith, looking anxiously between his betters, determined it was well for him to continue. "At first, begging your pardon, it was just a few things around the edge of the village. Nothing big, sir, not to start—

but odd. A fork with a load of hay, a handful of nails from my forge, a milking pail. No one noticed much to begin with, but the thief, whoever he was, became bold. In the last week, it was a flitch of bacon straight out of the smokehouse. And there was a bottle of wine from the church."

The smith glanced nervously over at the priest, who was now scowling at an innocent jay fluttering near the window ledge.

"Is this true, Father?"

Gilbert composed his features. "It is, Sir Hugo. I had thought the bottle misplaced, or the account books wrong. Half the shipments are never as the Ipswich merchants promise, the filthy—" He caught himself before he said something shocking in front of the peasants. "The, er, illiterate, innumerate lot of them."

Alice knew of the thefts from women's gossip. She had been annoyed at the trouble, though not overly concerned about it.

Hugo addressed the priest. "So you thought nothing more of it?"

Gilbert gave Hugo a puzzled look. "Oh, of course I checked the records, and looked to see whether the door had been forced. But in the end, it turned out to be two boys who stole it. From my house, not the church." He paused. "I found the lads drunk later—I won't mention their names. I didn't like to say anything more, as they'd both been violently ill behind the church. I made them clean it up, and they'll do chores to replace the cost of the wine."

"A beating would have served better," the baker muttered. "Robbing a churchman, and all."

"I know men's hearts," the priest said with an unusual and convincing authority. Suddenly the group, even the birds in the trees, went still. "I found no harm in the lads, and will remember them well enough should they sin again. I think it best to forgive a little, as our Lord would have us do, to behave with temperance and forbearance, when the matter is small. Charity and forgiveness, my good baker."

"Of course, Father Gilbert," the baker mumbled. "Better to forgive the little, ah, poor misguided lambs."

They all knew the baker didn't believe his own words, but as he himself had been in need of forgiveness once or twice, and the priest had interceded on his behalf with his wife, he knew enough about what was good for him and when to let the priest have his way.

Father Gilbert clapped his hands together, banishing the pall his stern reaction had brought to the men. The birds seemed to take their cue, and recommenced their song. "If you'd seen how green the boys were, at next Communion, you'd have seen they learned their lesson. They will recall it and repent every Mass of their lives."

A few knowing smiles, and the general humor was restored.

"Continue, Smith," said Hugo, gesturing politely for the priest to sit again. Alice knew Gilbert was fond of an audience, but they had to attend to business.

"Then things got nasty," the smith said. "Tuesday last, a goat was killed. Throat ripped out, blood…" He cleared his throat. "Well, it was a terrible blow for Taylor and his family, as they can't afford the loss."

"Perhaps someone was vexed with it escaping its shed again," the miller said.

A few dark looks followed the miller; one didn't joke about the death of a valuable animal, no matter how troublesome the beast was.

Alice made a mental note to increase the food she sent to Taylor's croft.

"It wasn't an animal? A dog, perhaps? It is early for wolves to be so bold, but perhaps a wild boar tangled with it?"

"No animal left a knife in the goat's eye, Sir Hugo." The blacksmith, reputedly the strongest man in the village, looked queasy. "And then there is the child, the weaver's youngest, gone missing now a day. Not even old enough to walk; we've been searching high and low for him. With no success."

Alice's heart contracted, and she leaned heavily against the windowsill, her hand instinctively covering her pronounced belly. She tried to put fear for her unborn child aside and concentrate on what she could do to help the missing one. She succeeded, only with effort.

"You think them connected?" her husband asked. "The other thefts—no, perhaps not the wine, Father—and the goat and the baby?"

"I don't know what to think for certain, sir." The smith glanced around and, seeing the nods of his fellows, was encouraged. "But I think they may be. And I'm afraid for the wee one."

Alice knew the parents would be frantic. Her own concerns sneaked back, doubled in intensity.

"Tell him about the prints." The miller, a coward, had no hesitation in prompting another to do what he himself ought to do.

"Ahem. Well, there have been strange sightings, Sir Hugo. I'm no tracker, but..."

"Out with it."

"We've seen wolf's prints, sir. An extremely large wolf."

"Ah." Hugo relaxed. "Wolves are always a problem, but not lately, not around here."

"Perhaps it carried off the baby?" the miller suggested.

"Not from inside a house. The door was shut, and no wolf I know of can open a door," said the priest.

"It's not only that." The smith paused again, looked around at his fellows, who gestured encouragement. "There were, some say they also saw…a giant serpent, Sir Hugo."

Now Hugo was truly disbelieving. "A serpent? Surely not—"

"It was Fletcher who saw him, sir, not to gainsay you, Sir Hugo."

Fletcher said nothing, but nodded vigorously.

Everyone else nodded, too. Fletcher had the keenest eyes of anyone.

"It was easily two spans long, sir, and very thick around," Fletcher said. He barely looked up, but reached into his pouch. "And more, sir, when I went to look, I found this."

Eyes still down, he held out his hand, on which rested a brown scale, the size of a man's fingernail. It shone in the light, as Hugo held it up to the window. He and Gilbert examined it carefully.

"It does appear to be like a snake's scale," the priest said, thoughtfully. Alice noticed his use of "like," her heart beating fast with fear.

Hugo nodded, too, soberly. "This is very serious. It is right you should come to me, and I shall take several men and my dogs to see what I can find."

The men nodded, rising, touching their forelocks or bowing awkwardly, relieved. The burden of bad news was off their shoulders now, and on Hugo's, where it rightly belonged.

"Only…" the miller started, still sitting as everyone moved to leave. "Only, will dogs and men be enough, sir?"

No one liked the miller. He lived on the edge of the village. There had been explosions at his place when too much flour dust had accumulated in his mill. He was also pompous and a braggart, as well as unkind and a coward.

Alice sighed. It was almost resolved, and the miller had to put in his oar.

"How so, Miller?" Alice recognized by his look of forced interest that Hugo's patience was thinning.

"Only a demon could wreak such havoc," the miller said with an accusing glare at the priest, who should have realized this, in the miller's opinion. "There's been something lurking in the shadows around my place recently. It moves fast and quiet, but I heard growling and muttering."

"A dog?"

"No dog in the village moves that fast, or is that big." The miller straightened himself, an air of mixed importance, titillation, and dread. "A demon's come to the village."

Hugo returned to the house after the villagers had left. He climbed the stairs to his chamber slowly, not liking the conversation he must have.

The chamber was locked. He turned his key. He frowned; the second, secret lock, known only to him and his Family, was unlatched. When locked and barred, it was a room more than safe from prying eyes and ears, and had unusually thick walls. A fine, secure refuge.

He opened the door cautiously, paused at the doorway.

His wife's gown was crumpled on the floor. On a pile of furs by the lit fire was a giant serpent. It raised its head, a narrow tongue flicking out, and then turned back to the fire. The snake coiled more tightly in on itself, as if protectively.

Hugo closed the door carefully, barring it behind him.

"Alice?"

The snake sluggishly moved across the floor to where the gown lay. A thickness in its body suggested it had recently fed, or was gravid. A frisson in the air sent a shiver down Hugo's back.

The giant snake vanished, and his pregnant wife stood before him, naked.

Desire kindled in Hugo; he found Alice even more beautiful now than the first time he'd met her, in her winter finery several years before. He recalled it hadn't been long before he found himself hoping to see her smile—or better, make her laugh. It was like magic, almost; he'd wish to see her and, suddenly, she'd appear.

Watching her husband stare, Alice put one hand on her hip and tilted her chin up, dark hair cascading down her back.

Hugo swallowed, but he shook his head. "We must speak, wife."

Her shoulders slumped, and she nodded. As she reached down for her clothing, she winced.

Hugo hurried over, stooped, and handed her the gown. "Have your pains started?"

"I thought this morning, but...they did not persist. I am only huge and clumsy and slow." She sighed, but dressed as hurriedly as she could.

"The door was not doubly locked, wife. You must be more than usually cautious, these days. The miller is—"

"The miller is a self-important idiot," Alice said, twisting her long hair into a braid and then a knot, which she fastened with a decorated bodkin pin, carefully weaving its sharp point through her hair without sticking herself.

"Yes, but he is not wrong. Trouble is afoot. It makes the villagers susceptible to everything. And I would not have them know my wife Changes into the form of a serpent, no matter how angelic her actions."

"And I would not have them know my husband is capable of turning into a giant wolf, no matter how noble the deeds he performs in that guise."

He reached over and tucked a fly-away strand of hair under her simple veil. "So, more caution, please."

"Yes, my lord." Alice attempted a look of contrition and did passably well. "But it feels so much more comfortable, even if I am without most of my powers while I carry this child."

"This will pass; you know well that your power to fight and to cure are redirected, as water through a course to a mill, in order to protect the baby while you assume your other forms. When the child is safely born, they will return to normal. You and I will find the source of these evildoings and remove it, as our people have done for generations. But I must ask..." He took her hand very carefully. "Were you outside, wife? The night the child went missing?"

She frowned and snatched her hand away, dismissing him with an impatient, tense wave and a furrowed brow. "Yes! I could not sleep. I made valerian tea, and then I walked in the garden until I tired. So."

He kept his frustration from his face. "Why so tart? It was a simple question." He moved to pat her hand again, and thought better of it.

Alice noticed the movement. "You treat me...." Another impatient gesture. "Sometimes you come at me like I was a feral cat, or a slow child, or...I do not know. Like I was not your wife. Like I was not in my right mind. Why not simply ask me, without all this...caution and reticence?"

They'd been married a long enough time for her to watch him consider many answers before determining the one least likely to cause more offense.

"I am sorry. My concern for you, and this worsening situation in the village? It makes me awkward."

"And now *you* make *me* feel ungrateful." He was honest and she loved his good heart. She sighed, and tilted her head again, with the small smile. "I am well. The baby is well, so please God. But a missing child? It cannot help but put us on edge."

"I do not like the coincidence of these events," Hugo said. "The missing items I might be able to explain, but the violence done to the goat and the vanished baby worry me greatly. These are dangerous times, and we must exercise more caution than ever."

"You always say that. Things are no better or worse than in years past. There are stupid people and clever ones, and those who are brave, and those who are afraid. Not worse, not more dangerous. Just...different."

He nodded, acknowledging her words, and began to pace. "Yes, but...I will be happier after the baby comes. In how many more years will it be born?" Hugo sighed, with great exaggeration.

"You know well it is not years, husband. Two weeks; perhaps more, perhaps less." Alice's mouth twitched. "And then you will be more worried still, when she learns to walk, and when she takes her time to talk, and then when she starts to notice boys."

"She will never leave this house. I will never let her out. There will be no boys; the moat will be dug twice as deep and a tall tower constructed." He smiled briefly. "So. You walked in the garden. Did you come straight back?"

"Yes. I came straight back, washed my hands, said my prayers, and climbed right back into your bed."

"Didn't go out, didn't leave the grounds?"

"No."

"Fletcher discovered a giant snake's scale." He gave her a pointed look.

She set her jaw and returned his look. "And there were traces of a giant wolf, I believe?"

Hugo nodded glumly. "I admit, I was remiss in covering my tracks. Fortunately, there *are* wolves around. England is not known for giant snakes. You must be careful, especially how you go abroad."

"I am; no one's seen me. And if I had ventured beyond the garden, or felt in the least afraid, you know I would have waked one of my women or taken one of your men."

"It is only to still wagging tongues, if not for your physical safety," he said while taking her hand. "I would not have you leave unattended. This is something we've discussed before, Alice. You know I'm not being unreasonable. Promise me you will not go out at night without me, or without a proper attendant. Your sister arrives when, to help you with the birth?"

She could tell that, as always, if he was looking forward to her sister Martha's visit, it was only because it would make her happy. "A few days. Less than a week, I hope."

"Well, at least Gilbert will be pleased, though I do not understand his fascination with her." Martha seemed to Hugo to have all Alice's bluntness and none of her charms.

"I think he delights in all that is good in the world," Alice said.

"In any case, if you go out, she can attend you, and I will be content."

The pursing of her lips was such that he almost apologized, but he said, "You know it is not me. I love and trust you. And if you want to put this life aside, we can find Cousins who will take our place. We will stage a horrible accident that suggests we are both dead, and move to some far-off corner of the country where no one knows us. I will be a shepherd, and you will tend geese—"

She started to smile at the notion.

"—and when the mood takes us, we shall seek out evil and destroy it, doing our Lord's will, in secret, as those who are born to the Fang. You and I and our little one shall be as wild as, well, wolves." He glanced at her. "But I do not think that is what you truly want."

"No." She sighed. This was no choice; neither of them would ever shirk their responsibility to Godestone. "No. I like this village, and I like these people, and if we are to follow our sacred calling, we must live among folk."

He nodded again, then frowned. "But if you were in the garden, and the scale was found in the field—you are *certain* you did not go into the fields?"

Alice believed Hugo's inclination to exactness sometimes outstripped his gentler instincts. She drew herself up, quite stern. "I said I went into the garden. You have no reason to doubt me."

"My apologies." Hugo's face was lined with weariness. "There is another talk I must have."

Hugo arrived at the Father's little house to find the priest instructing his servant Alwin in the ways of those born to the Fang.

"Welcome, welcome, Sir Hugo." Gilbert ushered Hugo in and sat him by the fire. The boy brought wine around.

"Alwin and I were just discussing our Family's Laws and Lessons. Why don't you ask Sir Hugo what you asked me, Alwin?"

"If this is our nature, sir, why must we study the rules so much? Why must we impose words and laws on that which is God-given and our true selves?"

"Ah." Hugo smiled. "We have many gifts, but we are not perfect. We are not quite angels. We have our flaws. We must live among men, and must remember that our duty comes first. These Laws and Lessons have been handed down and refined over centuries, to help us best perform our duty. We can only do that if we adhere to our Laws about the uses of our powers. For example: We must learn when one born to the Fang may first use his powers unguided, the punishment for intentionally harming another born to the Fang, and the importance of concealing our true natures from those men who do not Change. We put ourselves last. Only after destroying evil where we find it and protecting the innocent—those who do not Change—may we consider ourselves. Ours is ultimately a task of sacrifice. We hope to prepare you so that when you come into your powers in a few years, you will be ready."

He smiled at Alwin's somber face. "But if we follow our Laws, it is also a life of great adventure and noble deeds."

"Like King Arthur and his knights?" the boy breathed.

"Exactly so."

Alwin digested this. "And if we have such powers, why do we not rule? These are the same obligations of kings and queens, are they not, sir?"

"We have our stations, as does every man. And there are fewer of us, so we go where we are needed, as my lady did, and as you yourself came here to learn from us. There are some who say when our job is done, when we have struck down all evil, we shall rule. But until then..."

He nodded at the priest, his smile fading. "Until then, there is work to do."

"We will resume later, Alwin. You may listen, as this is part of your training, too."

After making sure nothing was wanted, Alwin took a stool at a respectful distance, mending clothes and paying attention.

"A scale has been found. You were out hunting, again?"

Gilbert shifted. "Well, perhaps."

"You know, Father, it is a sin to lie." There was no humor in Hugo's voice or his eyes.

And none in Gilbert's. "Do not preach to me, Cousin Hugo. You know the risks we run. You know what a superstitious villager would do to a priest with my talents who turns into a giant snake. I use all my discretion."

"But you *were* out close to the fields? Hunting?"

"Erm, yes."

The villagers believed Hugo winked at the priest's too-worldly delight in sport because of their kinship. They didn't complain about his preference for hunting over prayer because he shared the meat he took with those who most needed it. This convenient arrangement gave Gilbert leave to pursue activities even more dangerous than hunting.

"There was a boar," he explained, "and I only wounded him. I chased him until dark, but the beast was mad with pain and led me deep into the woods. I would not leave him to die slowly, in agony, and I couldn't leave him to attack a villager, so I followed. In my other aspect."

Hugo grunted. The superior senses of sight and smell, not to mention stamina and strength, in Gilbert's snake form would have been too valuable to leave unused in such a dangerous situation.

Enthusiasm carried Father Gilbert away. "I Changed to my snakeself in order to sneak up on the beast. I was quiet, so stealthy, I almost didn't stir the leaves. Oh, it was an epic battle, Hugo, you should have seen it! He fought like a dozen! Several times he nearly had me—I could barely sink my fangs into him to render him sleepy. It was something out of myth, a giant boar and a giant serpent!"

Gilbert loved talking about hunting almost as much as the doing of it. "He gored me, and I feared he would eventually succeed in killing me—the great, vicious brute! But I had him at last. I healed quickly, of course, but I must have lost a scale in the process." He chewed the inside of his cheek. "I had hoped it would go unfound, but we were too close to Fletcher's plot, and I daresay his dog led him to it. I would hope he think the scale a natural oddity, nothing more."

"Well, now, you've heard that the miller is talking about a demon being responsible for the events that have occurred."

The priest sighed. "I would have had a word with him, but the news is all around the village. I can't pen that pig now."

Father Gilbert could have convinced the miller, either by words, which seemed to have more than the usual powers of persuading ordinary humans, or by turning into his snake-man form and injecting him with a venom to either make him remember a different story or forget everything entirely.

"It's all our trouble, now, and can't be helped," Hugo said at last. "We must find the child immediately. Scatter and drench these coals before they burn into conflagration."

"Your men have found nothing?" Gilbert asked. "When I investigated the place where the goat was found, I picked up an unusual scent track today—but not of evil. I had no sense of foulness, no compulsion to take on a Fanged form and track it down. But there was something wrong. Almost familiar, but disturbing. It had the opposite effect than the scent of evil does, and I wished myself away from the places I found it, mostly at the farms on the edge of the village where the things went missing."

Hugo nodded gravely. "I sensed something similar—but it's definitely not one of our villagers, whose scents we would recognize, nor is it some strange evildoer from elsewhere. But if neither of us had the urge to Change...I'm not sure what it all means. My hounds have been behaving unlike themselves as well. They're either chasing their own tails or cowering from the track. I don't like all this oddness."

Gilbert's brow furrowed. "Something we have never seen before? Something we don't know if we are capable of tracking? Some new brand of evil? Hugo, we can't—"

Hugo raised a hand to quiet him. They both looked up.

A pounding. Alwin ran to the door. He returned with a sealed letter in his hand.

Gilbert recognized the seal immediately. "Who brought this?"

"One of our Family, from London. He gave me the correct signal. The rider was in great haste and on his way soon as he was assured this was the right place."

The priest opened the letter, scowling.

"It seems our troubles are multiplying. I have word from Cousin Gervase. We're about to have guests."

"Unwelcome guests?" Hugo asked.

"Very. The Order of Nicomedia is on their way here. It could not be worse timing."

Hugo took the letter his kinsman offered; the look on Gilbert's face suggested he would prefer to face a dozen wounded and vicious boars than the Order.

The Order of Nicomedia suspected the hidden existence of those born to the Fang, and hunted them down and killed them when they could.

Two men of the gentry appeared at the manor house door shortly thereafter, dressed in fine riding clothes besmirched with travel. Their well-favored features were haggard with worry and weariness. They accepted a cup of wine, a basin, and a late supper.

"What can I do for you, sirs?" Hugo asked. "It is late, and I cannot imagine that anything short of fire and war would have you out and on the roads at this hour."

"It is worse than that." The gentleman of the two was called Robert Fynch; his man was simply Toly, who vanished as soon as he'd eaten, on his master's errands. "We seek out an evil concealed among you."

"I deal with the earthly matters of this village. My friend and confessor, the Father here, deals with our spiritual health. Tell me how you presume to have authority or knowledge of my holding that I do not."

Fynch was unmoved by Hugo's commanding voice. "We are uniquely skilled in uncovering that which most men don't know about or deny exist."

"So, you hunt for witches, then?" Alice was quick to cross herself. "Surely that is better left to the Church itself, as I cannot approve of the taking on of such a great responsibility by...unaffiliated persons."

Hugo looked at his wife, frowning slightly.

Fynch nodded, as if to acknowledge that a lady of high social station had spoken. But as she *was* a lady, and he did not approve of ladies speaking, he did not answer her. "I will tell you something many do not know. There is a secret society battling sin and chaos in the world."

Gilbert took a deep sip from his cup. Hugo showed no change of demeanor.

"Our society, The Order of Nicomedia, is devoted to the eradication of demons. It is an awesome responsibility—the saints themselves undertook such efforts, slaying demons that took human or monstrous animal forms." Fynch tried to look as if he were not comparing himself to St. Michael or St. George, but the pride in his voice was obvious. "I understand from your miller there have been several thefts here lately, and now a child missing?"

"A child may go missing in any village," Hugo said. "And there is theft everywhere."

"Including holy wine?"

"The wine had not been blessed," the priest said. "It was taken from my house, not my church. And I apprehended the thieves myself. Took no Order I've never heard of to do that." Curse the miller and his self-important mouth, Gilbert thought. Rumors ran as fast as water downhill.

"So *you* say." Again, Fynch was unimpressed. "You are convinced you have the correct person."

"I am."

"But a child lost since yesterday, and a goat cruelly slaughtered. These events suggest we are here at a good hour. Now then, time is of the essence. I must demand that you—"

Hugo had enough. "I think you are here with a misguided collection of coincidences, and trespassing on my land."

"I come at the request of my cousin, and your lord, Denis. To inspect his lands on his behalf. And to report if I see anything amiss, which I do." He examined the bottom of his empty cup, shaking it a little in an obvious way, hoping someone would offer him more. "There are evil things in this land, things that are capable of changing form, of taking on the most monstrous of shapes: a wolf, a lion, a serpent, and a giant winged bat, almost like a dragon."

Alice nodded, her eyes lowered. "I have been preparing for motherhood all my life."

Fynch inclined his head to her, and if one can freight a gesture with an abstract notion, his nod might have said, "Dear sad creature, to make a non-sequitur pronouncement at once so bald and so inappropriate to the discussion."

Hugo remained impassive. Gilbert coughed nervously.

Alice continued. "I have helped raise my siblings and my cousins, and I enjoy children very, very much."

Robert Fynch was confused. "It is a wonderful thing, to be so happy in one's allotted role, my lady."

"Children might tell stories about monsters who change shape and do evil things, but that does not make it true. Every single time I have been told of demons or monsters or devils, do you know what I find?"

"My lady?"

"A dead leaf on a branch, its shadow magnified by moonlight. I find a mouse in a cupboard. I find a naughty sister in a silly hat with horns."

"My lady, you cannot imagine I am a child." His words were heavy with threat. "I have seen these things with my own eyes."

"And if *I* have not?"

Gilbert opened his mouth as if to speak, and Hugo shook his head almost imperceptibly, knowing no good could come of it. Alice was not stupid, though often too bold.

"I would not expect you to encounter such things," Fynch said, dismissing her. "You've probably never traveled more than five miles from your home. You've probably never seen the sea, but I expect you to believe in it. Sir Hugo, we have no time for this—"

"I have seen objects brought back by merchants from faraway lands," Alice said. "I have looked at maps, and I have seen illustrations. All corroborate more or less what I have heard." With some difficulty, she raised herself from her seat. "I've never heard reliably of demons from two people in succession—I come from a long line of scholars, and should know. I do not expect you will find monsters when you go looking, but I believe you will always find that which is monstrous. You'd best spend some time in self-examination, sir."

"My lady—" Gilbert spoke up now.

She paused in the doorway. "Also, I have in fact seen the sea, and have been as far as London. Twice. So."

"You allow her too much latitude," Fynch said to Hugo, impatient now. "You might consider sending her away when men would have talk."

"I do allow her much latitude, and she has given me good counsel, as a wife ought." Seeing Fynch was still not placated, Hugo thought to ameliorate the mood. "Breeding women are fractious, sometimes, and I would not have you take unconsidered babble to heart."

Gilbert looked downright alarmed now, and he stepped forward should he be needed to restrain Dame Alice.

There was no need. Alice bowed her head to conceal a smile. Her talk was never unconsidered and never babble, so Hugo had not demeaned her. She would, however, discuss the word "fractious" with him, sometime soon.

Fynch said, "In my experience, too much leniency and inattention to an orderly household invites every kind of evil."

Hugo turned to his wife. "Alice, you may go."

"My lords," she said, with a courtesy. The movement brought with it a pain in her belly; she winced, bowing her head to conceal it. "Father."

Fynch showed obvious relief in having been rid of Alice. "Which brings me to my errand here."

"You will forgive me—my wife raises the point of evidence, and it is one I must consider."

"The Order has evidence. I've seen it myself. We have been pursuing these demons since the time of our Lord, and before that. We have determined...ways of making them reveal themselves."

"You use torture, you mean." Hugo's jaw clenched, his anger barely in check.

"In the name of good and God, we do not shrink from what many might find distasteful. They have great strength—more than human strength. They have the power of transformation, taking on aspects of vicious animals, and can persuade you with the lies they concoct. So, yes, we extract information from them to make them reveal others. There are physical methods—starvation, depriving some of light renders them ill, and pain works remarkably well. Certain herbs of the *Helleborus* family are effective in distracting their minds and making them weak. Everything is necessary in this pursuit—what wouldn't you do, to protect that which is good and decent? To protect what you love?"

Hugo realized Fynch was earnest in his belief, misguided and fanatical as it was. He sniffed cautiously, but smelled nothing of the rank odor of rot and decay that true evil had. He didn't feel the urge to Change his form. Fynch believed he was doing something honorable, but what he was doing was endangering the world by seeking out and killing its true guardians.

He said, "Your methods concern me—anyone may say anything, under torture. Coerced words are not the same as proof."

Fynch waved his hand, unconcerned. "We have found relics associated with these creatures, which we guard jealously."

"Why not destroy these...relics?"

"Two reasons. The first is that they contain great power, and we may, with time, learn how to harness that power to good use. The second is that these demons *also* seek these relics, and if we have them, we may use the items as bait, to draw the demons out and destroy them. For example, rumors about one of these objects, a kind of pot, took my men as far as Asia Minor. In pagan stories, Pandora was the root of all evil, and if we find that pot, reputed to be the Box she opened, perhaps we can undo the evil she did by letting these monsters escape. We may even be able to banish them forever. We have men across the world gathering these objects and studying them."

Before Hugo could reply, Father Gilbert stood up, causing the others to stand as well. "Excellent, Fynch. May I visit you in your chamber this evening? I have many useful books on the subject of demons, and believe I could be of assistance—"

Toly coughed quietly at the doorway, holding up sealed letters.

Fynch nodded to him, then turned back to Gilbert. "If you will give me leave, Father, I will join you presently. I must attend these messages first."

He bowed and departed, with Toly following.

"You must be careful, Cousin," Hugo said in a low voice when the men had gone. "We cannot draw any more attention to ourselves. Especially not with Alice's time so near. You must be careful how you...persuade him to leave."

"You forget, my friend, what an old hand I am at this. Never fear; I will merely suggest to him there is nothing amiss in our village, and he can be on his way. Perhaps I will attempt to dissuade him from his radical views as well."

"But introduce only a nagging skepticism into his mind," Hugo said. "We cannot afford that every member of the Order who finds us should suddenly lose his purpose, nor can we simply kill them off. That would only raise suspicion. No." He poured more wine. "We must divert the Order away from us, and restore peace to our own village. You are absolutely sure you found nothing of the child? No tracks, no scent trail of that evil that calls us to Change and pursuit?"

Gilbert raised his hands helplessly. "No, nothing at Weaver's. Just that odd, repelling scent, same as where the goat was killed and things went missing. It made me feel ill."

They did not need to discuss the relationship between the callously slaughtered animal and a missing child. Those who started with animals often moved onto more significant quarries.

Both men were silent. "I think there must be a connection between that strange scent and these other matters."

"I agree."

Hugo nodded. "The curse of rank is that I can't simply go haring off on my own. I have sent the men to search this night, and you have your 'appointment' with Fynch, but if you would try again tomorrow, on your own? We haven't much time, a child that young."

The priest nodded. "That is the benefit of *my* position. I can always manufacture an excuse, a parishioner to visit."

"Then good night. Let us hope for better news with the dawn."

It was not four hours later, and dark as dark could be, when a tremendous banging roused the sleeping household. Hugo dressed hurriedly.

"Sir Hugo!" Father Gilbert supported one of the villagers, who was shivering, covered with scratches and dirt. Fynch and Toly were hard on his heels, a zealous light in Fynch's eyes.

"What news?"

"Bad news. The child's shirt has been found."

"And the baby?"

The anguished look on the villager's face was enough to tell the worst had come to pass. "Nothing. But the cloths were...bloodied. And bits of...flesh were found nearby."

The men crossed themselves. Hugo and Gilbert shared an anguished look: A savage killer they couldn't track? Who did not reek of evil? What was happening? What good were their powers if they couldn't trust them to reveal the truth?

"Where?" Hugo asked.

"By the river. In the woods, near Fletcher's place."

"The men are still there?"

"Gathering there, Sir Hugo. Some have twisted ankles from walking all night in the dark, and one has a bad cut."

"We'll all go," Fynch said. "I've just learned that the stolen items were discovered, interestingly, by the river. Also near Fletcher's place, if my source says rightly."

Hugo and Gilbert exchanged a glance. His source was, no doubt, the busybody miller, trying to make himself important.

"Sir Hugo, Father Gilbert—I think we've found our villain." Fynch was excited, his eyes ablaze. "He shall not escape me, or my Order's questions."

"Fletcher is a good man, an honest man. I know him well. It *cannot* be him." Hugo could not say he knew everyone in the village by scent and would have known immediately if one had descended into evil ways.

"Do not show yourself too partial, sir."

"And there are three homes at that end of the village," Hugo continued. "We must inspect the place carefully, make very certain before we accuse anyone. And you must leave the justice in my village to me."

"So long as it is full justice, and all involved are rooted out. If I am not convinced, I will go on my own. I'm perfectly ready to raze all three houses and, if need be, the entire village, to expose the villains. If you resist, I shall summon my lord kinsman's soldiers."

"Father," Hugo said, desperate, "I suspect we'll need your help before the night is through. If you would get the tools of your healing arts, and meet us?" He gave his Cousin a freighted look; they'd need all their powers at hand to save their villagers from the militant predations of the Order.

Gilbert nodded. "The child's family also will need comfort. I will fetch my things and meet you. It is a short distance from my house to that part of the village. I will not be long."

Hugo exhaled deeply; his kinsman had understood him.

"I trust you will hurry, Father," Hugo said. "We need all haste, to prevent more misfortune."

As men gathered together, lighting new torches, Hugo told Alice of the desperate situation they were in and of the plan he and Gilbert had communicated to each other. "I'll go with Fynch and my men on one road; Gilbert will take the other road near his house. My hope is that one way or the other, one of us will be able to find the true scent of the killer before Fynch starts 'questioning' the villagers," he said bitterly. "Bar the door after me. I'll send word when I can."

A nod, a quick kiss, and Hugo was away.

Increasingly uncomfortable, her pains returning, Alice had given up on sleep and moved to the firelight with her prayer book. There was a hurried rap on the door, a code agreed upon by those in her several-natured Family.

A dreadful cramp seized her in her belly as she opened the door for Alwin.

"I've just come from the village, following on an errand for my master. Fuller's Joan is nowhere to be seen. I thought it best to tell you, as it seems…you know." He hunched his shoulders. "Akin to the recent troubles."

It was unlike Joan to be out after dark, or disobedient; she was a good, diligent girl of nearly twelve.

"You did right to tell me…" Alice's mind raced. "Very well. Father Gilbert has returned to his house briefly, and then will trace the path up the stream to meet my husband. I want you to run as fast as you can and find Gilbert. Let him know…" What? "Tell Father Gilbert I've gone to the field between the two roads where he and my husband will be traveling. I hope that if Joan has been abducted, one of the three of us will be on the right track."

Alwin scrunched up his face in concentration. "Because if my master has not found the trail on his way, he can still cast about unseen as a snake-man. If Sir Hugo finds the trail as he travels with Fynch on their road, he can contrive to track the wrongdoer in some subtle way, as he will not be able take his wolf form."

"That is correct. Now go!"

"I should stay with you!" the boy protested. "To protect you! You should not be left alone because you are…" Although a farming lad, and well versed in the ways of nature, Alwin could not bring himself to say the word "expecting" to a lady. "Because you are…not at your full powers. My master would not thank me for leaving you!"

Apparently Gilbert had been instructing Alwin about the matters of birth of those born to the Fang. The boy was not even grown into his own power yet; she hid her smile at his bravado.

She drew herself up. "This is the best way. Would your master thank you for disobeying an elder, or for wasting time? You know the Laws and Lessons."

"No, my lady. Yes, my lady. I will go." He bowed, pulled the door open, and was off.

Alice felt another cramp and knew it certain she was now in labor. She couldn't call her ladies, and she couldn't wait. She might be the only thing between the killer and his next victim.

Alice pulled on a surcoat against the chill of the night and sneaked out of the house. She moved stealthily, if not as smoothly as she liked, and the baby was restless inside her. The quickest way to the field was behind the house, through the garden, and through the wooded area that separated the next set of fields.

Joan's life was at stake, she knew. But if she was not very careful of how she displayed the few powers she had remaining, Fynch in his fanaticism might jeopardize the lives of the rest of her Family of the Fang as well.

Once well away from the house, Alice took a moment to collect herself. She risked the half-Change, a human shape but with a serpent's features. It was a danger—she had to be in human form when she gave birth, as a human baby needs a human mother—but she immediately felt better, more at ease in her own skin and flesh. The babe seemed quieter, more content, too. Her labor pain receded, as if it were something perceived only distantly, through many layers of thick cloth.

There. A dark, humped form struggled across the field. There was an odd snuffling noise, and muttering. Alice was quick in her human-serpentine form, but the child bore her down and she was not as strong as usual.

The villain was also weighed down by a child. Joan, the fuller's daughter, unconscious, was thrown over his shoulder, her slight form hanging limply.

Alice's gown dragged heavily, her feet tripping over the unevenness of fields overgrown with cover after lying fallow. Her belly and clothing were slowing her down. Alice sniffed the air and detected a whiff of blood. She felt no call to attack the villain, but she hoped Alwin reached the men quickly and brought them even more quickly to her aid.

The ache from her belly suddenly became unbearable, even half-Changed. She was too close to her time for this.

Joan stirred faintly; the killer shook her roughly, and she fell still.

Hearing the distant barking of dogs, Alice knew the men were on their way. She paused and resumed her fully human form.

If she drew attention to herself, perhaps she could slow the killer down and give the nearing men a chance to help her. If she remained in human form, she was quick and skilled, but still very vulnerable. She couldn't let him succeed, but she couldn't let the Order or the villagers see her in another shape.

Sacrifice herself and her baby, for the girl? Or risk endangering her entire Family by revealing her hidden nature near Fynch? His maniac Order would not be stopped in their investigations once they found a "real" demon among the townspeople...

Save herself and damn her Family? Or imperil an unborn generation of warriors needed in the fight against true evil?

It was an impossible decision.

Alice paused, a dreadful, perfect thought seizing her. She rejected it, but now that she'd stopped, she could not get her body to move again. Her natures—of a wife, of a lady, of one born to the Fang, as a mother—warred. She had too many choices, all bad.

"Hugo, forgive me," she murmured. She raised her voice. "Stop! Halt, cur! I see you! I accuse you of murder! Come, stop, and be held accountable for your terrible deeds, and maybe God will have mercy on you! Stop, in the name of Hugo of Godestone!"

The killer did stop. As he turned, Alice could see a monstrous face, his face bestial with rage and purpose.

She moved closer, realizing that she felt positively ill now. The baby shifted, and Alice wanted nothing more than to run.

The killer dumped Joan down behind him. The girl moaned and clumsily tried to crawl away.

There was a slight movement of his now-freed hands. Alice saw his knife then, a terrible thing, sharp and oiled.

Her own work-a-day knife was also sharp, but very small. She pulled it out very slowly; Alice knew it was best when facing a mad dog to show it no fear, to be quiet in oneself, to make no sudden moves.

Across the field, she could hear the men were closer now. She hoped they would hasten, hoped the sight of her standing with the armed stranger in the early daylight would give them greater speed. She still resisted the urge to run.

She must wait, as a human woman. As bait. She would fight as a human woman, and she would die for her husband's sake and the sake of her people.

Alice stepped toward him. Her breath recovered, she took another step, and another. She would use the last of her strength to bring the monster down.

He swung the blade down, awkwardly but powerfully. She dodged it, but the long skirt of her surcoat was slashed.

Surprised at her having avoided his blow, he growled and struck out again. Alice stepped back, once, twice, and then jabbed at him. He fell to the uneven ground, but even as she advanced, she was halted by another contraction and cried aloud.

It was then she recognized that the odor that inspired her to flee reminded her of the herbs said to be dangerous to her kind. Her scholarly kin had made an extensive study of them.

And it was then she realized whom she was fighting.

Another born to the Fang.

She understood. He'd been drugged, made deranged. Tortured, too, she realized, her acute sense of smell detecting dried blood and fear. She noticed scars on his hands and chest. He had some wolfish aspect, but wasn't Changed fully to an upright wolf. He existed in some kind of horrible in-between state, a conflict of his natural aspects.

He'd been captured by the Order and turned to a true monster by his enemies' attempt to learn more about her Family. The Order had used the excuse of seeking out demons to recover him while concealing his escape.

Her startled realization made her too slow. He knocked the blade from her hand and left a cut across her upraised, defending palms. A guttural noise of triumph came from her attacker.

She could not hurt him, but she could not let him harm her or her baby. In his altered, unnatural state, he did not recognize one of his own Family.

He closed in; she stepped back, pulling the long bodkin from her hair, which tumbled down. Before he could register where she was, she stepped around quickly and slammed the bodkin into his shoulder, shoving him over onto the uneven ground.

She stooped to touch his empty hand. In an instant, her people's ability to see into the hearts of others told her what was going on.

He was no killer. The stolen babe was alive.

Born to the Fang, however, he quickly recovered. He pulled himself up, shaking his head as if confused and, baring his teeth, pulled the bodkin from his shoulder. He flung it away. She ducked, stumbling, and fell. Her heart raced with fear, knowing he was not his true self and would continue to attack her.

She had to Change if she wanted to survive. But what would happen to her baby if she was still Changed when it was born? It had never happened in her memory, or her mother's, or her mother's mother's, and Alice was terrified. She *must* be in human form to give birth to her baby. She could *not* be in human form if she were to survive long enough to reach that moment. She was caught between her duty to her unhinged kinsman and the preservation of herself and her baby.

It wasn't fair. No one should be asked to make this sacrifice. It was meant to be in her nature, this duty, but...

The shouts of the villagers were clear now, and the rising sun showed them plainly. She could hear Fynch's voice clearly over them all. But would they be fast enough?

Alice chose. She—

There was a long hiss, and the faintest rustle in the grass and leaves by the verge of the wood. It might have been ignored by anyone else, but to her wonderfully keen ears, it was music.

Salvation. A huge serpent slithered through the brush and into the field.

Never had Alice been so glad to see a snake in the grass.

"Gilbert, you must not kill him—he is one of our kinsmen! Send him only to sleep!"

Suddenly, her attacker faltered in his progress. The rage fled his face, to be replaced by confusion. He stopped, whimpered piteously, and clutched his leg.

Another hiss. The good Father Gilbert, in the shape of a thick serpent, had reared up, no higher than the tallest weeds. Unseen by anyone except Alice, the snake had sunk his fangs into the distraught creature's leg. He twined himself around the man's ankles, like a noose closing on a neck. The attacker, still whimpering, fell over. The serpent turned his head quizzically to Alice.

"He is one of us," she said hurriedly, glancing over her shoulder to mark the progress of the villagers. "He is born to the Fang, but tortured into this other horrid form by the Order, may God punish them! If you can make him appear to be dead, they will leave satisfied, and you may be able to heal him!"

The snake's head bobbed once and, summoning his strength, the serpent bit the fallen man again, administering venom that would cause sleep and ease the pain of the Order's torture. In the growing light, the man's chest seemed not to rise and fall, and his noises stilled. Alice knew he was still alive, though undetectably so. She watched, sighing with relief, as Gilbert removed the Order's poisons and healed the stranger, and his face returned to a human form, pale and scarred, but otherwise unhurt.

Alice nodded, then began to scream. She scuttled backward and got up clumsily. She kicked at the weeds, so that the villagers and Joan might imagine she was kicking the fallen man. No one must know that Father Gilbert had been there.

His healing work completed, the giant serpent head waved back and forth, seeming to smile in a familiar, gap-toothed way.

"You must go now, before the others arrive," she said. She caught up her knife—but then grabbed her belly. The labor had started again, made worse than before by all her exertions. "Nnngggahhh!"

The snake paused, and she shook her head. "It is well! Go now!" She made slight cuts on the man's body to suggest the fight and replace those deeper cuts she'd made in her defense. Those had disappeared when the human face returned, part of the camouflage of their people and part of the sign of their grace.

"Rest, friend," she said softly. "We will protect you now."

The pains started again, doubling and trebling in intensity, and her back ached awfully. She worried about the fall she'd taken, as well as the toll the fight might have had on the baby.

The search party, led by Hugo, was near to her now. Joan, who'd crawled away a little, stirred and raised her head. "My lady Alice? What...?"

"Hush," Alice said, biting her lip as another contraction took her. "All is well now."

The yard echoed with the clatter of hooves the next morning, and if Hugo could have found a way to make horses go quieter, or men remember their manners in a house with a new baby, he would have been a happier man. As it was, his worry that his new daughter, named Lucia, would remain asleep still kept his perfect joy to more-than-human, if not absolutely angelic, levels.

The weaver's baby had been found, squalling but safe, snugged down in a sort of nest of hay in an abandoned hermit's cell in the woods. The fork with which the hay had been stolen was found nearby; the stolen nails had been used to make some repairs—a large cobble nearby provided the hammer. The milk pail was found, stolen by the stranger, Martin, to give the baby something to eat; the bacon to feed the escapee himself.

Rather than a murderer inciting himself to greater and greater violence with minor thefts and increasingly cruelty Martin, in his madness created by torture and interrogation, had been acting out of the true instinct of those born to the Fang.

Once spirited away by a newly human Father Gilbert to be "buried," Martin revealed that he had escaped the Order and was trying to find his way home. The goat, once again having slipped out of its shed, had startled him, and believing in his fevered mind it was a monster, Martin had killed it. He had taken the baby believing it was his own and terrified he might have betrayed it to the Order. He was in the process of "saving" Joan, the fuller's daughter, when Alice had discovered him. Martin's own delight in eventually returning to his actual family was only matched by Gilbert's assurance that he had revealed nothing to Fynch that could harm any of them, and that his experiences would help arm those born to the Fang in evading the Order of Nicomedia.

Joan corroborated the story Alice told, of being surprised and carried away by a stranger. She remembered nothing but a bad dream—thanks to Gilbert's ministrations—until she woke up in the field, unharmed, and found her lady defending them both. The stranger had fallen over and hit his head on a rock, killing him. Alice claimed she had been abroad early seeking certain herbs to ease her labors.

Presented with the corpse of a sadly deranged man, and finding no demons—as well as no real murder—Robert Fynch was forced to admit there was nothing at all mysterious about the goings-on in Godestone. He and Toly spent a long time in discussion and confession with Father Gilbert, and they were so grateful for the happy outcome of their investigation that Fynch bestowed a pair of goats on Taylor. They also made a generous donation to the church's poor box, and although neither gave up a belief in demons, they developed a talent for examining the scene and evidence found where there had been theft or murder done. They later gained a reputation for the solving of crimes, all of which were mundane and secular.

Young Alwin took his notes during the discussion among Father Gilbert, Fynch, and Toly, using a shorthand invented by the priest himself. He learned much from his master that instructive afternoon. He longed for the day when he would be a healer like Father Gilbert, or a hunter, like Sir Hugo. Or even Dame Alice.

"More horses?" Alice turned over, her eyes squinting against the brightness of the window. Her next gesture was to feel for her well-wrapped baby, sleeping next to her, and feel the gentle movement of her tiny chest rising and falling. "Who now?"

"Your sister," said Hugo. "She might have taken a little longer, and been here for Lucia's first birthday." Even his sister-in-law, however, could not erase his fine mood. "I am glad for your sake she is here finally."

A quick rap, and the door flew open before anyone gave leave. Father Gilbert dashed in, his face suffused with happiness. "Alice! Your sister—!"

Too late he realized his inappropriate enthusiasm outstripped his manners and good sense.

All three looked at the baby, who yawned, frowned, and stayed asleep.

Gilbert closed the door behind him and made a great show of quietly moving away from the door to the window, where no doubt he could watch Lady Martha's progress into the house.

Alice suppressed a grin. "My sister tempts you?"

"I dare her to do her best."

The priest's tone was not one of resolution, but anticipation. Hugo gave him a bemused look. "Why don't you go welcome her, then?"

Gilbert vanished immediately, the door silently shutting behind him.

"I cannot for the life of me fathom his interest." Hugo turned to Alice and added hastily, "Not that your sister isn't a fine woman, of course. Perhaps it is the endeavor itself? A hunt, a chase, that can never end?"

Alice shrugged. She had no answers.

Hugo continued. "He's made his choice, though, taking holy orders. Now I find myself debased enough to enjoy watching him struggle with it."

"It is your only fault," Alice said, but her thoughts were much darker.

She still did not know what decision she would have made, had Gilbert arrived later than he did. Take on her true form, and betray her husband, and possibly all her Family, sacrificing them to the Order's ignorant hatred? The thought was tantamount to sacrificing humanity with the extinction of those born to the Fang.

But betray her baby, not to mention herself, in an unsought struggle? She looked down at Lucia and found the notion impossible.

"He's torn between the flesh and his calling," Hugo said, shaking his head.

"Mmmm," Alice said, closing her eyes to enjoy the warm sun on her face.

Pax Egyptica

Cleopatra has always fascinated me, and she's one reason I went into archaeology. This was my first crack at writing a true alternate history (beyond adding supernatural superheroes!): I wanted to explore how, if things had turned out just a little bit differently, Cleopatra might have waged war on Rome. It was also a fictional chance to visit the Library at Alexandria and the cosmopolitan world under the Empire. The animal-headed gods of Egypt shout "Fangborn" to me.

Light danced across the waters of the Middle Sea, producing a blinding glare against the pale stone of the lighthouse and government buildings. The princess ran along the quay, her sandals slapping against the sun-heated stones. Her lesson in navigation over, her destination was the great Library. Egypt was the center of the world, and this sliver of bustling, cosmopolitan Alexandria was the beating heart of Egypt, creating the world's history and its wealth. Her royal father's court was fascinating, but for the princess, the Library was the key, the source of all knowledge and learning.

Clouds darkened the sky so abruptly the princess stopped short. A terrible roaring noise was followed by fire raining from the sky, as arrows, trailing flames like comet tails, found their targets. The rigging of the ships caught, and sailors and merchants ran screaming, only to be caught by the fiery bolts themselves.

The princess was trapped, hedged in by burning ships and carts. At the far end of the quay, the magnificent lighthouse exploded when its entire fuel supply ignited. Ahead of her...

Ahead of her, the Library was ablaze, its thousand scrolls feeding the flames that consumed the building from the inside out. The princess cried out, running as if to save it.

The heat was so fierce, it stole the breath from her lungs, and finally, she felt her linen robes burning...

Cleopatra Auletes, Philopater, Queen of Two Lands, the New Isis, woke, gasping, from a nightmare of fire and loss. Her ships were gone, the Library, her Egypt—

She clutched at her heart, trying to still its pounding through her ribs. It was only the sound of the hard rain outside, and the biting cold of the salt air that roused her from one misery to another. As far as she knew, Alexandria still stood. The more immediate wretchedness was the weather of Germania, a Hell the likes of which she never imagined.

A slave hesitated by the doorway, shifting from foot to foot in anxiety. The slave smelled like sheep and resembled one, with her bland, pale features and lumpy, wool-cloaked figure. Still, she didn't seem to feel the cold as keenly as Cleopatra, so perhaps it was true that every country's inhabitants were bred to survive its particular hardships.

"It is the day, Queen. Our spies have reported that Caesar's legions in Gaul prepare to invade. It is the day we win or die."

"Never call him Caesar," the queen said. "I took one Caesar as consort and another as ally. Marcus Junius Brutus is an upstart puppy with an unbalanced mind poisoned against me."

The slave prostrated herself. "Forgive me, Queen!"

"Get up, and fetch me hot water. It is not your fault, but not every

Roman who leads an army this way is called Caesar."

The slave nodded obediently, rose, and scurried away.

Cleopatra shivered against the bite of the cold, but her warrior's heart sang. Trusting one Roman was not the same as trusting them all, and she'd always known this day might come. The slave was correct: Today meant only victory or death.

Just three years before, when the old woman appeared so suddenly in the desert, the refugee queen had wondered if the crone was some trick of the brutal sun. Cleopatra knew her death was likely near, either from starvation, or by military defeat followed by execution, so a hallucination was not out of the question. The desert was so barren that it eradicated the very memory of Alexandria's beautiful streets and brilliant society: there was no place from which the old woman could have appeared so suddenly. Her garments were of a material and color no longer identifiable; perhaps they had once been blue. Her face was as weather-worn as the markings on the ancient monuments, blurred and unreadable after many years of exposure.

"Hail, Cleopatra, Holy Vessel, Imperatrix, Empress of the lands from Britannia to Parthia. Why do you tarry here?" The cryptic use of nonsense titles and the heavily accented Greek—was that a hint of the Medic dialect?—by the old woman confirmed it: Cleopatra was delirious.

And yet...sometimes gods appeared in visions or dreams. In any case, it would be impolite not to answer.

"No queen, I," Cleopatra said. "If you haven't heard, I'm an exile. My little brother-husband, the co-king Ptolemy, and his scheming priests hunt me like an animal. My sister Arsinoe has fled, waiting to see which of us will win, so she may side with the victorious one. To call me queen of anything at the moment is cruel mockery."

The crone laughed. "No mockery; we must discuss how you will tear the world apart and restitch it anew. Your realms will far exceed those of your ancestor, Alexander."

The queen, though well trained in politics and composure, was exhausted and hopeless: She could not restrain a laugh. "Another time, I would be delighted to help you, sage. But my kingdom hangs by a thread and my people suffer from this uncivil war my brother wages against me." Though restoring peace to her people was paramount, this last saddened her. Her young brother had always been a favorite of hers, until they ascended the throne, and he fell prey to the poisonous whisperings of his priests. "I have more pressing matters at hand."

"Give me a drink of water, and I will explain how that can be changed."

The waft of onions and incense filled the queen's nose and she could hear the wind flapping the woman's loose garments around her bony frame: The old one was real. Cleopatra shrugged. As beggars went, it wasn't a bad line; it would be less trouble to hear her than to summon the guards to give the wretch a beating.

She handed the crone a cup and poured the last from her jug of water. The old woman nodded her thanks, took a sip, then gazed into the cup. "You will be banished to the edge of the world, triumphant, having had all power in your hands. You will return from that death to reign again. Your realm will exceed that of Alexander himself."

"As you've said." The queen was tired, now. "Enough."

"You have powers. Let me show you. If I disappoint, you may take my head."

She spoke like a queen herself, to suggest that the younger woman wouldn't take her life anyway. Cleopatra inclined her head. "You have the space of fifty heartbeats."

A feeling like lightning striking nearby raised the hairs on the back of the queen's neck. She watched as the crone's face became unrecognizable, bones shifting and features blurring and skin thickening.

The old woman turned into a massive serpent.

Cleopatra stifled a scream. No fever dream, but a miracle.

The giant serpent curled up, enjoying the warmth, and then darted, with inhuman speed, at a lizard. The lizard squirmed violently, its tail caught in the great serpent's mouth. The serpent then returned the lizard to the ground so it could scuttle away.

A shimmer in the air, then the crone returned to her human form, struggling into her robe. The young queen helped her. "Thank you. I can teach you to do the same. In exchange, you must do three things."

"Oh yes?"

"Make an ally of Rome. Preserve the great Library. Refuse the rituals of the priests."

Cleopatra laughed harshly. "If it were so easy to do those first two things, I should have done them already. And why the last?"

"I have seen that a united kingdom around the Middle Sea is closer to your hand than anyone's in several centuries. Do one task and the rest will follow. And if we are very lucky?"

"Yes?"

"We will see a return of the gods."

While Cleopatra was not certain seeing any god was a good thing, much less all of them returning, she was intrigued. "Very well."

"Give me your hand."

Without a second thought, Cleopatra extended her hand. The old woman grasped it, and suddenly, the queen's mind was filled with images. She saw

A race of powerful half-human creatures, some with the features of a snake or a wolf, who walked on two legs. She saw them as actors in a series of quick dramas, working to protect ordinary mortals and slay evil-doers.

The first, the walking snakes, had bright eyes and sharp fangs, but they healed with their venom, bringing the dead back to life, like Asclepius. They had killing venom, too, like boiling water, that ate the skin.

The second, the walking wolves, using their long snouts and keen ears to seek out and destroy villainy.

And there was a third, who took on no animal aspect, but possessed of myriad powers. Not drugged girls in caves, but true oracles—those who could communicate with thought—and those with tremendous luck. These guided the others in their fight against evil.

She saw the rise of Alexander; he could transform into a hunting wolf. She saw his mother Olympias, in the aspect of a snake. Then, too young, Alexander struck down before the world was united, by some Persian magic, in retaliation for the destruction of Persepolis. A great plague followed, destroying many of the Fanged and the Talented.

Those who survived were kept ignorant of their powers, drugged by priests, who saw the Talented as an affront to the gods. Behind their obsequiousness, the priests smirked, knowing that their rituals and potions controlled beings of great power.

The crone suddenly collapsed.

Cleopatra, reeling from all she saw, eased the older woman and wet her lips from the dregs in the cup.

The old woman pushed the water away. "Show me you can do as I did. Show me that you can Change your form."

The queen had always been a quick and clever student, capable of learning languages, mathematics, military tactics, as well as many kinds of physical activities, from sailing to hunting to dance. The idea that she might now have the power to truly protect Egypt and regain her rightful place inflamed her, so she did not hesitate. Recalling the images she saw, and the sensations she experienced watching the other woman change, she found that making the metamorphosis was as easy and agreeable as slipping into her favorite shift. She assumed the walking serpent aspect, then the full serpent form readily.

Cleopatra Changed back to her human form. When she looked down, giddy from her success, the crone was dead.

By the time she returned to camp, Cleopatra had a plan. She summoned her generals: A small force would escort her to within a day's march of Alexandria, and then a smaller group would smuggle her into the city, for General Julius Caesar had seized the palace. The idea of sneaking into her palace was ridiculous, but she could not enter with the pomp she deserved, and expect to live. She had to see Caesar—while avoiding her siblings, their generals and priests—and convince the Roman to take her part.

In disguise, she listened to the merchants outside the Alexandrine walls to see which of them had an audience with Caesar the next day. Picking the most likely one, she found the tent with his wares, found a place to hide, curled up, and fell asleep.

The next morning, General Gaius Julius Caesar was inspecting the pottery merchant's wares when he was surprised by a gargantuan snake. As the creature—all glittering black and gold and blue scales—uncoiled from inside the pot in which she had spent the night, he was struck temporarily speechless. Although he had an abhorrence of snakes he was careful to hide, the general soon realized that such a creature could only be an omen. This was confirmed when, with an explosion of dazzling light, the large snake turned into a small naked woman. She glanced up at him regally, and began to speak in perfect, courtly Greek.

When he did not answer, she repeated the speech in Egyptian. And then in Syrian, in Hebrew, then the Medic language.

"You may speak," she said finally, in decent, if accented, Latin. Truth be told, Cleopatra was rather enjoying the look of amazement the general could not conceal. His strong features and aquiline nose built authority into his face. She suspected it didn't happen often that confusion shone in his black eyes.

"Ahem—ah, thank you, er, Queen Cleopatra, for that lovely welcome, and for your condolences on the death of my friend Pompey. I would certainly entertain a discussion of alliance with you—"

Of course he would consider it. When a god shows up in the form of a serpent and a queen, you pay strict attention.

And when that imperious queen-god tells you she has a plan to create an empire for you to share, one that will exceed that of Alexander, you do exactly what she says.

First, however, once the courtesies had been extended, there were details to attend.

"Your brother? Husband? He's just a boy," Caesar said.

"If ten is old enough to overthrow a co-ruler, it is old enough to die," Cleopatra replied.

Caesar nodded. "And your sister?"

"We shall see," came the cool answer. She could see him evaluating her as a realist and a strategist. Patient. Cleopatra realized that, since she'd stopped taking the priests' potions, her insights were more acute than ever. She asked, "What is your intent for Egypt?"

"Nothing but peace and prosperity, a continuation of our long and happy friendship."

She held him in a commanding stare.

"With you as its rightful queen," he finished.

It was still not enough. "If we are to be allies, you must fully understand what Egypt is. It is not only grain to feed hungry Roman bellies. It is not merely a port or a piece of land for you and your enemies to squabble over. It is a kingdom with a pedigree going back to the sun-god, recently rediscovering its ancient powers, as you've just seen."

Her stare deepened; Caesar was fascinated, unable and unwilling to break it. It was ridiculous for her to lecture him or demand anything, and yet...

"If we ally, you must swear that Egypt shall be mine, and descend to my heirs forever. A friend, as you said, not just a vassal state feeding you tribute. You must swear to protect Egypt and her people. I will no longer have them be pawns in political squabbles. In return, we shall gladly share our bounty of grain and power with you."

"Agreed," was all he could say, and he meant it with all his soul.

She nodded once, and kissed him on the mouth, an agreement between princes. Inside she was trembling: She had succeeded in two of the crone's three commands.

She was also trembling because Caesar was. Their formal kiss had evolved into something much more passionate.

After the matter of her siblings' defeat and deaths had been accomplished, the queen received her brother's priests in the great hall of her palace, with all the courtiers, as well as Caesar and his advisors.

The priests bowed deeply. "Majesty, it has been far too long since you've undergone the purification ritual—"

"No. I have been given special insight directly from the gods themselves, and new powers, too. I will no longer be following your 'purification' rituals. No more potions. No more prayers. I am quite pure enough."

"I must warn you, my queen, that—"

Without warning, the queen hissed as if with the voice of a thousand serpents. Cleopatra began to tremble, and assumed the aspect of a snake-headed creature, covered in the sleek scales of a reptile. And yet she was still garbed in the white linen, golden collar, and the double crown she'd donned that morning, first making certain the two rearing cobras in the pschent had been polished until their gold shone.

She had practiced speaking clearly around her fangs. "You do not dare to disobey me."

"But my queen—!"

Hissing again, she struck the priest with a mighty blow. Claw marks appeared in lines of blood down his torso. Two more slashes, and the priest's body collapsed in two ragged pieces. She gestured to the priest's remains.

"You, priests—Achillas and Manetho! Take those with you as proof that I no longer require any priest's rituals," she ordered. "Either obey me in this, or pay the ultimate price for disobeying the gods. Any of you who feel I did wrong may leave. No harm will come to—"

As one, the crowd of attendant nobles and slaves prostrated themselves.

"Well, that's settled," the queen murmured. She took Julius Caesar's arm, and slowly returning to her fully-human form, left the audience chamber.

It was quite some time before the retainers raised their heads. They all left without speaking, each deep in their own thoughts. That is what happens when one is in the presence of the miraculous.

The two priests carried the remains of their colleague out of the palace, and dumped the body as quickly as they could. "I'm taking her part," Achillas said. "Blasphemy or no."

The other, Manetho, was still shaking from anger and fear; the blasphemy of his colleague's murder was so terrible, it was hard to imagine. "Maybe...I will go back with you."

But before they had gone halfway back, Manetho vanished into the crowds.

Revolution of a kind had begun. He swore to undo it.

Even before learning of the existence of those born to the Talents, Cleopatra had collected gods the way other monarchs collected jewels. It wasn't piety, or no more than that of the average Egyptian, but a thirst for knowledge. She was descended from gods, so it behove her to understand them. But now, with her new knowledge, she had her private scholars fill a secret annex of the Library with finding references to her Talented kin. Knowing the source of her powers would help protect her people, Talented and mortal alike. Histories of other cultures mentioned shape-shifters. Each of these descriptions was studied and filed away, into a set of scrolls that became known as the

Book of Talents.

But as diligent and clever as the scholars were, they were no closer to determining where the Talented came from. "Gods are unknowable, queen," they'd say, with as close to a shrug as one dared in the presence of a royal personage.

Even Julius Caesar, with all his erudition and knowledge of the classics, was little help. She took him to the Library, where he was stunned by the extent of the shelves of scrolls, room after room, the greatest repository of knowledge in the world. They expanded their search, sending couriers with instructions to search other libraries and private collections for anything that would tell them about the Talented Ones. They agreed that harnessing the abilities of the Talented, like understanding the rhythms of the Nile, was the clearest path to peace and power.

All through her first pregnancy—of course there was sex; there is nothing more erotic than shared intellect, friendship, and ambition— the queen and general worked. All was calculation and study before they would return to Rome, together. Oracles were scrutinized to see if they truly had the Talent. Philosophers were consulted, their studies of nature examined to find the roots of the Fanged and the Talented.

By the time their second set of sons—twins—was born, the civil war in Egypt was won and Caesar declared they would make no further progress learning about the Talented Ones. "It's time. We must leave."

Cleopatra nodded. "But our news must precede us. Such an upheaval of everything they know—men and women with the powers of gods—is potentially volatile. We must start slowly, and the news must appear to arise from the people themselves."

Caesar frowned. "I agree, but how?"

"Let our agents speak to potters and painters about a new style said to be favored by the great General Caesar himself, and all the rage in foreign parts. Graffiti might appear, made by unseen hands in the night, with wolf- or snake-headed men and women, with some of the happier classical references to the gods and their servants. From Ovid, perhaps."

Caesar's brow cleared, and he nodded. "I have had good success using poets. Let us hire a few to compose on the theme of heroic shape-shifting."

She took his hand, smiling. "The surest way to a welcome reception is to create the fashion before it is announced. We will secure the foundation of Rome, and heal her after this civil war."

As they traveled from Alexandria, they continued the search for other Talented within the army. Caesar proposed the idea of finding a convicted rapist and walking him through the ranks. Those who responded, compelled to attack the murderer, were chosen to form the new vanguard of each legion, and these were called "Victorious Janus."

The first stop in every city they passed through was to the temples. Sacrifices and prayers were offered up, and then a brief meeting with the priests and priestesses who guarded the treasure. In key cities, one or two of the newly discovered Fanged ones were left behind, and the priests and priestesses given strict instructions to obey them as if they were Caesar himself. The special trick the serpent-headed ones had of persuasion and delusion was very helpful.

The gates of Rome were thrown open with wild adulation. After a decent interval, Cleopatra met with Calpurnia, Caesar's wife, at a reception. After the formal greetings were exchanged, the two moved to a quiet room and got to business.

"My husband has appointed Octavian his heir," Calpurnia said briskly, arranging her veil around her.

"My sons are very young and will inherit Egypt," Cleopatra said. "I have no designs on either Rome or Caesar."

"Excellent. Then we have no quarrel." She paused. "I have foreseen Caesar's murder; you must help me prevent it. I hear no one can resist your arguments."

It was then Cleopatra realized the first lady of Rome was born to the Talent of prognostication. She had kept her abilities quiet, a secret protection for her husband.

The Egyptian queen nodded. "I shall prevent it."

Thus, encouraged by his wife's "dream," Cleopatra's skill at politics, and their joint efforts at bringing the senators and their wives to their side, Caesar assumed the role of dictator for life. He also gave the volatile Brutus the governorship of Asia and dispatched him at once. Octavian commenced the on-going campaign against Parthia. While Parthian chariots were nigh-on invincible over the open ground, the Victorious Janus units, with their fleet wolves and the terrible venom attacks of the serpents, helped ensure a Roman victory.

Two months later, disaster struck. Caesar was struck down, not by assassins, but by the illnesses that had plagued him all through life. Falling insensible, he struck his head upon a marble table and died. Cleopatra was distraught, not only for the loss of her love and her children's father. If she had been there when it happened, she might have used her healing powers to save him. But now...

Almost overnight, Brutus turned on Cleopatra. Rome was seized and held by the legions loyal to Brutus, who described this as a chance to rid Rome of the Egyptian witch and her heresies.

Cleopatra was devastated by Caesar's death, and now their plan for peace was threatened by Brutus on one side and the vanquished Pompey's sons on the other. She dispatched the bulk of her household with her two young sons, and a message for Octavian, who was now Caesar. After, she fled to the small temple housing copies of the Book of Talent. She would not allow Brutus to destroy such valuable work.

She raced ahead of her guard detail, her Talent alerting her that there was someone wishing her ill nearby. Cleopatra, tired of diplomacy and politics, thrilled to the idea of battle.

She gasped. The runaway priest, Manetho, was there. A basket of her scrolls was in his arms.

The queen felt the ecstatic rush of righteousness filling her as she transformed. Her mouth grew sharp, sharp fangs, her fingers grew into claws, and her reactions became quick as lightning. She spat and lunged at him.

Manetho was powerful, and much larger than she. When the venom hit the flesh of his neck, she could smell the burning flesh. He roared and slammed his fist against the side of her head. The queen was knocked from her feet; her speed and power informed by instinct rather than training. She rolled out of the way, and leaped up.

He did the unthinkable. He thrust a torch down into the basket of scrolls, then threw it at one of the walls of shelves.

With a cry to her guards, who were now arriving, the queen began to pull at the flaming baskets in an attempt to curtail the conflagration. "Find the priest, the one called Manetho! He's been wounded, but we need him alive! He is in league with Brutus, and I would interrogate him!"

In her half-Changed form, the queen suffered little injury, but many of the scrolls were lost.

The guard came back with the body of the priest. Rather than be captured, he had killed himself, but not before he had spoken a terrible curse against the queen and her kind. Cleopatra took the hand of one of the seers among the guard, and she saw a vision of a fire devouring everything from Gaul to Parthia, the flames reflected in bloody streets.

"And now? What do we do?" the captain asked, shaken.

"We go north," Cleopatra said. "I need an army. I'll find it among the German and Gaulish legions loyal to Caesar."

And so it was that, a month later, Erminia, queen of the Chatti tribe, entered Cleopatra's tent.

"Does it ever stop raining in this pestilential country of yours?" Cleopatra asked.

"Do you weak-shouldered Asians ever stop whining about the weather?" Erminia retorted.

They both smiled and embraced warmly, as much for reassurance as for formality. Today would be a test of them both. The fate of the world depended on the outcome.

"I've heard from my spies; the pro-Julian legions are holding well along the Rhine, but the Parisii are threatened from Brutus's legions in Hispania."

"I've heard from mine. Brutus's generals are building up his forces along the Black Sea and Rome is swaying dangerously in his favor." Cleopatra paced. "Octavian is holding Egypt, but we need to break the lines."

"So you think Brutus will take Byzantium, before returning to Rome?"

"I would." Cleopatra took out a map. "I think we have to go to

Byzantium and stop him there."

Erminia shook her head. "I cannot go so far. My time is too close." She spread her hands over her belly. "I will not leave the safety of my people nor my Family; I will go only as far as the borders of Pannonia."

Cleopatra nodded. "If the worst comes, I'll try to bring the survivors to aid you at the Rhine. We must protect the copies of the Alexandrian records of the Talented, especially if Egypt falls."

"That must not happen," Erminia said. "And what about our plan to preserve the Book of Talents? It's far too dangerous to attempt it now."

"It's the danger that makes it necessary to go ahead with the plan now," Cleopatra said. "No matter what the outcome, we must preserve our lore."

"It is risky to act, or to stay." Erminia shrugged. "Very well. I shall send word to Anglesey—the farthest outpost of our kind from Rome— and to our kin in the other tribes between here and there."

"Thank you. If I fall, I shall hold out as long as I can to ensure you have as much time as possible."

"We'll pray that doesn't happen." She paused, an idea suddenly blossoming. "Our priests have long spoken of a secret. A weapon, a warrior, I know not what, but something to be called in desperate times. I do not guarantee success—it may be naught but a legend—but your arrival put it in my mind. I will speak to them and see what can be done."

"These are the most desperate times. I thank you, sister."

They embraced again, and went to oversee preparations.

The intervening days en route from Germania to Byzantium

blurred together in a nightmare of fire and iron and blood. The renegade priest's dying curse seemed to follow them everywhere, and Cleopatra began to wonder whether her view toward the gods, the priests, and the revelation, was terribly wrong.

The battle at Athens was particularly brutal. The citizens were pro-Julian but the legions nearby were loyal to Brutus. At the last, Cleopatra's tribal allies and the faithful legions had to abandon hope, as the priests at the vaults of the Acropolis refused to turn over their history scrolls to either party. Blood flowed down the marble steps, as the Talented forces tore at other Roman soldiers, now their enemies. The terrible thing was that Cleopatra, and her Talented Family, healed so quickly. She was always ready to fight again—having insisted training as a soldier—but the toll on her mortal soldiers and citizens was disastrous.

But the defeat at Athens helped Cleopatra's cause a little, even as her army retreated. Her ranks were swelled by sympathizers and more of the Talented deserted the opposing troops. It was only these successes that kept spirits up, and by excruciatingly small increments, Cleopatra's army made their way to the far coast of the Aegean. And it was great good luck that a wealthy merchant league pledged them ships to carry their troops to Byzantium, because they had beaten Brutus's forces there by just a day.

The queen made her headquarters at the acropolis on the near side of the river and sea harbor. The hill gave an excellent view all around, a shout soon came from the lookout, echoing against the stone walls. "Ships! Ships coming from the northern sea!"

The river was soon so crowded by the enemy fleet, it was difficult to see the water. The hilly terrain made it possible to hold their position for a while, but the enemy's numbers were so great that defeat was inevitable. Indeed, Brutus was so sure of his victory that he himself had arrived, his flagship and standard visible at the back line of vessels.

"Will you retreat, my queen?" an African general, Rebilius, asked. "Best to escape and choose another battle."

"I will not."

"It is a miracle we have survived this long. This attack will be the end of us. Better to get you to safety; we have no more tricks left."

"I have."

Taking her bow, Cleopatra climbed to the roof of the acropolis, followed by other archers, and soldiers who were instructed to carry as many bundles of arrows as possible. Assuming her half-serpent form, she nocked an arrow, selected a target, and invoked her many gods. Each time it was the same prayer.

"Isis and Anubis, Athena and Hermes, Visucius and Sulis and Ahura Mazda, may all the gods, any god, hear me! Brutus and his army kill my people, undoing a peace that I hoped to make eternal. They destroy learning, and other of your gifts, out of fear. Aid me now. My people built the foundations of this upstart empire; I will tear it down, if need be! Help me now! I call on you directly, o, gods!"

She pulled and shot until her arms trembled with fatigue, even in that powerful, holy state of the Change. With each pronunciation, the other archers also pulled, until bows splintered and bow strings snapped. Those around her, even those who understood the nature of her transformation and power, marveled at her persistence and courage, and took heart, redoubling their efforts. Her voice grew hoarse and still the names flowed from her serpentine tongue.

But goodwill and stout hearts could not match an onslaught from sea and land by a well-rested force. When the last arrow flew, and found a mark, it was still not enough. Brutus's troops were starting to land and advanced up the hill of the acropolis.

There were no more gods to call on.

"Bring every one of our people into the fortress," Cleopatra ordered. Her bow was heavy, but her trembling hand would not release it. Her eyes were distant, her words almost rote, as if she was still in the thrall of her prayers. "If we are to fall, it will be here, fighting as Caesar and I planned, as one nation."

Screams from below. She could smell the edge of the city burning. The queen turned away, her eyes closing for a moment against the knowledge that her doom had come.

A terrible roar enveloped them like a flood. Cleopatra looked up, and saw what had until this day only been the stuff of poets' songs and cartographic warnings.

A beast like the giant serpent Ladon who guarded the Hesperides, or Pytho, the enemy of Apollo, appeared in the sky. Brilliant bronze and golden eyed, teeth like spears, a neck as long and sinuous as a river, and iron-boned wings that were like those of the Erinyes, the monster stooped like an eagle. It landed on the largest ship at the beachhead, and the weight of the beast tipped the galley over, blocking the next ship's way to the beach.

The great, thick dragon roared again, vanishing only to reappear at the next largest ship. Claws like swords raked the decks and rent sails, scattering rowers and archers alike, some sent flying into the water, some jumping of their own will to escape the dreadful beast. The next ship was a small one; the dragon simply picked it up and hurled it at two others.

By this time, some of the ships were fleeing, breaking ranks, and the assault had largely ceased against the city. The dragon amused itself by slowing their attempted escape, dropping wreckage of one ship upon another. The more clever rowers unshipped their oars and used them to float away from the wreckage before the dragon seized it.

Suddenly the queen's rapture at this unexpected ally was shattered. A booming voice, speaking in an ancient and unintelligible language, erupted in her head. She looked around, but none of her soldiers or advisors seemed to be affected. She sank to her knees, screaming, "Speak more quietly, or else you shall kill me!"

An image of Brutus, on the beach and fleeing, filled her mind, along with the irresistible urge to chase him down and kill him. She signaled her generals, but could not wait for them to join her. She would hunt him herself.

Seizing a discarded sword—her arrows all spent in prayers that had been answered—she all but flew up the stairs to the highest tower. Indeed, it seemed as if Hermes, Iris, Isimud, and Pappsukal aided her flight. The power of Sekmet, the lioness, and Innanna the Warrior suffused her being.

"To me! To me! Help me slay this traitorous pretender!" she cried to the dragon.

She hoped the dragon would pick her up and carry her down to the shore, but suddenly, there was an overwhelming sense of being...nowhere. She found herself alone in the streets along the river. She heard her guards shout with amazement, far above her.

As the fires raged through the streets, the queen felt the heat rising, heard the thunder-claps of great stones cracking. Past the temples, and down alleys into the heart of the city, she found Brutus's trail. It was as if the sound of his passing footsteps loitered, hanging in the air for her to follow. He was driven by the fire and chaos to seek shelter or an escape route.

But she could smell his desperation as easily as she could follow his tracks, and a part of her delighted in that. And then she saw him.

Brutus ran in a panic, discarding his armor as he fled. When the fire cut him off, and it was left to choose between the dragon, who was circling overhead, and the strong current of the river below, he chose the water and dove from the quay.

Cleopatra dove after him. Of course she could swim; Alexandria's wealth came from water, Egypt's life came from water. Her half-reptile form lent speed and strength to her strokes, as if the crocodile god Sobek himself had blessed her and Father Poseidon aided her against the strong current. The water was dark and cold, smelling of stone and decay, but was clear enough.

When she broke the surface, gasping for air, the queen felt a sharp biting pain above her left breast: Brutus's dagger had found her heart. Locking eyes with him, she pulled the dagger from her chest. His jaw dropped as he watched the wound close instantly and the blood washed away. She threw the dagger back at him, and he ducked away terrified.

Cleopatra dove back under the waves and swam as quickly as she could, until she saw the bottom of the wrecked ship Brutus had climbed upon. Summoning the full Change, she became a serpent, and slithered up the side as silently as the crocodile god himself. She darted, looping strong coils of her body around Brutus's arms, and rearing back, sank her fangs into his neck. Not to kill—no, the crone in the desert had taught her well. She had to bring Brutus back to Rome in chains.

The beneficence of every god from every pantheon seemed to flow through her for a moment. Cleopatra finally felt him cease to struggle. She Changed to her half-serpent form, and threw Brutus into the water and dove in after him, pulling him to the shore. She hoisted herself to the quay, dripping and exhausted, but exhilarated.

The guards had arrived and swarmed around her. She accepted a cloak from one of them, and pointed. "Fetch *that* out of the water. I have subdued the man who roused the people against the lawful empire and would have killed me. He will live, and return to Rome, but not as he imagined."

The guards regarded their slight queen with reverence and awe. "It's true! The gods came upon her and aided our cause!"

"How goes the rest of the battle?" she demanded.

"The dragon...it is hungry," one of the guards replied, tremulously.

"I shall deal with it," Cleopatra said, not knowing how she would do so. One of the officers quickly turned into a giant wolf, and she rode on his back through the burning streets of Byzantium to the acropolis. She found the dragon sunning itself on the rampart, idly gnawing the bones of a freshly slaughtered cow sticky with drying blood.

"Where did it get the cow?" she whispered to another officer.

"The marketplace," the guard whispered back, not taking his eyes off the sated beast. "The merchant...made no protest."

"Very well. Reimburse the merchant, and purchase another cow, or two or three, for our...ally. And deploy the troops to accept surrender; use the captured legions to help put out the fires."

By now, Cleopatra understood the dragon could hear her thoughts; she watched as the dragon inclined its head in thanks for her hospitality. The dragon cracked open the cow's skull, its eyes half closed with contentment as it gnawed.

"How did you know to come? What god sent you?" she called.

A feeling like laughter bubbled up inside the queen's mind. There was no deafening voice in her head, but the sure knowledge of the dragon's thoughts filled her.

No god, but your sister-queen Erminia summoned me from long slumbers. Your song of arrows guided me to you.

"What is your name?"

I was once called Saris. You may call me that.

"And what I can give you, my friend? What reward? For you have served me beyond reckoning today."

There is no reward but satisfaction for kin rendering duty to kin. But if I may, now that I am here, awake again after many long years, I would stay and view the world. Where best to do that?

"With me," Cleopatra said. "I am expanding the heart of the world from Alexandria. Stay with me, and watch."

A few weeks later, Brutus's legions surrendered and Queen Cleopatra entered the city of Rome. It was not a triumph, of course, but looked rather like one: piles of treasure confiscated from Brutus and his allies were scattered to the populace, Brutus and his generals marched in chains, and the queen wore armor made from the melted gold of the armor once worn by her traitorous brother.

If anyone thought about raising a protest at the unseemliness of a foreign queen inside the walls of Rome, or the spectacle with which she entered with the large number of soldiers, they were put off by the surrounding Janus guards, their banners bright with silver and gold embroidery of fierce wolves and fanged serpents. The sight of the dragon, Saris, well-fed and dozing, pulled into the city by elephants, also led potential naysayers to decide they were better off silent.

A note arrived from Octavian by the swiftest wolf-man couriers. The letter was polite and politic, but unable to conceal the fact that he was uneasy about a foreign monarch—even an ally—living in Rome. Discussing matters of state with the Senate. Entertaining on...an imperial scale. Perhaps it was time for her to depart for Alexandria, he wrote, with thanks for defeating the traitorous Brutus and securing the city.

Cleopatra wrote back: "I am delighted to be of service to Rome, the second city of my heart, and I will not rest easy until you've returned to Rome to prosecute Brutus. While Brutus is alive, there is always the chance of another uprising. After such a narrow victory, the dragon Saris—an ancient relative of mine, it turns out—has advised me to stay until your safe return. After that, we will certainly depart, for Saris has determined to visit Parthia and farther east, both to secure the new peace treaty and introduce me to more of my dragon kin. But rest assured, Saris has become just as attached to Rome as I have, and has chosen a part of the Tiber Island to dwell as a permanent guardian of the city."

"Perhaps some sort of more permanent alliance?" wrote Octavian. "It will be the joining of powerful families, Rome and Egypt, Fanged and Mortal. Perhaps we should discuss marriage."

"Perhaps," wrote Cleopatra. "Come to Rome and we shall see."

Queen Erminia watched as the children of the Chatti tribe studied reading and writing with one scribe, while another led older youths in a copying exercise. She was joined by a cohort of her priests as the Roman ship approached with its precious cargo. She shushed her baby, then handed him to a waiting attendant before going to greet the ship's captain. The captain bowed, a little unsteadily, for he had spent a great deal of time at sea. He handed a scroll to another attendant.

"Your voyage was uneventful, I hope?" Erminia took the scroll, and broke the seal.

"Pirates, majesty, but our Fanged warriors dispatched them easily." He stood a little straighter, pride lending steadiness to his joints. "I heard that the ship to Britannia has also arrived safely."

"This tells me that the other two reach their destinations, at Charax and Seleucia, but two others were lost to storms or enemies."

"Fewer and fewer every day, majesty. The empire is reinforced by the Empress's wisdom and our new found brethren."

"Good. The Library at Anglesey has started sending copies through Britannia and the northlands, and in the south, the Library of Hispania Baetica has almost completed another copy for Volubilis."

"First Citizen Octavian Augustus is making great inroads in Parthia."

"And from there, even farther east. There will be no civilized country on earth without its own Library."

She gave orders for the captain and his crew to be made welcome and comfortable while the cargo was transferred to the nearby stronghold. She traded the scroll for her son again, who promptly spat up. The queen wiped her son's mouth and proceeded up the hill to her home passing a group of adults sitting by a fire, being taught the new writing style. It was now the law of the land that every citizen be literate and numerate; rhetoric and logic were also obligatory. Students who showed the most aptitude were hired away to work as scholars in the new Libraries to further the availability of the texts to the world.

If it had been destroyed, the Library of Alexandria could never have been replaced. Indeed, as the new capital of the Empire, Alexandria was now even more important as a source of learning—but neither would it ever be endangered as it had been. Thus began the enlightened era of the Pax Egyptica.

The Curious Case of Miss Amelia Vernet

I'd been reading a lot of Sherlock Holmes, and imagined the inconsistencies in the Canon—the varying location of Watson's war wounds, the number and names of his wives, etc.—might be explained by the presence of a Fangborn vampire altering his memories. About the same time, I encountered Frances Glessner Lee's dollhouse crime scene reproductions, a tool that helped train forensic investigators in the first half of the 20th century.

It had been a very quiet September at 221B Baker Street, and the evening in question was almost unbearably so. I found myself nodding, yet again, over my volume of mathematics. I wished for the Irregulars to appear, so that I could go off with them and find trouble. But they were occupied elsewhere, and I was trapped in a tranquilly boring domestic snare.

I glanced across the sitting room at the workbench, where a vile green potion bubbled away madly, this one giving off an odor like rotten eggs. I was happy when my Cousin, Mr. Sherlock Holmes, finally developed his new test for bloodstains—but this was far more noxious and pervasive.

I sighed; the best I could hope for tonight was that one of Sherlock's eternal chemical experiments would go awry. Most frequently, there was awful smoke, but sometimes there was a fire, and once in a great while, there'd be a terrific explosion. It was wrong of me to wish for excitement, but I do love a good explosion.

The warm mugginess made my heavy skirts and petticoats unbearable. My Cousin was out investigating a string of thefts, though Scotland Yard was adamant that the crimes were unconnected. Not having that proof that would demonstrate his superiority put him into a bleak, distracted mood, but Sherlock forgave them their obtuseness because he himself could not yet positively gainsay them.

As a result, two-thirds of our little household was quite vexed, and the only one who was cheerful was Mrs. Hudson. Her obstinately pleasant demeanor was an affront to my pettishness, from across the whole length of the house.

There was a horrific pounding on the door, such that at first I thought it was the rumble of sudden thunder. I jumped up, glanced out the window, and my heart contracted painfully: I recognized all four figures. Doctor Watson supported a bleeding and unconscious youth, his medical bag fallen by his feet, while two other young men shouted and knocked.

The maid answered, and falling into my role, I gathered up my books and pencils and papers and scuttled off to the far side of the sitting room to await the moment when an Ordinary girl would be aware that something was badly amiss. Then crying, "What is the matter?" I raced to the top of the stairs and stopped, my fist to my mouth.

I watched as the good doctor stripped off his coat and put it under the unconscious lad's head. As he did so, the others were not idle: The maid looked as though she would faint, until Doctor Watson barked an order for hot water and clean rags. The second young man went to help her, and the last boy, covered in blood as well, stood wringing his hands, wheezing and coughing, moving from one foot to the other in his dismay.

I fancied that I saw the doctor as the military officer he had once been, and no longer a London gentleman. He was not tall, but very vital, and the ease with which he arranged the prone lad showed that he retained the strength of a younger man. If the vicissitudes of war had contributed to the premature graying of his light hair, his training also gave him an air of calm yet intense focus, which reassured me as he examined the boy, searching for deep wounds. I held my breath until he sat back and grunted with satisfaction. He rummaged through his medical bag, emerging with a surgeon's needle and suture as the maid and lad returned with the water and bandages.

Cousin Sherlock appeared from behind me, his hair damp-dark and sleeked back, a little disheveled. His long face was scrubbed clean of makeup, and the hair at his temples was artfully colored so that he appeared to be older. The carelessly tied sash on his dressing gown, the bulge in the sleeves that indicated his shirtsleeves were still rolled up, and his crooked collar were more than enough clues for me: My Cousin had come in through the back way, from an investigation, in a disguise that he'd shed too rapidly. The look on his face was mixed confusion and alarm, a combination I'd not seen him display before. He glanced down the stairs, then at me. I indicated his various untidinesses, and he adjusted them before he made a deliberate noise and caught the eye of his old friend.

Doctor Watson nodded to him and kept on with his work. The two conscious boys noticed me for the first time.

"Amelia, go to your room. This is nothing for you to see," my Cousin said sternly, an actor now intent on his role. He raced past me and down the stairs, his long legs moving so quickly that he seemed in danger of getting them tangled up in his dressing gown.

I, of course, went to the curtained recess where I might hear anything in the sitting room and most of downstairs, by virtue of an accommodating system of listening tubes. I kept a tight rein on my emotions—such an enormous quantity of blood!—and concentrated on what transpired below.

Mrs. Hudson appeared then and cried aloud at the sight of the dirtied and bloodied boys, the doctor, and the unconscious lad in her house. Dark-haired, trim of form, and an attractive young widow, Mrs. Hudson had the Scotswoman's hatred of disorder.

"Mrs. Hudson, we will no doubt do less harm to the kitchen flags than to your hallway parquet," Sherlock said. "Perhaps we could remove there and see to Tommy more comfortably?"

Mrs. Hudson said, "Och, Emily, run quick and warn Cook!" In her brisk directness, Mrs. H. almost echoed Doctor Watson's commanding manner; the maid scurried off, followed by the doctor and Sherlock, carrying the unconscious boy.

I stole down the stairs, keeping close to the walls so that I might observe the kitchen better and possibly help.

"It ain't just Tommy," one of them gasped. I recognized Jack Cooper's ginger hair and chronic cough, exacerbated by his exertions. Jack lowered his head, putting his hands on his knees, panting with exhaustion. "It's Billy, sir. Billy Wiggins."

Cousin Sherlock wheeled on him. "What about Wiggins?"

"'E's gone, Mr. 'olmes!" He looked up, and I saw his pug nose was bleeding steadily. He moved as if his ankle were tender. "The men what done for us—they—ahem—took 'im!"

A rush of voices and only a cry from Doctor Watson, not minding he was not in his own consulting room, but his friend's kitchen—"A little quiet, please!"—was enough to quell them.

Sherlock said hastily, "I believe I know something of this, Jack. Once we know Tommy will survive, we will discuss what you know about Wiggins and his abductors."

My eyes were only for the young man on the table, Thomas Turner. Doctor Watson worked busily. He seemed suddenly at a loss and looked up. "He has lost too much blood—I fear—"

Sherlock caught my eye and winked; he glanced across the room.

Mrs. Hudson nodded in response.

Tommy moaned and then went limp.

I gasped loudly, taking my cue, not needing it.

"Miss Amelia!" Mrs. Hudson said sharply.

All eyes but one pair were on me.

"Whatever are you doing, miss? This is no place for you—"

I cast my eyes down, but saw Sherlock, who had been examining the boy's hand, dart at the vein in his wrist. I saw Tommy's face relax, and my Cousin turned as if just noticing my intrusion.

No one had seen Sherlock Holmes bite Tommy.

Mrs. Hudson all but chased me out. "Miss Amelia, upstairs, immediately, if you please!"

"Yes, Mrs. Hudson." I wobbled a little, as if unnerved. The uninjured, dark-haired boy, Hal Schulz, scowled at me. I quickly retreated, though I wondered angrily why he should be unmarked when Tommy was all but killed.

"Bread and meat for these boys, if you would, Mrs. Hudson," Sherlock said.

Outwardly, she frowned, but I heard her whisper, "I can do a good deal better than that, Cousin."

I resumed my listening post off the sitting room. After a short time, order—such as it could be—was restored. Doctor Watson, reassured he'd done all possible for the injured boys, had given Tommy a sedative to keep him comfortable and asleep. The doctor washed and went to the sitting room, where he sat down to a plate of food that seemed to appear out of nowhere. Once he had wolfed it down—the sudden excitement of his arrival put aside—he settled back in his chair with a brandy and soda.

"Well, Watson," my Cousin said. A small, dry smile played at the corner of his lips. "It's good to see you. As always, you bring an enlivening air to your old rooms."

Doctor Watson, too tired to laugh, merely returned the smile, an acknowledgment of their adventures together. He leaned back with his brandy and soda and—all present needs met—relaxed. "I saw 'em as I turned into Baker Street. I recognized your "Irregulars," and as they were struggling to carry their fellow to your doorstep, I found myself able to attend to 'em even quicker than if you'd called, Holmes."

"It is more than good of you. Not many doctors would trouble themselves over street urchins."

Watson mumbled, "My blushes, Holmes" into his brandy.

"What is the nature of their wounds?" Cousin Sherlock asked.

"The unconscious boy—?"

"Thomas Turner—Tommy."

"He has a broken arm, some very bad bruising on his ribs, and a worrying knock to the back of his head. Badly beaten, and blood loss from a deep knife wound to the shoulder." He glanced up. "The boy can't be fifteen, surely?"

"Nearer eighteen, I think. His small frame is due to malnourishment."

"The other one who was injured, with the freckles and red hair? Has a worrying cough, asthma, I think. I do not know his name."

"Jack Cooper."

"Minor contusions to the head and a slightly sprained ankle. A street scuffle no doubt—he refused to tell me anything. The third lad I recognized from his brown hair and the badly healed scar on his arm— Hal Schulz. He was uninjured. He also said nothing."

Sherlock frowned. "I will speak with them presently. Is that all you observed?" he asked curtly.

"My dear fellow—it was quite enough!" The doctor blotted the sweat on his forehead; now that trouble was passed and he'd done all he could, his efforts took their toll.

"There is something distinctly odd going on in London, Watson. You know the case I've been troubled with?"

"*Cases*—plural, I thought. Have you determined the thefts are unrelated?"

"I have not. There is no geographical pattern to the scenes of the crimes; they are scattered randomly around England and Europe. The objects themselves have no cultural association and were of wildly disparate values. There is no pattern of social connection that binds their owners all together—no common church, no shared club. The one thing in common is that other, more valuable objects—art, jewelry, the usual ornaments of the well-to-do—were left untouched. The foci of the crimes were on specific items. A great deal of planning went into these robberies."

"All of the objects are antiquities," Doctor Watson offered. "They were artifacts taken from museums or heirlooms stolen from well-established families. The necklace with the Star of Bengal ruby, the collection of Japanese *netsuke*, a clay pot from Utah, the Moroccan—"

Sherlock held up a hand; he knew the items in question. "There has been one theft that breaks that pattern, but it is clearly unrelated. Mr. Page of Hertford reported the theft of a painting along with some valuable antique Spanish coins. It became clear to me very soon that he'd staged the burglary himself, to keep the property from the rightful heir. It is no comfort when gentlemen given every advantage in education make the rudimentary mistake of breaking the window glass from *inside* the house."

"No connections, no apparent relationship among them." The doctor poured more brandy and employed the gasogene again. "It is as though it were a puzzle created particularly for you, Holmes."

My Cousin startled and, with a glance at his friend, continued. "I spent the day at my old haunt, the British Museum, speaking with a Professor Emerson, an expert in antiquities. I was walking back to Baker Street, the better to clear my head, when someone ran straight into me. I was so deep in thought that by the time I had collected myself, he had vanished, possibly into a hansom. I feel certain that this incident, the attack on my Irregulars, and my investigation must be connected."

"Well? What did his face, his dress tell you about him?" Doctor Watson asked, after waiting expectantly, though in vain, for more detail.

"Nothing, not a clue. Male, dark clothing, above average height."

Now this was something quite extraordinary, and not just a bit worrying. I frowned, and Doctor Watson had almost the same response, perhaps for different reasons.

"It's unlike you to be so unperceptive, Holmes. Indeed, when *you* are so careless, something strange *is* afoot in London. Or else...look here, old man, I must ask—have you been indulging in that unhealthy pastime of yours?"

A noise of dismissal. "No, Watson. It is fatigue and distraction only."

There was the sound of movement, followed by a brief silence.

"I hope you've found my pulse to be normal, Watson," I heard my Cousin say, with the faintest tinge of annoyance in his voice.

"You're pale, Holmes. You've been burning the candle at both ends."

My Cousin rose suddenly. "I hope you will excuse me. You've come to visit and not only have I imposed on you, but I am very poor company."

It would have been a terrible shock to his readers if they could hear Doctor Watson make nary a protest, make no offer to stay and take notes. "Very good. Tomorrow, then, I'll stop by to check on the boy."

"Thank you. I'm certain Mrs. H. is very put out by all this. She suspects the lads will be as Visigoths and pillage the silver. She fears for the pristine nature of the anti-Macassars."

"Ah, well." The doctor chuckled. "I'll smooth her ruffled feathers as I see myself out."

I knew that Dr. Watson believed Mrs. Hudson didn't approve of the Baker Street Irregulars, as Cousin Sherlock called his army of ragged youths, but that was far from true. She worked hard to hide her affection for them—many of them children, sometimes girls—and used some of the household money to surreptitiously help them and their families. But no respectable lady would want them in her house, and Mrs. Hudson was the very image of respectability.

"Thank you, Watson."

They shook hands. As Doctor Watson's footsteps faded down the carpeted stairs, I followed him.

"Shall I ask the housekeeper to give you some steak and kidney pie, Doctor Watson? She's just finished one for tomorrow's dinner, and I know how you love it."

His demeanor brightened considerably. "What a kind thought! You always know what will cheer me up, Agatha!"

Doctor Watson always got my name wrong. He was so often preoccupied with medical matters and writing up Cousin Sherlock's cases that I didn't like to trouble him about it. He's a lovely, kind gentleman.

I feel sorry for him.

"You've had a trying day," I said. "A long day and your wife out of town, then to find a bloody and beaten lad on the doorstep? A bit of pie for your dinner tomorrow will help make up for your maid's dismal cooking." I trotted down the hall ahead of him.

"How on earth—?" I heard behind me.

It wasn't hard, my deduction, and as a medical man—indeed, as a soldier wary of ambush—he might have reached the same conclusions from the same evidence. But that final step of deduction always seemed just a little beyond him, clever as he was.

He still had his medical bag. If Mrs. Watson had been home, he would have gone straight there to dine. Such a simple observation, and yet...

The doctor made certain that Tommy was comfortable and gave a few instructions to the housekeeper, who looked none too pleased to be given the chore of nursing the boy. Mrs. Hudson had, rather presciently, wrapped up a piece of pie for him and we sent him on his way.

"My Cousin would like to talk to you both," I said to Hal and Jack.

"And we'd like a word wiv him," said Hal, a little ferociously. I looked away.

"It won't take long...ahem...miss," Jack said in a placating fashion. He'd recovered from the earlier excitement, but his chronic coughing persisted.

I led the way to the sitting room. Just before we went in, Hal seized my arm. "You keep away from Tommy, hear?" he hissed. "You're no good for him."

Hal had seen me talking to Tommy once and was not pleased about it.

"Take your hand off me," I said, holding his gaze until he did.

We found Cousin Sherlock seated, deep in thought.

He looked up as we entered. I departed the same way the boys and I had come, down the main hall stairs. I then sneaked up the backstairs to spy again from the curtained recess.

"Beggin' your pardon, Mr. 'olmes, sir, but before you go any furver, we'd like a word." Hal and Jack stood straight as they could, their caps in their hands. Hal was polite enough to my Cousin, I noticed.

"Yes?"

"We...ahem..." Jack started. "We...we want to hire you, like."

"You do, do you?" Sherlock rose from his chair, and indicated two seats opposite him. I could hear amusement in his voice. "Very well, gentlemen, if you'd take a seat, I'd be happy to hear your case."

"We can pay," Jack blurted. "We ain't asking no—ahem...favors, on account of you knowing us."

"We can, Mr. Holmes." Hal stuck out his hand. "If you need more...we...we'll get more. Somehow. Don't you worry."

Sherlock made a show of picking up each coin—three pennies, a dirty shilling, and a shiny new shilling—as if counting them, but it was really to show me.

"They're real enough," Hal said a trifle hotly. "Sir," he added.

"Indeed they are, but you've given me too much. I am already investigating a case I believe to be connected with this." He picked out the three pennies, leaving the two shillings behind. I had no doubt it was a great deal to the two boys, but any of the Irregulars would have sacked Rome to help Billy, and Sherlock's refusing any payment would have been an insult to their pride.

"Thank you, gentlemen. Now, pray, sit and tell me your problem."

"It's about Billy, sir," Jack said. "Billy Wiggins."

"As you've said. Please start from the beginning."

"Not much to tell, Mr. 'olmes, sir," Jack started. "We come back to our squat, Billy, Tommy, and me, and was set upon. Three big blokes, faces covered. They wanted Billy, that's sure. When they went after him, we fought back."

"Fought back hard," Hal said. "A proper barney."

"I went down," Jack continued. "and hit me 'ead. Don't know how long I was out."

"That's when I found them," Hal said. "I came in later, found Jack just coming 'round, Tommy out cold, and Wiggins gone. Blood all over. We got Tommy here, fast as we could, sir. Din't know what else to do, Mr. Holmes, sir."

Sherlock insisted they describe the scene over and over, until he was certain he knew all they knew. By the time they were done, I also knew the location and position of Tommy's prone body, where they'd walked, the number of men who'd barged in, and how they were dressed.

"We'll go now," Sherlock said. "I'll see the place myself. Two minutes, gentlemen."

He went by me, and I followed into his room as he dressed to go out. "You heard all?"

"Yes. Let me come with you!"

As soon as the words were out of my mouth, I regretted them. "Impossible. The lads would never understand, and I don't have time to make them. Prepare for action here, and consider the boys' story while I'm away, a mental exercise. Do you understand me?"

"I do, sir—only...who do you think beat Tommy? And why—" My interest in Tommy should not be so obvious, so I went on. "Where do you think Wiggins is? What if—"

I saw Cousin Sherlock's brow furrow and knew I'd been too hasty, too eager in my curiosity. "Amelia, so many questions, and the wrong ones. Why don't you attend to your dollhouse?"

"But Sherlock, I'm far too old—!"

"Amelia."

I was so angry, I very nearly told him to play with his own dollhouse, but when he took that tone, there was no more debating the matter. My shoulders slumped; I wanted to help—I didn't want to be stuck away in my room. "What will I need?"

"Mrs. Hudson will see you right." He relented as he pulled on his coat and gave me the barest hint of a smile, which almost made me press my protests. A slight narrowing of his eyes convinced me to save his goodwill against another time. "I'll be back shortly."

"Yes, Cousin."

I hurried to the kitchen and Mrs. Hudson's office. On my way in, I peeped in at the boys: Hal glared at me again. Jack never noticed me; he was patting Tommy's hand nervously.

Mrs. Hudson was just outside her office, discussing fine metalworking with the locksmith. Their discussion concluded, she gave him some money in exchange for a small package.

Lock picks, I wondered? No, it was too large a package for that.

Giving instructions to the housekeeper, Mrs. Hudson invited me into her office, shut the door, and from a locked cupboard, handed me a small basket.

"Amelia, dear, I thought you'd be wanting these," she said.

"Was that the Sight, Cousin Martha?" I preferred to call my Family by their true names when I could do so privately. As an orphan, I clung to my more distant relations, and they to me.

And being that we were all Fangborn and given special powers to protect Ordinary mankind from evil, our Family was all the more important to us. If you could heal wounds or detect truth or suggest a new truth, like Cousin Sherlock, who was a vampire, or if you could change into a wolf's shape and track down evildoers, like me, you would understand. But if you had no such knowledge of our lofty goals, you might be terrified. So we kept to ourselves and fought evil secretly.

The current craze for thrilling and fantastic literature amused me. What have we to do with walking corpses who can only be held in their grave by stakes driven through their hearts? We Fangborn are never wrong in detecting evil—in a thousand cases, I am not aware that I have ever used my powers on the wrong side. We cannot leave a case, once we undertake it, but are like racing engines connected to a powerful machinery for good.

"Och, nae, not the Sight. It's knowing you, and knowing Sherlock Holmes's habits." Martha laughed as she arranged a few small articles of clothing carefully over the top of the basket; it now looked as though I had a small pile of plain mending to do. "Not such a grand leap of guessery and deduction or what you will call it. There's a bookmark to the page, my dear, and do be careful with the blood. It stains."

I nodded, took the basket, and hastened to her office door. "Slowly, Amelia. Practice stealth, indoors!"

I would practice speed *and* stealth, I decided stubbornly, as I shut the door behind me. For if Cousin Martha couldn't hear me, she couldn't rebuke me for running in the house. I did reasonably well, for I startled the maid of all work on the stairs.

"Oh, miss!"

"I'm sorry, Emily."

"You ought to walk like a young lady," she reproved. "What with you coming out in two years."

Technically, I was older than she, but looked about sixteen. Those of us born to the Fangborn tend to mature more slowly, as if to make up for our great longevity, but I had "debuted" in my own society and was completing my training outside the safety of the Fangborn's secret academies, among the Ordinary population.

"Running about, and you seeing that awful sight in the hallway?" She sighed. "But Mr. Holmes will have his urchins upstairs and down, like a plague. Do you want me to bring you some warm milk?"

She had an air of disgust and concern, as if the mere presence of poor boys was a cause for distress.

"No, thank you, Emily."

"Then let me be about my work, so I can go to bed. And no more *running*, if you please, miss!"

Acting like a girl growing to a lady was my disguise. "I can walk very nicely, when I please." And I stuck my nose high in the air, made my back ramrod straight, and took the most mincing of steps up the stairs.

Emily couldn't help giggling. "It's no way for a young lady to behave, Miss Amelia."

Her laughter told me my imitation of an immature Ordinary girl had succeeded. "I am doing my best, I assure you."

I liked Emily, I thought as I climbed to my room, but there was no use cultivating a true friendship with her. She'd never allow it, her own sense of propriety regarding the classes far exceeded my own.

I shut the door behind me and set the basket down.

Moving to the part of the room most distant from the rest of the house, I burst into tears, so quietly, it was barely detectable even to me.

Tommy and I were terribly in love.

It had started off innocently enough. I saw him outside the Old Adelphi where he was reading the bill. I hadn't known Tommy could read, but managed to hide my surprise and greeted him. He spoke nervously to me at first, knowing who I was, then warmed as we chatted about theater.

He'd been living with his grandfather, who'd recently died. Rather than live with distant relations in Penzance, he'd run off to London.

The distant relations must have been unspeakable if these unkind streets proved more attractive.

Over the months our friendship had developed. He had been educated at home, for a while, and we shared many interests.

And he, too, was a kind of protégé of Sherlock Holmes, though he had no idea how extensively my training mirrored his own.

This was one of the reasons I was so in favor of Introducing ourselves to the Ordinary world. I envisioned a utopia, where humans were safe from evil, carefully guarded, and familiar with us. I believed that in doing so, there was a good chance that together with Ordinary humans, we Fangborn could remove the threat of war, forever. This was particularly important, as Cousin Mycroft had foretold conflict on an unheard-of scale within the coming century.

There would be no more lies. To anyone. No need to hide, no need to deceive those closest to us.

The thought of Tommy unconscious, injured, and me unable to do anything—I did not often regret my birth to the wolfish side of the Family, but I could not heal him as Sherlock, a vampire, could.

But there. Tommy was safe now, in the capable hands of Doctor Watson *and* Cousin Sherlock. If I was to keep our mutual friend Billy safe, I would have to apply myself as strictly as my Cousin to the case.

The notion that I might be able to save Billy with some observation of my own and make myself admirable in Tommy's eyes was perhaps unworthy, and I set it aside.

I pulled out the volume of housekeeping records from the basket. A little embroidered tag marked the page near the end of the small book, only a few blank pages left. The heading read "William Wiggins, Harold Schulz, John Cooper, and Thomas Turner," and on the page was a plan of the room where the lads had been living recently.

Mrs. Martha Hudson, née de Walden, kept plans of the many properties she owned; this was the fiftieth volume so far. In addition to the houses on Baker Street and her other properties, she kept and maintained a number of bolt-holes across London for use by Sherlock, me, or any member of our Family. Tracking and fighting evil sometimes required a safe place to recover, to change one's appearance, or simply to disappear.

The ink was still dark and fresh on this page. The four friends didn't have a fixed abode. This room, a sort of temporary camp in an empty house, was a luxury for them.

With many of the plans, there were fine sheets of tracing paper, showing the observations we'd made and recorded in the course of our investigations. Accordingly, I traced the room's dimensions on another piece of paper, then pulled the dollhouse furniture from the basket. Studying the page, I arranged the furniture as the lads had described. I took one small male doll, wonderfully articulated, and put it on the floor to show where Tommy had been found, according to Hal and Jack. I also took a tiny eyedropper, uncorked a small brown bottle, and again, carefully consulting the drawing, added small amounts to a fine brush, and delicately re-created the bloodstains. I consulted my memory of the boys' descriptions: there had been no unusual odors, no disturbances noticed by the neighbors, nothing awry but two boys beaten and one kidnapped.

Most of the blood must be Tommy's, I decided, because he lay there the longest and had the worst wounds of the boys. I hated the idea but put my affection for him out of my mind, the better to help him now. The roster of unhappy outcomes was already far too extensive.

An hour later, Sherlock returned. He'd learned nothing to add to what Jack and Hal had told us. "But neither one of them is telling the entire truth. I could not question them more deeply, as several other of the Irregulars appeared."

"I suppose it would not be unusual for those who live such lives to have secrets," I mused, thinking that Hal had kept my—or rather, Tommy's—secret.

"Perhaps not, but I will have to speak with one under vampiric compulsion. Oddly, I believe I have another part of the puzzle, but as yet, no notion as to how they fit. You heard me mention to Doctor Watson that someone nearly knocked me over earlier?"

I indicated my assent.

"Although I admit that I observed less than I would have liked, I immediately identified the coat and hat. They were from the bolt-hole near the museum, in Russell Square. There is only one other living human being who knows about it, too, and he had the strictest orders to use it only at the utmost necessity. That was young Wiggins. It was...a kind of test for him. You know to what I refer?"

I did. Cousin Sherlock was testing, very carefully, a plan by which we might Introduce ourselves to Ordinary mankind. It was only because he was so well respected among our Family that he was given license to explore whether he could take young people—those denizens of the street with no kin but skilled in discreet movement, theft, and survival—and trust them with our secrets. He must have been very sure of Wiggins, because our refuges are terribly important. Sherlock's notion was that, with certain unusually clever humans, those willing to think beyond the confines of society and who were academically or physically talented, we might form a kind of extraordinary league, Fangborn and Ordinary together. They would be the thin end of the wedge in our quest to Introduce ourselves to Ordinary humans. To my Cousin, it was another experiment, but of sociology or anthropology, rather than chemistry.

"Did you truly not recognize the person who bumped into you?" I asked hesitantly. "I notice you do not use 'gentleman' or 'lady.'"

"Only the stolen clothes."

I brought up the question I feared. "But *nothing* else?"

"Nothing else. It is fatigue, as I told Watson."

This was bad. Vampires are prone to exhaustion if they do not rest and get enough sun, which acts as a kind of fuel for them. So although it was possible that Cousin Sherlock was weak from exertion and too many nighttime investigations, it was unlikely that it would reduce his famous mental acuity so profoundly.

I nodded, making a note to ask Cousin Martha if he was eating properly. "And we must assume that the bolt-hole is found? Has Wiggins betrayed us, his abduction a ruse?"

"Wiggins is sea-green incorruptible," Sherlock said with some asperity. "I believe much worse than that, Amelia. Wiggins has been taken prisoner because of us. Me, specifically."

"What!"

"I believe Wiggins has been followed because of his connection to me. When he escaped his captors at the squat—or perhaps they let him escape—he sought refuge at the bolt-hole, as I instructed him. He was followed and the bolt-hole revealed, along with more of my operation."

Cousin Sherlock's face was hard and his mien grim. "I only hope for the kidnapper's sake that Wiggins lives still."

"What now?" If Sherlock was being followed, targeted, it was possible the entire Family was in danger, and therefore countless Ordinary lives at stake.

"We have an appointment, me in particular, you in the shadows. Later this evening. The disguised person, in addition to his clothing, left me an even more obvious message, shoved into my pocket." Here Cousin Sherlock looked abashed. "I was so deep in thought that I never noticed the note being placed there. An unforgivable offense on my part."

I could only stare. There was something desperately wrong, and I could no longer politely avoid it. "Cousin! It must be...did you detect the presence of black hellebore or any of the other things that may kill or weaken us?"

"I did not, and as you yourself know"—he nodded toward his bubbling experiment on the table—"I have conducted a comprehensive study of them and their effect on us."

"On *you*, you mean," I said, glancing at the battered syringe case on the mantel. "Perhaps you've reached the limit of what you can safely tolerate?"

"I think I know myself well enough, Amelia Vernet." To prove it, he bared his wrist and summoned his other self. His face shifted to a serpentine aspect, his fine brow and high cheekbones now showing pale-greenish scales, his hawk-like nose diminishing to a broad bump, his teeth extending to fangs. He bit into his own wrist, tasting the blood.

"I detect nothing that I know harms us," he said, turning back. He proffered his wrist.

I sniffed delicately. I am no vampire, but a wolf-woman, and know the scent of blood in many forms. I delicately lapped at the blood and frowned. My Cousin was correct, in that I could not detect any familiar toxins. However, Sherlock's blood was not the same as it usually was.

The difference might have been created by one of the many tests he made upon himself. My Cousin was Sherlock Holmes; he knows himself as no one else does. "I should not have doubted you."

He waved a hand, dismissing the notion. "We must always have proof. And so to business. The meeting is in two hours at the bolt-hole. You and I shall go, in disguise. Be ready to assist me or track the kidnapper, if necessary. I have a rather dreadful notion that this goes far deeper than young Wiggins putting his fist into the wrong pocket." Sherlock shook his head. "He's too good a thief for that."

"And Doctor Watson?"

"I think it best to leave the doctor to his ill-kept home this evening. I heard you were kind enough to offer him some pie to soften the lack of domestic comforts. And now—the results of your dollhouse study."

I handed him my drawing and notes. He observed the model I'd prepared for him, comparing it with his own deductions; he'd long been able to construct a sort of mental dollhouse to review the facts of a crime.

We agreed in every particular. We assumed disguises—a tradesman and his son—and began on our way to the Russell Square bolt-hole to meet Wiggins' captor.

We discussed the case along the way but made no progress until we walked past a shuttered butcher's shop. The smell of animal blood was heavy on the air.

"Wait!" The animal blood, and the memory of tasting Sherlock's blood, jarred a memory loose. An odor not quite right. "When I was there, at the room, two weeks ago—"

Sherlock's keen eyes turned to me. "What precisely were you doing in the boy's squat?"

I don't think Cousin Sherlock was angry, and yet I hesitated. He'd already suspected I was hiding something when I'd asked too quickly to accompany him earlier.

"If you were there to copulate or drink or take opium or anything else, I do not care," he said with some impatience. "No, that is not true. It is, rather, of no consequence. You have proven yourself trustworthy and reliable; I do not fear for your moral being. I seek context, that is all."

I nodded. "I was there in costume, as a street urchin, a boy, testing my disguise."

The final test of a good disguise was to appear in front of friends unrecognized. It was a variation on the one I used now, which had received no criticism from my meticulous Cousin.

"They did not know it was me," I said. I'd been scraping acquaintance with the Irregulars in disguise, hoping I could find my way with them to Sherlock's sitting room. Perhaps I would even fool him. "They offered to show me a clasp knife they'd found, and I could not have refused without raising suspicions, especially as I'd earlier admitted to having no particular plans for the evening."

"How long were you there?"

"Less than a half hour."

"Did you notice anything?"

"At first, I detected only those things one would associate with young men living in the most desperate of circumstances, but just now I remembered…"

He seized on my hesitation. "Yes?"

"I remembered I had noticed a very faint odor, familiar but misplaced. Bath soap. Lavender."

Cousin Sherlock clapped his hands together. "Excellent! And where was this odor the strongest? Was it localized, or was it ambient? It was not there when I arrived—that is certain. My head finally seems to be clearing!"

We stopped, and I tried to visualize the memory. "It was when I first stepped into their room. I realized something was out of place, but then Tommy showed me the knife at that moment, and I was taken away from the thought."

A slight narrowing of Cousin Sherlock's lips spoke volumes: I must do better to fend off distraction. And then a slight shrug: I had not been there on business; there had been no case at that moment; and I was attending to the requirements of my disguise.

But perhaps he suspected that it was Tommy himself who distracted me.

"I believe it was Jack, sir. I noticed it when I was closest to him. It was very weak and only on his side of the room."

"Did you see the soap?"

I opened my eyes, shook my head. "No. So he must have used it only once?"

"Or was hiding it, though I do not know why Billy should not have noticed. Excellent, Cousin Amelia; we shall start by observing young Mr. Cooper."

"But Hal wasn't wounded? Surely that puts some suspicion on him?" I didn't like Hal any better than he liked me, and thought he made a fine suspect.

"Bruises are easily had and make a good protestation of innocence." Sherlock shook his head. "No, Jack is a recent addition to the Irregulars, and based on that, and that shiny new shilling, I believe he was paid by someone to spy on the Irregulars and me. Possibly the Family."

I gasped.

"His spymaster will be someone with wealth and other resources—he knows about me and knows I trust Wiggins. He has an unnecessary niceness about him, and he asked that Jack wash his face and hands before they spoke—with the fine soap. This worries me, Amelia. Every instinct I have tells me that the kidnapping, the spying, and the thefts are all part of a broader, more dangerous plan."

"You believe that the thefts were intended to attract our attention?" I asked. "Or that the artifacts themselves might have something to do with the Fangborn?"

"Both. I just know it."

It was not unusual to hear Sherlock speak of "feeling" or "just knowing." Fangborn instincts, as well as imagination, are to be attended to. He preferred to emphasize deduction and scientific method in examining a case, as it not only gave us fresh eyes for noticing things out of order but also served to instruct Ordinary police detectives by example. This was merely one aspect of Sherlock's plan to teach Ordinary humans skills that would match some of the unusual talents we come by naturally. It would, he declared, one day create a world where humans would not fear the idea of our Fangborn kind, because we would have similar abilities, learned or natural.

"What I did not tell Watson was this: The thefts had one other thing in common. I have not been able to trace any scent at any of the crime scenes. My *nose* has never failed me before, but in each of these cases, it has been my eyes and my brain that revealed any clues I found. It is as though someone were aware of my peculiar powers and was doing his utmost to thwart me."

His eyes grew wide as soon as he said it. "The Order of Nicomedia. It must be."

"How is that possible?" I exclaimed, understanding immediately. The Order had hunted our Family for centuries, believing us demons rather than the guardians we truly were, because of our ferocity and shapeshifting abilities. Sherlock's files were filled with stories of the Order torturing unlucky Fangborn and destroying our homes with such a wanton hatred as to be nearly unfathomable. "You've said they were not well organized—because of this, we have been able to hide ourselves and our abilities for generations! They know of us, but surely...never so much as you suggest!"

"I found no toxins of the sort we know are dangerous to us," he murmured. "In my researches, both botanical and chemical, I've found nothing else that could possibly have that effect, and I don't believe the Order, with their crude research, has either. And yet, there must be such a thing, to confound me so. Amelia," he said, now taking notice of me again, "I believe we have found the answer!"

"What answer, Cousin?"

"That one constant in our equation: My distracted mind. It is the thread that we must follow to the end."

He took as much satisfaction in that very slender thread as if he'd already solved the case.

Satisfaction was the furthest thing from my mind. If Sherlock was correct, there was a new, dire danger to the Family. If a new foe had discovered our existence, and worse, had found the means of distracting us so thoroughly, then not only the short-term safety of the Ordinary populace but also the future of everything we worked for—Introduction and worldwide peace—was threatened.

"We must be very careful, now, Amelia. We dare not make one misstep." Cousin Sherlock's brow was deeply creased now, and anger flashed in his eyes.

With his anger, I saw that spark of interest that meant Sherlock was warming to the investigation. With that, we found our way to the Russell Square bolt-hole.

This bolt-hole was nothing but the most basic of hiding places. A small room—equipped with water for washing, disguises, and food—hidden by means of a false wall in the back of a shop. Ordinarily, the brick-covered door was opened by a triggering mechanism...

...but the door was already ajar.

We entered cautiously and found Jack Cooper lying on a pile of wigs and torn clothing, quite dead.

Sherlock ascertained that the secret cupboard with the weapons had not been found. "They came here, they found nothing of note, and they killed Jack."

I felt quite giddy at the sight of the lifeless Jack and barely attended to my Cousin's words.

Sherlock tried to rally his thoughts. "They didn't find anything—and yet we were not followed, no one is watching us now...the room is situated so that it is impossible to be observed..."

I realized it a moment sooner, having been under its influence less than my Cousin. "We must go out into the fresh air—"

"Yes, yes, they've brought us here, left the chemical compound about to slow us..."

We staggered outside and shortly our heads cleared.

"Billy is not here—Amelia!" My Cousin seemed much more like his usual self. "It is not us that they are looking for. They seek our friends, the Ordinary men and women of our acquaintance! Watson is in danger. I will go to him; you return to Baker Street and warn Martha to guard the household!"

Without waiting for an answer, he sprinted off toward the doctor's home.

I was frozen with the horror of that notion. Hal had been right: my Family and I were responsible for Tommy's injuries.

I sprang, moving as quickly as I could for Baker Street, but found my steps lagging when I passed one of the lecture halls of University College. I was slowed by the scent of an evildoer, rank and putrid. Somewhere behind that smell—that no perfume could hide—was a hint of lavender bath soap.

I had Jack's murderer.

What was so astonishing was that the man—I could not call him a gentleman, no matter his rank—entered the lecture hall.

I was terribly curious, for what could a murderer and kidnapper want with a presentation on the binomial equation?

I was able to watch him, and keep my hackles down, as he sat near the back; I spied from the open doorway. Giving only half an ear to the speaker—a skinny, older, cerebral-looking fellow who not only was incomprehensible in his mathematics but also had an off-putting habit of swaying his head side to side, a symptom, perhaps, of some nervous disorder—I noticed that my quarry had no particular interest in the lecture. Perhaps he'd only come in to get warm, or perhaps he was scouting out some new victim.

As soon as the lecture concluded, he left, and I followed him outside. He was nearly as slick as I was, quick and quiet, but he had no hesitation in shouldering someone out of the way when he thought he would be unobserved or unchallenged. As I followed him to an empty academic office, I suspected that he was the man who had bumped into Sherlock. There was no way any Fangborn, much less Cousin Sherlock, could have missed the unmistakable odor of evil that followed this man.

Whatever chemical had been used on us was very strong. Very dangerous.

A lamp was lit, and I hid in the anteroom. While I'd been caught up in my thoughts, the lecturer had entered from another doorway, and a conversation begun.

"—these creatures? And of what interest are they to this Order of...whatever you call it, Professor?"

"The Order of Nicomedia."

My blood froze at the words. Our Family's most storied enemies, dedicated to finding and destroying us. The sound of the lecturer's voice, cultured, low, suggesting deep water and the darkness beneath and his interest in the Order's goals, terrified me. I felt in him an inhuman malice.

"The Order? Pack of loonies, the ones I saw," my quarry said dismissively.

A sound of disagreement. "There are schemes to be found everywhere, Moran. I keep my ears and my mind open to any advantage

I might take. Even 'loonies,' as you call them, may present an opportunity, so when I first heard about the Order, I assumed another crackpot spiritualist group. But such may yield money or information or access. Then they proved to me, Moran—proved beyond a shadow of a doubt—that these creatures—these *Fangborn*—exist. More than that, they have an ancient pedigree, and there are objects that may enhance their strength. The excavations at Woodbridge yielded one such object, the Order claims. I've acquired many of these artifacts, and if they are the source of Fangborn abilities, I shall crack their code—and then crack *them*."

Another mumbling noise, and I knew my quarry expressed doubt. I strained to hear more closely. I could not bear the thought that this "professor" should turn his malignant attention and mathematical mind to "cracking" us.

"I understand your hesitation, however carefully phrased," came the sarcastic reply. "But I assure you—*I* assure you—that it is a mathematical certainty. And it explains much. There is not only money to be gained, Moran, but power beyond your wildest imaginings. I mean to have it. A former colleague of mine, from that dusty little so-called university I fled, used to mumble about such things as the Order does. I thought him mad, but now I believe I shall pay him a visit to renew acquaintance and to enlighten me further.

"These...creatures, these vampires and wolf-men, are subject to pain and death, and their prodigious senses can be baffled. I myself made several important adjustments to the crude concoction of black hellebore that the Order is using to disable these Fangborn. My formula is already far superior, for though it does not last as long, it is less detectable and causes confusion. It sometimes disguises the presence of their enemies—though why this is true I must study further. I'll keep my research to myself, for why give the Order any advantage?"

I shuddered. No wonder Sherlock had been so addled lately, with the use of this man's formula. Indeed, my true nature called for me to attack the two men, remove them from the face of God's green earth, but something told me to wait. Not only was it Cousin Sherlock's insistence that we always leave proof that Ordinary police might be able to follow logically—if only they would look!—but there was also something else bidding me, *Wait, stay just a moment…* That in itself was so unusual, I almost missed the next sentence.

"Now, things are settled at Baker Street?"

My heart thudded at the name—they knew where we lived? How did they—?

"Seven men down there soon, if not already."

"I told you to bring twenty."

"And how am I supposed to move a crowd through the center of London? Not a bit conspicuous that—no, sir. No, I sent my seven best."

"You should have gone yourself."

"Ah, but then I wouldn't have had the chance to see your latest acquisition, Professor."

"If you must, Moran." The professor unrolled a long bundle of burlap. A heavy thump, then a hissing intake of breath. I raised my head and saw a sword.

More proof that I'd found our thieves.

Like the other stolen items, it was old, ancient. The blade was fine and straight, just under three feet long, iron, and might have predated the Romans: It was truly a blade of Albion. Despite its obvious antiquity, I could still see a keen edge. When the professor held it up by its blade—the fool!—I saw the hilts were filled with a red enameling in a geometric pattern that reminded me of intricate paving bricks. The handle was breathtaking; I could not see well, but there was some sort of cross set into the end of the pommel.

I had to take it from them. I knew, as surely as I was born, that they must not keep this object and that this was what kept me lingering here.

"Very curious; you see, a medieval reliquary cross has been incorporated into the original Anglo-Saxon weapon. I wonder if that is their doing or some unknowing human's."

Another mumbled reply.

"Moran, I assure you. These are not human beings we are dealing with."

I had to stop them. I decided to go for the older one first...no—the one who had followed him seemed much more dangerous. But the other one was the brains...Far better to take him out...

Even as I realized that I was dithering to an unconscionable, unprecedented degree, I heard the noise behind me. Several men—how had I not detected their arrival?

They saw me at almost the same moment, and I cursed my foolishness. The professor had guarded his office with the same chemical compound he'd used in the bolt-hole! It was now acting on me, and because it did not have the sickening odor of the hellebore concoctions I recognized, it was far more insidious.

"What you doing in here, boy?"

At least my disguise still held. In my present uncertain state, I knew only two things. I needed to get out of here as soon as possible because my fighting skills and mental skills were utterly compromised.

And I needed to take the sword with me.

I feinted, making as if I'd dart past them, but then turned and barreled through the open door. I halted; the door the professor had used was blocked by his desk. Moran, the one I'd followed, immediately produced a pistol. The professor looked surprised, but only for a moment, and then his face cleared as he stared at me. "Ah. Not a lad at all."

The other said, "What do you mean, Professor?"

"I can detect the merest trace of theatrical gum. And the clothing hides much, but those are most certainly the hands of a girl."

I was surrounded now, three men behind me, two in front of me. Presumably, the pistol was not the only weapon. The smallest of the men outweighed me by thirty pounds.

Perhaps if I'd been more alert, I would have denied it, said I was lost, or simply told them to sod off. But instead, I did the worst thing possible and remained silent.

The professor, oddly, grinned at me. Then, as if something were not as he expected, he frowned and furrowed his forehead. He continued that odd motion of his head as he spoke: "Too small for a man, far too small for Holmes. The law of conservation of mass must hold; Lavoisier and Lomonov tell me this. So...who are you?" His eyes flicked over me. "Female, small, and if the other information is correct"—he pulled the wig from my head—"red hair and green eyes."

I growled. I was right; I didn't like him studying me so. His gaze was dissecting and merciless.

"Ah...my informant tells me of three of your kind in Baker Street. Not old enough, or if I may be so bold, large enough to be the formidable Mrs. Hudson. She's the one we want; our informant in the Order says she's the one with the location of all the Fangborn in the

Southeast. I wonder: Is hers a tartan pelt, the doughty Scot that she is? If not Martha Hudson, you must be the girl."

He didn't know Cousin Martha was an oracle. That was something, I suppose, but he knew entirely too much.

He drew something from his pocket. I did not wait to see if it was a gun.

Thinking how much I wanted, *needed*, to take the sword from them, my head cleared. I let myself sag and began to snivel. When Moran's pistol dipped, ever so slightly, I leaped onto the long oak table and somersaulted, snatching up the sword in its wrappings. I lunged forward; the Professor seized my arm. I raked my nails across his face. He screamed and released me. I threw myself at the window in just the manner I'd been taught.

I was lucky; it broke under my weight. I felt the glass tear at my disguise, and timing the act as best I could, Turned halfway through my fall. It wouldn't have done to Turn into a wolf-woman in front of so many who might not know as much as the Professor.

I hit the ground in my walking-wolf form, still feeling the pain of the glass and wood cutting me. No matter; I'd heal quickly. And now out of the room—and away from that horrible chemical compound— my head cleared even more.

I staggered up, and ran fast as I could, zigzagging through the streets, following a path no man could follow.

I ran with a kind of elation, an exaltation of the mind. This was the best part of my life. Dangerous, yes; violently fatal, inevitably. And yet, these moments where I could—*must*—throw off the shackles and conventions of Ordinary life were splendid, violent, wild, and joyful.

Then my nose picked out a familiar scent from the mélange of city dirt, horse droppings, garbage, and coal smoke: I detected Cousin Sherlock's tracks. He'd been here very recently, and with Doctor Watson. He must have reached the same conclusion that it was Cousin Martha and the Baker Street house that were threatened, using logic where I had learned by spying. I followed his trail, which led to Regent's Park just to the east of Baker Street.

As his scent grew stronger, so did the foul odor of men up to no good. Moran's men were gathering, in cover of the park's shadows, to descend on 221 Baker Street.

I ran faster—too fast to be seen. All that mattered was that I stop the army of thugs raised against the stronghold and stalwarts of my Fangborn Family.

I scaled the wrought iron fence with little effort and no noise at all. Cousin Martha would be proud of me: fast *and* stealthy. I landed, hid the precious sword under some bushes, and hid myself behind a tree to assess the situation.

My Cousin and the doctor were surrounded by seven men. Moran's shortsightedness had been a critical mistake. I knew that others of the professor's henchmen were on their way to aid them. I had to act quickly.

I pulled my cap down securely over my pointed ears and tied a dirty handkerchief across my face as a mask. It would not completely obscure my changed facial structure, but it would diminish the impact of a lupine jaw and nose. Gloves would only impede my claws, and with any luck I'd be moving too fast for anyone to see them.

I yipped several times to warn Cousin Sherlock that I was nearby and was coming to his aid. This was not the first time we'd used such a code. I vaulted into the fray.

The trick to our work is concealing our presence, so though my powers were greater than those of Ordinary humans, I had to mask the marks of wolf-bite and claw-rake as best I could. We'd spent a great deal of time practicing this, based on the various sorts of wounds found on murder victims. Sherlock had a comprehensive collection of such photographs in one of his many files.

I leaped onto the back of one man, using one claw to slit his throat so that it would look to the uneducated eye—those at Scotland Yard, say—to have been made with a knife.

I felt better as soon as he was dead, and caught up in the spirit of battle, searched for my next adversary. There was a man threatening Doctor Watson, who fought well against him but was clearly tiring. I kicked the man in the back so that he went down, giving the doctor a chance to pull his army pistol from his coat pocket. I kept running, fast and low, so that I could attack the man who was sneaking behind the doctor.

I dispatched that one with a quick twist of his neck, without the doctor's ever knowing he was threatened from two sides.

Show me another young lady who ever had such fun, and all in the service of mankind and the greater good!

A quick glance showed that Sherlock was holding his own in his human form. I noticed he was using boxing, kicking, and baritsu, in his experimental form of hand-to-hand combat designed for use against several opponents at once. He incapacitated two of his attackers, using nonlethal means, and focused on a large brute who had the stink of true evil on him.

It was then that a carriage pulled up with nearly a dozen more of the professor's men on its roof and clinging to its sides.

It had been a long day. We were getting tired and were now badly outnumbered.

I caught my Cousin's eye and nodded; he nodded back. Now there were more important things than being observed in our other selves.

He assumed his snake-man form, his face flattening, his prominent nose and brow receding, to be replaced with a scaled and serpentine aspect. I could see the glitter of his dark eyes and the shine of his fangs. It did not bode well for our enemies.

Two sharp noises, very quick: Sherlock spat toxic venom at his large attacker. The man was under the influence of some drug, because he didn't react to the sight of my Turned Cousin, and he did not seem to feel the poison. Two more cracks, and Sherlock's venom was depleted. He would have to fight with fang and claw the rest of the evening.

Two more men descended on him as the others arrived, fresh and eager to avenge their fallen fellows. They were brought up short by the sight of the strange creature in front of them.

I heard a shout of fear and astonishment. "My God, Holmes—what has become of you?"

I realized what Doctor Watson had seen, possibly not for the first time. Sherlock's soft workman's cap was gone, along with his visible humanity. The doctor saw only that his friend had been replaced by a snake-like beast.

"Believe me, my friend," Sherlock gasped. "I'm still my own man! On your left!"

The doctor, so amazed by the sight of Sherlock Holmes's transformation, had let his guard down and was attacked by the newcomers.

In for a penny, in for a pound. Our disguises were of no use now. I ripped off my mask, which was hot and foul smelling, and began to fight with less finesse than before but with more speed and fury. I sank my teeth into the neck of one of the men, making sure that Doctor Watson understood that I was on his side.

"Good evening, Doctor!" I said after I spat out a mouthful of malefactor.

"Annie's voice, but coming from a ragamuffin dressed as a dog?" he said, astounded. "What is happening?"

"Doctor, I will explain all later—look lively, to your right!" I ran after three men who were retreating, now terrified. I did not think anyone would believe their stories of fighting wolf-boys and long-fanged snake-men, but better to contain them until Sherlock could alter their memories.

I heard a shout: "Leave him to me!"

A figure on the carriage next to the driver—Moran—stood and raised a rifle.

Sherlock's opponent stepped away, out of range.

"Sherlock!" I cried. "By the gate!"

As the words left my mouth, I was shoved aside. I moved to strike back but held: It was the doctor brushing past me, running to his friend's aid.

A shot rang out.

That was when I realized that our grand plan might work, one day. The affection Watson had for Holmes was such that he willingly took

Moran's bullet in the leg for his friend, even when that friend resembled a monster.

I tackled the two closest men, rendering them unconscious. The third required a more permanent solution, and I reached up with both clawed hands and took his throat. I looked back; my Cousin's uncanny reflexes had saved him; he still stood, fighting, side by side with the wounded Watson.

I must reach the carriage. Moran could not be allowed to take another shot. The Baker Street household—indeed, my entire Family—required my last effort.

I tore through the dark of Regent's Park. Luck turned her face on Sherlock just as she turned her back on me. The professor, seeing me advance, screamed, "The little beast is upon us! Shoot now, Moran, or we are dead!"

Moran swung the rifle from Sherlock to me.

I took another three steps, then jumped directly into Moran's sights.

The horses caught a scent of me and, whinnying in panic, ran away, their driver unable to stop them.

I missed Moran. But he also missed me and fell back into his seat with a curse.

I landed on the foot rail of the carriage and slashed out. If not Moran, the professor would do.

He hurled himself out of reach. The carriage had hit a loose cobble, and I was thrown.

Collecting myself, I shook off my hurts. The carriage disappeared, rattling into the night. I turned my sharp eyes toward my Cousin.

All was well; Sherlock was wounded and the doctor was shot, but for now both were alive and safe. I recovered the sword I'd hidden and joined them.

We dispatched those whose evil required it. Sherlock whispered into the ears of the men who were wrongdoers but redeemable. Doctor Watson watched with awe as the detective convinced them that they had been at a brawl at a music hall and should never speak of it.

Sherlock turned back to Watson and resumed his human form. The wounds he'd sustained while fighting in that form remained; the wounds he'd received while in snake form were no longer visible.

"My friend, you have many questions, and I will explain all to you. But we need to make haste to Baker Street before a much greater harm is done! Will you help me a little more this night?"

The doctor was silent for a moment. "This...this is not the first time this has happened, is it?"

"No," my Cousin said simply.

"Now that I see you—again, it appears—there are vague stirrings of memory. I am confused, but I do know this. I am your friend. I believed you remarkable before this...transformation. I will help you now."

"Thank you." Sherlock turned to me. "Our home may be under siege, and it is more than us at stake, Amelia."

I nodded. "Cousin Martha and all the Fangborn in England depend on us."

He nodded in turn, and with Watson's permission, healed the doctor just enough to stop the bleeding.

And then we three ran.

When we arrived home, all was deathly quiet. No lights shone from any of the windows, and I knew that Martha had implemented the "castle protocol." Hidden shutters of iron slid from inside the walls on clockwork springs and gears, locking in place; the fronts were painted to look like curtained windows. I knew all the doors were equally reinforced.

221 Baker Street was now a fortress.

We assembled: I with the ancient sword at the ready; the doctor, pale but steady, with his pistol; and my Cousin, tensed and ready to spring.

We exchanged an anxious glance, and Sherlock produced a key that only the three of us Family had. He inserted the massive key into a cleverly concealed lock, and with a clicking and whirring, the door opened as the iron barricades retracted into the wall.

A tiny red light hovered in midair. Sherlock's breath caught a little, and his mouth twitched.

The entryway was dark. I smelled rough tobacco and human blood, some familiar. My hackles went up.

"It is all right," Sherlock breathed to me. "We're safe now, Amelia."

"How can it be?" I hissed back. "I smell—"

"Blood, yes. Trust me."

"Who's there?" a deep, booming male voice demanded. "Who dares?"

"One who has every right," Sherlock said, sagging a little with relief. "Brother Mycroft, will you give the countersign?"

"Enter and be safe; all is well," came the voice, as from a kettledrum in a cavern.

The gaslights flickered on with a hiss. On one side of the hallway, I could see the massive form of Cousin Mycroft sitting in a chair. Directly in front of us was our Mrs. Hudson, with an enormous shotgun of her own modification. Bandoliers weighed down with shells were partially covered by a long driving coat. The servants didn't dare go near her pantry, for fear of expulsion; she occasionally worked on her guns or filled her shells there.

Of course, it was all right. I cursed my fatigue and stupidity, and marveled once again at the quickness of my Cousin's brain. Cousin Martha never would have lit her cigarette if all was not well inside the house.

I hoped one day to be as quick and observant as Sherlock Holmes.

And yet, my other Cousin was armed and ready. She was confident but never would risk anything without full proof. I must find the Latin for "No rest without proof," for it seemed to be our household's motto.

Mycroft carefully disassembled the two components of a dead man's trigger, keeping their chemicals well apart. If he had been slain by the professor's men, our house would fall, and all its Family secrets with it. I did not love explosions so much as to ever want to see this one.

Cousin Martha glanced into a mirror that, with a series of other lenses, reflected the outside situation. It told her we had not been coerced and that all was safe.

She nodded to us, and we entered.

"Well, we've had quite a night," Martha said, matter of factly. "Those thugs had Billy Wiggins and threatened to kill him if I didn't let them in. So I did, closed the doors behind them, shot the one with Billy, and helped the lad away, closing off the hallway with the rest inside."

Hearing that Wiggins was alive, the doctor and Sherlock went to attend him.

"You gassed them?" I asked.

"Indeed, Amelia, I did. And as soon as they were out cold and the gas dispersed, I locked them in the cellar holding room." She spoke with a certain amount of pride in this extraordinary brand of housewifery.

"We took out the rest," I said. "But the two leaders escaped. Cousin Mycroft, sir, how do you come to be here? You seldom leave your haunts at Whitehall."

"When Martha invited me for a late whisky, I knew there would be trouble." He guffawed, and I swore I heard the windows rattling. His voice matched his body, which was necessarily of a size suitable to support his massive head and brain.

Cousin Martha nodded. "A sudden urge to see Mycroft here was so pressing, I realized we all were in danger and needed to close ranks. I paced and paced, inspecting the defenses and our weapons, never easy until I knew he'd arrived. We compared our visions. Then we readied the house for battle."

The two oracles beamed at each other, their abilities similar—to protect their domains—but the scale and emphasis different.

When the Doctor and Sherlock returned, both looked drained. But the Doctor was now free to be curious about the stranger aspects of the evening.

"Holmes, I would not pry for the world—" Watson was saying.

"Whereas I do little else but pry." My Cousin bowed ironically.

"—but you did offer me an explanation, and I confess myself curious. Very curious indeed."

"Doctor Watson, if you would allow me?" Mycroft said. The doctor looked surprised. He had been so concerned first with Mrs. Hudson's strange appearance and then the boys' welfare, he'd barely noticed anything else.

"Certainly, Mr. Holmes. A pleasure to see you again." The doctor extended his hand. "What is required?"

"Only this, sir," Mycroft said as he took the doctor's hand in both of his.

And then was a scene repeated many times since my coming to London and Baker Street: The doctor froze, perfectly safe, as Mycroft psychically communicated the whole, true history of his adventures with Sherlock Holmes. The nature and abilities of the Fangborn. That the only vampire in Sussex was Sherlock, that there was a large, hound-like creature—me—present at the Baskervilles investigation. And on and on, all in but a few moments.

Mycroft finished aloud. "Everyone in this household is part of an experiment. It is even more dangerous and volatile than Sherlock's test tubes and burners because the chemistry that we search for is...unknown. But we must not let that stop us. We four Cousins believe it is necessary that we must Introduce ourselves to the Ordinary populace. We are variously gifted, and Ordinary men have greater and lesser talents, so it's only logical to combine our strengths to improve the world. It is our duty. We are all English, after all."

A small ahem from Cousin Martha.

"Britons, I should say," Sherlock corrected his brother.

Mycroft ignored them both. "As Sherlock works with his young Irregulars, training the unwanted and uneducated—I am doing something similar. I have foreseen that there will be ghastly changes in the coming century, that the gentlemanly way of warfare—if war could ever be called such—will yield to increasingly brutal weapons and tactics. I am creating a governmental information-gathering organization that will use—well, plainly, *criminal* techniques to get the information vital to preventing as much bloodshed as we may."

He paused. "I've had a word in one or two ears about this plan. I have high hopes for a young aristocrat, half-American, name of Churchill. He will listen to me one day, I predict."

The doctor, accepting the information that Mycroft had conveyed to him, aloud and in silence, was deep in thought. He turned to Sherlock. "I must ask you then: What is my part in this?"

"Sir, I have the honor to call you my friend."

"And I yours, sir. But I am no homeless waif, nor am I a…spy." There was obvious distaste in that last word.

"You are exactly the sort of person we believe would be amenable to our cause of peace. An Englishman, through and through; a doctor; a man of science. You are, with the exception of your wife, without any living family now. You know excitement and adventure as a soldier and a gambler; you are loyal and a patriot who understands the need to fight and to sacrifice. You know how to speak to ladies in a way that I do not. Besides being my friend, you are the most perfect confederate I could wish for."

The doctor blushed, but the words were simple truth.

"And you are a writer—your thrilling stories attract a wide audience. New generations of investigators will use their interest in your instructive accounts to improve our methods of detection—I have hopes even for those blockheads at Scotland Yard—and to make us

Fangborn seem less strange if others can do much of what we can by logic rather than enhanced senses."

John Watson nodded, slowly. "And now you've told me all this."

My Cousin nodded. "I have. So I must ask you: Do you wish to remember this night? Or do you wish to continue as you were?"

"Every time, you must ask me this question, Holmes," the doctor said after a moment, smoothing his mustache with a finger and concentrating, "I must say exactly the same thing, must I not, my friend? If I have no memory of these strange events, I have my abiding affection and admiration for you. The inspectors at Scotland Yard are rightly in awe of you, so I know none of this is a lie. I am no philosopher; my science is a workman-like art, so me knowing does neither you nor your family any good. And worse, it may make me a liability, like young Wiggins."

"No liability, never, you or he," Sherlock demurred. "But yes, it is dangerous for you to know."

I thought with guilt and fear of Tommy's brush with death and the cause of that.

"And we would be vulnerable to those—the Order?—who wish you harm." The doctor shook his head. "Pray, take 'em away, the particulars of this case, and ease my mind. But I have one request."

"Name it."

"Let me help you again, if I can be of service. I may not remember everything precisely, but I know this. I feel quite rejuvenated after we've worked on a case together. I am a better man and a better doctor for it."

"It is the same request you make every time, and I am delighted to honor it. There is no man in England—in the *world*—I trust more and whose respect I crave more than yours. And if there is ever a time when we are able to put our little plan into action, I promise you: You will be the first to know. I owe you that, and you deserve that honor—yes, even ahead of the queen herself!"

Cousin Sherlock does have a flair for the dramatic.

Then he said, "You have my secrets, Doctor. Keep them well."

With that, Cousin Sherlock shook Doctor Watson's hand. He then took him by the shoulders and made as if to salute him in the French manner. Startled, as he was every time, the doctor said, "Oh, I say, Holmes!" But rather than kissing him on each cheek, Sherlock bit the doctor on the neck.

I knew he employed the venom that would cause Watson to forget, heal his wounds, and make him suggestible to the story we would give him, spiced with as much truth as was safe for us all.

"Mycroft, if you would be so kind as to oblige John Watson in his request?"

Mycroft again took Watson's hand, and closing his eyes, once again altered our history together. Mycroft and I vanished from this one; Billy's kidnapping and the assaults on the Irregulars were elided, too; and the thefts were maintained to be the work of a gang with a taste for antiquities. The bullet wound in the Doctor's leg was transformed into a second jezail bullet, another relic of his military service.

Doctor Watson sighed deeply, contentedly. His eyes fluttered open, and he started suddenly. "My apologies, Holmes. I'm asleep on my feet. Is there any chance my old room is free?"

"Of course—always. Good night, John."

"Good night, Sherlock."

We watched him climb the stairs.

"*'Si John Watson n'existait pas, il faudrait l'inventer,'* with apologies to Voltaire," Sherlock said to me. He paused a moment and shrugged. "And to the Deity."

"'If John Watson did not exist...you'd have to invent him?'" I shook my head. "I'm sorry sir, but I do not understand."

Cousin Sherlock sat down in his chair, stretched out his long legs, closed his eyes, and tented his fingers. "For many years, Amelia, I wrestled with the idea of a fictitious biographer. The idea would be to plant the seeds of an almost superhuman detective in the world's mind. There is no such thing, of course, but John is the perfect reporter of our adventures as well as the perfect friend."

"We need the stories to prepare the Ordinary world for our Introduction." I understood his intent at once. "Coming from so respectable a gentleman, it could not but help our cause."

"Amelia—Introduction? What's that?"

We looked around. Tommy stood in the doorway. His eyes were wide, and he'd heard Mycroft's story, no doubt. I was delighted to see that he was pale, but recovering, his arm in a splint.

"I'll give you two a moment," my Cousin said. He and Mycroft withdrew. Not too far away, I knew.

If the bolt-hole had been a test for Wiggins, this was a test for me.

Tommy took my hands. "What I've heard, Amelia! These things I've seen—Doctor Watson being healed! Your plans for the good of the world! It's wonderful, and I want to help you! You know I've always...been fond of you. You will let me help you, won't you? I...that is, if you feel the same way I do, we might take up your fight together."

"I do—you know I care for you, Tommy. Very much. And it would mean the world to me to have the life you describe. It would be...a dream." I shook my head. "But it is a dangerous dream, Thomas Turner, full of peril for us both. There would never be any quiet, any peace. The likelihood of our deaths by violent means would almost be assured. You must realize that."

"I'm not afraid if I'm with you. And I know that you, in addition to being the cleverest and loveliest of girls, are also the bravest."

"Danger is part of my Family's trade," I agreed. "All right, Tommy."

The look on his face was purest joy. "You have made me the happiest man in the world, Amelia."

"And I am delighted to be the author of your happiness, my dear." With that, I kissed him, very carefully, on his left cheek.

It was the same moment the needle went into his neck, below his right ear. Thomas went limp, and his eyes flickered closed.

I held his hand as he collapsed, Cousin Sherlock taking his shoulders to ease him to the ground.

"You chose correctly, I think, Amelia," he said as he worked. We brought Tommy back down to the kitchen, to make sure no one but the four of us would retain an accurate recollection of the evening. We retired to the sitting room. Mycroft handed a brandy to Sherlock, and to my surprise, one to me. The fire in the drink seemed to match the turmoil of my emotions.

"Then why do I feel so awful, Cousin Sherlock?" It was worse than seeing Tommy pale and unconscious on the table. My throat closed up, and I felt a sickening void yawn, wide and deep, before me.

"Because that is the terrible aspect of love; once given a glimpse and denied it, we never fully recover."

"What will you tell him?" I asked. "Tommy, I mean."

"Something good," Sherlock said sympathetically. "Something to divert him from you. Then tomorrow, when he's entirely recovered, I'll send him to fetch that young bulldog Lestrade to hear my tale of the antiquity thieves."

Sherlock narrowed his mouth. "And then I shall turn my wits to discover this new foe, this abstract thinker, this puppeteer of London criminals. As well as the sword—I do not like unknowns, and there are too many here. But, Amelia, will you be happy with Tommy not remembering you?"

I nodded, not trusting myself to speak for a moment. I wished I could take something to make me forget the pain of the decision I knew was correct. Perhaps I could go away from London, I thought. "Yes. Better he not recall any of this. Anything of me." And maybe Hal would like me now, too.

"I work to keep love at a distance," my Cousin said. "It is a dreadful thing, especially for our kind. Worse if we love Ordinary folk."

"'Keep love at a distance?'" Mycroft snorted, a stentorian noise, all disbelief. "Oh, *yes*, I recall many of these instances of swearing off, especially after our American Cousin was reassigned there. The moaning I heard. 'Oh, *she* was the daintiest thing under a wolf pelt, Mycroft!' he'd say, and 'Oh, *she* has no equal!' I suspect my brother's still mooning. Don't worry Amelia, his resolutions only last about twenty years or so. He'll recover and fall in love again about 1905, if my estimate is correct."

"Perhaps we could return to the matter at hand," Cousin Sherlock said. It was as if the room's temperature had dropped to freezing. He put a kind hand on my shoulder. "Amelia, it will fade over time."

"Say twenty years?" I stood straight, trying to be brave when I felt anything but. "We have our work to distract us, I suppose. But what of when we have no work? How can I bear it in idle times?"

Sherlock smiled sadly. "I recommend the violin."

Burning the Rule Book

I realized that when I started writing Seven Kinds of Hell, *I really didn't know anything about how Zoe's parents had met, and how she managed to grow up as a "stray" Fangborn. It became important later in the series, and especially in* Hellbender.

Somewhere outside his Portland apartment, Jack heard the televised sounds of the Red Sox losing. It had been nearly seventy years since they'd won a World Series, and as long-lived as his Fangborn Family was—and they were spectacularly long-lived—he had no expectation of ever seeing a Series win himself. Being an underdog and a perennial outsider, he felt sympathy but didn't feel compelled to root for them. He had no room in his life for more emotional violence.

The knock at his door took him by surprise, and he approached the peephole cautiously. Glancing through, he saw a tall redheaded woman in a faded Levi's jacket, acid-washed jeans, and white high-top Adidas sneakers. Her hair was pulled back with a black scrunchie. As he frowned in confusion, his partner, Sully, raised her hands in a gesture that was part "Yeah, it's me" and part impatience.

He opened the door and Sully walked in, glancing around, out of habit, for other visitors, for other danger. "You alone?" she asked in a Boston townie accent. "Good."

"I didn't expect you to come right over," he said. "Want a beer?"

"No time. Get your bag. We have work."

"Wait, I thought—?"

"You thought I was gonna rush right over with the illegally obtained confidential records you wanted, is that it?"

As Sully spoke, Jack felt the blood rush from his face and the panic well up inside him.

"They're background on the girl you've been seeing on the sly, right?" She shook her head. "Nope. But we'll have plenty of time to talk about that on the drive."

Jack was already in a precarious situation with the Family, and he'd hoped his clandestine, and therefore frowned-upon, romance was still a secret. "Oh, shit, how did you—? Does anyone else—?"

"I haven't told anyone—yet—and you'll have the drive to Boston to give me a good reason to keep it that way. But come on!" She clapped her hands. "We have a job, and time is of the essence."

"Can't I—can't we get someone else to fill in for me?" he said, grasping at straws. "Now's really not a good time for me to leave—"

Sully held up a hand and frowned. "You, better than anyone, know what happens when you go against the Family's orders, and we are on the clock, my friend."

He knew she was right, that he had no choice, but Jack stood another few seconds, trying to figure out how to keep disaster from crashing down on him. There was no solution, and further noncooperation wouldn't help, so he nodded once and went to the front closet. His bag was already packed—it was always packed. As much as the Family demanded obedience, it also required speed and preparation. "What's the job?"

"It's big, it's bad, and it's as weird as a snake with sneakers. We need to talk to an oracle."

"Yeah? What's so weird about that?"

"She's holed up in the Tower of London and won't come out until she talks to us."

"What?"

"Weird, like I said. I can tell you in the car. You ready?"

"Let me just call Emily, okay?"

Sully shrugged. "Keep it quick, okay?"

Jack dialed the number for the diner.

"Sunshine Diner. This is Emily." The voice wasn't impatient, but it was rushed.

"Hey, babe, it's me."

Her voice went softer, knowing it was him, like she was trying to keep the rest of the world from intruding on them. "Jack! What's up?"

"You're not gonna like it."

"Hang on a second." There was a sound of the phone being ineffectually muffled. "Yes, scrambled and wheat, just like I wrote!" she yelled at someone in the diner.

It drove Jack crazy when she did that, but Emily was at work. It also made him wonder how she, a short woman with a soft voice, could suddenly sound like a foghorn.

She took her hand away from the receiver, speaking normally again. "Let me guess—you've gotta work late."

"Yeah, I'm sorry. Actually, more than late; might be a few days." He sighed. "The life of an insurance adjuster is always intense."

"Ha. Funny."

"You gonna be okay?"

"Sure. Tracey Ullman's on tonight. They've got these weird little cartoons now; everyone's yellow. *The Simpsons*—it's pretty good. And I'll take a couple of late shifts. But I'll miss you."

"I'll miss you, too. I'll be back…I'm not sure when I'll be back, but I'll call as soon as I can and let you know."

"Okay. You give me enough notice, I'll bring home meat loaf."

"You're the best."

"No, you are."

He smiled into the receiver, and then caught Sully miming sticking a finger down her throat, pointing at her watch immediately afterward.

"Gotta go. Love you."

"Love you, too." He hung up.

"Gag me with a spoon," Sully said. "That was gross."

"Shut up and let's get going." But Jack still had a dumb smile on his face.

Jack threw his bag into the back of Sully's Trans Am and slid in with a little difficulty; whoever had been in the passenger seat last had been shorter than Jack, who was just medium height. He adjusted the seat to a more comfortable position. Sully, on the other hand, had to fold her long self into origami to get into the low-slung seat, which was already as far back as it could go. She glanced at the mirror and found nothing to complain about; Jack followed suit. It was almost second nature for the Fangborn to check their appearances, as it wouldn't do to get caught up in battle lust and then go out among the Normal population with a smear of blood on one's cheek. He sighed. There was nothing he could do about his hair; if he cut it too short he thought he looked like a bristling badger. Too long, and he thought it made his oval face with its fine features seem effeminate. The best compromise left him with a side part and a flop of black bangs, which hung in his eyes.

"You about done admiring yourself?"

He'd no sooner nodded when Sully took off from the curb with a screech.

"You know, I'm an officer of the court, and I have to watch my step getting information to the Family, else I'll lose my job as court stenographer." She started right in, making good on her promise to talk in the car. "I have to not only go by the book, I have to be like Caesar's wife and avoid even the *idea* of impropriety. If the Family understands why I can't just take whatever records I want, you know that I'm going to hold you to a higher standard. And given your past, I have to be even more careful. Spill it."

Jack couldn't decide if it was worse to reveal Emily's place in his life or to have Sully bring up the incidents that had made him practically an outcast. "How did you find out?" he asked, delaying the inevitable.

Sully knew exactly what he was doing. "I followed you, when *you* were following *her*. Couple months back, after we got that serial killer. You were out of sorts and wouldn't go out for a beer. I got curious and I followed you, and then when I found out what you were up to, I followed you a couple more times. I couldn't figure out why my newish partner hadn't told me about *her*, because, hey, his activities might reflect badly on *me*. I couldn't figure out why my partner wouldn't tell the Family he'd been seeing a Normal woman for weeks. I figured, he must have a good reason, he'll tell me; we're friends. He'll report his relationship soon; he knows what will happen if he doesn't. And yet, months went by and you did neither. So, enough stalling. Talk."

Jack stared at the spotless dashboard before he could bring himself to say it. The Fangborn had to adhere to strict rules. After all, the vampires, werewolves, and oracles of his Family were working in a world of Normal humans who didn't know they were being protected by supernatural creatures. For thousands of years, under the guise of being ordinary humans, the Fangborn took jobs that put them near human trouble—doctors, nuns, cops, lawyers, and even insurance adjusters—so they could better seek out true evil and eradicate it. In the presence of evil, werewolves might Change to the form of a large wolf, but more often that of a bipedal wolf-man—or wolf-woman. The vampires' half-Change made them look like a walking lizard-creature, which was even more unsettling than their full-Changed aspect of gigantic snakes. The Change was a glorious embrace of their true selves, and not the bone-crushing torment of legend; and while oracles did not shapeshift, they had powers of precognition, luck, or telepathy.

Long-lived and fast-healing, the Family was not immortal, and rather than being the monsters at the edge of every culture's nightmares, the Fangborn considered themselves saviors and angels. Acting in the shadows, disguising their activities had ever been their way, and, like any secret service, extended contact with Normals was always reported.

Except Jack hadn't done that.

Each time he opened his mouth to speak, he stopped himself. Confessing to Sully seemed fatally stupid, and it went against every fiber in his being to talk about Emily, but his partner already knew about his romance. And more, he trusted Sully. Her character, as well as her dedication to the Family laws, made her trustworthy, but it was those very qualities that might get him into hot water.

Finally, he said, "I love her. Emily—that's her name. I've loved her from the moment I saw her." Not given to sentiment or the expression thereof to others outside his relationship, he felt his face go hot.

"Okay," Sully said nonchalantly. "There have been relationships between Normals and Family before, even some marriages. Why not just tell the Family?"

This was the part Jack had the most difficulty with. He'd been working as hard as he could to toe the line and follow the regs, but for some reason, this was an absolute sticking point for him. Even now that Sully knew, he felt as though he'd give almost anything to keep his relationship with Emily a secret. It made no sense, but it was almost a physical urge, almost as great as the Call to Change.

Several more miles passed before he said, "She's...I think she's had a rough life, on the run from trouble. What kind, she refuses to say. Which is why I didn't want to say anything to the Family, at first, and then...it just got later and later, and the moment had passed and it all got too complicated, so I kept on keeping us a secret. The idea of the Family looking into her background...it just made me nervous that any kind of attention would scare her away."

"We're awful good at finding out things without being caught," Sully said as she pulled onto Route 95, heading south.

"But we're not perfect," he said. "I'm proof of that."

There was an awkward silence before Sully responded.

"What's the difference between me looking into her past—to 'help' her, as you say—and telling the Family?"

He sighed. "I think the fewer people who know, the better. Look, I know this doesn't make sense. She doesn't talk about her life, makes a point of asking me not to ask her, but I just have this feeling. If I find out more about her, I can help. I'd give anything to fix...to make her feel better. Keep her safe." He shrugged helplessly, hating himself for being so inarticulate about something that felt so primal to him. "I just want to protect her."

"Do you have any idea how creepy that sounds, Jack?" Sully shook her head and drove a little faster, the nonchalance fading from her voice. "This relationship already sounds pretty precarious to me; don't make it worse by going behind our backs *and* hers. As a friend, I'm telling you: Don't do this. It's against Family rules and it's against my better judgment. Just go to the Family."

Jack knew what Sully meant by "creepy." But he knew that, in spite of their obvious and not-so-obvious differences, he and Emily were in love. They were meant to be. It was a simple, immutable fact, just as he had green eyes and the best nose for trouble in the Family.

Realizing he'd been chewing his lip and staring out the window for too long, Jack glanced guiltily at Sully. "I can't do that. I *need* to find out more about her. I can help her, I feel it. Will you help me?"

She gave him a quick, evaluating glance, then turned back to the road, silent for so long he was certain she'd refuse. Eventually, he saw the shrug of her shoulders and the self-disgusted sigh that meant she'd help him. "But just this once. I won't do anything to endanger my place at work. It's too important to the Family's business."

He nodded hastily.

"And it won't be right away. Might be a couple of weeks. We have urgent business that requires our special talents."

"What is it?"

"I told you, one of our oracles locked herself up in the Tower of London with an artifact. Said she'd talk only to us."

Jack looked at Sully. "I don't know anyone in London. Do you?"

"Nope. Doesn't matter. Three other oracles, while having no idea the London Cousin was going to do this, saw big things happening for you and me. So we're it. Jack," Sully said hesitantly. "Look, I'm just a werewolf with a decent nose and better fists. I don't have any oracular talent whatsoever, and don't have any in my Family. But I get the impression that something big's coming down the pike very soon. There have been attacks on the Family lately, too many for coincidence."

He shrugged. "We're always being attacked."

"No, I'm not talking about the bad guys we're chasing." Sully chewed on her lip. "These are unprovoked and directed specifically at the Family strongholds and resources."

"The Order of Nicomedia?"

"Maybe. They might have finally found a way to spy on us. So when I say the oracles are getting into an uproar..."

"We get on the case." Jack nodded.

The drive from Portland down the coast to Boston was uneventful. At the halfway mark, they stopped at a Dunkin' Donuts for coffee. Jack ordered tea.

"I thought you were a coffee drinker?" she asked when they were back in the car and on the road.

"I hate the stuff."

"It's all you ever drink at that diner."

"Yeah, well...it's hard to explain."

Fortunately, Sully only raised one eyebrow. She turned the radio on to a rock station, and a saxophone solo wailed, filling the car and making it impossible to talk.

Jack was tired of talking anyway. The smell of the coffee brought back too many memories of meeting Emily for the first time.

Jack knew Emily was the one from the moment he saw her.

He'd felt it even as he walked into the Sunshine Diner for the first time, almost a year ago. At the time, it had seemed like a whim.

She'd poured him coffee, automatically, without looking at him. Transfixed by the sight of her, he was too stunned to ask for tea. So mesmerized by this sudden attraction, he barely tasted the brew at first, then didn't mind that it was coffee—weak, scalded, and bitter.

Emily wasn't beautiful in the traditional sense, and Jack wondered if that wasn't part of his attraction to her as he visited the diner over the next few months. She was short, with mousy brown hair in messy curls pulled back with a headband. There was a small, pale, puckered scar near her right eyebrow that he hoped was from some childhood misadventure and nothing else. She had a very small mole near the corner of her mouth, which she'd darkened into a beauty mark. That, and her fondness for a Fiorucci hot-pink lipstick, told him she was going for that Madonna look. The lipstick was the wrong shade for her skin, but you could tell it made her happy. If he could only make her happy like that, he'd—

Oh, for crissakes, Jack. Ask her out, or don't. Just do something other...than this...pining.

But he knew, deep down in his heart, that if he did anything so abrupt, it would ruin it. She'd flee as surely as a deer scents a hunter on a changing wind. From long years of watching people from the shadows, Jack knew she had secrets, that she was running from something. Her fear was real.

He got that. He had secrets, too.

So he drank the awful coffee, day after day, gradually drawing Emily out. He didn't mind that she was quiet; he was, too. He knew from the first she wasn't quite right, and that, for some reason, drew him even closer to her. It wasn't curiosity and it wasn't a Galahad complex. Jack didn't have time for most damsels in distress, because all too often, the drama was of their own creation. His own romantic experiences had mostly been the short-lived flings of his youth. Just when he might have considered something more serious, he'd gotten into the Family's bad books.

The attraction he felt to Emily was so strong that he sensed she might be Family, but she didn't act like it, didn't know any of the pass phrases, and he didn't dare push any further when she kept looking at him like he was crazy, saying things she didn't understand. It had to be going into the Sunshine, fresh from a job and taking out a serial killer that very first night they met that made her seem different, he reasoned.

But his desire never dimmed.

So he continued to stop by the diner whenever he could, and sometimes they'd chat, and he'd swallow the awful coffee, thinking, *Someday, it will be better than this. We'll be together.* Then he'd go home and try to sleep, and try to put her out of his mind, and fail at both.

His obsession took deep root. He hadn't really meant to follow her home three weeks after their first meeting; their respective paths didn't overlap in any way. He attributed the coincidental change in his route to his well-honed sense for trouble. And he thought he'd managed to keep from being observed following her, another Fangborn skill. It was the fourth time that it happened—what was becoming a habit of sorts— that he realized he was getting hung up on Emily Vargas. Maybe that's why he never picked up that Sully was following him.

"Hung up" was a nicer way to think of it than "obsessed."

He still avoided using the word "stalking" even as he recognized that his actions were those of a stalker. He knew better than most what that meant, and he shivered at the thought even as he brushed it away. Truth be told, there was that peculiar frisson of joy and anticipation that attended "stalker," and he tried to ignore that, too.

It wasn't a great way to live, but eventually his patience got him the results he wanted.

He woke up one day, three months after that first meeting, so filled with the idea of asking Emily out he could barely think of anything else. Jack had reached the breaking point, needing to know how she felt, and suddenly, finding out seemed of even greater importance than the possibility she might reject him. After an interminable day of filing boilerplate paperwork at his insurance job, he went to the diner that evening, reasoning that she'd feel safer than if he tried to catch up with her as she left her shift. As she poured him his usual, hated coffee, he started in.

"Look, I have to ask you something. I'd love to ask you out, but if you don't want to go, it's fine; I'll never bother you again." Once he'd started, the words seemed to come out in a torrent, and he felt his face going red with nerves, audacity, and hope. "I mean, you must have guys hitting on you all the time, but I really look forward to chatting with you, and I'd like to find out if there's something more. If you feel the same way—I mean, *of course*, if you feel the same way. If you don't, if it gets weird when I come in, I'll go someplace else, I promise. I just wanted you to know that I'd like to ask you out."

It took Emily a moment to tease out what he wanted from the rush of words, but when she did, she smiled. "Yeah, I think that would be nice. Thank you."

It had happened so quickly, that he blinked. "What?"

She laughed at his confusion, and it was a glorious sound, second only to her repeated, "Yeah, I'd like that. You pick out someplace, okay?"

He went home in a happy daze and couldn't even be upset that it had been so easy after so much agonizing. Somehow he knew he'd chosen precisely the right moment to ask her.

But Jack did agonize over where to take Emily. He didn't want to go for flat-out expensive, not wanting to come off as trying to overwhelm and impress her. And he didn't want to go too casual, because he wanted her to know that he cherished her. So he settled on a tapas restaurant, which was perfect.

Emily was shy and sharp and wary and wonderful. The small plates enchanted her, and she was delighted by the variety of flavors. They had sangria and, with none of the awkwardness that accompanies most first dates, began to talk. She asked what he was reading (hard science fiction and essays); she read history and biographies. That discussion branched into other topics that filled up the time between sitting down and most of the meal. Over dessert, he asked what she was listening to, and found out they shared a love of classical music and jazz. That took them through coffee and the waiters closing down the room. He couldn't know enough about her.

On the way out, he asked her, "If you could do anything in the world right now, what would it be?"

"Go roller skating," she answered promptly. Her cheeks were a little flushed with wine and food and...happiness, he thought.

Jack was thrilled. "We can do that! We can do that this minute!" Though he didn't know the first thing about skating or where one skated, he would find out for her.

"No!" She laughed. "I mean, I'd go skating in Versailles."

Jack wasn't sure if he'd had too much of the sangria. "Indiana?"

"No, France!" Another laugh, which made him feel silly and weak and invincible all at once. "I mean, I saw a documentary. There were all these long hallways with beautiful artwork. And the Hall of Mirrors? I think that would be just about the best place ever to roller-skate."

Jack was captivated by the boundlessness of her answer, the imagination, the quickness of it.

"And what about you? What would you do, if time and space and money were no object?"

"I'd ask you for another date," he answered, sincerely and truthfully.

She smiled and looked up at the stars. "We could do that."

He dropped her home, and after a quick kiss on the cheek, she ran to the front door of her apartment. He waited until he saw the light in what he knew was her window, and then took to the highway, cranking "The Marriage of Figaro" as he drove. Suddenly, the rotten tang of evil filled his nose, and he focused on a station wagon up ahead. Excitedly, he checked the license plate against a list taped to his dashboard and found a hit: the Family had identified the car as belonging to a serial sex offender. Jack followed, exalted by the chase, his nose so keen that he knew, even in a speeding car on a highway, that the suspect was the driver. His excitement grew to an almost fever pitch as Jack chased the man to his remote hideout, then gleefully, the strains of the Mozart overture still in his head, turned into a wolf-man and tore the predator's throat out.

It was, Jack considered, a perfect evening all in all.

When Emily quietly invited him to stay over the first time, the sex was quiet and calm and real and everything he'd hoped. She was not the tempest he'd known with other women. More like finding home. And as long as she stayed with him, he'd protect her from the entire world.

Even after she started staying over at his place, or he at hers, she never talked about her past. She said once that her background had been hard and, he sensed, dark, but after that, would say no more. That was part of their unspoken deal. She'd continue their relationship, however cautiously, however tentatively, as long as he stuck to the present, and didn't press her, didn't pry about her past. A contract to rival that of Bluebeard and his wives. He loved her enough to agree to such a ridiculous condition, but knew he had the means to find out what he needed to know.

That time had come, Jack had realized a week ago, just about six months after their first date. Emily had become distracted, high-strung, and monosyllabic almost to the point of rudeness. She claimed it had nothing to do with him, but he knew that was a lie. He had to know what had changed, what had made her so anxious, but the more he urged her to tell him, the more she retreated. And so, despite his promises, he began to investigate.

There weren't many people who could defy Fangborn detection skills and keep their lives hidden, but Emily did. There was no government paperwork—no birth certificate, no Social Security number, no license—and no one who knew her now seemed to know anything more of her past than Jack did. It was as if she'd fallen from the sky as an adult with no past at all.

Even as he promised her to let her work it out herself, Jack doubled down in his attempts to discover more about Emily and her past.

Nothing.

Eventually he had to admit he'd been defeated, and as much as he wanted to, it still took him three days to get up the courage to ask Sully for help.

And now everything he held dear was being threatened.

They arrived all too soon at the rendezvous, a darkened office building in the Financial District. Outside, a tall Asian-American Cousin was chain-smoking cigarettes. A pile of discarded butts lay at his feet. He introduced himself as Terrence Chang and led the way inside to an empty, anonymous conference room.

"Here's the situation," he said, all business. "There's a very important object that all our Fangborn Cousins agree needs to be moved. Apparently there have been warnings that it will be stolen, and we can't let that happen."

Sully nodded. "And she's locked herself up with it, in...?"

"The Tower of London, yes."

"Well, that should be *pretty* safe..." Sully said. "Why move it?"

Terrence shook his head. "No, you don't understand. All the portents indicate that it must not stay there. You know we've suffered an unusual number of targeted attacks lately? Someone who seems to be looking for and finding us?"

They nodded.

Terrence continued. "The oracles say the object—an ancient sword—needs to be moved. And the oracle refuses to give up the sword until she speaks to you two."

"Any idea why?" Sully asked.

Terrence shrugged. "She says she can't, until certain things happen. Certain things that *you* two must do. Apparently the old girl had something to do with the construction of our safes and defenses in the Tower somewhere back before the flood. She slipped in early this morning, GMT, and called us to explain her demands." Terrence pulled out another cigarette, frowned at it, and then replaced it in the pack. "We're gonna have to do this quick. I get the idea that a few of our London Cousins might be willing to chuck a grenade at the door to get in, and they wouldn't be upset if it took her out as well."

"Not really?" Jack asked. He knew what it was like to be on the wrong side of the Family.

"Not really, but they're completely thrown by this behavior, her going against the Family orders like this, taking things into her own hands. It's just not done."

There was an awkward silence as Terrence realized his gaffe. "I'm sorry. I wasn't saying you...I wasn't trying to—" he stammered.

Jack shook his head and looked away. "No sweat."

But Terrence couldn't seem to stop himself. "Of course, of course, if the Council decided not to...that you were...if they decided...in your favor, that's...it's all right, now. Ten years ago, uh, or whatever, water under the bridge—"

Sully broke in gently. "You've tried talking to her?"

Terrence and Jack both looked grateful. "We've tried reasoning with her, but she's old. Cussed. Even for an oracle." Terrence caught himself in a second misstep. "Sorry, God, I'm sorry. Neither of you is...?"

"No," Jack said.

Sully shook her head. "Werewolves."

"Well. No need to apologize, then. I'm a vampire, but you know what *they're* like."

Terrence made a gesture, which Jack interpreted as a ward against evil. Some of his Family were superstitious, a fact that Jack found hysterically funny.

"Wait, did any of our other folks have a clue this was coming? Or agree that she—what's her name?"

"Martha Hudson."

"Really? There's a name from Fangborn legend. You're certain it's actually her?" Sully asked. "You know about her, right, Jack?"

He nodded. "She was called 'the guardian of the Home Counties' and 'the Chatelaine of London.' She had a talent for anticipating trouble and protecting her domain, which included Family landholdings in London and the southeast of England." He whistled. "Who hasn't heard of her and the Baker Street Family?"

"It's her, all right. She gave all the passwords." Terrence laughed bitterly. "She *created* most of the passwords."

"So do the other oracles agree that Martha Hudson is doing the right thing?"

Terrence shook his head. "There was no discussion whatsoever. We told as few people as necessary, because there have been rumors that the sword would be stolen. We just didn't think it would be stolen by one of our Family. Martha wasn't in on the discussion, so she must have had a vision of her own. This is truly aberrant behavior for her. She's been dedicated to us all of her long life, which is long, indeed, as she's one of the oldest members of our Family in Britain. And she's never, ever gone rogue like this."

Jack looked at Sully, who shrugged. "How reliable has she been in the past? Have her prognostications and other efforts on the Family's behalf been accurate? Trustworthy?"

"Impeccably so."

"I guess that's our answer," Sully said. "Let's get busy."

The rebellious oracle answered on the first try. Jack heard the scratchy connection and wondered if the phone in the Tower was an original by Alexander Graham Bell. The Fangborn had been good at protecting humans undetected for millennia.

Terrence put the call on speakerphone.

"Martha Hudson."

Jack cleared his throat. "Um, Martha, this is Jack Parker. You asked to speak with me?"

"Prove it, if you would." Her voice was quiet and measured but still had a kind of authority that he could feel. The accent wasn't rich, upper-crusty, but it was polished. A hint of the Highlands, perhaps?

Jack was confused. "Do you want me to fax a picture of myself or something?" He glanced at Terrence and Sully. "Like, with my passport?"

"No, I want you to tell me a secret," the voice said, amused.

"Uh..."

"A secret only you know, something you've never told anyone."

Talking to her was eerie, like talking to a ghost. And Jack was feeling terribly protective of his secrets at the moment.

"How will that prove anything?"

"I'll know."

He glanced around at his two colleagues, who, in spite of themselves, perked up with interest and amused smiles. "Uh, I'm seeing this girl. Kind of."

Sully rolled her eyes. It was true, he *hadn't* told her. She'd found out only by snooping.

"Yes, yes," came the impatient reply. "What's her *name*?"

"Look, do we have to do this?" The panic in his voice was audible even to Jack. He could feel Terrence's gaze on him.

A breathy sigh from across the ocean. "Cousins, will you give Jack a moment's privacy, please?"

Terrence and Sully exchanged looks. "Sure. There's a vending machine down the hall. You hungry?"

"I'm always hungry," Sully said. She watched Terrence leave, then put a reassuring hand on Jack's arm, nodding. She left, shutting the door carefully behind her.

Jack shut down the speakerphone and picked up just in case; vampires and werewolves had sharp hearing. "Emily. Emily Vargas."

"And? What aren't you telling me?"

Jack sighed. "She's a Normal. I know it's irregular. I haven't reported her as a close friend to the Family, but I promise, I haven't told her anything about our powers or our purpose."

"Most Ordinary humans would not appreciate us taking the law into our own hands," Martha said. "Even if it is to protect them."

Jack caught himself before he brought up that most *Family* didn't appreciate when he'd taken Fangborn laws into his own hands. "Right."

Almost as if she could read his mind, Martha said, "And yet, if I understand correctly, you've been working very hard lately to keep your nose clean. Keeping your head down, no blots on your copybook. Why not tell them about Emily? You know that's one of the most ancient rules, reporting long-term relations with Ordinary humans. And it would make your situation far less precarious."

"Yes, it's just...it's complicated. I'm trying to protect her." He knew it sounded weak, suggesting that the Family would ever do Emily any harm. "The fewer people who know where she is, the better, I think. It's a gut feeling." He'd been balancing his desire to keep his nose clean with breaking another cardinal rule, and it had been eating him up.

His greatest fear coincided with the happiest time of his life.

"Very good," Martha answered after a moment. "I believe you are who you say you are, and I have a task for you."

Jack felt as if he was being sent to the principal's office after being pulled out of class. A pit opened up in his gut. It had been so long since he'd been this afraid, and that doubled his discomfort. "Okay."

"You need to go to East Eighty-First Street in New York City. There's an artifact there, a small clay figurine. It is fragile, it is ancient. It's about four inches tall, a male figure with an extended arm, with robes or a skirt of some sort. It is hugely important that you steal it."

"Why?"

There was a rasping sigh on the other end of the line, barely audible over the transatlantic hiss. "Because I have seen...others, generations of Fangborn, perhaps, will suffer. Ordinariels will suffer. Your line, Jack Parker, will suffer."

I don't have a line, he thought. *And never will, with Emily. But I still have Family.*

"All I can foretell is that it's imperative you do as I say. But, perhaps I can convey something of what your failure may mean—"

Suddenly, Jack's mind was filled with images of mobs, Normal humans overwhelming Fangborn Cousins.

The scenes resolved with piercing clarity: police and, eventually, the armed forces were co-opted to bring in the Fangborn population to so-called internment camps, now dotting the countryside. Allegedly constructed for the Fangborn population's own safety, families were separated, and those who resisted—for weren't they American citizens, guaranteed due process if accused of a crime?—were treated as criminals. As time progressed, fear of the Fangborn escalated. More extreme methods of finding Family and dealing with holdouts were rationalized and justified.

Another jump in time, and Jack saw a group of resisting Fangborn and Normals trapped in a parking garage. The harsh metallic bark of automatic weapons filled the air. He heard a scream as a grenade landed among the party—

Jack gasped, his clothing soaked through with cold sweat as he found himself back in the conference room. It was the nightmare vision of what would happen at Identification Day if it wasn't handled precisely right. Jack was convinced that the Fangborn had to voluntarily reveal themselves, and should have done so long ago to avoid this very scenario.

It would also have made his secrecy about Emily unnecessary.

"I...I can stop all that?"

"You can help. Other forces are at play, but until you get that object and bring it home with you, I can't see what comes next. If you and your partner play your parts, exactly as I tell you, I'll be able to tell you something about Emily. I may be able to direct you on how to find out more about your new love, and perhaps that will help her."

His heart soared. "I understand," he said, though it was a lie. Oracles had always baffled him, with their power to predict the future or create luck or communicate via telepathy. But his skepticism didn't matter now. She could tell him about Emily!

There was the breath of a chuckle on the other end of the line, as if she recognized that pause of disbelief. "I assure you, this is no whim of mine. I would not undertake what I have done lightly. And when that's been accomplished, you may ring me for my answers. That is, if I haven't been subject to Shedding or locked up somewhere."

"Answers, yes." Suddenly Jack was ashamed; he needed to consider the Family's business. "And if I do this, you'll give the sword to the Family?"

"Yes. Call the others back, if you would. I intend to keep your secrets; please don't tell them what we've discussed."

"I'd rather claw out my own eyes. I promise."

Jack opened the door and motioned the others back in. Sully pushed past him but held Terrence back, saying, "Jack, you can go straight out to the hall, and don't bother putting us back on speaker. If I gotta tell a secret, it's not going to be with an audience."

The door shut behind her. In the dimly lit hallway, Jack watched Terrence fiddle with his pack of cigarettes and finally put an unlit cigarette in his mouth. "I'd nearly stopped, before the oracles," he muttered. "Now look at me."

A few minutes later, Sully opened the door, beet red and scowling mightily. "She is crazy," she mouthed to Jack, who could only shrug as he and Terrence returned to the room.

Terrence spoke into the speaker. "How much time do we have to accomplish...whatever you've asked of Jack and Sully, Martha?"

"I've mentioned that there are enemy forces massing against us. Apart from that, I have two flasks of tea, a mess of sandwiches, and two good books. I'd say you have forty-eight hours before I start getting bored and hungry. I think at about that time, our Family will be finding a way to get me out of here, which I can't allow until you've succeeded. I won't let the sword out of my sight until I know."

Jack and Sully exchanged a glance. "Okay," Jack said finally. "We'll call as soon as we're done."

"Right-o."

The connection was broken.

"Not a lot of time," Sully said. "I'll drive."

The drive from Boston to New York City should have taken about four hours, but Sully seemed to have had a former life as a fighter pilot and drove the black Trans Am as if she was homing in on the Kremlin. She insisted on playing rap—Salt-N-Pepa—at full blast, which made Jack even more convinced they'd be pulled over, and neither of them was a vampire who could charm the inevitable ticket away. He would have said he enjoyed driving fast, but clearly he didn't know what the meaning of the word "fast" was until riding with his new partner.

"You really don't talk a lot, do you?" she asked two scary miles later after singing along to a track, advising some unseen someone to "push it real good."

He shrugged. "Most of my partners have been happier when I've kept my nose to the grindstone, kept quiet, and gotten the job done." When he saw she wasn't going to leave him be, he said, "Insurance claims adjuster by day, avenging werewolf by night. I live in Portland, but I grew up in Rhode Island. Moved up here after Academy. That's pretty much it."

"And that's pretty much what I got from the file," Sully replied. "Except for those other things."

Jack sighed. His partners—there had been seven over the ten years since the last incident—always claimed to want to talk about "those other things," but they almost always found an excuse to ask for a new partner shortly after he did. He'd resigned himself to it; he'd made his bed with his choices long ago, and they'd changed his life. "Those other things, they're in the file, too."

"Yeah—you were ordered to leave a hostage situation because the police and the news crews were getting too close. Instead, you clocked your partner, who was a good deal senior to you, and went in to take on the bank robbers yourself."

"I knew I could do it. We all make tough decisions," he said automatically.

"Sure, it's how we know we're ready to take on the job. But you went too far. Your partner took a couple of stray bullets in the chaos you caused. That's insubordination *and* imperiling Family."

"I got everyone out safely, including the bad guys. If we'd left, there would have been casualties for sure."

"You slugged your *senior* partner," Sully repeated. "He almost died. You were seen in your half-wolf form. The vampires had a huge number of false memories to implant, and it took the better part of an evening.

All with the press outside, just slavering to get a look inside the bank. You could have exposed us all, on the off chance someone might have died if you didn't."

"I thought I could keep everyone alive."

"We all think that, but we have to work as a team. And then there was the other thing, five years after that, just as you were starting to rebuild trust."

"It was a school bus crashing into a mall—how could I *not* act?"

"You could have acted without Changing."

"I wouldn't have been strong enough!"

"But you wouldn't have been seen. Again." She sighed. "It's not like you're strutting around, telling people you think you're better at making these decisions than everyone else, but you sure are demonstrating a real disdain for our rules—rules that have let us do our job for millennia."

"What's your point?" This was old news, something that had colored his entire life. He'd outshone everyone in his class at Fangborn Academy in tracking, but for every accolade he'd received, he'd received a demerit for not following Family protocols. "You seem to live for burning the rule book," one instructor had told him.

But what was the point of working in secret? Jack always asked. It complicated too much, and they'd be even more effective guardians and citizens if the Normal world knew the Fangborn existed. He'd almost failed his Finals, but his nose was too good and he was given a chance. And then a second and a third chance, but he knew that the Family was beginning to find him more of a liability than an asset.

So Jack had known the danger when he'd made the choices; the second time, he'd almost paid for it with his life. Or rather, his Fangborn abilities, which amounted to virtually the same thing. Shedding was the most severe punishment given a Fangborn, and he'd come within a whisker of a vampire draining him nearly to death and then injecting him with chemicals that would keep his powers from returning. The Shedding was rare, but it was ugly and it was permanent. Only his youth and his almost unparalleled ability to sniff out evil had swayed the Family in his favor again.

"Why start taking chances now? Why not walk away from this girl if you're afraid to bring attention to her?"

It was a different question than he'd been asked before, and Jack wasn't sure he knew the truth. "I've been living on the fringe of Family life for ten years now, working hard and trying to reduce the number of chances I have to screw up. I'm good at what I do. I save a lot of lives, and I can't stand to think that I might lose that ability because I act on the opportunities I see. If we'd Identified ourselves years ago, this wouldn't be a problem; I'd be a hero. But because we have to hide, I'm an outcast living on the fringe. Do you have any idea what it's like?"

"I'm a six-foot-tall lesbian who grew up in a conservative, working-class community known for its generations of career criminals," Sully said without emotion. "While the Family's politics might be more advanced than most of humanity's, I still have to live among Normals. So, yeah, I know about living in the margins."

"Okay, but you've still got the Family. I don't. And since I first saw Emily, I've had...something. I've been a part of something. And I wanted to protect it."

Sully drove a while longer, thinking it over. "So if it came down to sacrificing me or Emily...?"

It was Jack's turn to be silent. "Have you ever been in love?"

"Yeah."

"Then you know it's impossible to answer that."

"That's a shitty answer, but it's honest." Sully nudged the Trans Am's accelerator as if to express her frustration. "I hope we don't find out. In the meantime, Terrence filled me in while you were on the horn. There's a guard out in front of the house, on the street side. The owner has an antiques store, and sometimes brings his work home. He goes to the library every night for an hour—one of our people at the New York Public Library responded to our flash. You get in through the back, and I'll keep the guy in front busy."

Jack agreed, then begged for a turn picking a selection from the cassettes he had in his bag. He found one with a yellow label and slid it with a click into the player.

Sully made a face. "Awesome. Beethoven."

"Okay, where to?"

Jack rattled the map flat against the dash and located the block that he'd circled earlier. "Uh...ten more blocks, then head for East Eighty-First Street between First and Second."

"You got it."

They parked a couple of blocks away and did a quick walk around to check out the entrances and exits.

Just as promised, there was a guard outside the front door. "You sure you got to be the one to steal the, uh...dingus?" she asked. "I'm much better at B&E than you are, according to your file."

"I'm just going by what the oracle told me; I can't tell you more. Anyone on your radar?"

She pressed her lock picks into his hand. "Nary a tingle. And until I notice anything, I'll distract the guy out front."

He glanced at her Red Sox tee. "Well, we're deep in the heart of Yankees territory. Let's hope he's a Mets fan or that he's got a thing for big, nasty redheads."

Sully wagged her finger. "There's more than one way to distract, my friend." She paused. "And name one person who isn't into big, nasty redheads."

He smiled, just a bit. "You got me there. Go get him."

"Make it quick, homeboy. We're on the clock."

He slipped through the alleyway, blending perfectly with the shadows. He smiled to himself as he startled a cat from its prize—a fat rat—and delighted in parsing out the individual smells on the spring evening air: flowering trees, sizzling olive oil, the cracked vinyl of taxi seats. Well, most of the scents were pleasant; apparently trash collection was due. And...

Jack swore under his breath. Somewhere in the night air, he picked up the fetid stench of evil. It was faint—just faint enough to put him on edge—and he knew that Sully hadn't noticed it. He felt his gut tighten and his blood start to tingle as the Call to Change began to make its demands.

The lock to the back door was more complicated than he expected, and he was glad to have Sully's lock picks, which were far nicer than his own.

The house lock wasn't the problem, though it was just at the limits of Jack's abilities. As he entered, he saw that every square foot of the place was covered in cases. And every case was stuffed to the rafters with dolls of every sort—from baby dolls to Day of the Dead *calaveras* figures to tiny classical bronze statues. The rooms were spotlessly clean, but the floral wallpaper was curling at the edges, and the clutter of dolls and statues made Jack think of what happened when the frail Normal elderly were left alone for too long. If the brownstone was four stories, and each floor had two rooms off the side staircase, the number of objects he'd have to examine was in the thousands...

Martha Hudson had instructed him to look for a small clay figurine, but how would he ever find it amid all these things? It looked as though the collections of several museums had been crammed in here. There was no order that Jack could see—not by material, not by style, not by...anything. He was no expert and only had the description of a possibly rebellious oracle locked up—by self-inflicted choice—in the Tower of London.

And he had less than forty-five minutes to complete his search, according to the Cousin at the library. The smell of evil grew stronger and stronger over the smell of old floor wax as he climbed the creaking wooden stairs. His wolfish side cried to be unleashed, and his blood began to roar in his veins, insisting that Jack find the evildoer and destroy him.

Many things went bad as soon as he had that thought.

First, he heard shouts, faint, then increasingly distinct. One voice was Sully's.

From the front window of the second-floor hallway, Jack saw Sully run across the street, away from the man she was supposed to keep occupied. Her destination was a loud argument turning physical between another man and a blonde woman in front of a small family store. Sully's shout of "Yeah, well, I'm from Charlestown, Massachusetts, and we shit bigger things than you!" was drawing attention up and down the street. Her behavior went against everything the Fangborn prized.

Another curse—the "C-word"—and although he was no oracle, Jack could have foretold what would happen next. Sully hauled off and punched the guy in the nose. Blood poured from the guy's nose, and he swung back—

Jack almost called to her—he needed her to be a lookout and a distraction, not a concerned citizen and righter of social wrongs! How could she go against protocol like this? It was almost as if—

Then, a terrible smell, the purest of evil. Something like a dumpster filled with raw sewage and spoiled milk exploded in Jack's nose. He tried to resist with everything he had, but the Fangborn compulsion was too strong. He had to find whoever it was and stop them.

Fortunately, the offender giving off that rank odor of evil was not far.

Unfortunately, he was in the next room.

Jack froze as he realized this. Was it possible they were on the same errand?

He began to move silently from the hall to the door, somehow able to avoid another creaking floorboard. Carefully, he peered around the doorway, trying to suppress the urge to growl at whoever was there...

When Jack saw the source of his agitation, things got worse. A giant of a man stood there in a green tracksuit and tee, with a mane of carefully styled black hair and a bank vault's worth of gold chains and charms around his neck. He looked like any other guy you'd see in the city, but it was nearly a joke, camouflage for a dangerous predator. An untidy heap of crushed dolls and figurines lay at his feet; whatever the man was looking for, he wasn't finding, and he was removing the failed contenders from the competition.

Jack's sharp nose picked up traces of an unfamiliar shampoo and the heavy scent of borscht and sour cream.

Russian, maybe, he decided, and then, for the first time in many years, Jack felt real fear. The thrill of adrenaline raced through him—from the hairs on the back of his neck to the pit of his stomach—and he fought the tiny voice that wanted him to *run*.

It takes a lot to scare a werewolf.

It wasn't the size of the guy, which was huge, or the jacked-up, steroid-driven air of hostility that sat on him like a cloak, but...

Jack understood at last. He'd seen for himself: others, the old oracle had said, would suffer unspeakably.

Another, an early nineteenth-century porcelain doll, unbelievably rare, even to Jack's untutored eyes, was hurled to the floor with a sickening crack. The head lolled toward Jack, glass eyes looking as though they were pleading with him when the heavy Nike basketball shoe descended, leaving nothing but a pile of torn and yellowing lace dusted with grayish powder.

Already enraged by his Fangborn senses, Jack felt his anger reemerge anew. What if this monster had already destroyed the object of his mission?

Even as he had the thought, Jack knew they were looking for the same thing. Jack had to be the one who got it first. The Russian had to be stopped.

That broke the chains of his fear, sent his hackles up. Jack Changed. A rippling sensation of power washed over him, as if his blood was heating up in anticipation of the joy of fighting. His muscles grew and changed to accommodate shifting bones; his face elongated into a muzzle filled with sharp, sharp teeth; and his fingers turned into heavily nailed claws. There was no need for words when he was capable of such glorious transformation, and he was filled with a wonderful sense of purpose. Even if it was incongruous that a wolf-man should be wearing a blue Oxford cloth shirt and khakis, no one would laugh seeing the teeth that filled his mouth, or the ears, standing up from his head, go back with anger.

The transformation was barely complete as he launched himself at the big guy. He knew there was a good chance that if his enemy was Russian, he'd know combat *sambo*, so he decided to get in close, to avoid getting picked and punched. Get in close, stay there, and go to work at whatever target presented itself. He did not want to go to the ground and find out what kind of grappling moves the big bastard had.

He landed hard on the guy's back, taking him by surprise. The Russian was strong, beyond even steroid strong, and quicker than his bulk suggested. Jack felt something sharp against his leg and realized his enemy had a knife. He reached a claw around to rake the Russian's face, when something even more potent than the Fangborn urge to Change overtook him.

But that was impossible. There was nothing that could break the Fangborn compulsion to track evil.

And yet, the figurine he'd been sent to find caught his eye, as if a spotlight shone on it. He could *feel* its presence. It was on a shelf to Jack's left, sitting there just as plainly as the image the oracle had planted in his mind: a small male figure in ancient garb, arm outstretched. He gasped at the shock and clarity of his sureness, and the Russian took advantage of that to twist around and throw Jack away from him.

Nothing Jack had ever encountered, including other Fangborn, had been able to distract him from the Call to fight evil. His shock at that was almost as great as the wonder of seeing the figurine.

Two things happened then: The Russian saw the figurine, too, and was momentarily transfixed. As he darted for it, Jack moved back to block him.

The Russian got a look at Jack Parker the wolf-man. His jaw dropped.

The track-suited thief then did something unexpected. Most people, confronted with a werewolf, would scream, faint, run away or, in some cases, foolishly attack. The Russian did none of these. He paused, held up his hands, and cocked his head.

Jack wasn't buying it and moved almost imperceptibly to angle himself so that he'd get to the figurine first.

"Are you...*oboroten*? Are you truly a werewolf?"

The man's voice told Jack much more about his opponent. Russian and educated, despite his thuggish behavior and fighting skills. Used to commanding authority, sure of himself.

Curious, Jack couldn't help but nod.

"How were you made? How did you achieve this form?"

Jack, still nonplussed by the Russian's curiosity trumping fear, shook his head. "Born, not bitten. There's no 'making' involved, no curse."

Was this guy the threat Martha Hudson had warned of? If so, why wasn't he in London? *Keep him talking*, Jack thought, *and screw the rules of secrecy.*

Because it didn't matter. Either the guy would be dead and not capable of telling Jack's secret, or Jack would be dead and would revert to his human form, leaving no evidence.

"We're born this way," he repeated to the disbelieving Russian.

"Liar!"

The big man threw himself at Jack, trying to get at the figurine. Jack had a flash of intuition: his opponent believed the figurine would make him a werewolf. Even on the remote chance that the object was magic—there were many strange and mystical Fangborn artifacts in the world—he knew he could never let this thug become stronger.

Jack darted and grabbed the artifact. Unfortunately, trying to keep it safe left him fighting one-handed. He could still kick and bite, though, and even a one-handed werewolf was something to fear.

The Russian was just about Jack's match, and was also driven by his desire for the object. He was also fighting one-armed, as he tried to shove his hand into Jack's mouth. The idiot was trying to get Jack to bite him.

No problem. Jack bit down as hard as he could. The Russian screamed and pulled back in an attempt to free his hand, but Jack's wolfish jaws were strong, and he took insane pleasure in hurting his assailant.

More noise from the street, and Jack heard Sully shouting. Signaling him. A crowd was forming and the authorities were bound to take notice...

Jack cursed to himself. Time was getting short in other ways, too. The homeowner would soon return.

The Russian's desire to become a werewolf was no match for his self-preservation, and with a violent yank, he tore his hand away.

Falling back, blood running down his hand in rivers, the Russian pulled out a pistol and fired several times at Jack. Two bullets missed, while a third hit Jack in the shoulder and the last in the leg.

Reeling from impacts that were like being struck with cinder blocks, Jack felt the pain rush in as his body desperately tried to heal itself. He clutched at himself with his free hand, somehow trying to stanch the blood that insisted on gushing forth. Bullets could kill a Fangborn if they did more damage than quick healing could cure.

A shout from below. Lights went on around the house. "Police!"

The big Russian, crazed with getting the artifact, dropped the gun and tried to snatch the figurine away from Jack.

Jack's healing powers were enough—barely—that he could keep his mind focused on the mission. His claws curled tighter around the statuette as he growled.

The Russian knelt on Jack's shoulder and tried to pry his fingers off the figurine. Vision narrowing, Jack howled, fighting against the pain and blood loss.

Sirens in the distance. An ambulance, too—summoned by the shots, perhaps. More cops on the way, to join the ones now in and around the house. Outside it was a circus.

They needed to get out of here. As Jack knew all too well, the Fangborn avoided attention from the general public, and it would be impossible to explain his blood-soaked fur, long claws, and rapid healing. Even more difficult than explaining why he was fighting a muscle-bound Russian over a doll.

He Changed back to his human form and felt a world of pain erupt. He fought to keep his thoughts clear.

Heavy footsteps and more lights. The Russian grabbed desperately at the figurine one last time; Jack held on to it for more than dear life and groped for the dropped pistol. He jammed it into the Russian's shoulder and shot twice. The noise was ridiculous close up, and then there was another, smaller *crack*, like a tiny twig snapping. The man fell away, blood streaming from his two grievous wounds.

Relief surged through him as the Russian's weight was suddenly removed from his broken and bleeding body. Jack looked down at his hand. He still had the figurine. It would be all right.

"Freeze!" a slender, light-haired police officer shouted.

Exhausted, Jack felt oddly compelled to obey her.

More relief as he understood. He looked over at the Russian and would have laughed if he'd had the strength. The man was frozen—eyes ridiculously wide open, mouth agape, midshout, on his knees, blood soaking his clothing.

The cop was a vampire. Family.

He put the figurine in his pocket and watched her cuff him. "Thanks, uh, Officer—?"

"Rose. Verena Rose. No problem, Cousin. Can you walk?"

"Yes, with help."

"No time for that. Normal officers are on the way. Wrist?"

"Thanks." He held up his wrist and watched her half-Change into a walking serpent in an NYPD uniform. Her hair went darkly blue, and her nose vanished into a reptile's snout filled with sharp, piercing fangs. Her skin was replaced with blue-and-black scales. As her fangs broke his skin with the delicacy of hypodermics, Jack immediately felt better. The pain receded, his thoughts cleared, and he could feel his muscles and bones knitting up, his blood being replenished.

"Listen, we don't have much time," she said as she slowly reverted to human form, her body still reacting to the effort of healing him. She pocketed the bullets that had been ejected from his wounds. "Go back down the alley. There's an ambulance there blocking the entrance, so the crowd won't see you. My partner, Shawn Simmons, is there, one of the EMTs. She'll get you cleaned up and find you another shirt. We can blame that guy for the mess and the break-in; Shawn will get his story."

"What about *him*?"

Officer Rose smiled, and he saw the last glitter of fangs as they shrank away. "Hey, you! What's your name?"

"Dmitri Alexandrovich Parshin."

"Okay, Dmitri, you're going to come with me. You're going to make a lot of noise and act as though you're struggling, but you're not going to escape, and you're not going to hurt anyone. Until you meet the pretty EMT downstairs. Then you're going to charge her. Got it?"

He nodded. "You got it."

"Okay, now let me cuff you."

With a nod to Officer Rose, Jack raced down the stairs and outside.

He found the other woman, a petite blonde with stunning eyes and a stethoscope around her neck, just as Officer Rose had said. Working together with Fangborn speed and efficiency, they managed to get him presentable. By the time the other EMT, who was a Normal human, joined them, Jack looked like nothing more than a bystander wondering what all the fuss was about.

At that moment, Officer Rose appeared with a struggling Dmitri Parshin, hands cuffed behind his back. When he saw the EMT, he bellowed and broke away from the cop.

"Shawnie! Watch out! He's dusted to the gills!"

He charged into Shawn, all but overwhelming her with his bulk.

Officer Rose and Jack raced forward as if to pull Dmitri away, but they placed their bodies between the struggling pair and the onlookers on the street.

No one but Jack and Officer Rose saw Shawn Change briefly and sink her fangs into Parshin's shoulder. He pulled back, stunned, and she then clocked him with a solid roundhouse. Jack's jaw ached in sympathy as Parshin fell to the ground, unconscious.

Two other cops detached themselves from the fracas on the street; they and Shawn's Normal partner got Parshin cuffed to the gurney and locked in the ambulance. EMT Simmons reassured them she was okay, and they went back to dispersing the large and agitated crowd that had gathered around the shop where he'd last seen Sully.

Verena whispered to Jack as she pretended to take a statement. "She's got a real talent for getting folks to spill their guts. Her partner wouldn't have let her alone with him if he wasn't unconscious. This way, she'll have twenty minutes to revive him and get his story—then remove us from his memory as much as possible."

Jack nodded approvingly.

"Pretty good scheme your friend had, drawing so much attention to her with that fight. You never would have gotten away clean without this crowd and confusion."

Jack wasn't convinced, but it had all worked out. "Yeah, great...plan."

He joined up with Sully and they found her car. On the way to the New York safe house, he asked her, "So. Why'd you leave your post, Miss Rules and Regulations?"

It was dark, but the dash lights showed she was blushing. As she drove, the remaining bruises and cuts on her face and hands gradually healed. "I just did as the oracle told me. It all worked out, didn't it?"

"Yeah, but she told you to break protocol?"

"No." She sighed. "Okay, we're done, so I guess I can tell you now. She told me to do what my heart told me to do."

"What?"

"I know, I thought she was crazy. But across the street, I saw a guy yelling at a girl, calling her names. Then he started getting physical." She made the last turn, found a garage near the house, and parked. "My heart told me to break it up. It caused quite a ruckus. You'd think no one's ever seen an Amazon beating up a scumbag before." She grinned, relishing the memory. "Then some little jerk used our fight as a chance to try to rip off the store, and the owner saw him. Sharp words and knuckles were shortly exchanged, and it got worse when the jerk's buddies showed up. That gave me a chance to drag the woman out of there before the cops got to us."

"One of the cops was Family, so you lucked out." Jack thought about it for a minute. "Blondes, huh?"

"Oh, blondes are totally my weakness. Martina is her name. She's a flight attendant, and she's—" Sully caught herself getting off topic. "I just did what the oracle told me," she finished.

"It gave our Cousins enough time to get me away from the scene, with the, uh, thing I had to get," Jack agreed.

"And I got her number," Sully said, hating to leave out that detail. She smiled broadly. "I was right. Everyone *does* love a big, nasty redhead."

Once inside the Family safe house, they made the call to Martha Hudson, who seemed to already know that they'd succeeded. Her voice was filled with relief. "Thank you, Jack. Thank you, er, Sully. Am I on speaker?"

"Not anymore," Jack said, after pressing the button and picking up the receiver.

"Then I will tell you a secret in return for yours, Jack. You must never tell another soul, Fangborn or human. Do you swear?"

"I do."

"I have seen: Your Emily is an oracle. She doesn't know it and she doesn't appear on the rolls of the Family. She has a talent for hiding and for disguising her Fangborn nature; she's adept at anticipating danger, which she describes as 'nerves.' It is all-important that you never tell her this, and even more vital you keep the secret from everyone else."

"Why?" If he could reveal that Emily was an oracle, he could literally and figuratively introduce her to the Family! All would be well. "What will happen to her if I tell her?"

"I can't tell you that, only that her life, however hard it may be, will be infinitely easier than if she learns the truth. It is imperative the secret be sealed between us. And you must never tell anyone about the object of your mission: the figurine. The fewer who know of its existence, the better."

"I won't tell a soul," he said, his heart cracking a little at the thought of hurting Emily in any way.

"Thank you, Jack. I wish I had better news for you."

Martha's explanation removed a huge burden of worry about Emily from him, but added a new sadness. "You're welcome," he said, uncertain.

"Godspeed. Please put us back on speaker now."

He heard a faint click, and the opening of a huge and heavy door somewhere in the belly of the Tower of London. "All right, my darlings, this artifact can go where it needs to be." Her words echoed now that the door was open. "I've instructed the daring Ms. Sullivan to come here herself to take it to the repository in America. And be easy with me, you brute. I'm an old lady, after all, and our American Cousins are listening in."

Someone muttered, "*You're* the brute, my dear," and Martha laughed in response. Jack knew she'd be okay.

When they returned home to Portland the following day, Sully stayed just long enough to swap out dirty laundry for clean before she left for London. Jack stopped at his house to drop off the figurine and then went straight to visit Emily, who seemed much calmer and more relaxed. Jack was convinced that some weight, unknown to her, had been lifted. They spent the weekend in bed at his place, Jack not caring that they could never marry. He could never let the Family know about her. What they had was enough, as close to an ordinary life as two people with such secrets could manage.

The following week was ordinary bliss. An argument about the dishwasher. A missing bill found. Dinner at "their" tapas place.

Monday morning, they woke and gazed at each other. "Good morning, my Jack," Emily said.

"Good morning, my Emily," he replied.

She turned, laughing and groaning at the same time, and put a hand over his mouth. "I am not your Emily until you brush your teeth! Go!"

After breakfast, he dropped her off at the diner and went to work. This time he hummed along to the Boston Symphony's rendition of "The Magic Flute," with Gerald Elias on first violin.

That night, when he returned to her place, Emily was nowhere to be found. She was running late from the diner, he figured, but there were no messages on the answering machine. Emily was a stickler for such things.

Then he registered the emptiness of her apartment apart from the cheap furniture it had come with. The echo of his footsteps as he tore open cupboards and drawers. Not just her, but her meager belongings, everything she owned, which had never been much. No note, unless you counted the bright-pink lipstick letters on the mirror: *Please don't follow me.*

Huge relief; she'd left under her own steam. The note and his gut told him that. But then his stomach clenched. *Why?* No explanation, no reasons that he could fathom. As far as he knew, nothing had changed between last night when they'd gone to bed and this morning when they'd had breakfast and both had gone to work.

He stood, overwhelmed by his emotions, for nearly an hour, frozen in front of the mirror—shock, sadness, anger, hurt, and all the others taking turns, filling every part of his being and distorting his reflection.

When he felt himself getting cold, when he realized the sun had gone down, Jack collected himself. He had to wrap up the New York assignment.

Numbly, he drove to the Portland Jetport to pick up Sully. He was surprised to see his partner carrying what looked like a guitar case, but said nothing to indicate he'd seen anything unusual. He struggled to make commonplace chatter for the sake of any onlookers. "Um, good flight?"

"It was! Did you know Martina works at British Airways? She got me bumped up to first class! Man, I've never eaten food like that before, and the booze…it's all free! And she has a flat in London. I got to visit her while I was there. She is *totally* bitchin'!"

"Um, sure."

"We need to go someplace quiet," Sully said once they were in his car.

"Okay."

Sully glanced at him, saw something was wrong, and then continued to chat about London and Martina to fill up the silence around them.

Jack drove to his place, where he found that Emily had cleared out the few things she kept there. Something nudged him to check on the figurine.

It was gone, too.

Somehow, that felt right. Complete. The figurine hadn't been for him, ever. It was for Emily.

Still overwhelmed with emotions and questions about his love's whereabouts, Jack obeyed Sully's instructions mechanically. Open the case. Pick up the sword.

The sword was another antique: bronze, a few feet long, with several jewels fitted into it. Jack reached for the handle, and as he picked up the sword, his hand vanished. Make that, he could feel it, feel the handle of the sword biting into his flesh, but he couldn't see where his hand ended and the sword began. Then the burning started, and he wanted to scream, but could not. Jack felt as though magma was melting his flesh, combining it with the sword, but when he opened his eyes, all seemed as usual.

That didn't mean the pain had lessened. Now it was so bad that Jack didn't dare move for fear he would shatter. A thousand images, very few of which he recognized, filled his mind's eye, just as it had when Martha had given him the vision of a possible future.

He wept when he saw Emily as she had been just the week before, and knew at that instant, beyond the pain and the strangeness of his experiences, that she was pregnant. He tried to scream when he saw the image, years in the future, of a wasted and aged Emily in a hospital bed, a young woman holding her hand and then leaving the room. Emily dying alone with a different name on her medical chart.

"Emily!" came a breathy whisper from between his cracked lips. Another name sprang into his head: Zoe.

Was it Emily's real name? No. He knew as soon as the young woman returned to the room—green eyes, dark hair cut poorly and colored improbably, a turn of the mouth—that *she* was Zoe, and Zoe was his daughter.

Something in his head said, "Not this one," and suddenly, he was free. Hands, still attached, fingers wiggling and unsinged. The sword seemed untouched, the visions—pain-inspired or otherwise, having the ring of truth—fled.

Emily was pregnant, and she'd run away.

Finally, he replaced the sword in the case and brushed away a tear. He turned to Sully, who was anxiously waiting to hear what he'd seen.

Jack took a deep breath. "Can I make you some tea? I certainly need a cup."

"Jack—" Sully said.

"It won't take me a minute," he said as he fled into his tiny kitchen, thinking furiously.

To Hell with the Family's rules, he thought. *I'll break every last one of them if it means keeping her secret. Keeping them safe. I'll go after her, and I'll—*

He couldn't go after her, Jack realized, setting the kettle down on the stove more heavily than he intended. She'd asked him not to, and, as for telling her what she was, he'd promised Martha Hudson that he would not. Even Jack knew not to break a promise to such a powerful oracle. He also knew he might harm Emily in some way by revealing the truth.

Then I'll break with the Family, follow her from a distance, protect her without her knowing I'm there, he thought resolutely.

And instantly, he knew that, too, would only make things worse, drawing attention to himself and Emily. This time, there'd be no escaping the Shedding for him, and Emily would be exposed to the Family when the oracle had said they must not know of her.

There was only one choice: Act as if he had never met her, had never heard of her. Go about his day job and his Fangborn work so carefully that no one would give him a second glance. He would follow every rule, precisely, to avoid drawing notice to himself or Emily. Sully would keep his secret because there was no longer a girlfriend to report. He might still be able to keep an eye out for Emily and their daughter, but it would never be as much as he wanted to do. As much as he knew he could do. But it was what was best for her.

I can't believe I'm going to let her go. The idea of another new alias for him, always watching and protecting them from a distance when he could, but never getting to see or touch Emily again, was too much. As he reached for the tea, the tears came, burning almost as much as the sword had.

Dana Cameron writes across many genres, but especially crime and speculative fiction. Her work, inspired by her career in archaeology, has won multiple Anthony, Agatha, and Macavity Awards, and her short story "Femme Sole" was short-listed for the Edgar Award. Dana is best known for the Emma Fielding archaeology mysteries (now on Hallmark Movies & Mysteries) and the Fangborn urban fantasy novels. Since she hasn't been doing much traveling or visiting museums, she's been weaving, spinning, or yelling at the TV about historical inaccuracies. You can find out more about Dana and her writing on her author website and blog at danacameron.com.